The
MYSTERIOUS
DEATH of
MR. DARCY

A PRIDE & PREJUDICE MYSTERY

Regina Jeffers

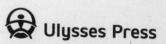Ulysses Press

Published in the United States by
Ulysses Press
P.O. Box 3440
Berkeley, CA 94703
www.ulyssespress.com

ISBN: 978-1-61243-173-4
Library of Congress Catalog Number: 2013930884

Acquisitions Editor: Kelly Reed
Managing Editor: Claire Chun
Editor: Sunah Cherwin
Proofreader: Elyce Berrigan-Dunlop
Editorial Associate: Lindsay Tamura
Cover design: what!design @ whatweb.com
Cover photo: © lolaira/istockphoto.com

Printed in Canada by Marquis Book Printing

10 9 8 7 6 5 4 3 2 1

Distributed by Publishers Group West

Character List

Characters from Jane Austen's *Pride and Prejudice*

FITZWILLIAM DARCY – the Master of Pemberley

ELIZABETH BENNET DARCY – Darcy's wife of six months

GEORGIANA DARCY – Darcy's seventeen-year-old sister; Darcy serves as her guardian

COLONEL EDWARD FITZWILLIAM – Darcy's cousin; second son of the Earl of Matlock; shares Georgiana's guardianship with Darcy

MRS. REYNOLDS – Darcy's housekeeper

MR. AND MRS. BENNET – Elizabeth's parents

MARY AND KITTY BENNET – Elizabeth's middle sisters

LYDIA BENNET WICKHAM – Elizabeth's youngest sister

GEORGE WICKHAM – Darcy's former friend; now his worst enemy

JANE BENNET BINGLEY – Elizabeth's older sister

CHARLES BINGLEY – Darcy's dearest friend; Jane's husband

CAROLINE BINGLEY – Charles's sister

LADY CATHERINE DE BOURGH – Darcy's aunt

ANNE DE BOURGH – Lady Catherine's daughter

Characters Unique to This Story

SAMUEL KINGSLEY DARCY – George Darcy's cousin; lives at Woodvine Hall in Dorset

GEORGE DARCY – Darcy's father

LADY ANNE FITZWILLIAM DARCY – Darcy's mother

MR. STALLING – Darcy's coachman

MURRAY AND JATSON – Darcy's footmen

MR. HENRY SHEFFIELD – Darcy's valet

HANNAH – Elizabeth's maid

MR. THOMAS COWAN – a former Bow Street Runner; served under Colonel Fitzwilliam during the war

THE EARL AND COUNTESS OF MATLOCK – Edward's parents

ROWLAND FITZWILLIAM, VISCOUNT LINDALE – Edward's older brother

MR. PEIFFER – Samuel Darcy's man of business

MR. FRANKLYN, MR. SEDGELOCK, AND MR. CHETLEY – members of the British Antiquarian Society

MR. MCKYE, MR. POORE, MR. CASTLE, MR. MAXTON, AND MR. DOUGLAS – men hired to protect Samuel Darcy's house from intruders

MR. BARRITON, MRS. RIDGEWAY, ELS, MRS. JACOBS, MRS. HOLBROOK, AND MR. HOLBROOK – servants in Samuel Darcy's employ

STEWART AND PERDITA DARCY – Samuel's elder brother and sister-in-law

BARTHOLOMEW AND CYNTHIA SANDERSON – the Earl and Countess of Rardin; Samuel's niece and heir to his property

MR. TOBIAS CRESCENT – Samuel Darcy's valet

MR. LOUIS STOWBRIDGE – the local magistrate; a squire in Wimborne

MR. GEOFFREY GLOVER – a local surgeon

MR. WILLIAMSON – the local curate

CAPTAIN LEWIS TREGONWELL – the real-life founder of Bournemouth

ANDRZEJ GRY – the leader of the gypsy band

Chapter 1

"Fitzwilliam, Mrs. Reynolds said you wished to speak to me."

Darcy looked up from the letter he clutched tightly in his grasp. It never ceased to amaze him—the effect her beguiling smile had on him. A moment earlier, he had read the Dorset-based solicitor's letter and had known immediate sorrow, but the moment the former Elizabeth Bennet had walked into the room, light returned to his heart. They had married a little over six months prior, and Darcy had not known one day of regret. For her regard, he would dare anything. Despite her poor connections, *his* Elizabeth was worth more than a hundred of Society's debutantes.

Darcy stood to greet her. "Yes, my dear." He extended his hand to her. "Please join me." When her fingers slid into his, Darcy automatically brought them to his lips. His self-control was sadly lacking when it came to his wife. He meant the kiss as a token of his affection, but Elizabeth caressed his jaw line; and one thing had led to another. Within seconds, he had forgotten the odious letter. Instead, Darcy had drawn her into his embrace. He inhaled her essence.

Months before, with her first raised eyebrow as he had entered the Meryton assembly, Elizabeth had claimed him. At the time, she had not realized the effect of her impudence toward a man exhausted by feigned regard from Society's overanxious mamas. Unknowingly, she had marked him as hers. Now, to his delight, Elizabeth lifted her chin and accepted his kiss. If it were not the middle of the afternoon, Darcy would lock his study door and enjoy the exquisite intimacy of his marriage.

Yet, Darcy realized that although Elizabeth had accepted his constant desire for her, she was still an innocent in many ways. As his lips released her, Darcy sighed with satisfaction. For months during their acquaintance, he had thought this moment might never be possible. From the first time he laid eyes on her across that crowded assembly hall, the woman's sheer force had possessed him. Uncharacteristically, Darcy had found himself on marshy footing when it came to their relationship: completely out of control. Elizabeth Bennet eclipsed every woman Darcy had ever encountered.

Elizabeth snuggled into his chest. "I hold no objection to knowing your regard, Mr. Darcy," she said on a rasp. "Yet, I find it hard to believe you sent for me in order to share this moment."

Darcy's lips trailed heat down the column of her neck. He whispered huskily against the creamy softness of her skin, "I can think of no better way to spend my day."

Elizabeth tilted her head to give him easier access. Under Darcy's jacket, her arms encircled his waist, and she pulled herself closer to him. "Mr. Darcy," she murmured, "the door remains open. The servants shall see us." Despite Elizabeth's words of protest, Darcy reveled in how she clung to him.

"The servant who dares to look upon our time together will be seeking employment elsewhere." His lips caressed her ear lobe. "God, Lizzy," he moaned. "You lead me to distraction." His arms came tightly about her. Darcy cupped her nape. As he fought to control his breathing, he rested his chin on the top of her head. "You are my bane, Elizabeth Darcy."

Elizabeth smiled secretly as she buried her cheek into his shoulder. How she had once declared that her dear husband was the last man in the world whom she could ever be prevailed upon to marry still dumbfounded her. He was her heart. On the day she married Fitzwilliam Darcy, she would have raced through her church's entrance if it had not been for her father's measured pace. She had been that anxious to become Mr. Darcy's wife. Throughout their short courtship, Elizabeth had had difficulty convincing herself of what Darcy had declared from the moment she had accepted his proposal: He had known no sacrifice in making her his wife—only pleasure. Yet, Elizabeth had been well aware that a man of Mr. Darcy's stature would encounter disdain when his choice became common knowledge.

Therefore, Elizabeth had made a private pledge to bring honor to the Darcy name. He had preferred her over the most beautiful and the most well-dowered young women of the *ton*. He had angered his aunt, Lady Catherine De Bourgh, by choosing Elizabeth over his cousin Anne. She would do everything in her power to make certain Mr. Darcy knew no regret in his choice.

Fortunately, her husband had never intimidated her—not the way he did most people he encountered. In fact, Elizabeth's unwavering honesty had proved the difference. She had obstinately told the world, "I could easily forgive Mr. Darcy's pride if he had not mortified mine." She was late to admit the man had fascinated her from their first encounter.

But then, when she thought her belated hopes dashed by her sister Lydia's absconding with George Wickham, the man intent on destroying the Darcys, Elizabeth had been quick to acknowledge her wretchedness.

Although at the time, she knew nothing of Mr. Darcy's rescue of her family's reputation, Elizabeth had found herself humbled by Darcy's wish of procuring her regard and the knowledge that, rationally, his pride would never allow him to form an alliance and relationship of the nearest kind with a man whom he so justly scorned. She had grieved; she had repented, though she hardly knew of what. She became jealous of his esteem, when she could no longer hope to be benefited by it. She wanted to hear of him when there seemed the least chance of gaining intelligence.

Before she had come to know Darcy, a happy marriage had appeared out of Elizabeth's reach, and her hopes of teaching the admiring multitudes what connubial felicity really could be had faded into the wallpaper of the Lambton inn.

Too late, Elizabeth had come to the conclusion Mr. Darcy was exactly the man who, in disposition and talents, would most suit her. His understanding and temper, though unlike her own, would answer all her wishes. It was a union that would be to the advantage of both; by her ease and liveliness his mind might be softened, his manners improved; and from his judgment, information, and knowledge of the world she would receive benefit of greater importance.

Somehow they had found their way, and Mr. Darcy had proposed a second time. From that point forward, Elizabeth had set herself the task of assuring that they would become the happiest couple in the world.

Elizabeth lifted her chin to study his countenance. "As much as I enjoy your attentions, I remain certain you held a different purpose in seeking my company. Your eyes speak of affection, but these frown lines," she teased, as her finger stroked his forehead, "know a different tale. Perhaps you should explain your earlier discontent."

His smile became soft and encouraging. "Had I known of your ability to read me so easily, Mrs. Darcy, I would have shuttered my thoughts early on in our relationship."

Elizabeth laughed easily. "A more indiscernible man never existed, Mr. Darcy."

He caught her hand and tugged Elizabeth toward a nearby chaise. Darcy caught the letter up in his grasp and settled himself beside her. With a deep steadying breath, he began, "I have received a letter from a Mr. Peiffer, a solicitor in Christchurch." Elizabeth moved closer, and Darcy appreciated how she instinctively knew her presence brought him comfort. "Mr. Peiffer reports my father's favorite cousin, Samuel Darcy, has passed."

"Oh, Fitzwilliam, I am grieved," Elizabeth sympathized. "From your tone, I assume Samuel Darcy and your father were great friends."

"As youths, they spent much of their time together, as did Edward and I when we were young rascals," he explained. "Cousin Samuel spent his adult life searching for the world's hidden treasures. I fear he was a bit of an eccentric."

Elizabeth laid her hand on Darcy's arm. He could feel her gaze sweep over him. "And your relationship with the gentleman?"

"When Father fell ill," Darcy began, "it was Cousin Samuel who rushed to his side. He left his expedition and returned to England so he might see Father through the worst of his sickness. Samuel moved into Pemberley, where he could oversee Father's care." Darcy looked off as if he could view the events anew. "I do not know how I might have survived those days without him. Cousin Samuel was my salvation. Although Father had groomed me to assume the role of Master of Pemberley, I was sadly lacking in how to proceed. How to become the estate's master and how to assume Georgiana's care. It was only with Samuel's sound advice that I was able to begin. And how easily Samuel led poor Georgiana through the grieving process…" Darcy's voice cracked with emotion.

"Your cousin is an acquaintance I shall regret not having," Elizabeth said softly. She interlaced her fingers with his. "As I am certain Mr. Peiffer's letter holds more than the details of your cousin's funeral, of what did you wish to speak to me?"

Self-consciously, Darcy kissed the back of her hand. "It is true. Cousin Samuel's death came a sennight prior. The most I can offer, at this point, is my respect."

Elizabeth nodded her understanding. "You wish to journey to Dorset?" He watched as his wife steeled her shoulders. Since their joining, they had spent but one night apart. He could almost see Elizabeth fortifying her composure. Darcy often felt foolish when he considered how much he required her in his life, but it was very satisfying to witness a like need in the woman he so dearly loved.

"I do," he said solemnly. "But I do not wish to be parted from you, my Lizzy." He caressed her cheek.

"Nor I, you," Elizabeth said sweetly.

Darcy cleared his throat. "This is not the best of circumstances. A man's death should not precipitate a pleasure journey, but after receiving Mr. Peiffer's missive, I began to consider the possibilities." He placed his arm about Elizabeth's shoulders and pulled her closer. "The solicitor has sent a similar letter to Lady Cynthia Sanderson. She is Cousin Samuel's niece, his brother Stewart's only child. It appears Samuel has named Lady Cynthia, Georgiana, and me as his heirs. Mr. Peiffer indicates Lady Cynthia has recently delivered her third child and cannot travel for at least another month."

"I am afraid I do not understand, Fitzwilliam." Elizabeth rested her head on his shoulder.

"Peiffer has requested that Georgiana and I attend the reading of Samuel's will. He has scheduled that reading one month from this Friday."

Elizabeth sighed in relief. "Then you will wait before your journey to Dorset?"

Darcy held her at arm's length from him so he might observe her reaction. "I have come upon a different plan. When we married in November, the weather did not permit us the pleasure of a celebratory journey. I am suggesting that we visit Dorset and enjoy the shore while we wait for Lady Cynthia's arrival. We may take a private cottage at Gundimore."

"But what of Pemberley?" she protested, but he noted the excitement in her voice.

"Pemberley will survive. Mr. Steventon and Mrs. Reynolds will oversee the house and the land. No one will object to our celebrating our joining." He gave her a thankful smile. "We could take the yacht from Liverpool to Bournemouth," he suggested. "Mr. Stalling would bring the coach across the land route."

Elizabeth bit her bottom lip. That innocent gesture told Darcy his proposition appealed to her, but his wife wondered how enthusiastically she should react. Darcy was well aware *his* Lizzy had set herself the task of proving herself a responsible and caring mistress for the estate. Truthfully, he had never considered that she would be anything less. Yet, occasionally, he worried his wife grasped too tightly the spontaneity he so adored in her. He also privately wondered if Elizabeth's striving for perfection had been the source of their recent loss. Darcy hoped this journey would help Elizabeth forget her sorrow and would bring life to her pale countenance. "I suppose we could spend some of our time in ordering your cousin's papers. Perhaps we could even place the late Mr. Darcy's affairs in order in preparation for Lady Cynthia's arrival," she said tentatively.

Darcy allowed Elizabeth her altruistic motives. "I believe yours is an amenable solution. We could speak to Peiffer personally. Possibly even direct the packing of Samuel's effects. I am certain his house holds many treasures. It has been several years since I spent time with my father's cousin, but Samuel was always a contributor to the British Antiquarian Society. I imagine his home is a museum dedicated to the past."

Elizabeth smiled widely. "Then it is settled. When do you wish to depart, Mr. Darcy?"

"I thought we could travel to Liverpool on Friday and set sail on Saturday. If you are of a mind, we could stop at several of the ports along the way. Our itinerary may remain open."

"Could we visit other parts of Dorset? I have always found the idea of walking along the Cobb at Lyme Regis a most intriguing prospect," Elizabeth said excitedly.

"Lyme has wonderful shale beaches," Darcy agreed. "And we could bathe in the sea at Mudeford. After all, the area is a favorite of our monarch."

Elizabeth rose and danced lightly about a low table. "A little sea bathing would set me up forever," she giggled.

Darcy followed her to his feet and swept her into his arms. He twirled her about the room. Elizabeth's laughter filled the air. He could not recall a time when he had known such contentment. "You are beautiful," he said as he spun them to an intimate halt.

They swayed in place. "I love your laugh," he confessed. "Promise me you will laugh more, Lizzy. I want to know you are happy."

"I promise," she whispered.

* * *

Elizabeth had never seen anything so beautiful. Her senses raced from one sight to another. From a vantage point marking the harbor, she had easily found the Darcy yacht, the *Derby*. A banner bearing the family seal floated above one of the two masts, and a bright blue stripe lined the hull. Her heart skipped a beat as Darcy assisted her from the carriage.

His men had awaited their arrival along the quay, and the Darcys had been ushered aboard. Now, she and Darcy stood along the railing to look out upon the rippling waves. The ship had everything. A highly polished wheel. A sharply raked bowsprit. Glistening brass work. A dark varnished rail and two crisp, white masts. The experience filled her senses to the brim. She tasted the salty air upon on her lips, saw the sun's glare above the glassy surfaces of ship and water, and heard the squawk of the sea birds overhead.

"What do you think of her, Lizzy?" Darcy asked as his arm tightened about Elizabeth's waist.

"She is magnificent, Fitzwilliam." Her mouth turned up in happiness. She closed her eyes against the bright sunshine and breathed in deeply. Elizabeth's countenance lit with excitement. It was as if her husband had laid a king's ransom at her feet, and that pleased her feminine conceit immensely. "Never in a million years would I have thought to be aboard my husband's ship. I have always wanted to sail off to foreign lands."

"As have I," Darcy confessed. "Unfortunately, as the only son, my course was defined at birth. Yet, I have often envied Colonel

Fitzwilliam. My cousin possesses a freedom of which I have only dreamed." He smiled easily, that boyish smile Elizabeth found so endearing. "Can you imagine me in Admiral of the Fleet regalia?"

She bit back a grin. "Admiral of the Fleet? No captain's dress for you, Mr. Darcy?" she teased good-naturedly.

"The colonel would outrank me if I were but a mere captain." Darcy winked at her.

"Ready about!" The ship's captain called, and Darcy caught Elizabeth to him. He leaned her forward as the boom swung over their heads. He pointed to where the ship broke through the waves. "The ship's tack changes because of the wind," he explained. "In order to keep the *Derby* on course, the sails must be swung around at the end of each tack."

"Hard alee!" the captain sang out, and the boom swung again. The ship heeled and set upon a new course.

Elizabeth squealed, "How exciting! This is my first adventure asea, Fitzwilliam. Thank you for providing me this moment."

He extended his hand to her, and Elizabeth, instinctively, slipped her fingers into his outstretched palm. She knew her husband was fully prepared to slay dragons and ogres for her. It was a satisfying thought for a woman who had never thought to marry for love. "I have asked for a special afternoon meal upon deck," he said huskily. "Perhaps we can go below to freshen our things."

Elizabeth recognized the desire reflected in his eyes. She interlaced her arm through his. "I can think of nothing more delightful."

* * *

"Your cousin spoke of you often, Mr. Darcy," Samuel's housekeeper said as she served tea. Darcy and Elizabeth had spent six deliriously glorious days aboard his yacht and at various ports. They had dined on regional delicacies, and they had known exquisite intimacies. The euphoria clung to him like a well-tailored coat.

Samuel Darcy's home had been much as Darcy had expected. Not a surface existed that did not bear some sort of ancient vase or dried bone. It would take many weeks to inventory Samuel's belongings. "I fear it has been several years since I last saw my cousin. It grieves me that Cousin Samuel might have suffered without someone in the family close at hand. I pray his passing was quick and painless." He studied the housekeeper charily. The house displayed many of his cousin's "treasures," but it also showed a lack of attention to care. Although Fitzwilliam Darcy was not so inclined, Samuel Darcy was known to be oblivious to such details.

The housekeeper's eyebrow rose in obvious dismay. "Oh, Mr. Darcy, did not Mr. Peiffer explain the circumstances surrounding your cousin's passing?"

Darcy shot a quick glance at Elizabeth to monitor her reaction to the woman's anxiousness. "I have yet to call upon Mr. Peiffer. We set in at Bournemouth a few hours prior." He placed his half-empty teacup on a nearby table. "In case Lady Cynthia arrived earlier than expected, I thought it best to inform you of my presence in the area." He reached for Elizabeth's hand. "Mayhap you might share the conditions contiguous to my cousin's death, Mrs. Ridgeway."

Darcy heard the swift, panicked catch in the older woman's voice. Mrs. Ridgeway drew out a handkerchief and dabbed at her eyes; yet, his instincts said something about the woman did not prove true. She was handsome enough, having one of those faces that did not display the passage of time. The lines around her eyes and mouth were barely noticeable. Although he suspected Mrs. Ridgeway to be nearing forty—after all, the woman had admitted to being a widow for some ten years—she seemed ageless. Her wavy blonde hair held streaks of silver-white, but there was nothing disagreeable about the woman's countenance: a strong chin, dark brown eyes and long lashes, a small face and nose, a low-vaulted forehead. She did not favor an Englishwoman. More in the form of the females of the Western European countries. Her eyes held tales of life well lived, and they were not tales of woe. He supposed that was what bothered him. Darcy had always imagined, if something should take him before his time, Mrs. Reynolds and all of Pemberley would truly grieve for his passing. Perhaps it was his pride to think so. He viewed Samuel Darcy to be a man of a similar vein, and Darcy expected his cousin's staff to grieve for Samuel's absence. "Poor Mr. Samuel," she began on a rasp. "Your cousin could not have known what happened."

"Did Cousin Samuel take a fall from his horse or a spill into the River Wey?" Darcy pressed. When he had learned of Samuel Darcy's passing, he had assumed his father's cousin had succumbed to some strange illness, likely contracted in Africa or India or the Orient—his cousin had explored the civilized and the uncivilized world. In addition, Samuel was two years George Darcy's senior, and Darcy's father had passed some six years prior. It had never crossed Darcy's mind that anything other than advanced age had taken his cousin Samuel.

"No, Mr. Darcy," Mrs. Ridgeway said softly from the folds of her handkerchief. "It was at more sinister hands that your cousin met his Maker." She hesitated in what appeared to be true anguish, but, again, Darcy could not shake the feeling something was amiss. "Mr. Samuel had spent an evening with some of his regular associates. Mr. Stowbridge often hosts an entertainment for several of the authors and artists in the area, and Mr. Samuel customarily attends when he is in the country." Mrs. Ridgeway flicked tears away. "Mr. Samuel customarily walked home from the Stowbridge house. Your cousin always said it cleared his head of all the philosophy Stowbridge's guests spouted throughout the evening, and it is less than a mile through the back pasture and the woods to Stowe Hall."

"Unlike many of his station, Samuel never avoided a bit of physical exertion," Darcy said fondly.

"Certainly, Mr. Samuel was unique in many ways," Mrs. Ridgeway continued. "Unfortunately, on the evening of his death, your cousin should have accepted Mr. Stowbridge's offer of his carriage. Despite both households' mounting an extensive search, Samuel Darcy's body remained undiscovered until noon of the following day. One of Mr. Stowbridge's staff found Mr. Samuel on a wooded path."

Darcy frowned. His brows pulled together in consternation. "You continue to dance around the truth. Please explain what happened to Cousin Samuel, Mrs. Ridgeway," Darcy said impatiently.

"It is a tale I prefer not to consider," the housekeeper said sadly.

Darcy set his mouth in a tight line. "Yet, I insist on knowing the details."

With a heavy sigh, Mrs. Ridgeway disclosed, "Someone must have followed your cousin. An ax handle lay close to Mr. Darcy's body. He had been struck soundly across the back of the head."

"Cousin Samuel was murdered? How is that possible? The man had not a selfish bone in his body. Surely if it had been a matter of a few coins…"

"Not a robbery, Sir," she said softly. "Nothing appeared to be missing. Your cousin's purse was not taken."

"I would think not," Darcy continued. "If someone wished to have his purse, Samuel would have handed it over and then invited his attacker home for a meal." His eyes narrowed. "Has my cousin's assailant been apprehended?"

"Regrettably, no," Mrs. Ridgeway answered.

"But it has been some three weeks," Darcy protested. "Are there possible suspects?"

Mrs. Ridgeway's shoulders stiffened. "As I am but Mr. Samuel's housekeeper, the authorities do not deem it necessary to keep me informed. The fact that I served your late cousin for more than six years holds no sway with the local magistrate."

Darcy stood and reached for Elizabeth's hand. "Then perhaps I should see if my concerns hold influence over the man. Might I impose on you, Ma'am, to tell me the gentleman's name and to provide me his directions?"

The woman rose. "I believe you already know the magistrate's name, Sir. It is Mr. Louis Stowbridge, and as to his directions, simply follow the main road around the orchard. Mr. Stowbridge's estate is the grey stone squire's house."

Darcy thanked the woman and escorted Elizabeth toward his carriage. "Do not assume culpability, Mr. Darcy," his wife chided as he assisted her into his traveling coach.

Curtly, he said, "I am unaware of the source of your censure, Mrs. Darcy." He climbed into the carriage to take the backward-facing seat.

"You have set your mind to blaming yourself for not arriving in Dorset sooner," Elizabeth insisted. "Yet, you must realize the outcome would have remained the same. Samuel Darcy lost his life to an unknown assailant."

Darcy sighed heavily. The fact his wife spoke his thoughts frustrated him. "Many days more than a fortnight, Elizabeth," he said in annoyance. "My cousin has known his Maker for nigh on a month, and no one has been brought to justice."

Elizabeth nodded her head sympathetically. "All you say is true, my husband, but do not cast fault upon your own shoulders for not having taken action prior to today. Although not timely to the course of the events, we *are* in Dorset, and you may see to a resolution."

"Yet…" he began, but a deep frown on his wife's perfect countenance curtailed Darcy's protest.

"I shall not hear of it, Fitzwilliam," she said adamantly. "If you regret our not rushing to Dorset, then it means you regret our time together on the *Derby*. I will treasure those days and would not have them tarnished."

Darcy knew she was correct. His tendency toward self-censure often ruled his thoughts—actually addressed them with rather an injudicious particularity. Not an incurable fault, but one where he had to practice how to dictate liberality to others, as well as himself. "I could never look with disdain upon any moment we spend together. You are my world, Elizabeth Darcy. Surely you are aware of my devotion."

She rewarded him with that easy smile Darcy so adored. "It is with shameful insensibility that I rejoice in your regard, my husband," Elizabeth assured. "Yet, because I return your sentiments, I would not have you assume the world's faults as your own. We will see to what is proper to honor your cousin's memory."

"But what of our wedding journey?" Darcy said softly. "I promised you sea bathing and time to mark our joining."

Elizabeth leaned forward, wrapping her arms about her knees. "We shall have more than enough time to do both. Lady Cynthia's arrival is several weeks in the future. We can press for a more comprehensive investigation, while spending time enjoying King George's favorite watering hole. One activity does not negate the other."

"Is it any wonder that I love you so dearly?" he asked earnestly.

Mischievously, she batted her eyes at him. "You could not resist my charms, Mr. Darcy," she teased.

He slid across the carriage to sit beside her. "I have possessed a strange attraction for your fine eyes for more days than I care to recall," he said as he planted a wet kiss on the column of her neck. "Now, I am aware of more alluring charms," he said huskily.

Elizabeth's eyes fluttered closed, but she quickly recovered her senses. "Mr. Darcy," she protested halfheartedly. Before Darcy could catch her to him, his wife slid across the seat to look pointedly out the coach's small window. "My goodness!" she gasped. "Are those gypsies, Fitzwilliam?" she asked in disbelief.

Darcy followed her across the bench to peer over her shoulder. "They are, my dear. Have you never seen a Roma band?"

Elizabeth turned her head slightly to him. Her eyes had widened, and they were full of excitement. "I have heard tales of gypsy bands, but I have never known of one camping near Meryton." Her gaze returned to the colorful wagons, and the young men taking a horse through its paces. "Shall they truly steal our purses if we are foolish enough to go near their camp?" she asked innocently.

Darcy watched as the men stopped their activity to scrutinize his coach's progress. As a group, they took several menacing steps in the direction of the road. Automatically, Darcy stiffened, and he slid an arm about Elizabeth's waist. Sensing his anxiety, his wife clung tightly to him, and he felt fiercely protective of her. "There

are many troops that offer no mischief," he said with little conviction. "However, my experience with those who annually visit
Derby is the Roma live by a different code." Mr. Stalling must have
considered the possible threat, for the horses' speed increased. "I
wonder how long this particular group has been in the area." Darcy
turned to see the men standing in the road as the carriage maneuvered its way around a curve at a quickened pace.

Elizabeth caught the strap to steady herself. She said intuitively,
"What you are asking, my husband, is whether the gypsies could
have played a part in your cousin's death."

Chapter 2

"Mr. Darcy." A smiling, elderly man entered the room, his hand extended in greeting. "I am very pleased to have your acquaintance, Sir. Over the years and on multiple occasions, your cousin has sung your praises."

Darcy accepted the man's hand. Directing Stowbridge's attention to Elizabeth, he said, "Permit me to present my wife, Mrs. Darcy."

Stowbridge executed a correct bow. "Ah, Mrs. Darcy, I cannot begin to speak of Samuel Darcy's elation with the news of your marriage to George Darcy's son. Samuel predicted that you would be quite beautiful—said a Darcy man recognizes a woman worthy of his attentions. I have always been of the persuasion that a man requires a beautiful bauble on his arm." Darcy felt Elizabeth's body stiffen with the condescending remark, and he cupped her hand with his free one to warn away her expected protest. Unaware of his affront, Stowbridge gestured to nearby chairs before continuing, "Listen to me, speaking so familiarly. It is only from the purest excitement at having your acquaintance. I am only sorry our dear Samuel could not celebrate with us." The man turned to Darcy. "Were you aware that Samuel had planned to journey to your home in Derbyshire? In June, your cousin had said of late."

Darcy assisted Elizabeth to her seat. "I have not heard from Cousin Samuel since he sent his congratulations on my joining with Mrs. Darcy." Darcy sat beside his wife on a narrow settee. He studied Stowbridge as the man rang for tea before joining them. The man had dark skin and eyes and was likely of European heritage, perhaps sixty years of age. Louis Stowbridge's wrinkles did nothing to dampen the animation crossing the man's countenance. Yet, despite Stowbridge's apparent joviality, the squire had yet to meet Darcy's eyes, a fact that caused Darcy instinctively to question the man's honesty. Looking a man in the eyes was a defining characteristic, the importance of which Darcy's father had drummed into his son's head. George Darcy had been quick to point out the necessity of doing so, especially when conducting business. Brushed to a fine gloss, the man's hair was thinning and peppered with gray, but by all appearances Stowbridge was a fit gentleman. Darcy continued, "Mrs. Darcy and I called at Samuel's home to inform the staff of our arrival in Wimborne. Mrs. Ridgeway suggested that we seek your knowledge of the events leading up to and those following Cousin Samuel's death."

Immediately, the benevolent smile disappeared from the squire's lips. "That old tabby," Stowbridge grumbled. "The lady does not know her place. She should have stood solidly by her husband rather than seeking her independence. Samuel should have pensioned off the woman years ago." Darcy thought it odd that the man spoke so bluntly about Samuel's housekeeper. Darcy was not privy to the woman's history, but he understood her to be a widow, which caused him to question what the magistrate meant by the lady standing "solidly beside her husband." Perhaps the woman and the late Mr. Ridgeway had gone their separate ways long before the man's passing. Such circumstances were commonplace among the aristocracy. Why should such difficulties not be so for the working class?

Elizabeth interrupted Darcy's thoughts and the magistrate's criticisms, "I found Mrs. Ridgeway quite pleasant, Mr. Stowbridge, and the lady appeared distraught over Mr. Darcy's passing." Darcy adored the way his wife never failed to speak her mind. It was one of the qualities that had attracted him to the former Elizabeth Bennet.

Pondering his pleasure in her straightforward speech, Darcy pleasantly recalled what his wife had asked one evening shortly after they had announced their engagement. "My beauty you had early withstood, and as for my manners—my behavior to you was, at least, always bordering on the uncivil, and I never spoke to you without rather wishing to give you pain than not. Now, be sincere, did you admire me for my impertinence?" And Darcy had reluctantly admitted, not for the first time, that Elizabeth's 'impertinence' had driven him happily to distraction. She was sadly correct. He had been disgusted with the women who were always speaking, and looking, and thinking for his approbation alone. *His* Elizabeth was so unlike every other woman of his acquaintance, and Darcy counted himself among the blessed because of it.

Evidently, the squire had never encountered a woman of Elizabeth's mettle, for the man blinked in surprise. He smiled benevolently, as if he were a loving grandfather offering a sugary treat to a child, but Stowbridge's tone was not so indulgent. "Of course, Mrs. Ridgeway thought kindly of her employer," he said placatingly. "However, the woman does not recognize that an upper servant should remain silent." A particularly false smile dressed the man's lips.

Darcy recognized Elizabeth's quickly rising ire. His wife's eyes narrowed, and her lips flattened into a sharply defined line. When her jaw hardened, he placed a hand over the back of her gloved one as a warning to still her tongue. "Then perhaps, Mr. Stowbridge, as the shire's magistrate, you might provide me the details of Samuel Darcy's passing. I am also interested in the steps taken to discover my cousin's assailant."

Stowbridge's shoulders slumped in defeat. "It is a sad tale, Mr. Darcy." He shot a glance of concern in Elizabeth's direction. "And it is not one fit for a lady's ears."

Elizabeth's fingers intertwined with Darcy's. "You do justice to the generosity and delicacy of your notions, Sir," Elizabeth said with feigned munificence—a tone of which Darcy had been the recipient on more than one occasion. "I assure you, Mr. Stowbridge, I am not a woman of weak sensibilities."

"Very well, Mrs. Darcy," the squire said brusquely, his irritation evident. "Samuel Darcy was my dearest friend, and his passing grieves me greatly. Not a day passes that I do not wish his return so I might tell him how every former frown or cold address has been forgotten." The tea arrived, and they waited for the service before the squire continued.

"The night of his death, Samuel joined me, Nicholas Drewe, and Liam Mason for a congenial evening. We played cards and spoke of Drewe's latest work, but Samuel appeared a bit distracted—very unlike himself. On that particular evening, Samuel displayed a true want of all laudable ambition, of a taste for good company, or of an inclination to take the trouble of being agreeable." An indefinable expression crossing the squire's countenance told Darcy things were not all what the magistrate pretended them to be. Stowbridge was sweetening his rendition of the night's happenings, but Darcy was uncertain as to why the man did not freely speak the whole truth. He hoped the magistrate's motive lay in delicacy for Elizabeth's weaker feminine sensibilities.

Darcy's brows rose slightly as he scrutinized every word the man spoke, as well as the unspoken ones. "Do you know the source of Cousin Samuel's distraction?" he asked.

"It is unlikely that anyone other than I took notice. I have spent a third of my life as Samuel Darcy's friend. Except for his absence during your cousin's many expeditions, Samuel and I have shared our memories. I have many fond recollections of our time together."

Darcy had no desire on this day to listen to Stowbridge's sentimental remembrances. He would make a point to call upon the squire on a future date to learn more of his cousin's recent years. For now, Darcy required details of Samuel's passing. "I do not wish to reject your memories as insignificant," Darcy said encouragingly, "but Mrs. Darcy and I have heard the most horrendous tale. Please allay our questions with earnest answers."

Stowbridge cleared his throat and assumed an air of importance. "Of course, Mr. Darcy. I have avoided mentioning the sordid details, for they are most distressing." The squire closed his eyes, and his grief was evident upon his countenance. Darcy thought it the first genuine moment they had shared since arriving at Stowe Hall. "Samuel insisted upon walking home that evening. Said it would clear his thinking. Said he had learned something of a distressing nature about a dear friend. Said the evening at cards had reminded him of a ritual from his latest expedition. I do not know which of the two matters most occupied Samuel's mind as he made his way to Woodvine Hall." Stowbridge opened his eyes slowly. "We did not discover Samuel's body until the following day."

Darcy asked softly, "Would it have made a difference if someone had come upon Samuel after his attack?"

Stowbridge shook his head in denial. "The surgeon assures me it would not; yet, when I think of how Samuel must have suffered…" his voice broke in sorrow.

Darcy's curiosity was piqued. The drama surrounding this tale had increased. "Then, the blow to his head did not kill Cousin Samuel?"

The squire reached for his handkerchief. He mopped his brow first and then wiped his mouth, as if shoving away a bad taste. "Evidently, Mrs. Ridgeway thought it best to keep her opinions to herself," Stowbridge grumbled. Again, the bitterness with which the magistrate spoke of Samuel's housekeeper rubbed at Darcy's inquisitiveness. From his last visit in Dorset with Samuel, Darcy recalled a troubling rumor that had plagued his cousin's usually cheery humor. Samuel had spoken of an acquaintance who had been accused of taking advantage of one of his servants. Had it been Stowbridge about whom Samuel had worried? If so, could that be the source of the magistrate's disdain for the Woodvine housekeeper? Had the squire made advances toward Samuel's servant? "The assault did not initially kill Samuel Darcy." The magistrate paused solemnly. "According to the surgeon, Mr. Glover, Samuel's injury was as unique as the man himself. The blow literally knocked your cousin's head from his shoulders; yet, it did not decapitate him."

Darcy's hand caught Elizabeth's. He held hers tightly in his grip. Such details would disturb his wife's customarily active imagination. "How is that possible?"

Stowbridge replied, "Glover says he has never seen such a case, but he insists it is possible. He claims the skull simply rests on the spine, or some such nonsense. Samuel's attacker delivered a strike, very much like one used in cricket. The impact lifted Samuel's head from his spine. With no skeletal support, your cousin's head drooped forward. Unable to raise his chin, Samuel could not take a breath. My dearest friend suffocated before anyone could discover him. Yet, even if we had found him in a timelier manner, Samuel's death would have only been a matter of time. Mr. Glover assures me that no surgeon could have repaired such damage. He says all he could have done would have been to give poor Samuel enough laudanum to ease his pain while your cousin waited for death. Likely, if someone had found him and attempted to move him, it would have exacerbated Samuel's suffering."

As if seeking guidance, Darcy's eyes searched the ceiling. He made a strangled sound deep in his throat. He had considered many scenarios, but he could never have foreseen something this out of the ordinary. He glanced to where Elizabeth sat quietly. His wife had paled, but she reached for his arm. She stared at him steadily. Her face twisted in horror. The fact that Darcy's voice sounded normal when he responded quite surprised him. It was strange because he felt so detached. A man whom he respected and admired had died an unspeakable death. Had died alone on a country path through the woods. "I wish I had been available to comfort him," Darcy said sadly.

"I am certain Samuel would have wanted that also," Stowbridge insisted. "Yet, we must remember that God guides us to his door in His time, not in ours."

Darcy's breath caught in his throat. "And what of my cousin's assailant? How has your investigation progressed?"

"Samuel's attacker was not content with your cousin's death," Stowbridge continued. "Several days following the discovery of Samuel's body, we found a man we assumed to be the killer. He was draped across Samuel's freshly dug grave. Multiple lacerations crossed the man's body. Part of your cousin's coffin had been shattered."

Darcy shook his head in disbelief. It was a crazy world in which they lived, one where a person's final resting place was not respected. He asked incredulously, "How did the man broach Cousin Samuel's crypt?"

Stowbridge explained, "This area suffered a series of storms in early March. Your cousin's intended resting place had been extensively damaged by a fallen tree. The curate and I thought it best to bury Samuel in the founders' section of the village cemetery until the repairs to his crypt could be sanctioned by the estate."

"I see," Darcy said tersely. But he really did not "see" how something as simple as addressing a man's final needs could have gone so wrong.

"You will excuse me, Mr. Stowbridge, but I fear I am decidedly confused. How do we know the man you have just described was the late Mr. Darcy's attacker?" Elizabeth asked before Darcy could utter the words.

"Who else could he have been? Most likely thought we had buried dear Samuel with his many treasures," Stowbridge persisted.

"Yet, Mrs. Ridgeway assured us that robbery was not the cause of Cousin Samuel's demise," Darcy argued.

Stowbridge's chest expanded with pride. "Mrs. Ridgeway knows nothing of my investigation. I have not spoken more than a dozen words to the lady regarding Samuel's passing. We initially assumed the incident leading to your cousin's death was not precipitated by a robbery. However, Samuel Darcy was known to carry one jewel or another in his pockets. Your cousin was always sharing glimpses of his latest treasure with the curious."

Darcy noted the line of Elizabeth's lips flattened in disapproval. He intercepted her likely chiding of the squire. Stowbridge appeared to have little tolerance for intelligent women, and the man's brusque replies only intensified the situation. "Let us assume for the moment that my cousin lost his life because of his eccentric habits, and let us also assume that the deceased man you found in the village cemetery truly wished to rob Cousin Samuel's coffin. Given these circumstances, please explain how the man was killed and who killed him."

Stowbridge frowned dramatically. "Unfortunately, beyond speculation, we have few clues as to what happened, and as the deceased was one of the gypsies..."

"A Rom?" Darcy scowled. "The man discovered as part of this madness was one of the band of gypsies currently camping on my cousin's property?"

Stowbridge said in contempt, "The gypsy leader awaits justice for the loss of his brother."

"I see," Darcy said evenly. This time his vision was clearer. He suspected that the squire had no intention of meeting the Roma leader's demands, nor would the magistrate escort the gypsy band from Darcy land. The fate of the gypsy band remained in Darcy's hands. "One thing more," he asked after a brief pause. "Were there treasures hidden in my cousin's gravesite?"

Stowbridge's eyes looked everywhere but at Darcy. "No treasures, Mr. Darcy. Other than his signet ring and a diamond pin, Samuel's body was unadorned."

"Then it is safe for Mrs. Darcy and I to visit the cemetery to pay our respects?" Darcy reached for his gloves. If the squire had known Darcy better, the man would have seen how difficult it was for his guest to remain calm. Darcy despised those of an insensible nature, and Stowbridge screamed of imprudence.

Stowbridge grimaced. "There is one issue of which you should be made aware, Mr. Darcy. Although we found the gypsy's brother lying across your cousin's opened gravesite, we found no body in Samuel Darcy's coffin."

Darcy was on his feet immediately. "No body!" he exclaimed. "How long ago did this travesty occur?"

"Only a day after your cousin's service."

His hands fisted at his side, and Darcy's heart seemed to falter, along with his reason. He shot a quick pleading glance at his wife, and, fortunately, she understood his need to be away from Stowbridge. "Mr. Darcy," Elizabeth said softly before placing her hand across her heart for effect, "I fear this situation has plagued me more than I anticipated." With her keen receptiveness, Elizabeth had sensed his tension and had come to his rescue.

With a deep steadying breath to calm his composure, Darcy gently caught her elbow and assisted Elizabeth to her feet. "Of course, my dear. The circumstances of Cousin Samuel's passing have played havoc with each of us. Permit me to escort you to our quarters." He gave Stowbridge a curt bow. "Please excuse us, Sir. I will call again once I am certain of Mrs. Darcy's well-being."

"Of course, Mr. Darcy," Stowbridge declared. "Our womenfolk possess a different disposition from us men."

Elizabeth clung to him until Darcy followed her into the darkness of the coach. "A different disposition!" she hissed. "One more word of female frailty, and I would have…"

"Have what, my darling?" His wife's testiness provided Darcy a brief respite from the craziness surrounding Samuel Darcy's passing.

"I swear, Fitzwilliam, I have never resorted to physicality, but Mr. Stowbridge brings out the worst of my faults."

Darcy slid an arm about his wife's shoulders. "I am very blessed to know all of your faults, Mrs. Darcy."

For a brief second, Elizabeth glared at him as if she meant to argue, but then she smiled and swatted his chest. "You have long suffered at my hand, Mr. Darcy. I am thankful you have forgiven my foibles." With that, she moved quickly into his welcoming embrace. The distraction would do him well for Darcy could not leave behind the idea that he had failed his cousin Samuel.

* * *

Darcy had arranged for a seaside cottage for their privacy. He had also hired a temporary staff to meet their needs. Despite his desire to analyze what they did and did not know of his cousin's mysterious death, he dutifully escorted his wife for a walk along the shoreline.

"Is it not magnificent?" Elizabeth sighed as she gazed out over the harbor's expanse.

Darcy had been staring at her, rather than the water's glassy surface. "I find it the most beautiful sight in the world," he said huskily.

Elizabeth glanced up at him. With her countenance no longer partially hidden by her bonnet's brim, he could enjoy the flush of color creeping across her cheeks. "I meant the harbor and the ocean beyond," she chastised, but her fingers caressed his forearm.

"And what makes you believe that I spoke of something beyond God's hand?" he said wryly.

Elizabeth tutted her disapproval. "Do not think me a simpleton, Mr. Darcy. I know your most excellent mind, and I recognize that particular tone."

Darcy smiled easily. "And what tone would that be, my love?"

"The one you use before…" she said with another blush, this one bringing a deeper red.

Darcy brought her gloved fingertips to his lips. "Before what?" he asked seductively.

Elizabeth leaned into him, and he gloried in how his wife responded to him. During April of the previous year, he had returned to Pemberley with his hopes of making Elizabeth Bennet his wife dashed by her venomous refusal. God! How he had pined for her! For months, he had suffered before discovering Elizabeth at Pemberley on a holiday in Derbyshire. His desire for her rekindled during those early days of August, and then his dreams were slashed to shreds by the elopement of his worst enemy, George Wickham, with Elizabeth's youngest sister, Lydia. Making Elizabeth his wife would have created a family bond with Mr. Wickham, and Darcy knew he could not place his sister Georgiana in such a fragile situation. However, Georgiana had insisted that Darcy should find love. He still did not understand where his often shy little sister found her strength, but he was thankful to have Georgiana in his life. He could learn a great deal about adversity from her.

Ironically, he and Elizabeth were indebted for their present good understanding to the efforts of his aunt, Lady Catherine De Bourgh, who had called on him at his London residence, and had there related the story of her journey to Elizabeth's home of Longbourn. Her Ladyship intended to stifle a rumor regarding Darcy's affection for Miss Elizabeth, and to discuss the substance of Lady

Catherine's conversation with Elizabeth; dwelling emphatically on every expression of the latter, which in Her Ladyship's apprehension, peculiarly denoted Elizabeth's perverseness and assurance; in the belief that such a relation must assist Lady Catherine's endeavors to obtain that promise from Darcy which Elizabeth had refused to give. But, unfortunately for Her Ladyship, its effect had been exactly contrariwise. It had taught Darcy to hope as he scarcely ever allowed himself to hope before.

He had consulted both his sister and his cousin, Colonel Fitzwilliam, and receiving their approval, as well as their encouragement, Darcy had immediately set out for Hertfordshire with the purpose of renewing his addresses to Elizabeth Bennet. Happily, she gave him to understand that her sentiments had undergone so material a change since the period of Darcy's first proposal, as to make Elizabeth receive with gratitude and pleasure his continued assurances. The happiness which this reply had produced, was such as he had probably never felt before; and Darcy expressed himself on the occasion as sensibly and as warmly as a man violently in love could be supposed to do. Had Elizabeth been able to encounter his eyes, she might have seen how well the expression of heartfelt delight, diffused over his face, became him; but though she did not meet his eyes, Elizabeth listened, and Darcy told her of feelings which, in proving of what importance she was to him, made his affection every moment more valuable.

"Be...before..." she stammered. Elizabeth cleared her throat, hesitated, and then playfully struck his arm with her fan. "Before you..." Another blush touched her cheeks.

Darcy leaned closer, where he might whisper into her ear. "Before I take you in my embrace and have my..."

However, before he could finish, Elizabeth struck him again, this time with more emphasis. "Mr. Darcy!" she exclaimed in protest. "I am not some trollop, Sir."

Darcy tightened his grip on her arm. "Elizabeth, you know that I delight in provoking a response from you, but I would never disparage your name. I love you more than life."

She paused, and a frown crossed her countenance. "I know, Fitzwilliam," she said contritely. "I truly have taken no offense. I suppose my mind remains on today's revelations. Perhaps we should curtail our walk and return to our quarters. Until we resolve this dilemma, I doubt we shall be at our best."

"Are you certain, Elizabeth?" he asked in concern. "I will not have you neglected."

Elizabeth pursed her lips. "Fitzwilliam Darcy," she began her mild chastisement. "How might I enjoy the area's beauty if I know you suffer? We will put aside our pleasures until you have satisfied your cousin's affairs."

"If I have not told you previously, you are a remarkable woman, Mrs. Darcy. How I ever laid claim to your affections, I do not pretend to understand, but I am fortunate among men."

"Some day, I shall share my secrets, Mr. Darcy." She turned him toward the cottages. "For now, come along, Fitzwilliam. We have much to discuss."

* * *

Some three hours later, Darcy and Elizabeth lingered over their evening meal. Darcy had excused the servants for the evening, and he and Elizabeth shared tea and some palate-cleansing fruit as they sat together in the cottage's small drawing room. Elizabeth had curled her legs up beneath her, and in contrast, Darcy had stretched out his long legs before him.

"Then we agree that we shall speak to Mr. Peiffer on the morrow," Elizabeth summarized.

"Agreed," Darcy said contentedly. It was as he had expected. Elizabeth complemented his natural inquisitiveness. She took notice of details which had eluded him, but his wife's keen intelligence was never in opposition to his. "Yet, I possess qualms about your accompanying me to speak to the Rom leader."

"Fitzwilliam, you would be in more danger alone than if I arrived on your arm. Even you admit that the gypsy band will act with honor toward a lady."

"I will consider your suggestion," he said begrudgingly.

Elizabeth dragged her teeth across her bottom lip in that familiar way, which he recognized as her deep consideration. She placed her cup and saucer on a nearby table. "Do you suppose we might discover someone besides Mr. Stowbridge who could address our questions regarding the events which took place after your cousin's interment?"

"I am not certain whom to ask," Darcy confessed. "It is not likely the local curate would offer much insight."

"We should speak to whomever was the first to come upon the Rom's body," Elizabeth reasoned.

"I fear, Mrs. Darcy, that in this matter, you and I will wear many hats, and I am most profusely sorry that you must be exposed to such sordid details; but please know how much I cherish your counsel."

* * *

"You are saying, Sir, that you have not involved yourself in the investigation of your client's death," Darcy said in incredulity. He and Elizabeth had called on the solicitor early in the man's day. Darcy's presence had sent the staff of Smythe and Osborn into a flurry. Yet, despite all the fawning and praise, Darcy remained unimpressed.

"We are the largest firm in the area," Mr. Peiffer said in self-importance. "And we serve many in the shire, but our clientele is solidly of the Christchurch community. Wimborne is some fifteen miles to the west. Events outside Christchurch cannot concern us."

Darcy's mouth set in a tight line. "Not even when Smythe and Osborn profit from those events?" he asked brusquely.

Elizabeth did not permit the solicitor a response. In his place, she said, "Mr. Darcy, perhaps it is best that we leave Mr. Peiffer to his duties. I have suddenly recalled that I promised Mrs. Ridgeway I would oversee the packing of Cousin Samuel's belongings." She stood and reached for her reticule.

Automatically, Darcy followed her to his feet. Whatever his wife planned would be better than dealing with the asinine Mr. Peiffer. "As you wish, my dear," he said obediently. Offering an abbreviated farewell to the solicitor, Darcy placed Elizabeth on his arm. He led her from the offices. "What was the purpose behind that charade?" he asked grumpily as he escorted her along the busy walkways.

Elizabeth purposely did not respond. Instead, she tightened her grip upon his arm. As they strolled toward the waiting carriage, she stopped periodically to glance into a shop window. If Darcy had not found her farce so amusing, he would have been quite angry. By the time they reached the coach's steps, he was shaking his head in disbelief. As he assisted Elizabeth into the carriage, he whispered into her ear. "Whatever scheme you have devised, I am your servant."

She caressed his cheek and pursed her lips in a pretty kiss before entering the coach. Darcy followed close behind her.

"Where to, Mr. Darcy?" his footman Murray asked.

Darcy nodded towards his wife. "Today, we take orders from your Mistress."

Elizabeth smiled knowingly. "Wimborne, Murray. We return to Samuel Darcy's home."

"Yes, Mrs. Darcy." The footman closed and secured the coach's door.

Darcy leaned easily into the squabs. He crossed his arms across his chest and closed his eyes. And then he waited. His wife was not known for her patience, and he knew it was only a matter of time before she would explain her scheme.

He sat, perhaps, five minutes before Elizabeth tutted her impatience. "I call a truce, Sir," she said contritely. "You recognize my weakness too well." Leaning toward him, she pleaded, "Please ask of my maneuverings."

Darcy opened his eyes slowly. He loved the moment in the early morning when he opened his eyes on the day, and they rested on Elizabeth's countenance. It brought him true peace. "Very well, my dear, please explain why you deemed it so important to end my conversation with Mr. Peiffer?"

Elizabeth sighed deeply in satisfaction. "First, Mr. Darcy, to engage in conversation, one must have a minimum of two relatively intelligent beings, not an exotic parroting bird such as Mr. Peiffer as one's partner."

"Very true," Darcy said through a pleased smile. He and Elizabeth customarily made like judgments of people. At least, they had done so once they had ceased their battle of wits and learned to love one another.

"Second, by announcing that I intended to supervise the consolidation of your cousin's effects, I earned permission from his man of business to do so," she declared.

Darcy's frown created deep lines in his forehead. "I did not hear Mr. Peiffer grant us such an allowance."

Elizabeth countered, "Neither did you hear him object. If we possessed no right to search through Cousin Samuel's belongings, surely his man of business would have made that fact known."

Darcy chuckled, "And as the events in Wimborne can be of no consequence to those in Christchurch, we hold an open invitation."

"Exactly, Mr. Darcy."

Chapter 3

Respectfully, Mrs. Ridgeway welcomed them to Woodvine Hall. "We thought it best if we separated Cousin Samuel's belongings. According to Mr. Peiffer, certain items have been designated for the Antiquarian Society." Darcy eyed the entranceway. When he and Elizabeth had called at Woodvine the previous day, the hall had been draped in the late afternoon shadows. On this day, he observed the unusual placement of many of Samuel Darcy's most bizarre treasures, specifically several carved Gorgons along the top of a magnificent grandfather clock. The Gorgons were certainly not items to his liking or taste.

Elizabeth chimed in, "We have procured a list." From her reticule, she retrieved the page Mr. Peiffer had provided them earlier.

Darcy had never considered her acting ability, but his wife was a natural. Or perhaps she had a mind for larceny. An expert thief required a quick mind for improvisation. The thought brought a light chuckle. "We would prefer to start in Samuel's study," he instructed.

Elizabeth added, "Perhaps, we might commission a room or two." She unfolded the list and glanced at it. "As we uncover each of the items to be donated, we could place them in the designated room to separate them from the remaining effects of the late Mr. Darcy."

Mrs. Ridgeway's frown spoke of disapproval, but she nodded her agreement. Darcy interjected, "We might also consider sep-

.arating Samuel's treasures from Egypt from those he secured in China and those from Africa. Lady Cynthia could choose which she prefers from her uncle's memories."

The housekeeper motioned one of the maids forward. She whispered instructions and sent the girl on her way. "I will have everything arranged whenever you are prepared to move Mr. Samuel's discoveries." She sighed deeply, "It is hard to imagine that Mr. Samuel will not be returning from an afternoon walk or a ride across his land. The staff and I have been at sixes and sevens as to what role we will play in the estate's future. Several expect to lose their positions."

"How long have you been with the late Mr. Darcy?" Elizabeth inquired sympathetically.

"Not quite seven years," the lady confided. "We met on a ship returning from America. I had just lost the late Mr. Ridgeway some three years prior, and I knew not what I would do when I returned to England. I am thankful Mr. Samuel showed me a great kindness."

"I recall Samuel's excursion to America. It was less than a year after my father's passing," Darcy explained. "Both my sister and I felt bereft of my cousin's counsel and his company, but we understood he had business that he had neglected while attending our family, and we had lives to set aright. We parted sadly, but with hope."

"Mr. Samuel was an excellent employer," Mrs. Ridgeway asserted. "Now, if you will follow me, I will show you the Master's study."

Within minutes, Darcy and Elizabeth were alone. Trying to take it all in, Elizabeth turned in a circle. "Mr. Darcy, if I ever complain about your need for order, remind me of this room."

Darcy assumed the seat behind his cousin's desk. "Do not permit the clutter to deceive you. Samuel Darcy had a brilliant mind."

Elizabeth seated herself before the desk. As she removed her bonnet and gloves, she said, "I would expect nothing less from a Darcy." She retrieved the correspondence from a nearby tray. "Where do we begin?"

Darcy reached for the foolscap on the corner of Samuel's desk. As he sharpened a pen, he said, "I think it best we list what we know and what we have yet to discover. Those lists should determine how we proceed."

For the next few minutes, they summarized the information they had learned from Mrs. Ridgeway, Mr. Peiffer, and Mr. Stowbridge. Unfortunately, the list was very short. "Not very promising," Elizabeth noted as she read over his shoulder.

Darcy frowned in dissatisfaction. "Evidently, we have stepped into a marshy predicament," he mumbled. Freshening his pen, he said, "Let us create the other list."

"We should start with Mr. Stowbridge's entertainment. The squire said something about your Cousin Samuel's remarking on the evening's discussion reminding him of an ancient ritual," Elizabeth suggested. "Someone should speak to Mr. Drewe and Mr. Mason to determine the source of your cousin's qualms."

Darcy added, "And the type of ritual." He jotted down their ideas. "Samuel often visited uncivilized societies. Did my cousin base his remark on something one of Mr. Stowbridge's guests said or on something the gentlemen were creating as part of their authorships?"

"Of course." Elizabeth's excitement grew. "I had forgotten that Mr. Stowbridge's guests are writers. Perhaps, they write a tale of haunted castles and darklings."

Darcy smiled easily. "You really must avoid Mrs. Ratcliffe's tales," he teased.

Elizabeth pointed to the list. "No commentary, Mr. Darcy. You are simply the scribe."

He winked at her and returned to the page. "We must determine with whom Samuel was disappointed."

"Mayhap your cousin has a journal that would provide us clues to his mindset," Elizabeth proposed.

"An excellent idea," Darcy concurred. "In the past, Samuel kept detailed reports of his expeditions. In addition to those logs providing us with information on the aforementioned ritual, they may also lead us to more personal notes."

Elizabeth thumbed through the stack of letters. Her brow furrowed in concentration. "Obviously, we must discover what happened to Cousin Samuel's body," she said matter-of-factly.

"Was Samuel ever in the grave?" Darcy asked, and the possibility surprised both of them.

Elizabeth said, "We have assumed that Samuel Darcy knew a traditional English burial."

Darcy shook his head in the disbelief. "At this point, we should avoid making assumptions. There are no assigned parameters in this scenario. And indeed it appears as if Cousin Samuel involved himself in something beyond the normal."

"I agree," she said softly.

As the list grew, Darcy realized how uncommon the events surrounding his cousin's death appeared. The events of Samuel Darcy's death went against the norm, and Darcy despised how control had been wrenched from his grasp. He regarded her with a somber expression. "What of the explosion?" he asked grudgingly. "Surely if someone wished to rob a grave, he would not do so by destroying the gravesite."

A terrible silence welled between them. "We must discover the reason a Rom would be in a cemetery at night," Elizabeth observed. "I would think the man might hold with too many superstitions to do so." Elizabeth's expression turned thoughtful.

He said, "I cannot imagine many souls taking comfort in a fresh gravesite, especially not late into the night."

"Was it late?"

Darcy frowned. "I *assumed* so, but perhaps it was not."

As if to share a secret, Elizabeth leaned closer. "No one mentioned a shovel, Fitzwilliam. Would not a grave robber require a shovel to do the deed?"

"If there was no shovel, then robbery was not the Rom's motive," Darcy said on a soft sigh.

Elizabeth's breath caught in her throat. She stared dumbly at the list. Even though not complete, her husband's second list had filled one page and half of another. "We cannot manage this alone, Fitzwilliam," she declared.

"I have come to the same conclusion." Conscious of the incongruity surrounding their efforts, Darcy agreed. "Likely, my first task is to send for reinforcements. My cousin is in London. I will ask the colonel to join us and to bring along someone with investigative experience."

"Ask the colonel also to secure the services of a person to catalog Mr. Darcy's archaeological finds. I believe the task beyond my skill," Elizabeth admitted.

Darcy said fiercely, "I doubt anything is beyond your abilities, Lizzy, but I suspect even Cousin Samuel would find the possibilities daunting." He drew out another sheet of foolscap. "Allow me to send for the colonel; then you and I will search for any information that might lead us to the truth."

Elizabeth fanned the letters. "Would it be insensate to read the late Mr. Darcy's correspondence?"

Darcy's countenance hardened. "Elizabeth, I would trust you with my cousin's deepest secrets, but you must act on your instincts in this matter."

She nodded her gratitude. "You should pen notes to Mr. Drewe, Mr. Mason, Mr. Glover, and the head of the gypsy band for a beginning. We must also learn something of who discovered the Rom's body."

"Our list may take the remainder of the day," Darcy grumbled.

Elizabeth reorganized the correspondence on a nearby table. She read each before placing it in one stack or another. "Our efforts will be for the good. Tomorrow, we will begin the necessary interviews."

Darcy lamented, "When I set Dorset as our destination, I possessed no idea of the hornet's nest into which we would slip."

* * *

"Mr. Darcy, my name is Andrzej Gry. You sent for me." Darcy and Elizabeth had returned to Woodvine Hall for a second day. He marveled at how his beautiful wife had taken on this odious task with an air of excitement that permeated his cousin's walls. Even after four hours of examining dusty volumes on the previous day, Elizabeth had awakened with a delightful light of curiosity in her eyes. Today, she oversaw the cleaning and cataloging of Cousin Samuel's private quarters. Darcy would not have her present when he met with the gypsy leader or with Mr. Drewe. Mr. Mason was reportedly unavailable until week's end. Knowing her disappointment with his decision, Darcy had reluctantly agreed to send for her when the surgeon called later in the afternoon.

"Mr. Gry. Thank you for coming so promptly." Darcy gestured to a nearby chair.

Gry smiled with wry amusement. "When a *gadje* sends for a Rom, a member of the band would be sorely lacking if he refused."

Darcy examined the man carefully. "You will pardon my saying so," he said cautiously, "but you have the look of no Roma I have ever encountered, and your accent lacks the rolling Germanic base."

With a tilt of his head, Gry acknowledged the truth of Darcy's words. "My branch of the family comes from the Nordic lines, hence the fairer skin tones and hair." The man smiled easily, but Darcy held the feeling the Rom despised the English idea of politeness. "When my family was driven from Wales to America, I found it judicious to speak as those with whom I dwelled and conducted business." He crossed his legs at the ankles and leaned leisurely into the chair's cushions, but tension remained in the taut lines of his muscles. "I have only recently returned to England to lead my family. We are a mixed band. My mother's people are from central Europe, Sinti, although they had carved out a life of respectability by the time she was born. My father was Roma. Of course, I am neither. As an unmarried man, I cannot be *Roma*, at least, not in the word's truest sense. Our home is in Essex."

Darcy fingered the gold thread that had worked itself free of the chair's braid. "I suppose you understand, Gry, why I have asked you to join me today."

"Rumors say you are Mr. Samuel's cousin and heir," the Rom said casually.

"The rumors are correct," Darcy said matter-of-factly. He took note of Gry's slight grimace. It was an odd reaction to something so simple—Darcy's suspicions increased. That niggling warning he had experienced since arriving in Dorset returned with a vengeance.

"As you are the legal heir to Mr. Samuel's property," Gry said cautiously, "I assume you wish to announce the eviction of my family from your relative's land."

It was Darcy's turn to scowl. "That was not my intent," he said honestly. "Why would I wish to rid myself of the man who might possess the answer to my cousin's mysterious death and disappearance?"

As if to divine the truth, Gry leaned forward. "But the squire mentioned that you objected to our presence on your cousin's land," he said suspiciously.

Darcy certainly did not appreciate Stowbridge's speaking for him. "I would not wish to see your family abuse my cousin's generosity. I would be greatly displeased if that were so, and I would utilize what power I possess to make your lives miserable."

Gry chuckled. "I see you are a man who speaks his mind."

Darcy thumbed the thread again. "In such matters as Mrs. Darcy and I have encountered in Dorset, it seems only prudent to act earnestly." When Gry did not respond, Darcy continued. "I hold many questions regarding the conduct of your family in my cousin's death."

Gry stiffened. "Then, like Stowbridge, you believe my brother held some responsibility in Mr. Samuel's disappearance."

"In reality," Darcy confessed, "I am sadly lacking in details. Perhaps I could convince you to share with me what you know of the events. I assure you I want only the truth."

The Rom studied Darcy closely, and Darcy was careful to school his countenance to match his words. Finally, Gry said, "Except for God's intervention in making me the first born, Besnik would have been our family's leader. His name means faithful, and Besnik was everything that is loyal to what the Roma hold most dear. I fear I am a poor alternative." Squaring his shoulders, the man continued, "I did not sanction Besnik's venture. My brother took it upon himself to meet two gadje in the cemetery on that fateful night."

Darcy's gaze narrowed, and his fingers tightened upon the chair's arms. "Your brother was to meet someone else in Wimborne's cemetery? No one has mentioned this fact previously."

"Because the squire said he would not believe the one witness that confirmed Besnik was not the only culprit in this matter. The magistrate refused to listen to one of my family, my cousin, Emilian. Evidently, our family had encountered Mr. Stowbridge when last my people stayed upon Mr. Samuel's land. It appears Emilian took offense at the squire's attentions to Emilian's betrothed, Luludya. Mr. Stowbridge thought he could treat our women as he might one of his maids," Gry said bitterly.

"I was unaware of these events," Darcy said apologetically. He found himself taken back by the gypsy leader's tone of vehemence. The Rom had hidden his open disdain until this instant, and it was a very telling moment. It seemed to Darcy that he had spoken of his lack of information often since his arrival in Dorset, but what was worse was he feared it was not the last time he would utter the words; and that went against his desire for absolute control.

"It is not uncommon in our travels," Gry confessed. "But with an episode of such importance, one would think Mr. Stowbridge might place his former prejudice aside."

Darcy's mouth set in a tight line. "I agree. Could you honestly explain to me why Besnik would choose to meet strangers over my cousin's gravesite?"

Gry asked ironically, "Who said the *gadje* were strangers?"

Darcy hid his irritation as the man spit out half truths. Darcy grimaced as he heaved a sigh. "I made a poor assumption. Please continue."

Gry apparently enjoyed having the upper hand. He smiled easily. "Besnik had met the men when several *gadje* came to our camp to play cards and to have their fortunes told. They offered my brother promises of *barvalimos*, with claims that if he aided them in opening Mr. Samuel's gravesite, they would share with him the riches they would find. If I had known, I would have forbidden Besnik's participation. My brother held dreams of a new wagon and team for his wife and child."

Darcy stared at the man in disbelief. It seemed a shame for a man to lose his life for something so trivial. Darcy imagined Besnik's wife and child would prefer the Rom's return to a new wagon. "What would make your brother and the others believe that my cousin would be buried with some sort of treasure?"

"It was common knowledge, Mr. Darcy, that Mr. Samuel had recently acquired what the late Mr. Darcy referred to as his 'most amazing find.' In Dorset, men and women are known to take their talismans to their graves. Besides, a sennight following your cousin's untimely death, someone thought to illegally enter Woodvine Hall."

Darcy refused to reveal any hint of his concern. "Was no one charged in that matter?"

"I assume Mr. Stowbridge thought the act occurred at my family's hand. Fortunately, Mrs. Ridgeway caught a glimpse of the intruder. She explained that the man was fair of head. And, of course, no one of that description lives among my people."

"No one but yourself," Darcy noted suspiciously.

A grim expression closed over Gry's countenance. "True, Mr. Darcy, but Mrs. Ridgeway assured the squire that I was much too tall to fit her description."

Darcy gave a slow shake of his head. "Was no one else questioned?" he asked warily.

Gry's eyes narrowed. "Even when the evidence says otherwise, a Rom is always the most likely culprit."

Darcy was more inclined to practice caution, especially when this interview brought more questions than answers. Needing to speak to his wife regarding these developments, he moved to end the conversation. "Is there anything else of which I should be made aware, Gry?"

"Only that my brother would never touch a dead man's body."

Darcy flicked a brow upward. "And how can you be so certain? Often, the temptation of great riches has men acting unconventionally."

Gry shifted his weight. As if sharing a secret, he leaned forward for a second time. "The Roma, Mr. Darcy, have a deep-set respect for both God's, or Del's, power and of Beng's evil intentions. My brother would fear that by opening the box he would unleash ills upon the world."

"Pandora's box?" Darcy murmured.

"Exactly, Mr. Darcy. Besnik, like most Roma, believe in predestination. My brother had asked Tshilaba to read his fortune prior to his departure. Nothing in the cards foretold of this tragedy." Gry stood slowly, and Darcy followed him to his feet. "I know my brother, Mr. Darcy. For money, he might dig a grave, but for no amount would he despoil a man's body."

Darcy accepted the man's assurance with a nod of his head. "May I call upon you if I have additional questions?"

Gry turned toward the door. "Perhaps it is best if you send word, and I will join you as I did today. Most of my family remains more suspicious than ever."

"Why not leave the area?" Darcy asked curiously.

"It is what is expected of a man who feels guilt. As I do not, I choose to remain; at least, until the May Day celebration."

Darcy motioned a footman forward. To Gry, he said, "If I learn of anything of importance, I will make it known to you." To the servant, he said, "Please see the gentleman out." With a nod, the Rom strolled away, but Darcy remained by the door where he might observe the man's retreat. Theirs had been a most convoluted conversation, and Darcy knew not what to make of it.

Once the Rom had had time to leave the property, Darcy sought his wife's counsel. From the time of their joining, Elizabeth had become his closest confidante. He found her staring out the window which overlooked the gardens, in his cousin's library. "Something of note?" he asked with amusement as he stepped up behind her.

Elizabeth glanced over her shoulder at him, but her concentration remained on the couple discreetly speaking under a rose arbor in the lower gardens. "I was ruminating on what a blond god with excessively broad shoulders might have in common with a woman of Mrs. Ridgeway's advanced years." She shifted to the right so Darcy might view the scene below. "Are you familiar with the gentleman, Fitzwilliam?"

Darcy watched the pair with more than a little curiosity. "The man is Mr. Gry. He is the leader of our gypsy band."

"Oh," Elizabeth said with disappointment. "I had hoped to have stumbled upon a compromising situation."

"Always the romantic," he said with true affection.

Elizabeth protested, "Obviously, Mrs. Ridgeway will require a new position once this investigation is complete. If the gentleman is too young for a flirtation, I could have wished for an offer of comparable employment for the lady."

Darcy slid his right arm about her waist. "As neither appears likely for Mrs. Ridgeway's near future, what do you suppose a genteel lady and a member of a gypsy band have in common to generate a conversation of such long duration?" He frowned dramatically as the couple moved closer to one another.

Elizabeth's mouth twisted in a tight line. "Perhaps the lady offers her sympathy for Mr. Gry's recent loss."

"Perhaps," Darcy said with undeniable curiosity. "Yet, in my conversation with the gentleman, I suspected Gry withheld information."

Elizabeth moved closer to the window. Leaning her forehead against the pane, she asked cautiously, "Have we taken Mrs. Ridgeway's amiability too liberally? Are we too gullible in this matter?"

Darcy automatically tightened his hold on her. Elizabeth's tone spoke of vulnerability and brought out his protective nature. In the past, even when he thought he might never claim Elizabeth Bennet as his own, Darcy had moved Heaven and Earth to allay her fears that her sister Jane would never know Mr. Bingley's regard and to save Elizabeth's, and all the Bennet sisters', reputations when Mr. Wickham had seduced the flighty, immature Lydia away from her family. "I suspect we should practice discretion in our interactions with those in the neighborhood. In reality, from Uncle Samuel's staff, I only recognize three who served him when I last visited," he cautioned.

"The conversation has ended," Elizabeth noted, "and Mrs. Ridgeway does not appear happy with the result."

Darcy suggested, "Move away from the window before the lady observes our interest."

Elizabeth stepped around him and returned to a stack of ledgers on his cousin's desk. "Mr. Gry's appearance is not one I would associate with those of Roman ancestry."

Darcy said teasingly, "Yes, I do not imagine many Roma are described as 'a blond god with excessively broad shoulders.'"

Elizabeth's eyes lit with delight. "A woman enjoys taking note of a man who fills out his jacket. Without the padding, of course. Mr. Gry's more casual attire fits him impeccably."

Darcy's eyes narrowed. "Was that your reaction to me? Did you take note of my shoulders, Mrs. Darcy?" he asked inquiringly. This was a conversation he and Elizabeth had never had.

Elizabeth's mouth formed a pretend kiss. "Your form was one of your finer qualities, Mr. Darcy," she confessed. "What quality would you consider your best?" she teased.

His mouth took on a sardonic slant. "I would have thought that my biting wit was your initial interest."

Elizabeth knowingly walked into Darcy's waiting embrace. Lacing her arms about his waist, she laid her cheek upon his chest. "When you walked into the Meryton assembly," she confessed, "I could not remove my eyes from you. I belatedly admit I envied your attentions to Mr. Bingley's sisters."

She paused, and Darcy apologized again for his abhorrent conceit at snubbing her during the dance. "I felt the attraction also, but my pride had convinced me that I would never find a woman of merit at a country assembly."

"We both acted foolishly," Elizabeth allowed. "My next attraction was your wit, and although it is shallow of me, I adored the sometimes less-than-delicate manner in which you addressed Miss Bingley's criticisms."

Darcy admitted, "The blame for Miss Bingley's attacks rested solely on my shoulders. It seemed only fair to defend you."

Elizabeth placed a kiss upon his cheek. "You were quite gallant, Mr. Darcy."

"Then what settled you upon accepting my hand?"

Elizabeth caressed his cheek. "Your fine form brought early girlish dreams, but such frippery cannot be the basis of a relationship. Some day your shoulders will slump and your waist will increase. Adieu to disappointment and spleen. After all, what are men to rocks and mountains?

"No, Mr. Darcy, a fine figure will not sustain a relationship." Elizabeth laughed at her earlier folly. "I once told Aunt Gardiner that stupid men were the only ones worth knowing. But I spoke in haste, and I soon realized that the proposals, which I had proudly spurned only months prior, would readily have been most gladly and gratefully received.

"The respect created by the conviction of your valuable qualities, though at first unwillingly admitted, had for some time ceased to be repugnant to my feelings. But above all, above respect and esteem, there was a motive within me of goodwill, which could not be overlooked. It was gratitude, not merely for having once loved me, for loving me still well enough to forgive all the petulance and acrimony of my manner in rejecting you, and all the unjust accusation accompanying my rejection." Darcy gazed at her in shock, but Elizabeth provided him no opportunity to object. She stepped from his arms, and, taking Darcy's hand, she gazed lovingly into his eyes. "You, who I had been persuaded would avoid me as your greatest enemy, seemed, on our accidental meeting at Pemberley, most eager to preserve the acquaintance, and without any indelicate display of regard, or any peculiarity of manner, where our two selves only were concerned, was soliciting the good opinion of my friends, and bent on making me known to your sister. Such a change in a man of so much pride excited not only astonishment but gratitude—for to love, ardent love, it must have been attributed; and as such, its impression on me was of a sort to be encouraged, as by no means unpleasing, though it could not be exactly defined."

She shrugged her shoulders in self-chastisement for her former naïveté before continuing, "I respected, I esteemed, I was grateful to you; I felt a real interest in your welfare; and I only wanted to know how far I wished that welfare to depend on me, and how far it would be for our happiness that I should employ the power, which my fancy told me I still possessed, of bringing on the renewal of your addresses."

Elizabeth tugged on his hand, and Darcy readily followed her to a nearby settee. Once they were settled, she continued, "No, my love, in essentials, you are very much what you ever were, and from knowing you better your disposition was better understood. By your dealings with Lydia and Mr. Wickham, I was humbled, and I was proud—proud that in a cause of compassion and honor, you were able to get the better of yourself."

She kissed his palm. "So, my husband, I willingly admit to taking note of your figure, but such vanity has no staying stick. It is your honor, your compassion, and your empathy that makes me love you so dearly." Darcy leaned closer as Elizabeth murmured, "And, of course, your lips. I love how your lips are intelligent enough to find mine at just the exact moment that I desire them."

Chapter 4

"And you can think of nothing that might provide an explanation for my cousin's unusual mood?" Darcy asked. He had entertained the young poet, and although he found the man quite amiable, the fact Mr. Drewe could shed no candle upon the mystery of Samuel Darcy's passing frustrated Darcy.

"Of late, Samuel has often been out of sorts." A sudden smile curved the man's lips. "I have repeatedly said your cousin should have been a poet. I have often felt the total bewilderment of knowing Samuel Darcy's empathy for others. He had the soul of a storyteller," Nicholas Drewe confided.

Darcy asked hopefully, "Do you recall what you said that triggered Cousin Samuel's maudlin mood?"

"I simply quoted a few lines from my latest *masterpiece*," Drewe said confidently.

Darcy gave of snort of grim amusement. "Might I convince you to share your excerpt with me, Drewe?"

"I would be honored, Mr. Darcy. I understand you are a great patron of the arts."

Darcy scowled. He had not anticipated that Drewe would dare to seek Darcy's patronage in the midst of what was likely a murder investigation. "Until we discover the disposition of my cousin's passing, I fear my attention rests elsewhere."

Darcy hoped Drewe was a better writer than he was a liar, because prevaricating convincingly was not among the man's talents. "Of course, Mr. Darcy, I did not mean to imply…"

Darcy interrupted, "The poem, Drewe."

"Certainly, Mr. Darcy," he said awkwardly. "I may need a moment to recall the lines as they were then. I have made several changes to the draft since that evening." When Darcy said nothing, Drewe continued,

> *Sharp be the stories*
> *That strike with pain*
> *Fairy-shot*
> *Windswept hills of ole*
> *In the bosom of isolated greens*
> *Invasion—overcome with despair.*
> *Peals of discordant laughter*
> *Come follow Mab you nomadic tribe*
> *Shabti and stolen child*
> *A warning of deceit*
> *Serenaded by the lark's sweetness*
> *A foliate mask dancing with Bacchus*
> *Freyr or Odin or Viridios*
> *No Robin Nottingham*
> *Delusion, nought but truth."*

Darcy listened carefully. "You take your inspiration from Dorset's tales of witches and changelings."

"A man must speak of what he knows," Drewe said with a meaningful look.

Darcy asked suspiciously, "Then you believe in the black arts?"

Drewe said with a sigh, "I believe you will discover in Dorset everyone holds a healthy respect for goblins and sprites. It is as

Chaucer said, 'In the old days of King Arthur; Of which Britons speak great honour; All was this land filled with fairy; The elf-queen with her jolly company.'"

"Yet, this is not Arthur's time," Darcy contested.

"No, ours is a darker one, Mr. Darcy."

* * *

"Fitzwilliam!" Elizabeth burst excitedly into the study. "I found them!" She clutched a small stack of leather-bound books to her chest.

Darcy rose upon her entrance. "Found what, my love?" he demanded in wry amusement. He smiled as she blew a loose curl away from where it drooped over her forehead. His wife had obviously hurried her steps, for her face displayed the flush of her exertion. He reached for his handkerchief and strolled leisurely toward her. "I mean, besides the dust and cobwebs in the corners of my cousin's room?" He lifted Elizabeth chin with his fingertips and dabbed away the smudge on her cheek with his linen.

She cocked one sardonic eyebrow at him. "I am pleased you find my efforts on your behalf a source of entertainment, Mr. Darcy."

He learned forward to return the errant curl to its rightful place. "Oh, my dearest Elizabeth," he whispered into her ear. "You bring me joy. Every day, I wake with a new happiness. It is not at your embarrassment that I smile." He took a half step back where he might look upon her countenance. "Being with you is perfection."

Elizabeth sighed heavily. "When you say such exquisite things, I cannot remain the least out of sorts with you, and I must tell you, Mr. Darcy, that I find my inability to do so most disconcerting. You save me from useless remonstrance."

"We each can no longer afford to cherish pride or resentment," he suggested. "Now, tell me of your discovery."

Her hands tightly gripped the still-dusty volumes. She thrust them into Darcy's open palms. "The late Mr. Darcy's journals," she announced royally. "There was a locked chest hidden under a false bottom in your cousin's wardrobe. I found the key earlier today, but I had no idea, at the time, what lock it might match," she said on a rush. "I brought these. The dates show them to be samples I have chosen to represent the past ten years." She reclaimed one of the leather tomes and thumbed through it. "From what I can tell upon my initial perusal, your cousin religiously summarized his thoughts each day. There are six books representing each year. The ones in your hands are from the prior two years." She pointed to a date on one of the entries.

Her spontaneous, untaught felicity regarding the discovery warmed Darcy's heart. "You are magnificent," he praised her honestly. "Have Murray move the chest to my carriage. I would not wish to leave Samuel's private musings to just anyone. We will read them together at the cottage." He wrapped the twine-tied stacks in his handkerchief and returned them to her. "Mr. Glover will arrive soon, if you care to join me."

Elizabeth smiled brightly. "Thank you, Fitzwilliam, for including me. I shan't be long. I shall freshen my things." She turned toward the door, but Elizabeth paused in her exit. "Perhaps it might be best if we do not share our discoveries with those of the late Mr. Darcy's staff. We agreed to be less credulous in our dealings with those who knew your cousin."

Darcy looked pointedly at his wife. "Although I suspect you are correct, what else has triggered your hesitation?"

Elizabeth winced visibly. "It is odd. I imagined a man of Samuel Darcy's obvious intelligence not to succumb to superstitious talismans."

"I fear you hold me at a disadvantage, my dear." Darcy stared at his wife impassively.

Elizabeth shivered in disgust. "There are small painted eyes upon the walls and witch balls hanging at each window in your cousin's bedchamber."

"And these are…" Darcy's voice rose in question.

"Are symbols for protection against spirits," Elizabeth finished his sentence. "Do you know nothing of Witas and fairies, Fitzwilliam?" she asked in frustration.

Darcy smiled with bemusement. "Obviously, my university education was greatly lacking in folklore."

Elizabeth sighed heavily. "Then I must bring you up to snuff, Mr. Darcy."

"Tonight, my dear," he said seductively. "I will be an apt pupil for all your whims."

Elizabeth's cheeks flushed a becoming shade of pink before she turned once more toward the door. "If you had had a mind to do so, you would have made a fine London rake, my husband. You manage to turn every conversation to your benefit," she teased. Elizabeth presented him with a brief curtsy. "I shall return momentarily. Order tea, Fitzwilliam."

Looking after her in an ecstasy of admiration of all her many virtues from her obliging manners down to her light and graceful tread, Darcy sighed contentedly. It was very vexatious how much he required her in his life. Now that Elizabeth had placed herself under his protection, Darcy was inclined to credit what she wished. "When she is happy, my days are favorable to tenderness and sentiment."

* * *

"It was a most unusual case," Mr. Glover shared. The surgeon was a younger man than Darcy had expected, likely in his late thirties or early forties. "Your cousin's body showed early signs of deterioration. After all, Samuel had lain on a wooded path for many hours before one of Stowbridge's footmen found him. It was prudent to see to Samuel's services as quickly as possible." Glover presented Darcy and Elizabeth the branch without a bark. "Per the late Mr. Darcy's instructions, his man prepared your cousin's body, but Mr. Williamson refused to allow Mr. Crescent to practice the uncivilized arts the man learned in Egypt. They are too primitive by English standards. The good Christians in this community would have no man's body mutilated, even at the gentleman's final wishes," he said pompously.

Sorrow and horror clouded Darcy's countenance. He protested, "If my cousin's last wishes were to have his body mummified in the ancient arts he had studied, then I do not understand how others presumed to choose otherwise."

Glover shot a quick glance of concern at Elizabeth, but he described the Egyptian process nevertheless. "Christians consider the practice barbarous, Mr. Darcy. No Englishman would tolerate such tomfoolery," he declared in repugnance. "As a surgeon, I am not unaccustomed to cutting into the human body, but most Christians believe that God never intended for a man to have his lungs, liver, stomach, and intestines removed and placed in a jar. Nor would any in Wimborne permit a man's brain to be violently ripped from his skull."

Darcy tightened his grasp on Elizabeth's hand, but his wife did not appear squeamish. On the contrary, her countenance reflected her genuine interest in what Glover had said. "I understand how a person might find the possibilities appalling," Darcy said evenly. "Yet, I am equally aghast that Cousin Samuel's last wishes were ignored. What I know of Samuel Darcy says he would not have made such a choice without careful analysis. If Samuel came to a difficult decision regarding his resting state, I would have been inclined to honor it."

Glover apparently was not one to admit an injury or a weakness, for he said, "What was or was not addressed cannot be undone. Samuel's body had obviously served him well in this world, and as we have no idea what became of him, we must follow the example set by Mr. Williamson's parishioners and simply pray for your cousin's eternal soul."

Darcy bit back his retort. "Do you have a theory as to what happened the night the Rom was killed?"

"I examined Besnik Gry after the explosion. Mr. Gry likely died immediately. The gunpowder blew away part of the man's countenance and left a gaping hole in Gry's chest," Glover reported. The surgeon shifted his gaze to where Darcy studied him. News of an explosion a revelation. "By the time of my arrival, Mr. Gry had expired, and the villagers had whisked his contact to the Wimborne gaol."

Darcy's dark eyes were troubled. He was never at ease when a puzzle required solving. "I was led to believe only Besnik Gry had been found that evening. Has Gry's contact been properly questioned regarding the theft of Samuel's body?"

A shadow of sorrow crossed the surgeon's countenance. "Unfortunately, the stranger did not survive. The explosion had sent shrapnel crisscrossing the man's chest, and then again, the villagers had taken their ire out on the man. I treated the stranger, but he never awakened from his injuries. Two days after his incarceration, the accused passed quietly in his sleep."

A dark brow flicked upward. Regret and anger tinged Darcy's voice. "And what of the other assailant?"

"The first of the villagers to arrive in their nightshirts and gowns reported observing someone running away from the scene, but no one gave pursuit."

Darcy tipped his head back and closed his eyes. *Another broken trail.* He blew out a frustrated sigh. "Is there no end to this madness?" The uncertainty played havoc with Darcy's need to control everything in his world. "Mrs. Darcy and I are being led on a merry chase, and I, for one, am exhausted by the duplicity."

* * *

They had enjoyed another stroll on the beach and a leisurely meal when they returned to their let cottage. "Obviously, we cannot trust anyone involved in this matter," Elizabeth had declared.

"It would appear so," Darcy said as he sat heavily in his chair. "We should likely reconstruct our list."

"And burn the previous one," Elizabeth observed. "I want no proof of what we suspect."

The continued quagmire pricked Darcy's pride. A puzzle as complicated as discovering his cousin's murderer had not been what he had expected when he had set a course for Dorset. "I would not consider documenting our concerns except I fear forgetting an important detail. I anticipate the colonel and whomever he has hired to aid in the investigation to arrive on Monday."

"I shall be pleased to speak to someone who does not believe we have lost our senses," Elizabeth said. "When we first began to question the handling of the late Mr. Darcy's death, I thought it simply some provincial malfeasance. Unfortunately, I now suspect more nefarious designs."

"I worry that I have placed you in danger," Darcy confessed.

Elizabeth sat on the chair's arm and leaned her head on his shoulder. Darcy brought his arms about her. "I do not think either of us is in immediate danger," she assured. "I feel this crime is more one of silence than it is of violence. It is as if everyone speaks in half truths."

* * *

Darcy and Elizabeth stepped from a millinery shop in Christ-church's busy business district into the strong April sunshine. "It is a beautiful day," Elizabeth observed. Darcy had insisted they not return to Woodvine Hall for a third day. "It may lessen suspicion," he had reasoned. The more he had considered the evident dangers of their investigation, the more his protective instincts had increased. It was his duty to seek an answer to the question of his cousin's death, but he held a more pressing duty to Elizabeth.

He turned when he heard his name called. Recognizing the approaching gentleman, Darcy placed Elizabeth on his arm and prepared to greet a former acquaintance. "Tregonwell," he called as he offered the man a bow. "What brings you from Cranborne's doors to Christchurch?" Lewis Tregonwell had served as a captain in the Dorset Rangers. Darcy had made the man's acquaintance at a house party several years prior, and they had corresponded with some regularity over the years since Darcy's father's passing and his coming into Pemberley's ownership.

"You have not heard?" Tregonwell asked as he amiably bowed to the Darcys. "I have purchased land from Sir George Ivison Tapps on Bourne Heath. Mrs. Tregonwell and I have built a summer home. We have been there a year last month. We spend more time at Bourne than we do at Cranborne Lodge," he said jovially.

Darcy explained, "Mrs. Darcy and I have set in at Bourne's harbor."

Tregonwell smiled widely. "And this lovely lady must be the aforementioned Mrs. Darcy."

Darcy chuckled. "I have forgotten my manners. Mr. Tregonwell, allow me to present my wife, Mrs. Elizabeth Darcy. Elizabeth, this is Captain Lewis Tregonwell."

Elizabeth curtsied. "I am pleased for the acquaintance, Captain Tregonwell."

"Have you come to Dorset for Mudeford's famous healing waters?" Tregonwell asked.

"We have, Sir," Elizabeth said softly.

Darcy added, "After we see to my cousin's estate. Lady Cynthia Sanderson and I are his heirs."

Tregonwell said in disbelief, "Samuel Darcy. Of course, I should have made the connection."

Darcy said with hesitation. "You knew my cousin."

"Only by reputation," Tregonwell confessed. "The loss of any man of letters leaves a gaping hole in Dorset's future. I extend my condolences."

"Thank you," Darcy said sincerely.

Tregonwell nodded his understanding. "Despite the circumstances of your presence in Dorset, I am more than pleased to know of your recent marriage and to claim the acquaintance of

Mrs. Darcy." He motioned his waiting servant to precede him to his carriage. "Mrs. Tregonwell and I are hosting a small gathering tomorrow evening to celebrate our first year at Bourne. Please say you and Mrs. Darcy will join us. It is an intimate gathering of family and friends."

Darcy glanced at Elizabeth. He liked the idea of introducing her to his acquaintances. A country society would not be too intimidating for Elizabeth to assume her role as his wife. At Pemberley, during Derbyshire's winter months, they had enjoyed their isolated existence, but it was time they claimed their place as a couple. "It would be our honor, Tregonwell."

"Excellent." The captain made to leave them. "I will send a man around with a proper invitation. Where might you be staying, Darcy?"

"The cottages."

Tregonwell grinned slyly. "Wonderful accommodations."

* * *

"Mr. Darcy," Mrs. Barrows said, "it is my understanding you are in Dorset to tend to your late cousin's affairs."

"Yes, Ma'am," Darcy said absentmindedly. He watched his wife charm her tablemates. Elizabeth's eyes sparkled with mischief, and Darcy imagined how she had manipulated her words to offer the young Mr. Grantham a double entendre. Grantham sighed deeply, and Darcy smiled. He had once presented the world a similar countenance. Elizabeth Bennet had besotted him with her dazzling smile and her sharp wit. His wife shot him a quick glance, and Darcy winked at her.

"And do you intend to be in Dorset long?" Mrs. Barrows continued.

Reluctantly, Darcy turned his attention upon the woman. "My cousin's niece is not expected until month's end. Lady Cynthia is recovering from her lying-in. Mrs. Darcy and I have chosen to celebrate our joining by partaking of Mudeford's waters."

Mr. Carnes, Tregonwell's man of business, asked, "Recently married, Mr. Darcy?"

Darcy nodded. "Since November. But Mrs. Darcy and I took no time for a holiday. I stand as guardian for my sister, and Miss Darcy and my wife wished to return to our family estate of Pemberley to open the manor's doors for the neighborhood during the Festive Days. Unfortunately, Derbyshire's winters often prevent travel. This has been our first opportunity to enjoy other parts of England."

"Yet, it is a sad occasion," Mrs. Barrows noted. "Will you wear mourning, Mr. Darcy?"

Darcy felt a sudden rush of protectiveness for his family's name. "As Samuel Darcy was my second cousin and as he passed nearly a month prior, I see no need for my wife or I to don black. The honor we do my cousin is to organize his affairs."

Carnes added, "I am familiar with the late Mr. Darcy. He was a great collector of the unusual."

Darcy gazed steadily at his tablemates. His eyes darkened, and his expression became serious. "Samuel Darcy was a man of science. A man of great intelligence, but also a man of compassion. My family was blessed to count him among us."

Later, when the gentlemen rejoined the ladies in the drawing room, Darcy sought his wife among the chattering women. She thumbed through the sheet music left behind on the pianoforte. He looked over her shoulder at the song titles. "Do you intend to entertain us, my dear?"

Elizabeth glanced up at him. "I did not wish to commit myself to the card tables," she confided.

Darcy asked softly, "Would you prefer to make our departure? I hold no qualms regarding making our apologies."

Elizabeth chose several pieces from the stack. "Perhaps you would join me on the bench, my husband. I will play if you will turn the pages."

"Promise me you will sing at least one," he said intimately. "Your voice provides me such contentment. It is as if I hear *home* calling to me."

Elizabeth blushed. "Likely you mistake my caterwauling for 'home'" she said, but he noted how his compliment had pleased her.

Darcy sat close enough to whisper intimacies in her ear. Elizabeth smiled and giggled. Her skills on the pianoforte had improved dramatically, thanks to his sister. Georgiana practiced very constantly, and his sister's influence showed in Elizabeth's performance. "Well, Mr. Darcy, what do I play next? My fingers wait your orders."

"I care not which song you choose; I care only for the woman who performs it. My wish is to remain by your side all evening, Lizzy," he said huskily. "You mesmerize me as much as you do the rest of Mr. Tregonwell's guests. You have captured the room's complete attention."

Elizabeth shrugged away his praise. This was typical for his wife: Elizabeth set her shoulders to the task at hand, but he noted how her gaze flickered with unspoken passion. Her protest was reflexive. "My fingers," said Elizabeth, "do not move over this instrument in the masterly manner which I see so many women's do. They have not the same force or rapidity, and do not produce the same expression. But then I have always supposed it to be my own fault—because I would not take the trouble of practicing. It is not that I do not believe my fingers as capable as any other woman's of superior execution. For example, my sisters Georgiana and Mary greatly outshine my effort."

"Yet, neither possesses your easy and unaffected touch. Although another may eagerly succeed you at the instrument, your audience will appreciate your efforts with much more pleasure."

* * *

Although it was a Sunday, they had made an unannounced visit to Woodvine Hall. After having purposely stayed away for the two days, Elizabeth had insisted that they attend services in Cousin Samuel's parish. "We could learn more of the Woodvine household if we mingle among the locals," she assured Darcy. "You understand the *ton* and the maneuverings of the aristocracy, and I bow to your expertise, but in a country neighborhood, I hold the advantage. Although some believe," she alluded to a remark he had once made during their days at Netherfield, "that in a country neighborhood one moves in a very confined and unvarying society, I contend that people themselves alter so much that there is something new to be observed in them forever. We may discover much by speaking to those with whom Cousin Samuel did business."

He regarded her in a searching manner. "Do you suppose Mr. Crescent remains in the neighborhood?"

"I think Mr. Crescent will have found it prudent to seek employment elsewhere. Mr. Glover's description of the criticism leveled at Mr. Crescent's willingness to follow Cousin Samuel's last wishes has painted the man in an unfavorable pose. However, I pray Mr. Crescent has lingered for, I fear, only he holds the answer to several of our questions."

With a commitment to learn all they could from the neighborhood, they had arrived early to be ushered to the Darcy box by the Wimborne village curate. However, after the service, Elizabeth had suggested that they join the crowds socializing before the church doors.

"Mr. Darcy," a man running his hat's brim through his fingers said as he offered a respectful bow, "I wish to extend my family's condolences for your loss. I am Lucas Snow. I own the local mercantile."

Darcy nodded aristocratically, but Elizabeth offered the man her most beguiling smile. "Thank you, Mr. Snow. Mr. Darcy and I are gratified to know how much the late Mr. Darcy was loved and respected."

Snow's nervousness faded, and Darcy marveled at how easily his wife had conquered the stranger's hesitation. "The late Mr. Darcy was an excellent customer," Snow related. "But more importantly, Samuel Darcy was a true gentleman. He treated everyone with compassion. The late Mr. Darcy spoke to the individual rather than to society."

Darcy said fondly, "My cousin held a reputation for his benevolence, but it is an honor to hear such sentiments upon your lips."

Snow smiled widely. "I speak the truth, Mr. Darcy. There were few in the neighborhood who would speak ill of your cousin."

Darcy asked astutely, "But there were some?"

Snow flinched under Darcy's direct gaze. "Samuel Darcy knew value when he saw it, and there are always those who offer inferior products," the man said privately.

"Such as the gypsies?" Darcy said softly.

"Yes, the gypsies, but others who pass through. Those who were on the open end of Samuel Darcy's evaluations were not always pleased by his words."

As Snow made his excuses to depart, Darcy nodded his understanding. Several others offered their condolences before the Darcys made to board his carriage. Mr. Williamson, the curate, found them awaiting Murray's setting of the step.

"Mr. Darcy," Williamson said genially, "you have done our simple church an honor with your presence, Sir. Hopefully, you will join us again. I understand you plan to remain in the neighborhood for several weeks."

"We do." Darcy placed Elizabeth's hand on his arm. "I have promised Mrs. Darcy a holiday while we await the appearance of my cousins Lady Cynthia Sanderson and Colonel Fitzwilliam."

Williamson cocked his head. "I was unaware of the colonel's anticipated arrival."

"The colonel is visiting with acquaintances in Cornwall. I have asked him to join us for a few days. As he has regularly traveled beyond England's shores as part of his service to the King, the colonel will provide us new insights on how best to proceed in identifying the value of Cousin Samuel's effects."

Williamson gave a self-conscious laugh. "I did not mean to intrude, Mr. Darcy. Our little village will rejoice with the news of the colonel's and Lady Cynthia's appearances. It is not often we entertain those of the aristocracy."

Elizabeth's dry voice interrupted. "We had hoped, Mr. Williamson, to encounter Mr. Crescent at services this morning. Mr. Darcy wished to acknowledge Mr. Crescent's long service to his cousin."

"According to Mr. Glover, Mr. Crescent has located a new position."

"So soon?" Elizabeth asked innocently; yet, Darcy took note of how quickly she had pounced on Williamson's innocent words.

Did Mr. Glover present a Janus face? The man had spun a contradictory tale regarding the absent Mr. Crescent.

Williamson puzzled. "I had not considered Mr. Crescent's departure a problem."

Darcy was quick to say. "It is not of a problematic nature. I will speak privately to Mr. Crescent with his new employer's permission. Would you happen to know with whom Crescent has taken a position?"

The curate regarded them in surprise. "Truthfully, Mr. Darcy, I do not believe I have heard the man's direction—with a gentleman of some merit in London, if I understood correctly. At least, I believe that is what Doctor Glover confided."

Elizabeth's countenance betrayed her wry curiosity. "I did not notice Mr. Glover among today's parishioners."

Williamson shrugged. "That is not unusual. Perhaps Glover tends a patient."

Elizabeth said nonchalantly, "I also did not take note of Mrs. Ridgeway. I observed many from Woodvine's staff among the worshippers, but not Cousin Samuel's housekeeper."

Williamson confided, "In her some six years in the neighborhood, Mrs. Ridgeway has yet to step over the church's threshold."

Chapter 5

"Fitzwilliam! Look!" Elizabeth gasped. He glanced up at the L-shaped house, which had been built in the Renaissance fashion, but somehow now sported a Baroque exterior. The detailed façade did not appeal to Darcy's need for clean lines, but he could understand how the unique look would capture Samuel Darcy's attention. They had entered the Woodvine lands from the village road rather than the main entrance. Now, as they approached his cousin's manor house, the presence of Mr. Glover's equipage parked behind the stables surprised both Darcy and Elizabeth.

"Interesting," Darcy said distractedly.

Elizabeth murmured, "Perhaps someone within is ill."

Darcy gave a sharp shake of his head. He observed, "But Glover is a surgeon, not a gentleman physician. Let us discover if someone from Woodvine requires Glover's services or whether there is a more questionable reason for his presence under my cousin's roof."

Darcy ordered Mr. Stalling to leave the coach on the far side of the manor below the gardens, and he and Elizabeth approached the main house on foot. "Mr. Darcy!" the Woodvine butler exclaimed as he opened the door to Darcy's entreaty. "I did not hear your coach, Sir. Please come in. Mrs. Darcy, may I assist you with your things?"

Darcy glanced toward the staircase. From the driveway, he could hear Stalling's approach and was certain others in the household could, as well. "Is Mrs. Ridgeway not available?"

"I believe the lady entertains Mr. Glover in her sitting room."

Elizabeth asked innocently, "Is the lady ill? Although we noted many from Woodvine among the parishioners, we did not see Mrs. Ridgeway among those at worship this morning." Elizabeth feigned concern for the Woodvine housekeeper. "It is too early for calls, Fitzwilliam. We should see to Mrs. Ridgeway immediately. I fear the poor woman must be quite ill. Come along." Before the butler could block her way, Elizabeth handed her bonnet to Mr. Barriton and started toward the stairs.

Darcy marveled at how well she had improvised. This journey had brought to his recognition new facets of his wife's personality. He must keep Elizabeth's skills in mind for future encounters. The thought of matching wits with her had always excited him. Obediently, he said, "Of course, my dear," before following her to the third story, where the housekeeper maintained her quarters.

Surprisingly, Elizabeth slowed her steps as they neared Mrs. Ridgeway's door, and instead of knocking, she stepped into an empty room and pulled Darcy in behind her. Before he could question her, Elizabeth's fingers stopped his words. "Shush," she whispered. "Just listen." Within seconds, a maid frantically tapped on the housekeeper's door. As they peered through the crack between the open door and the portals' framing, Darcy and Elizabeth viewed Mrs. Ridgeway's countenance when the maid informed her of their approach.

"Send Mr. Barriton my gratitude," Mrs. Ridgeway said as she shot an anxious glance toward the hallway.

"Yes, Ma'am." The maid rushed away.

Glover joined the lady at the door. "What is amiss?"

Mrs. Ridgeway scowled. "Nothing of consequence. The Darcys fear I am ill. They are coming this way."

"Perhaps, I should leave before they arrive," Glover suggested.

"Barriton told them you joined me for tea. The Darcys will be here momentarily. Just have a seat. We have done nothing wrong." She turned Glover toward their waiting tea service before glancing at the empty passageway once more. Then Mrs. Ridgeway followed the surgeon into the sitting room. She pointedly left the door open.

Elizabeth breathed her order. "Stay here. Your boots are too heavy." Then she tiptoed some ten feet along the passage they had just traversed. Saying loudly enough to be easily heard, "This way, Mr. Darcy. I believe Mrs. Ridgeway's rooms are down this passageway," Elizabeth walked heavily toward the housekeeper's room. As she passed the open doorway, Darcy fell into step behind her. God! How he loved her deviousness and the way her hips swayed when she walked smartly. Her close presence sent a rash of awareness over Darcy's skin, and the scent of lavender filled the air with fond remembrances. The whole situation was quite exhilarating.

"Mrs. Darcy?" Mrs. Ridgeway asked in affected surprise, as they appeared framed in the open doorway. "I had no idea you planned to call at Woodvine today. It is Sunday, is it not?"

"Of course, it is Sunday," Elizabeth said sweetly. "Mr. Darcy and I took advantage of his cousin's pew this fine morning." For effect, his wife glanced with concern at the housekeeper. "When we did not observe you in attendance, I thought perhaps you had taken ill. You can imagine my horror when Mr. Barriton informed us of Mr. Glover's presence in your quarters." It was another of the double entendres that his wife so loved to use in her speech. They truly had been horrified to discover the close connection between Glover and the lady. Another missing detail. It was the source of Darcy's unease.

Mrs. Ridgeway offered the Darcys a belated curtsy. "I am most apologetic for causing you grief, Mrs. Darcy. It was never my intention."

Darcy asked pointedly, "Then Mr. Glover has made a social call?"

Glover stuttered an "Uh…um," before Mrs. Ridgeway answered for the man. "Mr. Glover made an overnight call upon one of Mr. Samuel's tenants. He simply stopped at the main house to report upon his treatments. I naturally asked him to join me for tea before he returned home for some restorative sleep."

Glover immediately reached for his gloves. "And I should be taking my leave. If I dwell longer, I will have to ask Mrs. Ridgeway to provide me a room for the day."

"I am certain the lady would gladly comply," Elizabeth said congenially, but Darcy understood her unspoken conclusion.

Mrs. Ridgeway's tone held a hint of censure. "Of course, I would be pleased to see to the doctor's needs."

"That shan't be necessary," Glover announced. Giving everyone an amiable smile, the surgeon stepped around Elizabeth, but Darcy caught the man's arm to stay him.

"Who was your patient, Glover? I would see to the family's needs in my cousin's absence," Darcy said in mock seriousness.

Glover glanced around nervously. "There is no need, Mr. Darcy."

Darcy waved off the surgeon's words. "I insist. Cousin Samuel would expect it."

Glover glowered. He swallowed convulsively. "Mr. Winters. But keep in mind, Mr. Darcy, not every cottager takes kindly to those who show benevolence."

Elizabeth said defensively, "I assure you, Mr. Glover, that my husband is renowned for his compassionate approach with Pemberley's tenants. His father was an excellent man, and his son is just like him—just as affable to the poor. He is the best landlord and the best master."

Glover looked about helplessly. "I have no doubt of Mr. Darcy's condescension. Now, if you will excuse me." With a curt bow, the surgeon disappeared through the servants' hallway, a fact of which Darcy readily took note.

Mrs. Ridgeway's voice cut the silence. "Am I to assume you planned to continue your accounting of Mr. Samuel's belongings today?"

Elizabeth hovered in the open doorway. Darcy watched as his wife surreptitiously examined the housekeeper's quarters. "I had not planned to return to Cousin Samuel's effects today, but since we're here, perhaps we should spend some time with the late Mr. Darcy's library. Mr. Peiffer sent over a list of books we should separate from the others. I suppose God would forgive us for spending time on the Sabbath with this task. What is your opinion, Mr. Darcy?"

"As you love books nearly as much as you cherish your Christian upbringing, I suspect God will be lenient in his judgment. I believe each of God's children should add something substantial to his education by the improvement of his mind by extensive reading." Darcy hoped his wife would use the reference to Christ's teachings to return to the question of the housekeeper's avoiding the Wimborne village church.

As if part of dramatic farce, Elizabeth asked, "What is your opinion, Mrs. Ridgeway? Would I go against God's tenets if I chose to spend time in completing a duty? Speak to me of what God would intend."

The housekeeper's shoulders stiffened. "I fear, Mrs. Darcy, that I am far from being a student of the Scriptures. You should accept Mr. Darcy's counsel. Your husband means to protect you."

With a slow nod of her head, Elizabeth said, "Of course, you are correct. Mr. Darcy means to protect me in this world, as well as the next."

* * *

They had enjoyed each other's company as they had leisurely perused his cousin's books. By silent consent, the Darcys had avoided a discussion of what most interested them: the true relationship between Mr. Glover and the housekeeper. Instead, they had kept a running chatter between them—the kind one would not expect between those only recently married. Darcy marveled at how well they had assimilated into married life. If an observer had been unaware of their young joining, he might think them of a longer-standing relationship. It was as if they were of one mind. How well they had adapted to each other's temperament was a true testimony to the genius of Darcy's choosing Elizabeth as his wife. He would know a comfortable home, whereas many of his friends would suffer with their choices.

Darcy had once told the colonel, "I cannot fix on the hour, or the spot, or the look, or the words, which laid the foundation. It is too long ago. I was in the middle before I knew that I had begun." And so it was. Darcy had futilely fought his desire for *his* Elizabeth. She had taught him a lesson, hard indeed at first, but most advantageous. She had properly humbled him. He had initially come to Elizabeth without a doubt of his reception, and she had showed him how insufficient were all his pretensions to please a woman worthy of being pleased.

Darcy glanced toward the open door. "I suspect we should finish for the day," he said loud enough for those lurking in the hallway to hear. And Darcy held no doubt that others listened to their conversation. More than one of Samuel Darcy's servants had paused outside the library as they had gone about their duties.

In many ways, Darcy admired how the household staff had rallied about the housekeeper; yet, their actions had rubbed against his deep-rooted sense of loyalty. Their efforts were misplaced. Each member of Woodvine Hall's staff owed his fidelity to Darcy's late cousin. It was Samuel Darcy's estate that continued to pay their wages. He would be glad for Lady Cynthia's arrival. Darcy would encourage her husband, the Earl of Rardin, to join him in releasing each of the fickle wastrels without notice.

"Fitzwilliam," Elizabeth's voice spoke of frustration, and he turned to see her struggling with a heavy tome on one of the higher shelves.

"May I be of assistance, my dear?" Darcy stepped behind her and caught the hefty manuscript in his large grasp.

Still a bit irritated, Elizabeth said, "It adheres to the surface." She stepped to the side to allow Darcy an easier access to the shelf.

Darcy wedged his fingers under the spine. "Perhaps the binding has suffered damage." He carefully lifted the volume, but it would not budge. "Would you place the stool where I might reach it?" he asked as he attempted once more to work the book free.

Elizabeth quickly retrieved the small three-legged wooden stool she had commandeered from one of the maids. "The book is on Mr. Peiffer's list," she disclosed as she placed the stool close to where Darcy waited.

He stilled; his eyes narrowed. Darcy read the title aloud: *The Demon Necromancer*. Fingers flexing at his side, he was left gaping.

"Why ever would Cousin Samuel choose such a book for his donation? The title reeks of something a schoolgirl might read late into the night."

Elizabeth glanced again at the book resting above both their heads. "It is thicker than any novel I have ever read." As Darcy stepped upon the stool, she cautioned, "Be careful, Fitzwilliam." She placed her hand on the back of his long leg to steady him, and Darcy felt the instant heat of her touch. Delicious warmth cascaded through his body.

"Permit me to see what keeps this title in its place," he murmured as he laced his fingers about the book. Yet, still it did not readily come free. "Perhaps," he said teasingly, "the casing is hollow, and Cousin Samuel's latest treasure is within."

He glanced at Elizabeth, and his wife's eyes sparkled with anticipation. "Would that not be grand?" Elizabeth asked with wonderment.

With a bit more force, Darcy carefully lifted the tome. "The binding is caught on a nail, which has worked itself free from the wall," he explained. As he loved books, Darcy worked diligently to avoid destroying the title in his haste to free it. "Cousin Samuel would not want his donation to know harm," he said with a grunt as the book slid free of its holdings.

"I am pleased we uncovered the problem," Elizabeth said with relief. "Another might have ripped the book from its shelf and injured it irreparably."

Darcy grasped the book solidly and lowered it into Elizabeth's outstretched hands. "I should see to the nail," he said as his wife stepped away to examine the book. However, when he reached for the nail, Darcy's fingers found a recessed notch and a lever instead. He paused, his stomach suddenly queasy. Without removing his eyes from the shelf, he instructed, "Elizabeth, close and lock the door."

Thankfully, his wife did not argue or protest. "What is amiss, Fitzwilliam?" she asked as she returned to stand below where he balanced on the stool.

Darcy stared at the lever. He had seen such mechanisms in both the Earl of Matlock's and Lady Catherine's homes, but he had never suspected that he would discover one in Samuel Darcy's house. After all, Samuel's manor was a modest abode in comparison to the sprawling estates of Matley Manor or Rosings Park. "Lizzy," he said cautiously, "I need for you to make some sort of noise to cover what I do next. I do not want Samuel's servants to know what I have discovered."

Her hazel gaze lifted at his strange request. "Fitzwilliam, I do not understand," his wife said in concern.

Darcy glanced at her. "I know, my dear," he said softly. "Just trust me for a moment more."

Elizabeth held his gaze for an elongated moment, and then his incomparable wife nodded her agreement. She opened her mouth and began to sing a Scottish love song, the same one she had sung that memorable evening at Sir William Lucas's home in their early days together at Hertfordshire. It was one of the most exquisite evenings he could ever recall. She had mesmerized him with her song.

Darcy smiled at her and then returned to the lever. Lifting the protruding metal tip with two fingers, Darcy focused on the sound of the bookshelf's separation from the wall. It was a disquieting sensation echoing through his body. A sucking noise signaled the release.

As the air filtered through the small opening, Elizabeth stammered to a halt, but with a sly smile, she renewed her efforts and broke into another verse.

Darcy scrambled from the stool. Pulling the drapes partially closed to prevent anyone from observing their actions, he turned to kiss her cheek. "Keep singing for a few minutes more, my love," he whispered close to her ear.

Quickly, he lit several candles before he wedged his fingers into the opening and pulled with all his might. As if on a silent cloud, the shelving wall slid open. He saw Elizabeth's eyes widen, and he reached for her. Expecting that someone eavesdropped beyond the locked door, he said loudly, "You have a beautiful voice, my dear. Come to me, Lizzy." The servants would gossip about his infatuation with his wife, but the rumors would be a fair price for the privacy they required. Darcy handed his wife a candle and pulled her through the opening.

As she came to a stumbling standstill behind him, Elizabeth gasped, "My goodness, Fitzwilliam! What in the world is this?"

Darcy, too, stared in disbelief. "Cousin Samuel's treasure trove," he said reverently as he descended the last few steps into the hidden room.

Elizabeth's hand rested on the small of his back. She asked curiously, "Do you suppose there are armed traps?"

Despite his wife's trepidation, Darcy smiled. "I doubt Cousin Samuel would go to such extremes. What my cousin considered of value might not pique the interest of those who have never studied ancient civilizations."

Elizabeth stepped beside him, and they surveyed the room together. Darcy held his candle high, allowing the light to creep into the dark shadows. "It is amazing," Elizabeth said in awe. "I have seen nothing to compare—even in London when Uncle Gardiner escorted my sister and me to the museum."

"Perhaps that will change with Cousin Samuel's donation," he said with pride. "It will be a great legacy—one bearing the Darcy name."

"May we make a quick tour of what the room holds?"

Darcy caught her hand. "Watch your step." He turned to the left where row after row of glass cases displayed a variety of weapons, eating implements, bones, and jewels. "These appear to be from Egypt," he said as he set his candle on the corner of one of the cases. He glanced to another nearby row of glass boxes. "Those items appear to have come from India or Persia."

"What are these?" Elizabeth asked as she leaned over the case closest to where she had stopped to wait for Darcy. The possibilities touched Elizabeth's cheeks with a flush of excited intensity.

He shoved aside an unfurled set of diagrams for a primitive weapon to join her search of a dusty glass shelf. Removing his handkerchief, Darcy wiped away the grime. "They appear to be some sort of sickle swords," he said, as engrossed in the find as his wife. "Samuel once explained to Georgiana and me how Egypt imported the tin required to make bronze, meaning that those without wealth carried stone tools well into the time of the Middle Kingdom. Egypt was at a disadvantage during the first millennium because it had to import iron."

Elizabeth pointed to what appeared to be a piece of armor. "Are those real jewels?"

"The Pharaohs often wore armor with inlaid semiprecious stones because the stones were harder than the metal used for arrow tips."

Elizabeth nodded her understanding. "We should likely make a quick perusal of the room. We may study the individual pieces at our leisure at another time."

"Excellent suggestion," Darcy said as he retrieved his candle. "We do not want the staff to become aware of this room."

Elizabeth poorly hid her wince. "Do you suppose them ignorant of it?"

Darcy considered her question. He glanced toward the steps. "If any of Cousin Samuel's present staff has knowledge of this room, he or she has not inspected it for some time. Ours are the only footprints in the dust on the stairs and the floor. And no one has touched the cases. I suspect Cousin Samuel kept this room a secret."

"Then what of those?" She lifted her candle higher and pointed to several books and amulets on the table half-hidden by the steps. She reached for one of the items. "These do not appear to be of ancient origins."

Darcy joined her at the table. Grasping one of the leather-bound books, he read the title: *Pagan Covens and Apotropaios.*

Elizabeth unrolled a manuscript. She gave a faint frown. "This appears to be a map of the area. Are there Stonehenge-type stones in Dorset?"

Darcy studied the document. "I am unaware of any stones as close as this map would indicate." His finger traced the lines from one symbol to another. "What does all this mean?"

The shadows, past and present, filled every corner of the dimly lit room. She quickly thumbed through a ragged volume that held incantations and prayers. "I would say your cousin had developed a recent interest in witchcraft."

He conjured a nervous smile. "In ancient medicines and religious beliefs, definitely, but not in superstition and the dark arts.

Such practiced ignorance was not in Samuel Darcy's nature," Darcy protested.

Elizabeth said with a bit of irritation, "Samuel Darcy was more than a man of science. He was a man who embraced the unusual. Perhaps, he feared a witches' coven had made him a target."

Darcy felt his temper rising and quickly restrained it. There was so much out of his control that he responded with more vinegar than he intended. "You know nothing of my cousin."

Her husband's chastisement rubbed raw against Elizabeth's vague sense of disquiet. She retrieved her candle and turned for the stairs. "Then perhaps I should leave you to discover your own realities, Mr. Darcy," she said tersely.

Darcy cleared his dry throat before catching her arm. He said resignedly, "I am a fool, Elizabeth. You are the one person I trust in this insanity, and I have made you my enemy."

Framing his face with her hands, Elizabeth smiled warmly. "You were my enemy once, Mr. Darcy, but those days are long forgotten. Now, you are the man I revere above all others. Even though I may speak in opposition, I would never be your critic." She leaned against his chest, pressing her cheek to his heart.

"I love you, Elizabeth Darcy," he said sincerely. His arms snaked about her to hold his wife to him.

"And I you, my husband."

They remained in the embrace for an elongated moment. Finally, Darcy kissed her forehead. "We should have a quick look around before we return to the library. Surely someone will take note of our absence soon." He reluctantly released her.

Circling the room's perimeter, each went a separate direction. They peered quickly into the glass display cases and pulled at the locks to be certain of their security. Along the back wall, Darcy's toe caught on a loose floorboard, and he tapped it in place with his heel. Cursing under his breath at the mark on his favorite pair of boots, he grumbled, "Personally, I have had enough mystery and mayhem for one day." He raised his candle higher for additional lighting. Turning to his wife, he said, "Lead the way, Mrs. Darcy. We may explore Samuel's sanctuary in more leisure in the near future." Within seconds, they emerged into the draped afternoon light. As Elizabeth extinguished the candles, Darcy placed his shoulder to the shelf to return it to a locked position. "Hand me *The Demon Necromancer*. I will replace it to cover the lever."

Elizabeth busied herself with smoothing away their dusty footprints on the carpet as Darcy balanced on the stool to slide the book's cover over the protruding lever to disguise the secret latch. Just as he stepped down and reached for his wife to bring her into another embrace, the library door latch turned, and the door swung wide. Darcy spun to see Samuel Darcy's housekeeper framed by the hall's backlight.

"Mr. Darcy!" The woman said in obvious surprise.

Darcy placed Elizabeth behind him in a protective manner. "How dare you?" he growled. "How dare you intrude upon my private time with my wife!"

"We…we thought…we thought something amiss," Mrs. Ridgeway stammered. "We heard no sound from within."

Darcy lorded over her. "And why should you have? Have you set the household to spy on us? I must say that I find your interference in my efforts to bring a resolution to the mystery of my cousin's death and disappearance beyond the pale. You have taken upon yourself too many liberties, Ma'am. With my cousin's absence you have assumed this household to be yours, but you have erred greatly, Mrs. Ridgeway." Darcy glanced to his wife, who now stood beside him and who clutched his flexed arm. "If this manor is to have a Mistress, it shall be Mrs. Darcy. From this point forward, you will take your orders from her. Is that understood, Mrs. Ridgeway?"

"Absolutely, Mr. Darcy," she said with feigned resignation.

Darcy stepped around the woman. His voice carried through the supposedly empty passageway. "Mr. Barriton, I want to see you and the rest of the household staff immediately in the library." Without waiting to see if his wish would be attended to, Darcy returned to Elizabeth's side. From nowhere and everywhere at once, the room filled with servants dressed in his cousin's livery.

Eyes refused to meet his, but Darcy was accustomed to such deference. He spoke in hard tones. "Mrs. Darcy and I came to Dorset to pay our respects to my late cousin's memory. Unfortunately, because of the bizarre events surrounding Samuel Darcy's death, our journey's purpose has changed. Yet, never once did we consider that we would be treated with complete disregard by my cousin's staff. By my staff," Darcy said with emphasis. "Along with the Earl and Countess of Rardin, I am your current employer."

Darcy paused to allow the reality of what he had just announced to settle. "If any of you wish to leave my employment, I will reconcile your wages immediately." As suspected, no one spoke. Darcy placed Elizabeth's hand on his arm. "I believe Mrs. Darcy and I have accomplished all we may as distant participants in this charade. With Mrs. Darcy's consent, we will be changing our residence to Woodvine Hall tomorrow morning."

With her silence, Elizabeth obediently supported Darcy's plan. His expression uncommonly somber, he continued, "Mr. Barriton, you will see that an appropriate suite of rooms is prepared for Mrs. Darcy's needs and another for mine."

Barriton bowed low. "Yes, Sir."

Darcy's focus remained on the housekeeper. "You will also prepare rooms for my cousin, Colonel Fitzwilliam, and two of his associates. Be certain the colonel's rooms befit an earl's son. Later, we will discuss preparations for the Sandersons' arrivals." Darcy said aristocratically, "That will be all for now, Barriton."

Barriton bowed again. "I will see to it personally, Mr. Darcy." The butler ushered the staff from the room.

When Mrs. Ridgeway made to follow, Darcy said, "A moment, Mrs. Ridgeway." Although he assumed a few of those who had departed would tarry in the passageway to hear his words to the housekeeper, Darcy purposely waited until only he, Elizabeth, and the woman remained. "I will not forget your affront, Ma'am," he said threateningly. "You will bring this household to a proper order, or you will be seeking another position. When I lock a door, it is to remain locked. When I give an order, I expect it to be followed without comment. Is that understood?"

"Yes, Mr. Darcy."

Darcy's temper had not lessened. "I am not the amiable employer of your past, Ma'am, and you would do well to remember that fact."

Chapter 6

She had been quiet: Far too quiet for Darcy's peace of mind. "Say it," he dejectedly insisted. They had departed Woodvine Hall shortly after he had delivered his ultimatum. However, his wife had yet to speak her mind, and Darcy had fretted over her silence.

Obediently, she drew her gaze from the passing scenery to meet his eyes. Elizabeth gritted her teeth. "What is there to say, Mr. Darcy?"

"You might say I overreacted. You might say I failed my cousin by showing the opposition my Achilles heel. You might say I promised you a holiday, but I have dragged you into a developing scandal."

She lifted her shoulder in a casual shrug. "Why should I speak such disparagements? You obviously recognize your weaknesses, Mr. Darcy." She smiled wryly.

Darcy moved to sit upon the bench seat beside her. "I could not control my anger, Elizabeth," he confessed. "I kept thinking how Mrs. Ridgeway's intrusion might have brought degradation to your door. What if instead of the secret room we had partaken of…" He broke off when his wife blushed thoroughly.

"Mrs. Ridgeway has been permitted too many liberties," Elizabeth conceded. "With your cousin's frequent and extended absences, Mrs. Ridgeway has experienced complete freedom in the running of the late Mr. Darcy's household. Yet, it would not serve us well in discovering Woodvine's secrets to announce our intentions, and I readily admit that I have no desire to sleep under

Samuel Darcy's roof." His wife's immediate understanding of the situation brought a bit of relief to Darcy's mind.

He declared, "I will protect you, Lizzy. I would never purposely place you in danger."

"I know your nature, Fitzwilliam," Elizabeth persisted. "But it does not lessen my trepidation. We are caught in a game, and we hold no understanding of the rules or of the players. Nor are we aware of the true dangers. Despite your reassurances, my husband, we must recall that your cousin lost his life to an unknown assailant and in the most improbable manner, and the late Mr. Darcy can find no rest because either the same culprits or a different set have removed his corpse from its final resting place. I cannot feel easy about our relocating to the hornet's nest."

Darcy touched her arm lightly. "When I made my decision, I did not consider how this situation might worry you. I am truly apologetic." He stared into his wife's beautiful countenance. "In my defense, I have always seen you as *my* doughty spirit. You are incomparable, Elizabeth."

Elizabeth sighed in exasperation. She rolled her eyes heavenward, but she asked, "How may I object when you speak thus?" She rested her head on his shoulder, and Darcy drew her nearer.

He did not think he could survive if his wife lost faith in him. Beyond her passion—beyond her companionship, Darcy desired Elizabeth's belief in his steadfastness. "Place your trust in me, Lizzy. I will not fail you."

* * *

"I do not like it, Fitz," his cousin, Colonel Edward Fitzwilliam, said, as he scowled for the third time in less than ten minutes.

As expected, the colonel had arrived in midmorning with a former Bow Street Runner and an expert from the British Antiquarian Society in tow. Without permitting his cousin or the colonel's associates the leisure of unpacking their belongings, Darcy had set about explaining the events surrounding Samuel Darcy's passing and the series of surprises he and Elizabeth had encountered since their arrival in Dorset. "I am not pleased with the circumstances," Darcy said seriously, "but I am content that this is the most prudent means to discover Woodvine Hall's secrets."

"Why should we not simply dismiss the staff and hire one we can trust?" the colonel argued.

"I agree with your cousin," Elizabeth said pleadingly.

He could not claim his cousin's cunning nor his wife's pure bravado, but there was one area in which he excelled: Darcy knew something of human nature and all its foibles. Darcy caressed the back of Elizabeth's hand before catching it and bringing it to rest in his lap. "As one may hear, Mrs. Darcy holds her own qualms regarding this matter." He interlaced their fingers. "Yet, I am unswayed. I have considered my rash response to Mrs. Ridgeway's intrusion into Cousin Samuel's library last evening. It is my opinion the Woodvine staff seeks Cousin Samuel's reported treasures. I have observed that most of the items on display about the house are valuable to a man of science or of history, such as Mr. Franklyn," he said as he gestured to the bespectacled archaeologist sitting unobtrusively in the corner. "But they lack value to those in service. Based on what little I observed of the secret room, Cousin Samuel's wealth rests within," Darcy said definitively. "I suspect that last evening when Mrs. Darcy and I drew the drapes, those spying on us thought we had discovered Cousin Samuel's secrets."

"Which we did." Elizabeth shivered with hesitation.

Darcy smiled lovingly at her before tugging her closer. "Yes, but Samuel's staff has no knowledge of our find. We had set the library to right before Mrs. Ridgeway made her entrance. The housekeeper only discovered a newly married couple in an embrace." He noticed Elizabeth's blush, but his wife did not drop her chin nor did she divert her eyes. That was why he had always considered her indomitable. Elizabeth would face down any form of censure. "However, it is simply a matter of time before they uncover what we did," Darcy insisted. "The only means to prevent that from happening is to take occupancy of Samuel's manor house. Otherwise, his company of less than reputable employees will have free rein."

"I, for one, agree with Mr. Darcy's reasoning," the Runner said. He moved to stand beside the marble chimneypiece. Thomas Cowan's hair showed touches of gray at his temple, but there was nothing "elderly" about the man. Perhaps five and thirty, Cowan stood close to six foot and weighed some fifteen stone. There were dark circles under the man's eyes and a faint haggardness in his attire, but Darcy had liked the man immediately. "Sometimes, a man must take control of an investigation by making a preemptive move."

"I could go alone," Darcy suggested.

"Absolutely not!" Edward and Elizabeth said in unison.

Elizabeth protested, "I shall not have you be a Daniel in the lion's den."

The colonel added, "We will face the chaos of Woodvine Hall together."

Darcy nodded his gratitude. "We should set out when everyone has had the opportunity to partake of the nuncheon Mrs. Fox has prepared."

* * *

Their heated discussion continued on the journey to Woodvine. Darcy had described to the colonel and Cowan the background story he had created for the villagers as to why he had sent for Edward. "I think it safe to say," Darcy had explained, "that we may *discover* Samuel's cache on the morrow, and then Mr. Franklyn may begin his inventory."

Their expressions thoughtful, his cousin and the former Runner agreed. "Afterwards, we may concentrate on solving this mystery," Cowan said as he leaned forward. Darcy, Edward, and Cowan had ridden in Edward's carriage, while Mr. Franklyn had kept Elizabeth company in the Pemberley coach. Cowan said cautiously, "Are you willing to accept the fact that we may never uncover the truth of your cousin's death? The perpetrators have had nearly a month to set right their mistakes."

Darcy hesitated. "I would hate to walk away from this without a resolution, but I can live with the idea of our performing to our best, but still knowing failure."

Within minutes, the company disembarked the carriages before Woodvine Hall. Darcy had previously instructed his and the colonel's servants on how to treat the Woodvine staff. "Be receptive to any overtures, but do not trust any among the current employees. And more importantly, if you overhear anything out of the ordinary, confide your suspicions to Murray or Jatson."

Elizabeth accepted Darcy's hand as she stepped from the coach. "My objections remain," she said softly.

"I understand, but I am most appreciative of your support," he acknowledged.

He stared deeply into emerald green eyes. The eyes disclosed the depths of her soul, and Darcy had once called them "fine," but that word did not come close to defining the pure exuberance, which danced within them. "I shall never fail you, Fitzwilliam," she whispered, and Darcy knew without a doubt that Elizabeth spoke the truth. Despite his familial arrogance and her initial insensibility, from the onset of their acquaintance, he had known her to be the one person upon whom he could rely—the person who would complete him.

He inhaled his wife's essence and permitted it to mark him as hers. "Nor I you, my love," he said as he escorted her through Woodvine's entrance. He turned to the waiting butler. "Mr. Barriton, I assume everything is in order," he said aristocratically.

"It is, Mr. Darcy."

Darcy shot a glance about the foyer, but Mrs. Ridgeway was nowhere to be found. "This is my cousin, Colonel Fitzwilliam, and his associate Mr. Cowan." Barriton bowed to both gentlemen. Darcy continued, "And the gentleman sent to authenticate Cousin Samuel's donations to the British Antiquarian Society is Mr. Franklyn. I am certain, when necessary, Mr. Franklyn will send for others to assist him."

"I understand, Mr. Darcy." Barriton's tone and manners had changed dramatically from the time of their previous encounter.

"Mrs. Darcy and I prefer to keep country hours. We will settle into our quarters. If we have not come down prior to that time, you will send someone to inform us of supper. Tomorrow, Mrs. Darcy will meet with Mrs. Ridgeway and the manor's cook regarding menus and other requirements for our stay."

"Yes, Sir."

"Now, please have someone escort us to our quarters."

While Hannah and Mr. Sheffield saw to the unpacking, Darcy and Elizabeth relaxed in their adjoining sitting room. "You were quite demanding," Elizabeth teased as she stroked his brow.

Darcy leaned against the settee's cushions and enjoyed his wife's ministrations. His eyes remained closed, but he said, "I thought you enjoyed my Master of Pemberley persona."

Elizabeth brushed her lips across his ear lobe, her touch making Darcy forget the importance of breathing in and out. "I cannot say that I have always appreciated the power of your persuasion," she said playfully. "However, I have grown quite found of it over the past year. Your understanding and opinions all please me. In fact, you want for nothing but a little more liveliness, and as you have married prudently, your wife may teach you."

"Liveliness, is it?" Darcy asked as he caught her and pulled Elizabeth into his lap. "I will demonstrate *liveliness* to my most *sensible* wife." Without giving her time to consider the desire she created in him, Darcy kissed her passionately, smothering Elizabeth's squeals as he took her mouth.

At first, as if to escape, she wriggled in his embrace, but soon she clung to him. "Fitzwilliam," she murmured as Darcy broke the kiss. He treasured those moments when his name was both a prayer and a demand.

"Yes, my love," he said with an easy smile.

"You are incorrigible," Elizabeth complained, but she snuggled closer.

Darcy tilted her chin up where he might look upon her countenance. "Yet, you love being my wife?" he teased. However, there was always that moment of hesitation where he questioned his happiness as a providential stroke of luck.

"More than anything." She said sincerely, "When we are old, and it is our time to know God's will, I pray that our Lord takes us together. I cannot imagine living even one additional minute without you."

Her sentiments had spoken to his soul in ways that no simple "I love you" could. Elizabeth had put into words Darcy's greatest fear—that one day they would no longer be together. In the past six months, he had repeatedly asked God to take him first because he did not believe he could go on without her. "We will pray for God's benevolence. Surely He knows of our love."

* * *

Mr. Franklyn spoke in agitation. "Mr. Darcy, you do not understand." They had gathered in the smallest of the drawing rooms while their party awaited the supper service. "Someone has purposely removed the jewels from the Head of Thiruvadhiral." The man thrust a small figurine into Darcy's hands.

Darcy examined the unusual statue in which the figure's head dwarfed the remainder of its body. Carved from a polished granite-type material, the figurine displayed a slight scratch where Franklyn had declared the three jewels should be. "Perhaps the jewels were removed many years prior to my cousin finding this piece," Darcy suggested.

Franklyn was far from appeased; the man said in dismissal, "That is impossible, Mr. Darcy. Samuel Darcy sent a detailed listing of his most recent findings to the Society in January. I brought tidings from the Society's chair, at the time, and later, in mid-February, Mr. Sedgelock and Mr. Chetley visited with your cousin. During that short stay, Sedgelock and Chetley verified the existence of and the condition of each piece in the late Mr. Darcy's collection, as well as the items he indicated that he would have the Society display at the Grand Exhibition in September. I have that original list with me. I have studied it extensively, and I can assure you, Sir, that Thiruvadhiral's head held three small jewels, each perhaps the size of a small pebble: two rubies and one sapphire."

Elizabeth shared, "Reportedly, there was an attempted robbery some three weeks prior to our arrival."

Franklyn paled. "I pray nothing else is missing."

Darcy leveled a steady gaze on the man. "You may begin your detailed search on the morrow. If you believe it necessary, Sir, to send for reinforcements, I hold no objections. I am certain the Earl of Rardin would want his wife's inheritance handled by experts."

* * *

Darcy woke early the following morning. The heat from Elizabeth's body nestled against him reminded him how fortunate he was to have found her. He was also very fortunate not to have lost her. In reality, his idea of a holiday had come about because Elizabeth had not been herself of late. Since February, his wife had silently grieved for what was not to be. Elizabeth had not realized she carried his child until after she had lost it.

Neither he nor Elizabeth had fully understood what had caused her to double over in pain and had sent her tumbling down Pemberley's main stairway. Fearing the worst, Darcy had sent immediately for the surgeon. He had never known such incapacitating fear in his whole life. Only after Mr. Spencer had come and gone had Mrs. Reynolds explained that Elizabeth's bruises would easily heal, but his wife's disposition had suffered the greatest injury. He had held her in his embrace as Elizabeth had sobbed for their loss and had uttered the question both of them feared most: "What did I do wrong?"

Darcy had had no answer, but he had not blamed Elizabeth. Even before Darcy's loyal housekeeper had assured him that the fall had not cost him his heir, Darcy had known the truth. "Mrs. Darcy's body must learn to nourish the child," Mrs. Reynolds had insisted. "Your lady was not prepared to carry a babe. Each woman is different. Mrs. Darcy will become enceinte again."

Darcy had nodded his understanding, but that evening as he said his prayers, he had begged God not to take her from him. "Even if it means no heir for Pemberley, give me Elizabeth. She is all I require."

"You always wake so early," she murmured against his skin. Her breath tickled his chest.

He stroked her hair and nudged her closer. "I promised my cousin that we would ride out this morning. The colonel has an idea where the ancient stones may be found. Several men in his previous command were from Dorsetshire."

Elizabeth kissed the line of his chin, nipping gently at the point where his neck met his shoulder. "And your wife cannot induce you to remain in her bed?" she asked huskily.

Darcy rolled her to her back and draped himself over her. "My wife has only to walk into a room or to share a smile, and I am lost to her presence." He tasted the curve of her shoulder.

"Poor Mr. Darcy," she said with sugary sweetness. "Such a terrible ailment. However will we cure you?" She brushed the hair from Darcy's forehead.

"Love me," he growled as he claimed her mouth. "Just love me, Lizzy."

* * *

An hour later, Darcy and the colonel strode toward the Woodvine stables. Edward had brought his mount from London, but Darcy would ride one of Samuel's horses. "Mr. Darcy?" The head grooms-man bowed respectfully.

Darcy closely examined the man's countenance. "I have seen you previously, have I not? You have been in the late Mr. Darcy's employment for some time."

"Aye, Sir. For a bit over twenty years. Since I be a boy. Me father served Samuel Darcy before me. Holbrook, Sir."

Darcy's wall of reserve relaxed. "I sent word for a proper mount, Mr. Holbrook."

The groom's smile faded. "I must apologize, Mr. Darcy. Other than the carriage horses there be none to be had, Sir."

Darcy scowled. "How is that possible? Cousin Samuel was never one to keep a large stable, but my cousin surely maintained cattle for his own pleasure."

Holbrook took a half step backward. His voice spoke of his discomfort. "The late Mr. Darcy kept three thoroughbreds. The former master be a competent horseman."

He was wound tight and seriously ready to explode. Darcy demanded, "Then where are Samuel Darcy's horses? My cousin has been but three weeks deceased."

Holbrook swallowed hard. "The horses be sold, Sir. Less than a week following Mr. Darcy's untimely death."

"Sold!" The word exploded into the damp morning air. "Sold to whom? And under whose orders?"

The groom glanced toward the manor house. "A man comes with a bill of conveyance. He claims Mr. Darcy's stock be his. I read the papers meself."

Instantly, Darcy understood the groom's unspoken explanation. He asked dangerously, "Was it Mrs. Ridgeway or Mr. Barriton who negotiated the purchase?"

Holbrook's eyes did not meet Darcy's. "The housekeeper, Sir." The groom hesitated before saying adamantly, "Master Darcy would have been fit to be hanged before he would have parted with them animals."

Darcy's anger seethed. Not only had his father's favorite cousin lost his life, but also those Samuel Darcy had trusted most had betrayed Samuel over and over. Darcy set his step in the direction of the house, but the colonel's hand on his shoulder stayed him.

"You cannot dismiss the woman," Edward insisted. "Only yesterday, you argued that this mystery revolves around Mrs. Ridgeway's arrogance. Our only hope to disentangle this situation is to keep her close. To date, she has committed no crime."

He rubbed one hand across his face. Darcy growled, "The woman is a thief. I will see her at Newgate."

Edward reasoned, "All Mrs. Ridgeway must do is claim your father's cousin had instructed her before his death to sell the horses." He lowered his voice. "You must play the game more intelligently, Darcy. Do not show your cards too soon."

Elizabeth had said something similar the day prior. "Only once previously have I known a person so full of deceit," Darcy said unevenly.

Edward understood immediately. "If I had held no previous acquaintance with the late Mrs. Wickham, I might have considered Mrs. Ridgeway the mother of our favorite miscreant. They come from the same stock."

He thought his cousin's comparison a true evaluation of the Woodvine housekeeper. As young men, he and Edward had often attempted to understand Darcy's former friend's vicious propensities and want of principle. They had laid the blame for George Wickham's many manipulations at Mrs. Wickham's feet. The Wickhams were always poor from the extravagance of Mrs. Wickham. Darcy sighed heavily. "What do I do instead of strangling the woman?"

Edward chuckled. "We provide Mrs. Ridgeway with a length of hemp and pray the lady hangs herself with it."

Darcy looked toward the house. His brain was racing, and anger had lodged in the center of his chest. "To what den of deceit have I brought my bride? Elizabeth requires time to heal. To rediscover her joy. Instead, we are embroiled in a never-ending quagmire."

Edward assured, "Mrs. Darcy is resilient. She will survive this adventure. Perhaps," he said cautiously, "it will force Mrs. Darcy to move beyond her recent loss."

Darcy despised the guilt that seemed to cling to the edges of his mind. "I pray you speak the truth. Elizabeth is my life. Beyond my duty to my father's cousin, my duty to Mrs. Darcy remains paramount."

The colonel said, "This is more than a simple theft. Those involved have composed their crimes. We have a mysterious death, a missing corpse, stolen horses, and disappearing gems. We cannot walk away from this, and we must keep control. It is important, Darcy, that you use most astute judgment. You cannot permit your anger to outweigh your good sense."

After a long moment of silence, Darcy said grudgingly, "I know your tactical nature, and I will follow your lead."

Edward motioned the groom to them. "Mr. Holbrook, my cousin intends to retain the services only of those who faithfully serve Samuel Darcy's memory. We hope to count you among them."

Holbrook puffed up with pride. "I have spent me whole life at Woodvine, and I's don't be approvin' of all the changes made at the manor. It not be right, Sir. Some of them let go previously had been with Master Darcy for years. Give Woodvine their lives and service and be released without pension or letter."

Edward did not permit Darcy to respond. To the groom, he said, "If you serve us, we will right the wrongs you describe." The colonel paused for emphasis. "Mr. Darcy requires you to keep this conversation private. Can we count on you to follow orders, Holbrook?"

"Aye, Sir," the man said earnestly. "And any other task ye need done. I not be afraid of them who set themselves above the Master."

"Excellent." The colonel rested his hand on the groom's shoulder. "First, we will require you to let a horse or two for my cousin's use while he is in residence at Woodvine. Do you know where one might be found?"

"Aye, Sir."

Edward continued, "Then you will make the proper arrangements."

Darcy added, "If possible, please find a gentle mount and a side saddle for Mrs. Darcy."

Holbrook smiled warmly. "I know just the mount for yer lady. Over at Bournemouth."

Darcy told the man, "I am well acquainted with Captain Tregonwell. He can likely aid in our search. Are you familiar with the captain's home in Bourne?"

"I am, Mr. Darcy. Me cousin been hired on by Tregonwell's steward."

Darcy assured, "I would trust Captain Tregonwell to recommend a proper horse for Mrs. Darcy."

The groom offered a quick bow. "I'll hitch up the cart and set out right away, Sir."

Edward halted the man's retreat. "Do you know who purchased Samuel Darcy's horses?"

The groom snarled his displeasure. "Them be fine animals, Colonel. I sees to them meself. Master Darcy thinks mighty grand of his hidden treasures, but the late Mr. Darcy also be a good judge of horses. He kept some of the best in the area, and it be a shame to permit that riffraff to be off with them."

Darcy and Edward replied in unison, "The gypsies?"

"Aye, Sir."

Edward's frown deepened. "We will see to the sale of the Woodvine horses. For now, set about your mission." With the groom's withdrawal, the colonel said privately, "Did you not say that you and Elizabeth observed Mrs. Ridgeway and the gypsy leader in what appeared to be a contentious discussion?"

"Andrzej Gry," Darcy confirmed. "At the time, Mrs. Darcy and I wondered of their connection."

"Perhaps they argued over the horses. Mrs. Ridgeway must have known it would be only a matter of time before you discovered her perfidy."

"What do we do now?"

Edward said, "We will have one of the assistant grooms prepare a proper carriage for us and Cowan, and we will pay a call on the Roma band."

Darcy explained, "Gry suggested that I send for him rather than to make an unexpected call on their campsite."

Edward countered, "Likely the Rom wished to keep you away while Gry's troop disposed of the evidence."

Darcy shook his head in disbelief. He heard the forcefully restrained anger in his voice, and Darcy made no effort to disguise it. "From the time of my arrival in Dorset, I have silently criticized my father's cousin for his gullibility, but I find myself just as vulnerable to those who practice obscurantism."

Chapter 7

Edward assured, "With estate business or savvy investments, you are the expert, but when it comes to comprehending the psyche of the common thief or murderer, you have had no experience. You must allow Mr. Cowan and me to lead. Let us return to the house and rouse the Runner from his bed. I am certain Cowan will take note of discrepancies of which we have not."

A little over an hour later, Darcy, the colonel, and Cowan climbed down from the late Samuel Darcy's less-than-stylish chariot to be greeted by a wary group clustered about a dying campfire. Darcy spied Andrzej Gry stepping from the back of a brightly decorated wagon. The Rom had a few highly contested words with a man whose appearance held a familiar look, but one which Darcy could not place. A jauntily slanted felt hat covered the man's countenance, and the stranger disappeared behind the wagons before Darcy could get the right of it. As the gypsy leader approached, several men formed a protective semicircle behind Gry.

The gypsy said with a tone of strained congeniality, "Mr. Darcy. What a pleasant surprise. To what do we owe this visit?" The man's smile did not quite reach his eyes. Wariness clouded Gry's countenance. A lack of a respectful bow spoke the words the man omitted. The Rom did not appreciate their intrusion.

"Mr. Gry," Darcy said with feigned politeness, "my cousin and I have discovered some inconsistencies in the late Mr. Darcy's business transactions. We had hoped you might consent to answering a few questions." The idea of conducting business in the middle of an open field disoriented Darcy, and a shiver of foreboding racked his spine. He glanced to the stolid countenances of his cousin and the Runner, and Darcy purposely schooled his features in a similar vein.

With the slightest nod of his head, Gry told his men to hold their tongues. The dark-skinned protectors stepped away to attend to their camp duties, but Darcy was not fooled by the pretense. These men expected trouble, and they were prepared to defend their camp. "Of course." The Roma leader smiled easily. "The accommodations are not of your caliber, but if you possess no objections, then who am I to complain?" He gestured to the wooden bench placed beside the wagon he had exited earlier.

Darcy nodded curtly and strode toward the offered seating. Edward followed close behind. With a snap of his fingers, Gry ordered up two roughly hewn chairs. When the four men were seated in a tight circle, and Darcy had made brief introductions, Edward spoke for the first time. "My cousin and I have taken on the odious task of setting to right Samuel Darcy's affairs."

Gry said warily, "I understood Mr. Samuel's man of business held those loathsome duties."

Edward's authoritative tone spoke of how the diversion had not taken. "My cousin and I honor our family duties," the colonel declared. He did not allow the Rom the opportunity to interrupt. "In doing so, we have discovered that your followers have been the recipient of goods that belonged to the late Mr. Darcy. Unfortunately, the person who sold you the property, held no legal right to do so."

Gry said defiantly. "Yet, we are to blame. Is that how it is, Colonel?"

"No one is making accusations," Edward said calmly. Darcy admired how his cousin had taken control of the situation. He would attempt to emulate Edward's perceived influence, but it would cost him to keep his fury trapped inside.

Gry scowled before a half smile curved the corners of his mouth. "I suppose you expect us to return the animals?"

Darcy watched Gry's countenance closely. The man had mastered the art of negotiation: Gry betrayed nothing unusual. "It would be for the best," Darcy insisted. "I am certain your men would not wish the community to believe you have taken advantage of Mrs. Ridgeway's grief." He noted the slight flinch of Gry's shoulders, but the source of the Rom's anxiety remained unclear. He benevolently said, "Of course, we would return your payment." The gypsy leader gave a silent signal to the men who had edged closer, and Darcy saw Cowan palm a small pistol. To allay a confrontation, he added, "No one from Woodvine wishes to bring censure to your door."

The gypsy leader's response was sharp and to the point. "Yet, that is exactly what has happened. We are blamed for acting honorably," Gry argued. He gestured wildly. "My men have treated the animals well, but all of Dorset will claim we have earned the cattle by devious methods. We paid a fair price for the Darcy horses. It is not as if we have stolen them."

Edward shot Darcy a knowing glance. They both knew the price was half what it should have been. His cousin responded calmly, "And we are willing to assure the community of your earnest dealings."

The Rom took a long, steady measure of Darcy and Edward, but the gypsy ignored Cowan. Watching the former Runner's perceptive glaze, Darcy realized Gry had made a tactical error. Of the three of them, Cowan was by far the most dangerous. After an elongated pause, Gry related, "We have retained possession of only one of the horses. Several of my men have taken the other two to London to sell."

Cowan asked suspiciously, "When did your men leave?"

Gry turned finally to look upon the Runner, and the Rom's frown lines spoke of his initial wariness. "Some three days prior. I fear it will be impossible to stop the animals' sale at this late thought."

"Then we will claim the single horse," Edward said as he stood. "At a more appropriate time, we will discuss how best to handle the fraudulent sale of the others. If you will ask your men to produce the animal, we will leave you to your business." The colonel drew on his gloves.

Darcy extended his hand to Gry. "If you call at the manor, I will see to your compensation." He stood beside his cousin.

Gry reluctantly accepted Darcy's hand before giving his guests a proper bow. "Thank you for accepting the truth, Mr. Darcy."

Darcy said enigmatically, "I knew the truth before I called upon your encampment." He had expected many things from this tense confrontation, but Darcy had not expected the look of confusion that skidded across Gry's countenance before the Rom quashed it.

When the Roma brought the horse forward, Darcy recognized the stallion as being the one the gypsies had put through its paces on the day he and Elizabeth had called upon Mr. Stowbridge. In his world, the one of Pemberley, things ran to suit his pleasure. Unfortunately, in Dorset, that was not the case. Had he recognized the perfidy upon which he would unknowingly stumble, Darcy would have ordered Mr. Stalling to set a return journey to Pemberley's safety. He easily recalled the trepidation he had felt when he had gazed upon the gypsy band.

Edward accepted the horse's reins and tied it to the back of the carriage. "Let us be about it, Darcy," his cousin ordered. "I promised Mr. Franklyn I would assist him with the issue of the missing gems. Another of the many mysteries my cousin has encountered in Dorset," Edward said innocently, as if he were unaware that the gypsies hung on his every word. "Come along, Gentlemen."

Darcy had taken note of the shift in the Roma's composures. He followed Edward into the carriage. "Ask for me personally when you call upon Woodvine," he said in parting.

"How long might you be at the house today?" Gry asked as he closed the side door of the chariot.

Darcy smiled wryly. "You may call at your leisure. Mrs. Darcy, as well as my cousin, Mr. Cowan, several curators from the British Antiquarian Society, and I have taken possession of Woodvine while we await the Earl and Countess of Rardin. By the way, Gry, you should consider leaving before Rardin makes his appearance. The Earl holds a strong disdain for the Roma." With that, Darcy tapped on the chariot's side to signal their departure to Mr. Stalling.

When they were out of earshot, Cowan said, "The gypsy leader knows more of what is amiss at Woodvine Hall than he discloses."

Edward inclined his head. "How so?"

Cowan continued, "To begin, Gry never asked what property had passed illegally to his followers. He knew he had received the horses without proper arrangements."

Darcy regarded the man with a searching gaze. He reasoned, "Perhaps the horses were the Rom's only purchase from Samuel's estate."

"But even a Rom would know a housekeeper possessed no legal right to sell off her employer's stable," Cowan countered. "Obviously, Gry did not take advantage of Mrs. Ridgeway. The housekeeper likely recognized a means to supplement her income after Mr. Darcy's passing."

The colonel concurred, "I have come to the conclusion that the woman maintains her own agenda."

Cowan suggested, "Did you not say the late Mr. Darcy had met Mrs. Ridgeway on a journey from America?"

Darcy quickly drew the same conclusion as the Runner. "And Gry admitted to having lived in the Americas after his family's forced exodus from Wales. Mayhap, the Rom and Mrs. Ridgeway held a former acquaintance."

Edward frowned noticeably. "Although the housekeeper is a handsome woman, there is a great disparity in age between the woman and the Rom. Besides, Mrs. Ridgeway has genteel ways. A woman in such a position would avoid any connection with a known gypsy. Even in America, it is just not acceptable."

Something fiery gnawed at the pit of his stomach. Darcy asked cautiously, "What if Gry's identity had not been *known* in America? The man's features might have permitted him more freedom on the American shores."

A long silence followed as each man considered Darcy's supposition. "We should carefully observe Gry when he calls upon the manor later today," Edward declared. "If a woman had placed my family in a tenuous position, I would not be pleased to speak to the lady further."

"Or perhaps I might choose to insist upon a few brief moments alone with the woman," Cowan said ironically. Silence descended as they each came to his own conclusions. Finally, the Runner asked, "Do you wish me to send word to London? My former associates might discover word of the other horses. There are only a few places, even in London's stews, that will do business with gypsies."

Edward said decisively, "That is an excellent idea. At least, we will know for certain whether Gry speaks the truth, and whether the gypsies hold the other two horses hidden somewhere in the forest."

Darcy had thought to make a comment about the tales of gypsies painting horses to disguise them, but before the words could escape his lips, a shot rang out. More accustomed to seeking shelter when danger called, both the colonel and Cowan dove for the floor of the open chariot. A second later, Edward's tight grip on Darcy's waistcoat brought Darcy tumbling forward on top of them.

"What the hell?" Darcy expelled as he looked wildly about him. Mr. Stalling had set the Woodvine horses at a gallop, but the carriage rocked as if something pulled it in opposition. Fighting for control, Stalling pulled tight on the reins. As the animals slowed, the colonel and Cowan crouched on either side of the carriage in a defensive stance. Both held guns and surveyed the open area.

Darcy scrambled to his cousin's side. "Did you see the shooter?"

"No!" Edward grumbled. He cautiously reached for the door latch and eased his way to the ground. "Are you hurt, Stalling?" he asked without turning his head.

"No, Sir," Darcy's long-time coachman cursed under his breath. "But me shoulder will need some of Mrs. Reynolds's special liniment tonight."

Darcy followed Edward from the coach. His eyes scanned the tree line. The colonel declared, "It is too quiet, which means someone is there or has been there. Nature goes silent when men invade it."

"I have it. See to the horses," Cowan said as he pushed past them. With a gun in each hand, the Runner raced away into the surrounding brush.

Edward's eyes traced the Runner's steps while Darcy turned to the animal. "Stalling!" he called as he sprang to where the horse leaned heavily against the chariot's back boot.

"Easy, Boy," the coachman said as he approached. To Darcy's horror, a small wound trickled blood on his side, but a sticky red fluid gushed over Stalling's fingertips as his coachman pressed a dirty handkerchief to the animal's neck. "I fear it's too late, Mr. Darcy," Stalling said sadly. "This one be gone, Sir."

Darcy swallowed hard. "Finish it, Mr. Stalling." He turned heavily toward where his cousin waited at the team's head. Edward soothed the skittish animals as Stalling led the injured animal away.

With the wheezing and snorting of the frightened animals as a backdrop, a second shot rang out, and the proud gelding collapsed with a heavy thud.

Edward spoke though clenched teeth, "I have seen many men and their animals fall in battle, but I will never grow accustomed to the loss of life, no matter whether it be man or beast."

The Runner reappeared beside them. "Whoever it was is gone," he confirmed. "I found this." He extended his upturned palm. "It is like no ammunition fragment I have ever encountered."

Edward scooped the shard of evidence from Cowan's hand. He held up the scrap of metal to the light. As he turned it in his fingers, he said, "It is from an American long gun. I have seen only a few of them, but I have no doubt of its origin. That is why we did not see our assailant. With such a weapon, one does not require close proximity to be accurate."

* * *

Elizabeth shivered involuntarily. As Darcy had directed, she had met with the Woodvine cook regarding the weekly menu. They had finished their task when dread had physically rocked her spine. Despite the feeling of dizziness drowning her senses in its sweep, Elizabeth desperately pushed the swirling sensation away.

"Is something amiss, Mrs. Darcy?" the cook asked with what sounded of true concern.

Elizabeth shook her head in denial. "Just one of those intuitive moments we women experience daily. Likely, Mr. Darcy has turned his ankle or one of my sisters has spotted a snake along the road to Meryton." She laughed at her foolish nature.

The gray-haired woman with the sparkling, equally gray eyes pushed her spectacles farther up her nose. "It be the way of women," she said sympathetically. "Me boy, Arnie, be one of Mr. Darcy's grooms. We both have served the old master for many years. Whenever Arnie gets himself kicked by one of them ornery beasts, I knows before he ever shows himself on me doorstep and looking fer some of me herbs to ease the pain."

Elizabeth again wondered if something had happened to Darcy. Her husband had spoken of the possibility that the gypsy band had posed an unknown threat. At home, at Pemberley, she had often sensed Darcy's presence before he appeared on the threshold of her sitting room, but this was different. The lingering dread that currently wrapped itself about her shoulders had nothing to do with the pleasant anticipation she often experienced when her husband surprised her in the middle of the day. This was a warning of danger. She cleared her throat, refusing to consider the possibilities. Bravely, she said, "I am certain it is nothing. Mr. Darcy's cousin, a seasoned military commander, as well as Mr. Cowan, accompanied my husband. I am being foolish."

Mrs. Holbrook's eyebrow rose in sharp denial, but the lady wisely said, "If that be all, Mrs. Darcy, I's best return to me duties."

Elizabeth gathered her notes. "Remember, Mrs. Holbrook, no sauces on the meats. The colonel prefers his dishes plain. Serve the dressings in a separate dish."

"Yes, Ma'am. I's understand."

Elizabeth stood slowly to follow the woman to the door. "I expected Mrs. Ridgeway to join us," she said as nonchalantly as she could muster. In reality, the housekeeper's absence had irritated Elizabeth. It was another affront to Darcy's authority, and she planned to express her anger over the woman's slight.

Mrs. Holbrook paused in her speech, as well as her step. The woman looked about quickly—as if she suspected someone could be eavesdropping on her conversation. "Mrs. Ridgeway sent word, Ma'am, that she be experiencing a megrim."

"I see," Elizabeth said knowingly. "I suppose a headache might keep Mrs. Ridgeway from her duties."

Mrs. Holbrook smiled wryly. "I suspect that be true, Mrs. Darcy." The woman disappeared into Woodvine's apparently empty halls.

Elizabeth stood silently by the still-open door and listened carefully to what were obviously exchanged whispers. Someone, or several people, concealed themselves in Woodvine's late afternoon shadows. The thought of others watching her every move, on one hand, shook her resolve, but on the other, it irritated her. She would permit no one to intimidate her. After all, had she not withstood the imperious Lady Catherine De Bourgh? "We shall see how they perceive their positions when I have my say," she said privately to fortify her resolve.

Then she was on the move, climbing to the house's third level again. As she turned the corner, Elizabeth declared boldly aloud, "I know you have hidden yourself from my view, but I am aware of your presence. If you have any sense of self-preservation, you will disperse immediately and attend to your duties." As she climbed, Elizabeth did not turn her head to observe which of Woodvine's staff broke from his hidden security, but she was well aware of the sound of scrambling feet and the quick opening and closing of doors. "They have chosen to make me their enemy," she declared. "But they do not know that I am well seasoned in the comings and goings of servants."

She thought immediately of how Darcy had early on complimented her on her quick assimilation into the role of Pemberley's mistress. Little had her husband known that at Longbourn, Elizabeth and Jane had equally shared in the running of their parents' estate. Their mother had taught all her daughters of the responsibilities of an estate's mistress. As she and Jane had matured, Mrs. Bennet had relinquished more and more of her duties to her eldest children. Elizabeth had arrived on Pemberley's threshold well versed in preparing menus, balancing expenses, and settling service disputes. Her transition into the role of Pemberley's mistress had come easily.

She paused at the top of the stairs and set her shoulders in a stubborn slant. "You mean to frighten me, but I will not be alarmed. There is a stubbornness about me that never can bear to be frightened at the will of others. My courage always rises with every attempt to intimidate me," she declared to the empty passageway.

With renewed determination, Elizabeth entered Mrs. Ridgeway's quarters unannounced. "I believe I requested to speak to you this morning," she said tersely.

It did not surprise Elizabeth to find the woman dressed and working on an embroidery pattern. The housekeeper sprang to her feet. "Mrs. Darcy, I...I had...I had a severe headache," she stammered. She tucked her sewing hoop behind her, but Elizabeth had observed the meticulous work of the pattern.

Taking a satisfyingly slow breath, Elizabeth's mouth set in a tight line. "Evidently, you have recovered remarkably." She gestured to the tea set upon a low table. "That being said, I will see you in my chambers in a quarter hour." Elizabeth turned on her heels to leave.

However, Mrs. Ridgeway's offer slowed Elizabeth's retreat. "Why do we not share tea here?"

Elizabeth turned haltingly to the woman. "I think not. You will attend me. It is not acceptable for the mistress to attend those she employs. You did understand that my husband has assumed control of this household?"

"Yes, Ma'am." Mrs. Ridgeway dropped her eyes.

The act infuriated Elizabeth. "Do not offer me a false face." She turned again for the door. "A quarter hour, Mrs. Ridgeway." To emphasize her indignation, Elizabeth launched the door against the wall. The sound echoed throughout the dark passageway.

Returning to her quarters, Elizabeth fought hard to rein in her temper. "It would not do to permit Mrs. Ridgeway to know how much I dread this interview," she declared as she punched one of the pillows decorating the bed. "Concentrate, Elizabeth," she chastised her image in the cheval mirror. "You must see this through for Fitzwilliam's sake." The thought of her husband brought an immediate smile to Elizabeth's lips. "Everything he has done he has done for me," she thought.

When Lydia had inadvertently disclosed Mr. Darcy's part in bringing about her sister's match to Mr. Wickham, Elizabeth could not fathom how his regard for her had allowed him to act without pride. The vague and unsettled suspicions which uncertainty had produced of what Mr. Darcy might have been doing to forward her sister's match, which Elizabeth had feared to encourage as an exertion of goodness too great to be probably, and at the same time dreaded to be just, from the pain of obligation, were proved beyond their greatest extent to be true: Darcy had followed Lydia and Mr. Wickham purposely to Town; he had taken on himself all the trouble and mortification attendant on such a research; in supplication had been necessary to a woman whom he abominated and despised, and where he was reduced to meet—frequently meet, reason with, persuade, and finally bribe—the man whom he always most wished to avoid, and whose very name it was punishment to Darcy to pronounce. He had done it for her. For a woman who had already refused him.

Even as she considered her husband's benevolence in the matter, Elizabeth blushed with embarrassment. Every kind of pride must have revolted from the connection. She was ashamed to think how much. Though, at the time, she could not place herself as his principal inducement, she had perhaps believed that Darcy's remaining partiality for her might have assisted his endeavors in a cause where her peace of mind must be materially concerned. "If Fitzwilliam could place his qualms aside, then I will follow his lead." Darcy's ability to overcome a sentiment so natural as abhorrence would serve as her model.

When Mrs. Ridgeway arrived, Elizabeth bade the woman's entrance in a perfectly calm voice. She motioned the woman to a chair across from where she sat at the small desk before setting the ledger, which she had used like a stage prop to make herself appear not to be awaiting the housekeeper's appearance, aside. In reality, to compose her erratic heart and to soften her anger, Elizabeth had retrieved several of the notes which Darcy had left for her over their few months of marriage. Beginning with the morning following their first night as man and wife, her husband had periodically presented her an eloquent reminder of their time together: a reminder of their one month anniversary and again to mark their first half year of marital bliss; one for the night that they would spend apart when Darcy had been called away on business; and the one where he consoled her during the loss of the child she had not known she carried. Her magnificent husband had grieved silently for their lost child while she openly nursed her broken heart. Today, Elizabeth had read the two "anniversary" letters. They were full of love's awe, and they had bolstered her spirits immensely.

Elizabeth did not permit Mrs. Ridgeway to speak. Instead, she assumed the offensive. "I had expected better of you, Ma'am. When we first met, I presumed you to be a woman possessed of kindness, but also a woman well aware of her place in the world. I thought you displayed an independent nature and were capable of overcoming adversity."

Mrs. Ridgeway asked earnestly, "And you no longer hold the same opinion, Mrs. Darcy?"

Elizabeth's forthright nature never faltered. "You have proven yourself, Ma'am, to be a coward."

"Do not think ill of me, Mrs. Darcy," the woman challenged.

"How may I not?" Elizabeth asked aristocratically. She considered the possibility that Darcy's air had found a new home in her. "Mr. Darcy gave specific orders for you to present yourself in the role of Woodvine's housekeeper; yet, last evening, you made no appearance after our arrival, nor did you sit with me and Mrs. Holbrook this morning."

"And did you find something lacking in your quarters? In Mrs. Holbrook's attention to your needs?" Mrs. Ridgeway asked confidently.

Elizabeth's chin rose with the challenge. A prickle of antagonism shimmed up her body. This was her first real test as Darcy's wife. Her transition at Pemberley had gone smoothly: partly because of her mother's training, but partly because of Mrs. Reynolds' guidance. Pemberley's long-time housekeeper had brought Elizabeth along and had instilled the confidence of a fine lady in a country miss. "Do you dare claim to be the source of efficiency I have observed from certain members of the late Mr. Darcy's staff?" Elizabeth would not mention those she suspected had found hiding places to shirk their duties. Her cold tone announced her disdain.

Mrs. Ridgeway's countenance betrayed a momentary lapse of confidence, but the woman quickly schooled her features. "And why should I not? Mr. Darcy blamed me for the deficiencies he discovered among those Mr. Samuel had hired. Why should I not glory in the household's successes?"

If the older woman thought Elizabeth's age would provide the housekeeper an advantage, Mrs. Ridgeway would discover otherwise. Elizabeth's shoulder shifted, and she presented the Woodvine housekeeper with a look of scorn she had once seen displayed upon the countenance of Lady Catherine De Bourgh when the grand lady had instructed Mr. Collins on the state of the cleric's gardens. "I am pleased to hear it, Mrs. Ridgeway." The housekeeper's forehead crinkled with disappointment, and Elizabeth knew satisfaction. She would definitely share her "disapproving" glower with Darcy when they were alone. She would ask her husband's opinion of its effectiveness as compared to the one of his imperious aunt. "Then you will have no difficulty in overseeing a thorough cleaning of each of Woodvine's rooms. I shall not have the Earl and Countess of Rardin determining Woodvine lacking. Lady Cynthia holds her uncle in loving regard. I shall not tolerate having Her Ladyship's memories of the late Mr. Darcy tarnished by finding Samuel Darcy's home in anything but pristine condition."

Elizabeth noted how the housekeeper recoiled, but the lady wisely held her tongue. Elizabeth continued, "Every shelf will be dusted. Every rug beaten. Every piece of silver polished." Elizabeth snarled her nose in disgust. "Cousin Samuel's propensity for clutter will create additional responsibilities, but with your discipline, the staff shall rise to the challenge. You must inform me immediately if any of our current employees choose to seek other positions. As I have noted several among the staff who appear less than enthusiastic about fulfilling their duties, I assume we shall need to replace them. If you do not feel comfortable in making those decisions, I assure you I hold no such qualms. At home in Hertfordshire, I often dispensed with the servants." That was a stretch of the truth, but Elizabeth would never permit the woman an advantage.

She stood to end the conversation. "I am pleased that we have had the opportunity to address Mr. Darcy's perceived grievances. It shall make our stay more agreeable. Now, as I know you have many duties of which to attend, I shall excuse you." Mrs. Ridgeway looked dismayed, but she managed a proper curtsy. Elizabeth led the way to the door. "Is this not more pleasant?" she asked sweetly. "To have a complete understanding between us?"

Mrs. Ridgeway spoke through tight lips, "As you say, Mrs. Darcy."

* * *

Darcy had resumed his seat in the chariot. His cousin had pocketed the shell fragment, and they had reluctantly returned to their ride. Silence reigned as Mr. Stalling set the horses in motion.

Edward's cross expression spoke of his cousin's frustration. "Could the gypsy leader be sending you a message, Darcy? That if he cannot have the horse then neither may you."

Darcy rubbed a weary hand across his face to clear his thinking. "Obviously, we should examine the American connection?" They did not speak for several minutes, each man lost in his thoughts. Finally, Darcy cautioned, "I would prefer that Mrs. Darcy possessed no knowledge of today's events. I would not worry my wife with news of this attack." Another elongated silence followed. "I am thankful no one was injured in this folly," Darcy said sadly.

Cowan warned, "You must not permit your guard to become lax, Mr. Darcy."

Darcy's brows lowered into a pronounced frown. "I do not understand. Surely, you do not think this was more than a dispute about a horse's ownership."

The former Runner's eyes scanned the passing countryside. "I believe, Mr. Darcy, that your insistence on discovering the disposition of your cousin's estate has brought a warning. We might think the shooter made an unfortunate shot, but the bullet was placed in the animal's neck. It was an admonition that a skilled marksman could easily achieve a smaller target. Say a man's head."

"You are saying someone wants me dead!" Darcy said incredulously. He felt the air rush from his lungs.

"I am saying, Sir, that someone knows desperation, and he holds no reservations about exercising mayhem in order to relieve himself of your interference."

Chapter 8

Darcy entered Woodvine Hall to find a flurry of activity. Servants scurried forth and back in a frenzied state. Whatever Elizabeth had said to the Woodvine housekeeper in his absence had been effective: Mrs. Ridgeway oversaw the moving of furniture in the front drawing room. Two footmen rolled a heavy carpet, likely one brought to Dorset from the East. Its intricate patterns spoke of looms accustomed to prideful artisans. As they passed the room's open door, Darcy noted his cousin's wry smile. Edward leaned closer to say, "Mrs. Darcy has worked a miracle."

"My wife never ceases to amaze me," Darcy said honestly. His need to see her, to spend a few moments in his wife's presence, had increased dramatically with his survival of an unprecedented attack upon his person. Cowan's words had shaken Darcy to his core. He desperately wished to look upon Elizabeth's countenance. To observe how his wife fared. To speak of his admiration. It was the way with him. Darcy despised being separated from her more than a few minutes. At Pemberley, he had set up a desk for her in his study. He had found he accomplished more work whenever his wife was in the room. If she were elsewhere in the house, he was often on the move: in search of *his* Elizabeth.

Yet, before he could search her out, Mr. Franklyn appeared on Woodvine's steps. "Thank goodness you have returned. I must speak to you, Mr. Darcy. It is a matter of great urgency."

Silently, Darcy groaned. He turned to his cousin. "If you would please inform Mrs. Darcy of our return, I would appreciate it. And tell my wife she is welcome to join me in Samuel's study."

Edward's mouth widened into a sly grin. A familiar tease followed. "Your wife likely holds no taste for this loathsome business. Perhaps I will convince Mrs. Darcy to join me for a walk in the gardens."

Darcy could not stifle his chuckle. He and Edward had competed in every facet of their lives: physical strength, education, marksmanship, and women. Darcy had excelled in the first three, Edward in the last. "I am certain Mrs. Darcy would prefer experiencing the gardens on my arm," he said confidently.

"At Rosings Park, over your illustrious company, the lady sought mine," Edward teased good-naturedly. "Miss Elizabeth liked me first."

Darcy bowed to his cousin. If it had not been for Edward's good counsel, Darcy would never have approached Elizabeth Bennet a second time. "'Tis true, Cousin. First impressions are often mistaken ones. The lady may have preferred your acquaintance first, but she loves me last."

Edward returned a flamboyant obesiance. "I concede to your mastery, Darcy." With a hearty laugh, Edward attacked the steps two at a time.

Darcy motioned to the archaeologist to follow him. Entering his cousin's study, he asked, "What service may I offer, Franklyn?"

The man rushed to close the door behind him. He nervously cleared his throat before saying, "I have taken the liberty of sending for others to assist me in this task."

Darcy nodded his agreement. "I have previously given my permission to do so. You have a phenomenal duty before you, and I fear that neither the colonel nor I hold any expertise in the field."

Franklyn appeared relieved. "I have some concerns on how the many artifacts displayed upon Woodvine's tables and shelves have been handled, and I am, obviously, anxious to witness the items in the secret room you have described previously."

Darcy sighed heavily. The archaeologist was singular in his passion. "I had thought that we might *accidentally discover* the vault some time after supper."

Franklyn's anticipation was not what Darcy had thought it would be; the man hesitated. "I will be glad to look upon such wonders, but with second thought, I must admit I hold misgivings regarding the Woodvine staff knowing of the room's existence. Just today I have seen evidence that someone has rifled through the displayed treasures of the late Mr. Darcy—someone likely looking for items to pawn. Once the staff knows of the room, it must be guarded at all hours of the day and night."

Although he thought the man exaggerated the greed found among Samuel's employees, Darcy agreed in principle. He said, "Permit me to speak to the colonel and Mr. Cowan on how best to handle your concern. Perhaps Cowan knows of men in the area that we can trust. Or I could seek the aid of Captain Tregonwell."

Franklyn's expression had lightened. "I would find that most satisfying, Mr. Darcy. Such treasures must be secured as part of the world's ancient history."

Having finally excused Franklyn to his own devices, Darcy made his way quickly through Woodvine's passages. He had hoped Elizabeth would have joined him in Samuel's study, but his wife had yet to make an appearance. After the earlier drama, he possessed a distracted need to hold her in his embrace. Cowan's warning clung to Darcy's shoulders. He could not shake the foreboding that the man's words had left behind. All he had wanted since he, Cowan, and his cousin had set their sights on Woodvine was to catch Elizabeth up in his arms and bury his face in his wife's scent. He only felt alive in her presence, and with death closing in on everything Darcy held dear, he desperately required his wife's closeness.

He had just turned into the passageway to their quarters when the blood-leaching scream filled the ground floor and ricocheted off the high ceilings. Darcy froze in midstride. Immediately, he was on the move, skipping steps and vaulting over the landing. "Elizabeth!" he bellowed. "Elizabeth! Where are you?" He did not think it his wife's voice that he had heard, but Darcy could not shed the dread building in him.

He heard a heavy tread behind him and realized it was his cousin. Both men skidded to a halt in the front foyer as Cowan burst through a side entrance. "What is amiss?" the Runner asked in an anxious exhale.

"Not certain." Darcy's eyes scanned the hall. "Where are the servants?"

He motioned his cousin to search a side hallway, but before either man could take a step, Elizabeth called, "In here, Fitzwilliam!"

Darcy followed her voice to come upon a most unusual scene. "What has happened?" he asked as he knelt beside his wife. Elizabeth cradled Mrs. Ridgeway's head in her lap. Meanwhile, one of the younger maids wrapped the housekeeper's bloody hand with a strip of cloth that he suspected had come from Elizabeth's petticoat. Shared secrets and trust passed between them, and Darcy breathed easier knowing she was well.

"Mrs. Ridgeway has suffered some sort of injury," Elizabeth explained. "I have sent for Mr. Glover."

Edward slowly circled the room's periphery. From his eye's corner, Darcy noted that his cousin palmed a small pistol. "Why such drama?" the colonel asked suspiciously.

"I am uncertain," Elizabeth confessed. She directed the maid cleaning the housekeeper's wound to fetch some water.

An older woman eyeing the proceedings from her place in the corner said, "The lady be burned when she tuched the witch's bottle."

Darcy stood slowly. He surveyed the room. From where his wife nursed the housekeeper, soft sobs and whispers continued. "Explain," he demanded as his eyes rested on the woman's wrinkled countenance. Although a servant in his late cousin's house, the woman did not act the part; she showed no signs of alarm. In fact, she appeared almost gleeful in her attitude.

"Thar be a witch's bottle under the lose hearth stone. None of us be tuching it, but Mrs. Ridgeway said we be fools. Yet, when she grasped it, it burned her skin. Brought the blood."

"A witch's bottle," Edward said with some amusement. "Why would there be a witch's bottle in this house?"

"Protect those within," the woman insisted. "We not be overlooked by a witch from without. No familiar either."

Cowan retrieved pieces of the offending item from the floor where Mrs. Ridgeway had dropped it. "Not many use such conjurings these days." Shifting through a knotted twist of metal, he closely inspected the bottle's contents. "Appears to be some bent iron nails. As well as thorns. Some pins." He touched the spilled liquid with his fingertip before sniffing the fluid. "Blood. Maybe some holy water. Very likely a person's urine."

Darcy gave himself a mental shake. "You jest," he said incredulously.

"No. Seen them many times in Cornwall." The Runner stood slowly.

Darcy was uncertain whether the reference to Cornwall was part of the story he and Cowan had concocted for the villagers or whether Cowan truly knew something of England's historic shire. "I still do not understand what could have burned Mrs. Ridgeway's hand."

Cowan explained, "Generally, several pins are set within the stoneware. When Mrs. Ridgeway dropped the Bellarmine Jar, she was cut by the jar and the items within. Then the liquid poured over the wounds." The Runner's dark gaze spoke of the man's inquisitive mind.

The old woman scowled. "Perhaps it be as you say or perhaps not. Thar be many among those who live about that believe those which the bottle burns know the worst of the arts."

The woman's remark annoyed Darcy with all that it implied. "We will have no such talk in this house. Do you understand?"

A tangible thread of doom filled the space. The maid obediently dropped her eyes, but he did not think it was from a subservient deference to his position in this household. "Yes, Mr. Darcy."

Elizabeth assisted Mrs. Ridgeway to a seated position. She examined the woman's hand again. Darcy noted her frown of disapproval. "There are several lacerations." She sighed heavily. "We have done all we can until Mr. Glover arrives. Els, would you see Mrs. Ridgeway to her quarters?"

"Yes, Mrs. Darcy."

The housekeeper struggled to her feet. With what appeared to resemble fear, Mrs. Ridgeway glanced toward the hearth. "When Dunstan returns, I want him to check each of the fireplaces. I want no more accidents."

After the maid had assisted Mrs. Ridgeway from the room, Darcy caught his wife's hand, and his long fingers closed around it. Immediately, Elizabeth's presence brought him comfort. To the remaining Woodvine staff he ordered, "I want this situation resolved before the bottle's contents stain the floor."

Darcy led Elizabeth from the room, but in the main foyer, he turned to speak privately with Cowan and the colonel. "Edward, if you would join Elizabeth and me in her sitting room, I would appreciate it."

"Of course, Darcy."

To the Runner, he said, "Please locate Mr. Franklyn and then join us also. It is odd that the gentleman did not respond to the chaos." Cowan nodded before disappearing into the servants' passageway. Darcy supposed the Runner had already surveyed the house's many entrances and exits.

Darcy placed his wife on his arm. Before the audience of Woodvine servants, they would carry on as if nothing unusual had happened. "I have asked Mr. Holbrook to speak to Captain Tregonwell about a proper horse for you to ride. If the groom is successful, perhaps we might share a short outing tomorrow and a longer journey the next day. The horses should have some rest after the journey from Bournemouth. I have made the assumption that you have missed our rides across Pemberley."

As if she understood the need to underplay the drawing room incident, Elizabeth smiled brightly at him. "That world be wonderful, Mr. Darcy." She caught Edward's arm also so she might walk between them. It was Elizabeth's way: to include those she affected. "Will you join us, Colonel? I would enjoy that very much."

Edward's easy smile followed hers. "If your husband holds no objections, a ride would do me well."

Elizabeth shot a mischievous grimace in Darcy's direction. In a playful stage whisper, she said, "We shall ignore Mr. Darcy's normal dudgeon. I refuse to allow it to defer my pleasures."

Darcy laughed good-naturedly. He could do so now that Elizabeth was his wife, but when he was so violently in love with her, and she had shunned his advances, it was a different story. At Rosings Park, anything was a welcome relief to the tedium of his aunt's manipulations, and Elizabeth had caught his cousin's fancy very much. Edward had seated himself by her, and had talked so agreeably of Kent and Hertfordshire, of traveling and staying at home, of new books and music, that Darcy could not withdraw his eyes from them, and, in that time, he would have gladly devised devious means of disposing of his cousin. "I would never deprive you, my dear, of such delightful pleasures."

As he held the door for her, his wife pursed her lips as if to leave a kiss floating in the air before his countenance. He inhaled the pleasure of her honey breath and squeezed her hand. With the door firmly closed behind them, Darcy seated Elizabeth beside him while Edward pulled over a straight-backed chair to form a tight semicircle.

His cousin leaned forward and kept his voice low to maintain their secrecy. "What do you make of what has occurred below?"

Elizabeth said in exasperation, "Every time I think we have uncovered the depth of deception in this house, another layer is exposed. Why would anyone permit such a foul superstition under his roof? I understand a horseshoe over the door or even a trail of salt spread around a bed, but I cannot comprehend the use of human secretions as part of a witch's potion. Neither a horseshoe nor sprinkled salt will cause harm to others, but the witch's bottle was meant to do injury."

Edward noted, "Obviously, Mrs. Ridgeway possessed no prior knowledge of the bottle or else she would have handled the situation differently."

"I actually held sympathy for the woman," Elizabeth confided. "What say you, Fitzwilliam?"

A frown tugged at Darcy's brow. "Since our arrival in Dorset, I have learned to question all my instincts."

A light knock at the door signaled Cowan's appearance. As he settled among them, the Runner explained, "Located Franklyn with his head buried in Samuel Darcy's travel chest. The man claims he heard none of the uproar. I left him to his own distractions."

Darcy accepted the Runner's explanation. "I am of the persuasion that your identity as a top-notch investigator should become common knowledge. I would like to place you in charge of locating my cousin's body. It grieves me greatly to know Samuel has been deprived of his proper resting place." The Runner accepted his assignment with a curt nod. "Franklyn and his associates will catalog my cousin's collection. We will hire protection for the items that Franklyn deems as worthy."

"Then what role do you and I play in this intrigue?" the colonel asked solemnly.

"We will assist Cowan in his search, but we will concentrate our efforts on discovering the truth of Cousin Samuel's death and how superstition has colored this investigation."

Elizabeth asked softly, "And what part do I play in this charade, Mr. Darcy?"

"You are the steel that binds us, Mrs. Darcy. You will listen to the murmurs of the servants to discern hidden facts. You will be the voice of reason when the colonel, Cowan, and I have lost ours.

You will keep the eccentric Mr. Franklyn from carrying off Lady Cynthia's legacy, and, most importantly, you will observe Mrs. Ridgeway's every move. The woman is involved in every facet of this duplicity. I feel it in my bones," Darcy declared.

* * *

Early the next morning, they set out for an open field some three miles from Wimborne Minster, along the River Stour. Despite his personal objections, Darcy had agreed to allow Elizabeth to accompany them. Beside the fact Darcy had foolishly promised his wife an outing, Elizabeth had argued that the servants would permit their guards to slip if they did not suspect that she watched their every move.

"I will assist Mrs. Darcy," he told Mr. Holbrook when the groom brought forth a mounting block for Elizabeth. His wife had quickly become a fair horsewoman. Elizabeth possessed a bit of daring, which displaced any fear she might have of the animal. That daring also occasionally prompted his wife to ride beyond her skill. So noting, Darcy instructed the groom, "You will ride beside Mrs. Darcy."

"Yes, Sir," Holbrook responded as he steadied the mare's head while Darcy lifted Elizabeth to the side saddle.

He tightened the strap and placed her heel into the stirrup. Darcy loved touching her, and he allowed his fingers to caress the back of Elizabeth's calf beneath the hem of her riding habit. He handed Elizabeth the reins. "If you tire, you must tell Mr. Holbrook," he instructed. "This is not Pandora. We know nothing of this mare's temperament, nor does she have knowledge of your sometimes heavy hand on the reins," he teased.

"I understand, Mr. Darcy," Elizabeth said with a pert smile.

Darcy stared deeply into his wife's emerald-green eyes. "Indulge me, Mrs. Darcy. I worry for your well-being."

Elizabeth leaned down to whisper, "I am honored by your love, Fitzwilliam."

Edward called, "Come along, Darcy. Mrs. Darcy has always practiced good sense."

Darcy shook his head in exasperation. His cousin did not understand. Some day Edward would give his heart to one woman, and then he and his favorite cousin would be equal. Only then would Edward comprehend the overwhelming fear of God snatching away Darcy's only true happiness.

Darcy mounted, and they turned their horses toward the field that Edward's former soldiers had described. When they had asked Holbrook if he knew of such a place, the groom had confirmed Edward's information. "There be a mighty stone close to the road," Holbrook had said. "Don't know of no circle, but I's rarely travel that direction, and I'd have no reason to cross the farm on foot."

They had traveled a different section of Samuel's property, one of which Darcy was not familiar. Upon the few occasions he had called upon Samuel over the past few years, they had hunted the forested areas, but little else; yet, since arriving in the neighborhood, Darcy had crisscrossed between the shires of Hampshire and Dorset, where he had noted the broad elevated chalk downs and their characteristic rolling hills and valleys and the shallow soil structure which was poor for farming. Farther inland, there were steep limestone ridges and low-lying clay valleys. The limestone ridges were mostly covered in arable fields or grasslands supporting sheep. Some parts resembled a heathland, with the low shrubs of that landscape. Dorset certainly held nothing of the look of Darcy's beloved Derbyshire.

His party had had no difficulty in finding the area known as the "Great Wood." It was on the west side of Wimborne on the Roman Road leading from Badbury to Hamworthy, where a minor loop of the river came close to the road. It was a place of meadows and pastures dotted by hawthorn hedgerows and large ash trees.

One of the stones they sought had recently been marked off from the adjoining field by a sturdy fence. "Best not appear as if ye want to place a claim on the land," Holbrook warned as he reined in one of the four horses the groom had let from Lewis Tregonwell. "You in yer fine attire might remind the locals of the Inclosure Act."

Darcy nodded his understanding. He carefully organized his thoughts. "We will take shelter under the shade of that copse of trees." He gestured off to his right. "You ride to the house and tell whoever claims this land that all I want is a quick look at the stone formation. If this is the only stone, we have mistaken the place."

With a simple doff of his hat, the groom turned toward the house in the distance. Darcy nudged his horse forward and quickly dismounted. He rushed to assist Elizabeth to her feet.

As Edward slid from the saddle, he said, "I will have a look around." He walked off toward the tree line.

Elizabeth watched him go. "What remains amiss for your cousin? In private moments, he appears less than his amiable self."

Darcy's mouth twisted in a wry grin. She met his steady gaze squarely. "How do you always manage to notice when a person disguises his true nature?" He seated her on an uprooted tree trunk.

His wife blushed. "I would not call my opinions astute. I greatly misjudged you, my husband."

Darcy sat beside her. "True. But in your defense, I admit to hiding my feelings even from myself. Perhaps what you saw as pride was, in fact, my awkward attempts to mask my emotional need for you in my life."

Elizabeth chuckled lightly. "How like you, Fitzwilliam, to assume the blame for my ill behavior, but I shall not permit you to do so. I acted most discommodiously. Yet, we shall not assign culpability," she said to stifle his objection. "We both have learned from our failures." She nodded toward the path Edward had taken. "What should I know of the colonel?"

Darcy's eyes followed hers. "My cousin has received notice for the American front," he said solemnly.

"Oh, no!" Elizabeth shook her head in denial. "It cannot be! The colonel has served the King on one front previously," she protested. "Is that not enough?"

Darcy watched the path. He would not want his cousin to overhear their discussing Edward's life. "Yet, it is so. As soon as the colonel has trained his men for the American conflict, they will set sail. Likely, by summer's end."

"I had hoped…" Elizabeth said wistfully.

He stilled at her words. "Hoped what, my love?"

She shrugged her shoulder to indicate her nonchalance, but his wife's tone spoke of a very female romantic slant. "I had hoped that the colonel might find someone who would claim his heart."

Darcy caught her hand to hold between his two. "I pray you have no plans of playing matchmaker, Mrs. Darcy," he said lightly.

Elizabeth teased, "I am my mother's daughter."

"Heaven forbid!" Darcy exclaimed in feigned alarm.

Elizabeth laughed openly. "You sound like my father," she chastised. "And we both know that my mother's motivations are purely unselfish. She seeks husbands for her daughters." She hesitated before saying, "I would not purposely place any young lady in the colonel's way, but I would see him know happiness."

Darcy confessed, "I had thought perhaps Edward held a true affection for Anne, but that appears to have turned."

Elizabeth observed, "I should not speak poorly of Miss De Bourgh; however, even with her advanced years, your cousin Anne is more naïve than is Georgiana. Miss Darcy's experience with Mr. Wickham provided our sister a more resilient nature. It proved the making of Miss Darcy. Georgiana did not succumb to the distracted spiral of possible shame, and she has emerged as reliable and independent."

Despite his contempt for the nefarious Mr. Wickham, Darcy had to agree with his wife. Georgiana had weathered the scandal well, but unlike his wife, Darcy placed the credit for his sister's recovery on Elizabeth's shoulders. His wife had shown Georgiana the love of a sister and of an honest confidante. Elizabeth's caring nature had altered Georgiana's confidence. "As a second son, Edward must marry an heiress. He likely will not know the pleasure of choosing with his heart."

"That fact does not prevent me from wishing for the colonel's faithful happiness," Elizabeth countered.

Before they could finish their conversation, Holbrook reappeared with a local farmer in tow. As the men approached, the colonel emerged from the thick copse. Darcy stood and assisted Elizabeth to her feet.

The farmer removed his hat in a respectful gesture when the men came to a halt before Darcy's party; yet, Darcy noted the man appeared nervous and ill at ease. Holbrook cleared his throat. "Mr. Darcy. Colonel Fitzwilliam. Mrs. Darcy. This be Mr. Rupp." Darcy's party nodded to the man, who offered an awkward bow. "I be explaining to Mr. Rupp that you wished to see the stones found upon yer cousin's map. Rupp assures me there be five stones of various sizes and another farther on used as a field marker."

Darcy dipped his head in another nod of approval. "I thank you, Sir, for granting us permission to survey the area. My father's cousin was a famous archaeologist, and he wished for me to know this place." It was a bit of an exaggeration, but Darcy was certain Cousin Samuel did intend for Darcy to discover the hidden room's secrets.

"It be me honor, Mr. Darcy. If'n yer wife be requirin' more rest, Mrs. Rupp would be pleased for the company," Rupp offered with a bit of strain in his tone. Automatically, Darcy thought perhaps the farmer was not as welcoming as he pretended; however, a quick glance at both Edward and Elizabeth gave him no indication that either his cousin or his wife had taken note of Rupp's tight-lipped offer of greeting. Mayhap after encountering so many unanswered questions of late, Darcy looked for mystery where none could be found.

He shot a quick glance at Elizabeth, but she shook off the offer. "Mrs. Darcy has always considered herself a great walker. I am certain she can easily traverse the distance."

Rupp returned his hat to his head. "This way then, Sir."

Holbrook tied off his horse with the others and followed behind Darcy's party. The colonel remained beside Elizabeth, and so Darcy took the opportunity to converse with Rupp. "Is that the Wimborne Minster steeple?" he asked as he looked off across the horizon.

"Aye, Sir. On Sundays, one kin hear the bells calling souls home." Rupp gestured to a path through the field. "This be the way, Sir."

"I did not realize we were so close to my cousin's estate. It must be less than two miles," Darcy noted as he glanced around to locate his bearings.

Rupp confided, "The main road wraps around the course of the river. Through the woods be just over a mile."

Within a few minutes, the field opened to a flattened area to expose five large stones, likely from the Purbeck quarry. Darcy paused to scan the area, and as he did so Elizabeth stepped beside him and slid her hand into his. "It is not much to see," she said softly.

"In reality, neither is Stonehenge. At least, not a grand or spectacular experience. It is simply our contemporary desire to view the world through a narrow lens—one buried solidly in the past. It is more the history and its significance that creates the mystique," he said. "Otherwise, they are simply large stones from the Neolithic and Bronze Ages. Only the civilization that placed them in the circular formation remains in question. That and the several hundred burial mounds." Darcy squeezed her hand. "Wait for me in the shade, Mrs. Darcy. I wish to walk the circle." He motioned to his cousin. "Join me, Colonel."

He and Edward strode away toward the nearest stone. "For what are we searching?" his cousin asked when they were out of earshot of the others.

"Any evidence of whether this field might serve as a meeting place for those who fancy themselves as dark witches," Darcy said softly as he searched the ground for telltale signs of torches, unusual etchings, or small animal sacrifices.

The colonel squatted near a conical-shaped stone and ran his fingers through the loose dirt. "Do you really suppose this place is used for pagan worship?"

Darcy looked off to the other stones and the rough circular area. "We have seen firsthand how superstition takes hold in a community: In Derbyshire, we celebrate how the well dressing ceremonies prevented the Great Plague. Then there are those who dance with druids in the moonlight." He took note of his cousin's deep frown. After all, all this talk of magic and spells was little more than a leap of faith. "It is not beyond comprehension that among Dorset's citizenry we would discover those who serve the dark arts."

"I do not like it, Darcy," the colonel said as he stood once more.

Darcy's eyes continued to search the open area for anything out of the ordinary. "Neither do I." They stood in companionable silence and looked out over the land. "Let us divine what we can before Rupp becomes suspicious. I am hoping Mrs. Darcy will charm the man to the point where Rupp does not recognize our search for what it is."

Elizabeth strolled slowly toward the shade of three lonely trees in the field's middle. "You are fortunate, Mr. Rupp, to have such fine fields. My father, Mr. Bennet, owns some five hundred acres in Hertfordshire, but part of the land is too rocky to plant." As soon as her husband had directed her steps toward the spot of shade in this open field, Elizabeth had understood her role in this farce. Mr. Darcy was often more than a bit protective of her, but her dear husband had long ago accepted the fact that time outdoors each day best suited her nature. He would not relegate her to a shady spot unless he required a distraction.

"This be good land," Rupp acknowledged. "Me wife's father had the claim before me. It takes hard work to make the land prosperous."

Elizabeth interrupted, "But so satisfying. You have a legacy for your children."

"Aye, Ma'am." Rupp's chest expanded with pride. "That be every man's dream, and I found mine."

Elizabeth smiled brightly at the man. "Then you owe God your most heartfelt gratitude. Not many men may make that claim."

"Yer Mister has his own estate?" Rupp asked.

"Oh, my, yes," Elizabeth gushed. "I recall my first sighting. The park is very large and contains a great variety of ground. When one has reached the top of a considerable eminence, the wood ceases, and the eye is instantly caught by Pemberley House, which is situated on the opposite side of the valley, into which the road, with some abruptness, winds. I have never seen a place for which nature has done more."

"It sounds quite grand, Ma'am," Rupp said reverently.

Elizabeth blushed. "It is very unbecoming behavior, and I should not brag so, but Mr. Darcy's father and grandfather have bestowed him with one of England's finest estates. I am very proud to be a Darcy and to know my children will honor the name."

Before Rupp could respond, Holbrook noted, "Mr. Darcy and the colonel return."

Elizabeth looked up to see her husband's distant approach. "If you will excuse me," she said politely. "I have a pebble in my boot. I shall step on the other side of the trees to loosen it from its place."

Darcy had observed how his wife had disappeared behind the trees as he and his cousin returned to the waiting trio. They had found only some broken fragments of what could have been hag stones and a skeleton of a small cat. Weather had crushed the bones of the animal to the point of making them nearly unrecognizable. Yet, neither find identified this as a place of dark secrets. Both could be coincidental. Darcy wished they had had more time to search, but he and Edward could not bring suspicion their way. They were some one hundred yards from where the men awaited them when he heard his wife's scream. "Elizabeth!" her name exploded as his heart twisted in pain. Immediately, he was at a run to reach her.

Chapter 9

Darcy broke through the vegetation to catch Elizabeth up in a tight embrace. How he and Edward had covered the distance so quickly, he would never know. All he knew was that Elizabeth was in distress. Thoughts of poisonous snakes or other dangerous wildlife rushed through his frantic mind as he covered the area in long, looping strides.

"I have you," he said into Elizabeth's ear. Immediately, she went limp in his arms, and Darcy staggered backward with the force of her weight. "Lizzy," he demanded as he adjusted his grasp about her to lift his wife to him. "Are you hurt?" She gulped for air, but Elizabeth shook her head in denial. As tears pooled in her eyes, she buried her face in his shirt.

"Tell me," he insisted.

Elizabeth did not raise her head from his shoulder, but she threw her arm backward to point toward a row of small shrubs. "Over there," she said huskily.

Darcy nodded to Edward to investigate while he calmed his wife. "Allow me to place you on your feet," he whispered into her hair. When he had set her upon solid ground, Darcy took a half step back so he might observe her countenance. Holding her chin in one large palm, he dabbed at Elizabeth's tears with his linen. "Can you tell me what occurred?" he asked encouragingly.

She sighed deeply and her body sagged heavily against his side. Finally, Elizabeth sniffed loudly. "I…I loosened…loosened my boot…to dislodge…a pebble," she stammered. "Then I saw… saw something colorful…beside the bushes. When I took…several steps…in that direction…"

Again, the tears slid down her cheeks, and Darcy flicked them away with his thumbs. "I will observe the scene for myself," he said definitively. "Will you be well while I do so?"

His cousin stood beside the last bush. "Darcy!" Edward called with an urgent tone.

Darcy nodded. "Mr. Rupp," he said evenly. "May I importune upon your goodwill to escort Mrs. Darcy away from this area?"

"Aye, Sir." The man offered Elizabeth his arm. "This way, Ma'am."

Darcy watched her go. His heart had nearly stopped when he had heard her scream. The woman held too much control over him, but he would have it no other way. He joined his cousin and Holbrook as they knelt by the bush. "What is the mystery?"

"This." Edward leaned away to expose what appeared to be a relatively new grave. From it an arm and hand stood erect at a quarter angle—as if in some sort of salute. The skeletal hand grasped several golden threads of fabric.

"My God!" Darcy exclaimed. "Has someone planted a severed arm in this chalky soil?"

Edward scooped away the loose stones and dirt. "I think not." His cousin pointed to the makeshift grave. "Note how the site is marked." He and Holbrook began to dig dirt from the hole with their hands. "The arm remains attached."

Darcy swallowed hard. "Why would someone bury another in this deserted place?"

"It is not deep," Edward observed. "I am accustomed to this type of grave on the battlefield." He continued to scoop away the loose dirt. "It is a necessity in war because the troops are always on the move, and there is little time to bury the dead properly. But why would it be so here?"

Holbrook remarked, "The ground be hard underneath the topsoil."

Darcy asked aloud what they all wondered. "Could this person have been alive when he was buried?"

Edward groaned as he lifted a heavy stone from the victim's chest. "I suppose we should first identify who our skeleton may be." He set the stone to the side and ran his fingers into the watch pocket of the tattered clothing the skeletal frame sported. "Obviously, this man's clothes will not aid us in the identification. I hope there is other evidence which has not rotted away. Whoever he is he must have been here several months. The body is not wrapped properly for burial either. This appears to be a hastily dug grave. It is shallow and covered with stones." Edward withdrew an ornate watch and a snuffbox from the pocket. He brushed the dirt from the timepiece and opened the face.

Darcy looked over his cousin's shoulder. "Perhaps someone will recognize the sketch within."

Holbrook glanced up from his digging. "Allow me to have a look," he said as he wiped his brow.

Edward handed the timepiece to the groom and waited for the man's assessment.

"This belongs to Mr. Hotchkiss," Holbrook declared.

Darcy regarded the groom with a curious expression. "Hotchkiss? I thought Mr. Hotchkiss was my cousin's steward."

"Previously," Holbrook explained. "Hotchkiss just up and disappeared between Christmastide and Twelfth Night. Nobody knows where he goes. Most thought he returned to York, where his daughter lives. That be her likeness." The groom returned the watch to the colonel. "I seen the image many times. When Mr. Darcy returns from India, he hires Mr. Gaylord. That be in late January. No one hear from Hotchkiss as best I know. No one speaks of him other than to wonder why he leaves without notice. Mr. Darcy be mighty upset with the news. The Master writes to York, but heard nothing from Hotchkiss."

"That answers one question," Darcy said solemnly.

Edward stood slowly and glanced in the direction that Elizabeth and Rupp had gone. "We should send someone for the magistrate."

Darcy reached for the threads and pried them from the bony grasp before sliding them into his watch pocket. "I should see Mrs. Darcy to Woodvine. Would you mind speaking to Stowbridge?" he asked his cousin.

The colonel nodded his agreement. "It will allow me to take a measure of the man. Cowan was to call on the magistrate in regards to Samuel Darcy's disappearance. This new development should bring out Stowbridge's true mettle." They walked toward where Rupp and Elizabeth obediently waited. "Perhaps Cowan might attend me. If you will see that the Runner knows of this new predicament, I would appreciate it." A curt nod indicated Darcy's agreement.

"I'll go for Mr. Stowbridge," Holbrook volunteered. He started toward where they had left the horses.

Darcy caught the groom's arm to stay the man's retreat. "Not a word of this incident to anyone at Woodvine."

"I understand, Sir."

* * *

They met in the library after the supper hour. It had quickly become his party's private sanctuary. "Glover could not give a cause for

Reuben Hotchkiss's death," Edward explained. While his cousin summarized what happened after his departure, Darcy carefully observed his wife. Elizabeth had insisted that she was not one to lose her composure, and despite her earlier hysterics, his wife had assured him that she wanted to know the truth of what they had discovered on Mr. Rupp's farm.

Elizabeth said without emotion. "It is the not knowing which can create havoc with a person's imagination. It is less frightening to face reality." Earlier, when they had returned to the manor and the privacy of their quarters, Elizabeth had sat on his lap and had curled herself about him. As always, her presence had both calmed and excited him simultaneously. "If we know something of our foe, we are better armed to defeat him."

However, Darcy had not experienced the same level of confidence, as had his wife. Edward had told Darcy of the futility of speaking to either Stowbridge or Glover. "With the military, I have often known incompetence, but not of such a marked nature," his cousin had observed with discernible contempt. Now, as he half listened to the colonel's poorly disguised opinions, Darcy wondered, not for the first time, what course he should choose. Part of him wished to turn his back on the bedlam surrounding his Cousin Samuel's death. His involvement in the investigation had placed him in danger and had given Elizabeth a terrible fright—one he suspected had affected her more than his wife was willing to admit. Further, his loyalty must lie with Pemberley and the legacy he had sworn to honor. However, part of that honor meant that Darcy must do all he could to restore order to Samuel Darcy's inheritance.

"There was no apparent blow or gun wound," Edward announced. "Yet, obviously, Hotchkiss did not die from natural causes."

Cowan grumbled, "A man does not lie down in a field to die with his arm sticking from the ground. Hotchkiss certainly did not cover himself with dirt."

Darcy noted the shiver, which Elizabeth attempted to mask. He asked evenly, "Is it significant that Mr. Hotchkiss met his demise less than a fortnight before my cousin's return from the East? Is there evidence to connect Hotchkiss's passing with my family loss?"

Edward set his lips into a tight line. "Like everything else we have uncovered, there are no clear connections. It is very vexatious. Yet, the number of coincidences indicates we are missing this puzzle's centerpiece: the one that holds it together."

Elizabeth stood, and the gentlemen scrambled to their feet. "I find today's incident has robbed me of my good manners this evening. If you will excuse me." She made a quick curtsy.

In concern, Darcy stepped before her. "Allow me to escort you to your chambers, Mrs. Darcy."

Elizabeth glanced about her: He knew what she would say before the words slipped her lips. "That is not necessary," she said softly.

Darcy smiled easily. He had thought at one time to never know this woman; now he took great comfort in her being his other half. "I did not say it was a necessity. Rather, it is my pleasure." Darcy extended his arm, and Elizabeth slipped her hand about his forearm. "I will return in a moment," he said to the others.

As they departed, he overheard Cowan saying, "I think we should make inquiries into other recent disappearances or deaths, especially those directly associated with Woodvine Manor."

Darcy observed his wife's countenance as she leaned heavily against him. They remained silent as they slowly climbed the main staircase. It was not like Elizabeth to know fear, and Darcy suspected her recovery from their recent personal loss had been less efficient than Mrs. Reynolds had assured him it would be. When they reached her room, Darcy held the door for her and then followed his wife into her sitting room. "Do you wish me to ring for Hannah?" he asked as she circled behind the chairs to reach for a small box on her escritoire.

"No." Elizabeth took a seat in a nearby chair. "But if you will light a brace, I would appreciate it."

Darcy retrieved the candelabra while Elizabeth opened the box. "What have you there?" he asked over his shoulder.

"The journals. Your cousin's words," she said as she returned to the page she had marked. "It is apparent that we must discover this house's secrets, and who better from which to learn them than Samuel Darcy. Mr. Franklyn also reads the late Mr. Darcy's words, but the gentleman reads only about your cousin's scientific discoveries and not of Mr. Darcy's home and his relationships. I cannot believe there is no news within these pages regarding Mr. Hotchkiss's withdrawal."

Darcy set the brace on the table beside her chair. "I have been thinking," he said as he casually sat upon a stool at her feet, "that if we do not have a definitive answer to what has occurred here by Monday next that we should leave it to the authorities. Or Rardin and I could hire a bevy of investigators more experienced in the fine art of deception to do the job. I will dismiss the staff, except for the Holbrooks, and you and I will visit Lyme or Bath for the remainder of our time away from Pemberley."

Although he had attempted an untailored tone, his wife had seen through his ruse. "Oh, Fitzwilliam, I do so love your need to protect those you affect. How we could know such happiness if you had not is unfathomable. In a cause of compassion and honor, you were able to get the better of yourself, but I shall not have you make another sacrifice for my sake. Your family's name is my mine, and some day it shall be our child's name. I shall not have it soiled by those working outside the law."

Darcy protested, "But it is too much. A woman should not be exposed to such perfidy."

Elizabeth's eyebrow rose in a familiar challenge. "I am not of the set with which you are most familiar, Mr. Darcy."

He leaned forward to kiss her nose's tip. "I am well aware of the differences, Mrs. Darcy, and I offer no complaints."

Elizabeth caressed the line of his jaw. "Then be the man with whom I fell in love. Restore your family name, and then escort me home to Pemberley."

Darcy's finger brushed her lips. "I remain your servant, my love."

* * *

Darcy woke from a deep sleep. He and the colonel and Cowan had sat up late devising a plan of action. By the time he had returned to her quarters, Elizabeth had been sleeping soundly. On silent feet, he had undressed and crawled in beside her. With a loving nudge, he had snuggled Elizabeth in beside him and closed his eyes. That had been some three hours prior. Now, with only the darkness surrounding him, Darcy was immediately on his feet. Slipping on his breeches and his discarded shirt, he trailed a dim light under his wife's sitting room door. "Elizabeth," he said softly as he stepped into the room, but it was empty. "Elizabeth?" he said automatically.

Since they had married, Darcy had found it impossible to sleep alone; yet, occasionally, his wife had accused him of stealing away the bed's warmth, and so she had left her own bed to find comfort in his. Therefore, expecting to find Elizabeth wrapped in his bedclothes, Darcy crossed through his dressing room and into his own dark chamber, but it, too, was empty. "Where in bloody hell?" he grumbled as he exited through the exterior door.

Taking a candle, which he lit from the waning wall sconce, he set out on a search for his wife. Unfortunately, his exploration revealed nothing: not in the library or his cousin's study or the drawing rooms or the estate's kitchen. And with each failure, Darcy's panic rose.

He shook a sleeping footman awake. "Have you knowledge of Mrs. Darcy's whereabouts?" he demanded.

The man scrambled to his feet and straightened his uniform. "No, Sir. Would you have me look for your wife, Sir?"

Darcy shook his head in the negative. "Tend your post. I will send word if I require your assistance. My wife is likely asleep in one of the empty rooms with a book across her lap," he said casually, although he felt anything but casual. He had previously searched all the rooms to emerge empty-handed.

He turned toward the back staircase. Circling through the servant passageways, he peered into closets and pantries and was just about to mount the stairs to his cousin's rooms to seek Edward's assistance when the kitchen door to the vegetable garden opened and his wife slipped into the muted light of his candle.

Elizabeth gasped when she saw him and clutched at her chest. "Fitzwilliam!" she hissed. Her hand fluttered to her slender neck. "You gave me such a start!"

One part of him wanted to bind her to him. He had never been so happy to see anyone. The other part wished to scold her for providing him an avenue for his worst nightmares. Thankfully, his desire to have her in his arms won out, and Darcy clasped her to him. "Thank God," he whispered as he caressed her hair. "I was so frightened." Darcy kissed the top of her head. "Where have you been?"

Elizabeth stepped from his embrace. She glanced toward the half-open door leading to Mrs. Holbrook's small room. "Perhaps we might take our conversation upstairs," she suggested before stepping around him and mounting the servants' stairs to the family quarters.

Darcy scowled. He almost wished he had chosen the scolding instead of the embrace. He snatched up the candle and shielded the light with his free hand. With his frustration building with each step, he followed his wife through the narrow passageway. Once inside their shared sitting room, Elizabeth tossed her cloak across a nearby chair, and Darcy realized that she wore her nightshift and a light wrapper. On her feet were her evening slippers.

He closed the door silently behind him and pointedly set the candleholder upon the table. "What were you thinking?" he asked before he thought to soften his tone. "You went out in the night's middle dressed so!" He gestured with a fluttery flick of his wrist.

Immediately, Elizabeth's ire rose as well. She said coldly, "I was thinking, Mr. Darcy, of solving this mystery so we might return to the safety of Pemberley."

He said flippantly, "It is fortunate that your inclination and your spontaneity should accord so well."

She strode into her bedchamber, and Darcy was forced to follow once more. By the time he had reached the room, his wife had relit the candles with a strike of a flint and a rolled paper tube. When she turned to him, she said bluntly, "I do not wonder at your disapprobation, upon my word. Obviously, by your mind, I possess a great defect of temper, made worse by a very faulty habit of self-indulgence. Yet, you should know my mind, Mr. Darcy, and I shall not have it!"

"Have what?" Darcy said boldly. "If I recall, it was you who left our bed and sought the dark recesses of the vegetable garden."

"Do not be ridiculous!" she asserted.

Darcy stormed toward her. She stood before the hearth with her arms wrapped about herself as if for protection, but her chin rose in defiance. Even though Darcy recognized her vulnerability, he did not guard his tongue. "First, I have offered you a yet-to-be-disclosed offense, and then I was ridiculous for worrying over your disappearance."

Hot tears sprang to his wife's eyes, and Darcy knew instant regret. Through trembling lips, Elizabeth rasped, "I have discovered it all, Fitzwilliam. I know of the dead horse and how close you came to meeting God today." He felt each of her words as if someone had physically struck him.

Instantly, he scooped her into his arms and sank into an over-stuffed two-armed chaise. Darcy cradled her on his lap as he covered her face with a storm of kisses. "Oh, Sweetheart," he whispered into her hair. "I never meant to deceive you. You must realize, Lizzy, that my intentions are always to protect you." He lifted Elizabeth's chin with his fingertips and lowered his mouth to hers. Since the first time Darcy had held her in his arms and had kissed her with all the passion he possessed for her, this was where he felt most complete. He could spend the rest of his life as such and never complain.

When his lips slid to her neck's column, Elizabeth warned, "You shall not wish to live with the woman I shall become if you ever lie to me again, whether on purpose or by omission."

Despite the tension of the last few minutes, Darcy smiled against her skin. "Yes, Ma'am," he teased as his tongue drew a line along her collarbone. With a deep sigh of satisfaction, Darcy set her from him. "What else must you know of the incident with the horse?"

Elizabeth lowered her eyes. It was a trick she had learned among the Bennets and one he had noted after their betrothal. His wife hid her smile of triumph when she managed to discover the truth of forbidden subjects. On the occasion of his discovery, he and Elizabeth had known each other intimately, and his wife had lingered in that wonderful stupor, which fogs a person's brain following such splendor. In a moment of weakness, Elizabeth had told him of how her mother had kept seedier tales from her daughters' notices, and how she and her sisters always discovered the sordid details. "Ours was a house rife with tattle. The servants. The tradesmen. My sisters. Both Jane and I held knowledge of a man's expectations long before we were Out in Society." So, despite her subservient pose, Darcy knew her curiosity would win out.

Dutifully and honestly, he explained what had happened during his encounter with the gypsy band. "Evidently, Mr. Gry held some responsibility for our attack. I told the man to call at Woodvine, and I would return his purse to him, but the gypsy leader never made an appearance."

"Oh, but he did," Elizabeth hastened to assure him. "I observed him speaking to one of the kitchen maids in the back garden while you met with Mr. Franklyn, but Mr. Gry did not call upon the household."

Darcy wondered aloud. "There is no way a maid would know of the shooting. I swore the colonel, Holbrook, and Cowan to secrecy, as well as Mr. Stalling."

"Did you not say Cowan suspected that Gry would call on Mrs. Ridgeway?" Darcy nodded his agreement. Elizabeth continued, "Before the gypsy spoke to the maid, I had set Cousin Samuel's staff a line of duties that would not permit the housekeeper time to meet with Mr. Gry. Mayhap Mrs. Ridgeway sent the maid to the gypsy with news of her indisposition."

"Perhaps," Darcy said thoughtfully. Then with a wry smile, he asked, "How did you learn of my perfidy?"

Elizabeth confessed, "Hannah observed Mr. Sheffield working diligently to remove the mud from your favorite jacket. She overheard his grumblings and reported them to me." Elizabeth wiggled her behind against Darcy's leg to distract him. It was exquisite torture, which Darcy gladly encouraged. He would never complain of Elizabeth's manipulations. "In truth, Mr. Sheffield said very little that made sense until I ventured into the stables to discover the lack of horses."

Darcy could not feel more at a disadvantage. Had his wife practiced her own half truths? "Then your accusations were based purely on conjecture?" he asked with a bit more irritation than he intended. "You rip out my heart with your tears!" He could not quite read her expression.

"The tears were real, Mr. Darcy," she asserted. "The terror I felt when I placed the clues together was real." She swallowed hard. "True. I only knew a few of the details, but I knew enough."

Immediately, his ire disappeared. Darcy's chest ached. He had never seen her so vulnerable. "Lizzy, you are my world." Darcy briefly closed his eyes in hopes of finding the right words. "The day you agreed to become my wife, my dreams came true. The one woman designed especially for me had, quite literally, tottered into my life's path. I recognized the awe that you would experience as Pemberley's Mistress and in assuming your place in my social circle. Yet, I never doubted your success."

"I can do none of it without you." She laid her head upon his chest and sunk heavily against him. Darcy encircled her with his arms. "Do not think of leaving me, Fitzwilliam Darcy." She hiccupped her order. "It would not be fair for me to know such happiness and then have it snatched away by some crazy plot to buy a horse that is not for sale." She tightened her hold on him. "I mean to grow old with you. To raise our children. I will tolerate nothing less than thirty years of bliss from you, Mr. Darcy. Set your mind to it."

Darcy smiled. Farce was his wife's middle name. Her innocent charm and caustic wit had enchanted him from their first introduction. "I had thought forty," he whispered into her hair. The lavender oil gave her auburn tresses a soft glow in the candlelight. "We will argue no more of the horse or the gypsy band. Perhaps you might explain your moonlight stroll instead."

Elizabeth kissed his neck before sitting upright again. She dabbed her eyes with the blousy part of her wrapper's sleeve. "I read part of your cousin's journals. Samuel Darcy mentioned the possibility that one or more members of his staff was involved with witchcraft."

"Does he say who?" Darcy's interest piqued.

Elizabeth shook her head, and a stray curl escaped her loose braid. "Not from what I have read to date. Mr. Darcy simply mentioned that there were signs of witchery about his house. He did not enumerate the signs. Just stated that he held suspicions."

Darcy gave her a speaking look. "And these suspicions sent you out into the blackness of the night?"

Elizabeth answered tartly. "Of course not. As you well know, Mr. Darcy, I am not so easily persuaded." She took his hand in her two. "I had waited patiently for your return so I might share what I had discovered, but you were later than I had expected, and I had fallen asleep. However, you know my imagination. It would not permit me to forget the diary's words, and soon I lay staring at the crown's drapery. Even though I wanted your opinion on the matter, I foolishly refused to wake you."

She shifted to lie in Darcy's embrace. Darcy lifted her long braid and draped it over her shoulder. With a soul-cleansing sigh, Elizabeth continued her tale. "I slipped from the bed to order my thoughts, and as I peered from the window into the deserted garden below, I saw a figure moving along the side pathway."

"Mrs. Ridgeway?" Darcy asked.

Elizabeth stroked his arm absentmindedly. "I thought so also. At least, at first. That is until I roused Hannah from her room across the hall and insisted that she accompany me to the housekeeper's rooms. Surprisingly, Mrs. Ridgeway was there, snoring quite pronouncedly. I assume Mr. Glover had given her a hefty dose of laudanum to cover the pain of her injured hand. Mrs. Ridgeway did not stir as Hannah and I moved about her room."

"Is that when Hannah told you of Mr. Sheffield's complaints?"

"Yes. She thought perhaps your valet had knowledge of what had occurred and had kept it from me." She took a deep breath. "I sent Hannah to bed, and I sneaked from the house to confirm my own suspicions. You discovered me upon my return."

Darcy ran his fingers through his hair. "Then you did not chase after the shadowy figure you observed in the garden?"

Elizabeth allowed her fingers to slide slowly down his arm. She interlaced their fingers. "At first, I thought to do so. Especially when I thought it to be Mrs. Ridgeway. But when I discovered the lady still tightly wrapped in her bedclothes, my interest turned from Woodvine's mystery to my husband's welfare. All of which I could think was you, Fitzwilliam."

Darcy brought her hand to rest above his heart. "Tomorrow we will think more on the why and the wherefore of this fatuity. Tonight, I wish to hold my beautiful wife in my arms. I find I have quite forgotten how to sleep without her warmth lining my body and her scent filling my lungs."

Chapter 10

"On her midnight trek to the stables, did Mrs. Darcy see any evidence of the person she had observed in the kitchen garden?" the colonel asked with an amused smile upon his lips.

Darcy had disclosed the incident to his cousin and Mr. Cowan over their morning repast. Darcy had insisted that his wife remain in bed for a few extra hours of restorative sleep. After their late-night adventure, they had known marital intimacies in that slow deliberate way Darcy preferred. The one in which Elizabeth clung to him and called out his name on a husky rasp. It was as near to Heaven as Darcy could find on Earth. "Mrs. Darcy realized that by the time she and Hannah had checked on Mrs. Ridgeway, the opportunity had passed."

Edward smirked, "Knowing Mrs. Darcy's propensity for challenging you, Cousin, your wife likely relished the idea of catching you in a half truth more than she did divining Woodvine's secrets."

Darcy recalled the tears glazing his wife's eyes and the earnestness of her words, but he would not betray Elizabeth's desolation to his cousin. Nor to the world. "I suspect you are correct," he said sagely. Darcy directed his attention to Cowan. "Do you suppose you could search for evidence of a coven without stirring up too much interest?"

"I will see to it," Cowan said as he placed his serviette beside his empty plate and prepared to make his exit.

Edward added blueberry jam to a second wedge of toast. "Likely some maid on a midnight assignation."

Cowan scowled. "I'll be asking questions in the kitchen." The Runner stood and disappeared through the room's service entrance.

"A valuable man," Darcy noted as the door closed behind Cowan. "Where did you form his acquaintance?"

"Served under me in Spain," Edward said stiffly. "Was wounded at that disaster in Corunna in '09. That nincompoop Sir John Moore possessed no idea what to do with Marshal Soult." Edward's shoulders tensed in a painful slant, and the colonel's countenance betrayed the serious darkness of his thoughts. The implacable look in his cousin's eyes spoke of the horrors, which Edward had witnessed as part of his service to the King.

"Soult had pursued us across Castile and Galacia, but we rendezvoused with the evacuation fleet at Corunna. Moore thought it best if we would provide a diversion while our forces were loaded on the fleet." Darcy saw his cousin's eyes glaze over, as if Edward relived each volley. He had observed his cousin as such previously. Whenever Edward spoke of the battles, and those incidents were few, Darcy listened carefully. He thought it best if the colonel freed his conscience of the witnessed devastation.

"Moore set up his position on a hill called Monte Mero, a point north of Piedralonga. Hope's and Baird's brigades held the east-west line, but we possessed a weak, open right flank close to the village of Elvina. Moore placed Paget's and Fraser's units in a position to cover his weak one, while Moore secured a position lower than the Heights of Penasquedo, which was an easy cannon shot on the south." Edward pointedly set his cup on the table.

"Out of sight of the French, Cowan and I were among those stationed with Fraser. We were backed up nearly to Corunna's outer fortifications. Delaborde and Merle managed to hold our troops in place, while Mermet turned Baird's flanks. The French cavalry under La Houssaye and Franceschi eliminated both Baird and Moore. Thank goodness Paget's forces turned back Mermet and La Houssaye. My men, under Fraser, prevented Franceschi from flanking our position.

"During the siege, Cowan was badly injured. In our escape, I carried him to the ship and then tended his injuries. Cowan has an ugly scar across his abdomen. I do not profess to handle a needle as well as Mrs. Darcy, but it was enough to save Cowan's life. His injuries earned him a trip across the Channel. I met him again some two years prior. He had joined Bow Street, but I do not think it suited him."

Darcy's interest piqued. "How so?"

Edward shrugged his shoulders. "Cowan was always a thinking man. Even in Spain, he would question the officers' decisions. You should have heard him when Moore chose to engage Soult. I thought the officers might order him directly in the line of fire, but he stood beside me throughout the battle. Never left my side until the Frenchy cut him down with a volley meant for me. I was the one with the epaulets on my shoulders. I was the target."

Darcy swallowed hard. He had liked Cowan from the beginning of their acquaintance. Now, he realized he would forever be in the former Runner's debt. Edward Fitzwilliam lived because of Thomas Cowan's unselfish bravery. Instead of speaking words of gratitude that would embarrass them both and which choked his throat, Darcy turned the conversation with a teasing quip. "Were you not Cowan's commanding officer? Should he not have despised you?"

The smile returned to Edward's lips, and Darcy breathed a sigh of relief. He had chosen well in distracting his cousin. "Cowan always said I was an aberration. That I had too much sense for an earl's son."

Darcy nodded his agreement. "I expect Cowan is correct. You were always the odd one in the family."

Edward quipped, "And you were always the haughty one. Is it not evident why we continue to see eye to eye?"

Darcy understood immediately. "It takes a loose screw to recognize the tight one and vice versa. Yet, they work to hold the wood together."

* * *

"Mr. Darcy." Mr. Barriton interrupted Darcy's time with the Woodvine estate ledgers. "Mr. Sedgelock and Mr. Chetley from the British Antiquarian Society have arrived. Evidently, Mr. Franklyn had sent to London for them."

"Sedgelock and Chetley?" Darcy mused. "Are they not the gentlemen who assisted my cousin previously?"

The butler did not hide his surprise at Darcy's knowledge of the workings of Woodvine Hall. "I believe they are, Sir."

Darcy stood. "Are the gentlemen in the receiving room?" He straightened his coat's lines.

"No, Sir. The gentlemen have joined Mr. Franklyn." He paused awkwardly. "Am I to see to the gentlemen's accommodations?"

Darcy came around the desk. "Naturally," Darcy said aristocratically. "I assume Sedgelock and Chetley have brought their own company?"

"Several gentlemen arrived with their entourage, Sir, but I heard one of the men say that Captain Tregonwell had arranged for his party to meet with Mr. Sedgelock and Mr. Chetley in Christ-church," Barriton said evenly.

"Place the gentlemen in the wing with Mr. Franklyn." Barriton nodded. "And the others in the smaller bedrooms at the rear of the house." Darcy glanced out the study's windows to see Cowan crossing toward the wooded parkland. The man amazed Darcy: Cowan was driven to perfection. "How many men did the good captain send as escorts for the Antiquarians?"

"Three, Sir."

His cousin's finds must be true treasures if the Society had sent three of its most noted archaeologists to retrieve them. "Inform Mrs. Holbrook that our numbers have increased by five." Barriton bowed to exit. "I will pay my respects to the gentlemen before I seek my wife's company."

Barriton said, "I believe Mrs. Darcy is in her quarters, Sir."

Some twenty minutes later, he slipped through the interior door to his wife's bedchamber. Elizabeth lay across the counterpane on her stomach. Her day slipper dangled from a toe as her foot twitched in that characteristic distraction of deep concentration. When studying something enthusiastically, his wife often flexed her foot and held her largest toe at an odd angle. The harder she bit into her lip in concentration, the stiffer her toe became. It was a lovable quirk, and Darcy enjoyed watching her mind at work. He waited by the door for Elizabeth to become aware of his presence.

Finally, she amusedly said, "Quit skulking, Fitzwilliam." She did not look away from the book she held.

"Skulking, is it?" he said as he approached the bed. "What an odd word, Mrs. Darcy," he teased. "Is it one of your own invention?"

Elizabeth rolled to her back and sat up. She marked her place in the book. "Actually, it is one of Kitty's. My younger sister could not say the word *sulk* correctly. Eventually, *skulking* became our favorite word for all sorts of tasks." Elizabeth smiled in reminiscence. "In reality, it is the first time I have used it in what seems forever. Thank you for the memory."

Darcy sat beside her on the bed. "If you wish, we could call at Longbourn before we return to Derbyshire. I am certain Mr. and Mrs. Bingley would welcome our company."

Without preamble, Elizabeth flung herself into his arms and kissed him happily. "If I have not told you previously, I have pronounced you to be the most perfect of husbands."

"I am only perfect for you, my Lizzy." Bringing her with him, he leaned back to rest across the counterpane. Elizabeth lay atop him. He kissed her tenderly. Darcy so enjoyed these moments; he counted himself among the few of his class who had married for love, but his luck was more than that. Elizabeth had accepted all his overtures, and she had turned into a passionate lover. Among his peers, their relationship was an anomaly, and Darcy held no complaints. One would think after some six months of marriage that he might tire of her, but his wife needed only to offer a pouty smile across a crowded ballroom, and he was like a randy schoolboy. His hands skimmed her hips. Even through the layers of clothing, he could feel her warmth, and Elizabeth's lips pressed harder against his. "I love you, Elizabeth Darcy," he said huskily as she relaxed into him.

Elizabeth rested her head on his chest. "And I you, Mr. Darcy," she said contentedly.

Darcy could have remained as such for many hours. Elizabeth's closeness was all he required, but he was sensible to the fact that the household had increased by five males. He would not embarrass his wife by giving credence to the gossip that would follow their spending an afternoon in Elizabeth's bed. With a sigh of disappointment, Darcy assisted her to a seated position and then righted himself. "I came to tell you that the Antiquarian Society has sent Mr. Sedgelock and Mr. Chetley to assist Mr. Franklyn. The gentlemen are most eager to examine my cousin's various finds."

"Are those not the gentlemen who spent time at Woodvine in the winter?" Elizabeth asked as she stood to straighten her dress and to mend her chignon.

Darcy remained seated on the bed's edge. "They are. The Society fears several of Samuel's treasures could have been lost due to a lack of oversight. Sedgelock and Chetley have brought three others to supervise the care and removal of Samuel's donations. They come to us via Captain Tregonwell."

Elizabeth said softly, "Five more."

Darcy clasped her shoulders to turn her to him. "Nothing untoward will happen, Elizabeth."

His wife's delicate features tightened. "I cannot say that I am comfortable with the prospect of serving as hostess to a table of gentlemen. After all, at Longbourn, frills dominated the service. Yet, my hesitation rests upon the fact that we now number ten, and we are no closer to solving the mystery than the day we arrived at Woodvine Hall. We have yet to discover the whereabouts of your cousin's body or the reason for Samuel Darcy's demise."

It was now Darcy's turn to grimace. Even if no solutions were available to this house's mysteries, he had not abandoned his idea of departing from Woodvine. "Perhaps the additional eyes will assist us in seeing what we have not observed previously." He released her and straightened his waistcoat. "Was there nothing of notice in my cousin's journals that might lead us to answers?"

Elizabeth's countenance lit with excitement. "I nearly forgot," she said as she reached for a slender volume. "I finished the entries for last year and have begun the ones for this." She turned to an entry date for the last week of January. "See here." Elizabeth pointed to a passage. "Your cousin describes his dismay at returning to Woodvine to discover Mr. Hotchkiss's absence." She read as Darcy looked over her shoulder. "He says, 'My anger was improperly placed as Hotchkiss would never have departed without good reason. Hotchkiss has served the estate some twenty years, and he had written me in November to encourage my speedy return. Reuben spoke of evil residing beneath Woodvine's roof, and although I have been home but a sennight, I see his words hold truth.'"

Unconsciously, Darcy shivered. "It is a shame that Samuel did not heed his steward's warning."

Elizabeth thumbed through the journal's pages. "Your cousin had resolved to write to Hotchkiss in York."

"Mr. Holbrook informed us of Samuel's intentions to do so," Darcy said. "The groom told the colonel and me that my cousin's efforts were to no avail."

Elizabeth found the page she sought. "Mr. Holbrook erred," she insisted. "In this entry, the late Mr. Darcy records a most unusual message from a Mrs. Wickersham, reportedly Reuben Hotchkiss's sister." Darcy took the journal from her outstretched hands. As he read, Elizabeth encapsulated, "Mrs. Wickersham explained that her brother had not returned to his childhood home. In fact, Mr. Hotchkiss's family was most distressed. Your cousin's steward would regularly send part of his wages for the care of his invalid mother. At the time of her writing, Mrs. Wickersham said it had been some six weeks since they had heard from Mr. Hotchkiss. The family had expected his semi-annual wages to be paid in January."

Darcy read the words a second time to assure himself of the accuracy of his wife's précis. "I will send word to Rardin. It seems only appropriate that a small settlement be made in Hotchkiss's name. If the man had remained at Woodvine, Samuel would have seen to his steward's care and pension," he said distractedly.

Elizabeth reached for the book. She flipped the pages backwards to rest on another of Samuel's daily posts. "In this one," she returned the book into Darcy's open palms, "Mr. Darcy speaks of his uneasiness with Mr. Gaylord. It appears that Cousin Samuel intended to replace Gaylord as soon as he located a competent candidate for the position." It was a revelation that had not surprised Darcy. He had spoken to Gaylord only twice since his arrival at Woodvine. Neither interview had proved productive. Gaylord had not impressed. In fact, Darcy had sent Rardin a message suggesting that they replace the steward as soon as possible.

Again, Darcy read as Elizabeth excitedly explained her discoveries. Tonight, he would choose the journals for his own reading "pleasures." "We should share this information with the colonel. You have done well, my dear." He kissed the tip of Elizabeth's upturned nose. Returning the book to her care, he said, "We should join Franklyn. I assured the man that we would greet his associates properly. The gentlemen are most eager to discover Samuel's treasure trove."

"I shall ask the colonel to join us." Elizabeth secured the journal with a string. She placed it with the others in a shallow box before hiding the box under her intimates in her dressing room.

Darcy smiled at her precautions. "Should I ask the colonel to bring Mr. Cowan with him?" she asked as she patted her hair into place.

Darcy held the door for her. "I espied Mr. Cowan earlier in the parklands. He may not have returned to the manor, but ask Edward to bring the Runner if Cowan is available."

They separated in the upper passageway, and Darcy made his way to the library, only to find the Antiquarians waiting for him. "Ah, Gentlemen. I pray you have not been too inconvenienced by my delay."

Mr. Franklyn looked up from the book over which he and his associates hunched. "Not at all, Mr. Darcy. Mr. Sedgelock brought a detailed inventory of what we should find among your cousin's belongings."

Darcy nodded his understanding. Although he was more than a bit obsessive over relics from the Middle Ages, especially items of military interest, Darcy had never known such abstracted attentions as the Antiquarians displayed. Of course, the only exception was a particular young lady of a recent acquaintance whose affections he had eventually won. The thought brought a smile to Darcy's lips. Unlike the men gathered into a tight group around the handwritten list, Darcy's cousin had been more than a man of science. Samuel Darcy held many interests: music, art, languages, and agriculture. His cousin had lived in the present and planned for the future. To Franklyn, Sedgelock, and Chetley, only the past existed. "I have asked my maternal cousin, Colonel Fitzwilliam, to join us, as well as Mrs. Darcy and Mr. Cowan. I assume you hold no objections."

"Certainly not," Chetley mumbled distractedly as he closed the ledger containing the inventory list.

Darcy glanced toward the door to see Elizabeth enter on his cousin's arm. Despite a bit of jealousy, which always plagued him when Elizabeth gave Edward her attentions, Darcy had to admit they made a handsome couple. If Fate had not taken a twisted turn, Elizabeth could easily have become his cousin in marriage, rather than his wife. She had initially preferred Edward's company to his. Another errant thought crossed Darcy's mind: If something should happen to him, Elizabeth would be wealthy enough to choose another. Would she turn to Edward? Although the thought of another man knowing her could easily drive him insane, Darcy reluctantly had to concede that he would rather see her with Edward than with any other. His cousin would protect both Elizabeth and Georgiana.

Behind him, men scrambled to their feet. Darcy reached to accept her hand, and Elizabeth left Edward's side to join him. "Gentleman, may I present my cousin, Colonel Fitzwilliam, and my wife, Mrs. Darcy."

Sedgelock, as the senior member of the group, politely extended his greetings to Elizabeth, but to Edward, he said, "I am quite familiar with your father, Sir. The Earl of Matlock is a great contributor to the Society."

Edward acknowledged the man with an aristocratic nod. "My father believes in God, King, and Country. If your work brings glory to England, Matlock considers your group worthy of his financial support."

Darcy wondered if his cousin and the Earl had quarreled recently. Edward's tone held notes of strain. His cousin and Matlock were often at odds. As much as Darcy respected his mother's only brother, he disagreed with the disparity with which the Earl of Matlock treated his children. Matlock favored his older son to the detriment of the younger. Darcy had always told Edward that Matlock had to coddle Viscount Lindale because Edward's brother was too inept to survive on his own. Although Edward loved and respected his father, Darcy suspected his cousin still harbored a bit of resentment at being born second. Likely, Edward's previous interest in their cousin Anne had been founded in Edward's drive to marry well and prove himself to his father.

"The Earl speaks well of your service," Sedgelock continued. "Matlock is quite proud of your accomplishments, Sir."

Darcy noted a slight blush and a definite frown upon his cousin's countenance. It was as if Edward had never heard another speak of Matlock's admiration. Darcy cleared his throat. "Perhaps we should resume our seats and become acquainted."

Edward reached for the bell cord. "I will order tea."

Darcy seated Elizabeth on a nearby settee. "First, permit me to introduce to you the others traveling with Mr. Sedgelock and Mr. Chetley, my dear. Mrs. Darcy, this is Mr. Poore, Mr. Maxton, and Mr. McKye." Each man bowed in turn. "I have left word for Mr. Cowan to join us when he returns to the house."

When everyone was settled, Mr. Sedgelock said, "Mr. Franklyn has performed admirably in organizing the late Mr. Darcy's acquisitions; yet, we are most impatient to examine the items hidden within."

Darcy said authoritatively, "Normally, I would embrace your enthusiasm for Samuel's finds. My cousin's legacy will bring honor to the Darcy name, and it would please Samuel to know so. However, I am at Woodvine for one purpose: to recover Samuel Darcy's body for a proper burial and to identify those who have executed his degradation."

Chetley stammered, "Of…of course, Mr. Darcy. We did not mean to imply that Samuel Darcy's acquisitions took precedence over justice."

Darcy continued, "Once you begin your assessment of Samuel's finds, my family and I will leave you to your examinations, but I demand a daily accounting of your activities. I deem it my duty to assure that Cousin Samuel's collection is treated with the reverence it deserves. Either the colonel or I will oversee the work. I am certain Matlock would wish his son to assume the role. After all, Lady Anne Fitzwilliam married George Darcy. Samuel's legacy reflects upon Matlock's family name." Darcy noted the twitch of Edward's lips. Despite his cousin's and his uncle's continuing battle of wills, Darcy and Edward occasionally invoked the earl's name as a negotiating tool. It was a common practice among the aristocracy. "The bulk of Samuel's estate has been left to his niece, the Countess of Rardin." Adding another earl to the scenario certainly would not hurt the chances of the Society's agreement.

Mr. Franklyn cleared his throat. Obviously, Sedgelock was the senior Society member, but it was Franklyn who quickly comprehended Darcy's implications. The Society would answer to the Darcy family in this manner or know disappointment. "We agree to your stipulations, Mr. Darcy."

"Excellent." He extended his hand for the ledger resting on Sedgelock's lap. Reluctantly, the man handed it to Darcy, who passed it to Edward. "My cousin will make a copy of the list and then return the book to you." He smiled amiably at the group. "Are there items on the list of which we should be made aware? Any of great worth or rarity?" he asked casually.

"Many are invaluable examples of ancient civilizations," Chetley explained. "A monetary estimation cannot be placed on history."

From beside him, Elizabeth asked softly, "What of the Lemegeton?"

Edward asked suspiciously, "The Lesser Key of Solomon? What does a grimoire have to do with Samuel Darcy?"

Elizabeth said with confidence, "The late Mr. Darcy mentions the Lemegeton in one of his journals. Samuel Darcy thought he had discovered one of the original texts."

As if his wife had consulted him regarding the new information, Darcy asked the Antiquarians, "What is the historical context of the manuscript?"

Chetley explained, "There are references to the text in the seventeenth century. Some claim King Solomon authored the Lesser, but experts disagree on this matter. The text contains Johann Weyer's sixteenth century *Pseudomonarchia Daemonum,* as well as material from the fourteenth century."

"The titles of nobility assigned to the demons are of a more modern language," Sedgelock added. "Needless to say, Solomon lived long before any of these events."

Darcy asked, "Is it possible that my cousin could have uncovered a copy of this document during his travels?"

"Easily so," Chetley assured.

Elizabeth's voice cut through the archaeologist's confidence. "I suspect the late Mr. Darcy did not discover the grimoire in foreign lands."

Edward insisted, "Please clarify, Mrs. Darcy."

Elizabeth glanced at her husband for his agreement. He nodded almost imperceptibly, and she continued, "The late Mr. Darcy wrote daily in his journal. In a series of entries, my husband's Cousin Samuel described coming upon the book quite unexpectedly in the lower garden under a column bedside the sundial.

Samuel Darcy thought it had been placed there in haste. He hid it in his secret room. I suspect it is among the items my husband and I found below. Cousin Samuel also mentions a stang and an arthame."

In serious contemplation, Darcy cocked his head to one side. "You are saying that Samuel thought witches practiced their arts under his roof?"

Elizabeth shook her head in denial. "Samuel Darcy does not make such an assertion; yet, I do believe he thought some of his employees delved in evil spells and magic potions. We have seen evidence of this with the witch's bottle, my husband."

Edward said adamantly, "I find the prospects of such rumors ridiculous."

Elizabeth countered, "Ridiculous or not, there are many, especially in the country shires, who strongly follow their superstitions. I assume from the late Mr. Darcy's words that he was of the colonel's persuasion, but Samuel Darcy understood how the dark arts motivated others."

Ironically, the elderly maid who had been present when the witch's bottle was found entered with the teacart and set it before Elizabeth. "Shall I serve, Missus?" she asked softly.

Elizabeth whispered, "I shall serve the gentlemen if you will bring in a second pot."

"There be one waiting in the hall, Mrs. Darcy. I will fetch it immediately, Ma'am."

Sedgelock asked, "When should we commence with our cataloging?"

Darcy said, "After tea, we can be about our business." He reached for the cup, which Elizabeth extended in his direction to hand off to Sedgelock. As he accepted the second cup his wife had prepared to serve Chetley, Darcy asked, "What is the Latin name for the Lemegeton?"

From behind him, a crash of china quieted the room. Darcy spun to see a white-faced maid in distress. "Mrs. Jacobs?" Elizabeth asked as she directed the woman's steps from the broken porcelain. "Are you safe?" Darcy rang the bell for additional assistance.

Mrs. Jacobs murmured, "I beg your pardon, Missus. I be...I be splashing the hot tea on me hand, and then I lose me grip."

Elizabeth assured, "It is fine, Mrs. Jacobs. See Mrs. Holbrook regarding a bandage for your hand and send Els to attend me."

"Yes, Ma'am." The maid executed a half curtsy and disappeared into the hallway.

Elizabeth turned to face the room. "I apologize," she offered. "The late Mr. Darcy's staff is adjusting to my preferences."

However, before she could say more, Cowan burst through the door. "Mr. Darcy, you must come!"

Darcy turned to discover the Runner covered in dirt. "What is it, Cowan?"

The man sucked in a deep breath; whether in agitation or exasperation, Darcy could not say. "I have found another grave in the woods!"

Darcy asked the obvious, "Is it my cousin's body?"

"Unfortunately, no. The clothes are of a gentleman, but not so refined, and there is no apparent damage to the head. Dead perhaps a fortnight."

Elizabeth's voice caught in her throat, but she managed to ask, "Mr. Crescent?"

"Very likely, Mrs. Darcy."

Chapter 11

"Elizabeth, I do not think it is wise for you to accompany us. Perhaps you should return to the house." They rushed to keep pace with Cowan and the colonel.

"I am well," she said as they crossed the rugged terrain leading to the tree line.

Darcy struggled to shorten his stride so he would not outpace her. "But…"

Elizabeth stopped suddenly, and Darcy had to circle his return to her side. Her hands fisted at her waist, and Darcy prepared himself for a tongue-lashing. "I shall not embarrass you, Fitzwilliam," she asserted.

"I never thought you would," he conceded. "It is just that…" Darcy hesitated.

Looking sad and lonely, she gazed up at him. "That I would what, Fitzwilliam? That I would crumble into a watering pot?"

Darcy's fingers caught hers. "I would not see you suffer in any manner," he said for his wife's ears only. "I could not stand your countenance dressed up in woe and paleness."

Her expression softened. "I am not so fragile, Mr. Darcy. And we both know that this is not about Mr. Cowan's find. It is simple: I am a woman who has lost her first child. However, I am not the only female who has known such sorrow. Yet, we may begin again. Together. Is that not what you wish? Or are we to dwell forever in the past?"

Darcy gave no indication of how much the question bothered him. Of course he desired the future Elizabeth described, but he would never abandon his desire to protect her. Not while he breathed life into his lungs. "I want the future. I want you and our children at Pemberley."

"Then allow me to recover in my own way—to distract myself with the mystery and then to enjoy the holiday my husband has promised me."

The colonel called from the hedgerow. "Come along, Darcy!"

He did not turn his head to acknowledge Edward's entreaty. Instead, Darcy tugged Elizabeth closer. He remained inclined to credit what she wished. "We should hurry, Mrs. Darcy."

Elizabeth smiled brilliantly. "Yes, we should." She double-stepped to maintain the pace Darcy set. He was so proud of her. Even if his wife raised her skirts and set off at a run, Darcy would not censure her. A woman of the *ton* would have demanded that he remove her from this madness. Would have thought him foolish to fret over clearing his cousin's name. But not *his* Elizabeth. His wife had embraced every facet of Darcy's life and had made it her own.

They joined Edward and Cowan beside a loosely disguised grave. "How in the world did you discover this site?" Darcy asked as he surveyed the area. They were deep in the woods where the sun rarely reached because of the thick foliage overhead. Brush and fallen leaves covered the ground.

Cowan said matter-of-factly, "I listen. To the servants. To those in the village shops. To those gathered after services. I listen for common phrases."

"Are we certain Mr. Crescent rests below?" Elizabeth asked softly. His wife looked everywhere but at the unmarked gravesite.

Upon the chance she might swoon, Darcy instinctively rested his hand on the small of her back.

Cowan's frown lines met. "Just a suspicion until we exhume the body." He kicked at the loose dirt. "I dug down as far as I could on both sides to guarantee there is a body under all this forest debris." Cowan gestured to the slightly raised mound. "I wanted everyone to view the site before we searched further."

"I do not understand," Darcy said as he nudged Elizabeth closer to his side.

Edward explained, "The rocks. It is the same pattern as those we found on Mr. Hotchkiss's grave. The V. A mark of the witch. A mark to represent a sacred place."

Darcy ran his fingers through his hair. "That makes little sense. I have heard of those who mark a mantelpiece with ritualistic symbols, but never a grave. A house with its doors and chimneys and windows are considered vulnerable to evil spirits, and the marks are meant to ward off the spirit. Placing the mark above the grave would keep the evil within."

Elizabeth asked, "Why a V?"

Franklyn explained, "For the Virgin Mary. Occasionally an M is used."

Before anyone could respond, Sedgelock declared, "Mr. Darcy is correct. For the past twenty years, I have studied ancient civilizations and the use of the black arts. Never once have I encountered a report where a society marked the grave to seal the evil within."

Cowan suggested, "Perhaps the mark is to keep the cursed without. To protect the dearly departed. The same as the marks of protection drive the witches from the house."

Mr. Franklyn countered, "What of those uncivilized societies that mark gravesites and houses with crosses and iron horseshoes to ward off vampiric creatures?"

Edward grumbled, "Such as the English?"

His cousin's cynicism brought a smile to Darcy's lips. "It is not as if I doubt you, Mr. Cowan. Obviously, someone has gone to great lengths to conceal the body. The fact that this grave and the one in the field with the monoliths display similar symbols only adds to our body of knowledge regarding our culprit."

Edward summarized, "If we all agree that the markings are not a coincidence, then we will exhume whoever rests below." No one said a word as Murray, Jatson, and Edward's man Fletcher picked up the shovels, which Mr. Holbrook had retrieved from the stable. The four men set their backs to the task. Uncertain what they would uncover, Darcy had purposely left the Wood-vine staff at the house. He did not trust those recently hired by his cousin Samuel.

Within minutes, the blanket-draped body lay before them. The grave had not been very deep, just deep enough to keep animal predators from abusing the body.

Keeping his voice low, Darcy leaned close to his wife to catch her gaze with his. "Step away for a moment, Mrs. Darcy. I will not have you look upon death."

Surprisingly, Elizabeth did not argue. She walked away toward where he could hear water running. Darcy watched her departure to assure himself of her steady steps. When she was out of sight, he nodded to Holbrook to remove the thin wool dressing covering what remained of the body. Both Fletcher and Jatson turned away from the disgusting sight, but Darcy searched the disfigured countenance for the familiarity of Crescent's face. "From what I recall of the man, that is not Mr. Crescent," he said solemnly.

Holbrook cleared his throat. "No, not Mr. Crescent. Me mother will be thankful. Crescent be a favorite of hers." The groom leaned over for a closer examination. "It not be Crescent, but I thinks it might be Bieder Bates."

Steel in his tone, Darcy demanded, "Who in bloody hell is Bieder Bates?"

Holbrook leaned against his shovel. "Bates bought the old Eastman place on the other side of the village. Haven't seen him for a while, but that not be unusual. He mostly kept to himself, excepting he came regular to the assembly. Bates liked to socialize with the ladies."

Edward asked the obvious, "If this Mr. Bates was from a farm some five miles distant, why is his body on Woodvine land? And how did Bates lose his life?"

Darcy said skeptically, "I do not suppose it would do much good to ask Mr. Glover to provide his best assessment."

Edward shook his head in disbelief. "Perhaps it might be best to send to London for a more competent surgeon."

Darcy argued, "Perhaps there is one closer at Christchurch or Lyme Regis or Hampshire." He gestured to the body. "Mr. Holbrook, do you suppose we might find some hearty parishioners who would prepare Mr. Bates for a proper burial?"

"I'll see to it, Mr. Darcy. The church's sexton will know who to trust."

"Murray, please call upon the vicar and make him aware that we require his services again."

"Immediately, Sir."

"And summon the good doctor," Darcy instructed as his servant moved away. "Jatson, you and Fletcher should make yourselves comfortable. You will watch over the body until Mr. Glover arrives."

Edward said, "We should return to the house."

Darcy started toward where his wife had disappeared. "I will retrieve Mrs. Darcy, and we will join you in a few minutes." He did not wait for his cousin's agreement. The realization that Elizabeth was alone in the woods drove Darcy to lengthen his stride. He had not gone far before he found her staring off toward a small waterfall, a steady stream of water rushing through the rocks. The refreshing sound provided the feeling of a private grotto. The season, the scene, and the air were all favorable to tenderness and sentiment.

Darcy stepped up behind and encircled her waist in a comforting embrace. "We should return to the manor," he said as she laid her head against his shoulder.

"I was saying a prayer for the soul of a man I did not know," she confessed. "It seemed only appropriate to find God here in this beautifully heartening place."

Darcy tightened his embrace. "Mr. Holbrook has identified our stranger as Mr. Bates, a farmer who lived on the other side of Wimborne."

Elizabeth turned in his arms. "Then it was not your cousin's manservant?"

"No." He kissed her forehead. "It may sound odd, but I pray Mr. Crescent escaped. I do not know what shadow has crossed Woodvine's threshold, but I would like to think someone survived this idiocy."

Elizabeth asked, "Do you think Mrs. Ridgeway has practiced witchcraft? Could she have orchestrated these men's deaths?"

Darcy shook his head in disbelief. "It is frustrating that we are no closer to solving the mystery of Samuel's death than we were upon our arrival in Dorset. I suspect we may never know the truth." He released Elizabeth before catching her hand to interlace their fingers. They would return to Woodvine to face the unknown together. "We now have two additional deaths," he continued.

"With similarly marked graves," Elizabeth added.

"A witch's bottle and unusual maps," he recited.

Elizabeth thought aloud also, "A gypsy band and missing horses."

Darcy muttered, "One of which has been killed.

"The Clavicula Salomonis."

Darcy stopped suddenly. "The list never ends," he declared. "How can we possibly create order out of such chaos? So much perfidy has made grievous inroads on the tranquility of all."

Elizabeth clenched her jaw in determination. "We shall finish this, Mr. Darcy. There is one missing piece that will lead to multiple solutions."

Despite his own frustration, Darcy smiled. She had shifted her shoulders and raised her chin in that adorable challenge that had won his heart at Netherfield. Perhaps his wife should provide ladies of the *ton* lessons on bringing a gentleman to the line. She was forever *his* Elizabeth. Levelheaded, yet impetuous. Calm, yet intractable. Always with his best interest at heart. "Yes, we will, Mrs. Darcy. Then I will take you sea bathing and to London for part of the Season and to Longbourn for a long-overdue visit."

"I plan to hold you to those promises, Mr. Darcy," she said as she caught his hand again.

They entered Woodvine through a side entrance only to be informed that Mr. Gry awaited Darcy in the small drawing room. "What could he want?" he grumbled. After instructing the servant to have Mrs. Holbrook deliver tea, Darcy brought the back of Elizabeth's hand to his lips. "Would you ask the colonel and Mr. Cowan to join me?"

Elizabeth observed, "I thought we had seen the last of the gypsy leader when he did not claim payment for the horse."

"As did I," Darcy said dryly.

Elizabeth caressed his cheek. "As I am certain Mr. Franklyn and company are engrossed in their relics, I plan to construct a list of what we do know and another of what we must still discover. The process will assist me in ordering my thoughts."

"The 'must discover's will greatly outnumber the 'do know's," Darcy said with a self-mocking smile. "Perhaps a third list of items we assume have some bearing on this mystery, but which we have no basis for connection."

With an expectant expression, Elizabeth asked, "Such as why Mrs. Ridgeway has never set foot in the Wimborne church or what is her true relationship to the good doctor?"

"Or why the lady has chosen to set herself against me?"

Elizabeth ironically said, "It appears many of our 'some bearing's are connected to Mrs. Ridgeway."

Darcy squeezed her fingertips. "I will find you once I have finished my interview with Mr. Gry. I am most eager to view this list."

"I shall see to the scientists' comforts and then retreat to my chambers, Mr. Darcy."

He watched her walk away. The sway of her hips fascinated him. Although his wife was not a woman who required constant reminders of her fine looks, Darcy appreciated her form, and he made a point of assuring Elizabeth of her effect on him. He looked after her in an ecstasy of admiration of all her many virtues, from her obliging manners down to her light and graceful tread. "For it is many months since I have considered her as one of the handsomest women of my acquaintance," he had once told Caroline Bingley to ward off one of Miss Bingley's catty attacks on the woman Darcy loved with every fiber of his being. From the beginning, Darcy had found it charmingly refreshing to encounter a woman who would challenge him. One who would not bore him with her inane chatter, and one who inflamed his passions. With a deep sigh of contentment, Darcy turned toward the sitting room and the awaiting gypsy leader.

"Mr. Gry," he said as he entered the drawing room. Darcy purposely did not return the Rom's obeisance. Instead, he strode past the man to assume a seat of dominance. "I had not expected to see you again." He motioned the man to a nearby chair.

"I saw no cause to intrude on your good humor," the gypsy said sheepishly. "I came across the gelding shortly after your departure." Of course, Darcy understood that Gry offered a false face. He was well aware the gypsy had called at Woodvine before being sent away by one of the maids. Darcy still did not know the gist of the conversation between Gry and Samuel's servant, but he meant to discover the truth of the matter.

The colonel and Cowan entered before Darcy could respond. "Ah, you are here," he said to his cousin and the Runner. "It seems we erred in our estimation of Mr. Gry. He saw the dead animal and chose not to make a demand on my time." Darcy spoke as if the man did not sit some five feet from him. It reminded him of Edward's father. The Earl of Matlock had perfected the art of the indirect cut.

"Is that not what we first surmised," Edward said conspiratorially. The colonel and Cowan pulled over chairs to join the pair.

When everyone was settled, Darcy asked, "If your business is not the stallion, Gry, what brings you to Woodvine?"

The Rom shifted uncomfortably. "Actually, I have come with news of our impending departure. I have promised my men that we will leave Dorset."

Cowan asked suspiciously, "And your destination?"

The gypsy leader was not so successful in hiding his previous disdain for his Anglo tormentors when he spoke to the Runner. Darcy supposed that Gry saw Cowan as a man of little consequence, or perhaps, the Rom understood that Cowan's mind would not rest until the investigator knew the truth. "If it is of any importance, we will spend part of the summer in Wales."

The colonel asked, "And your departure?"

"On Monday," Gry said obligingly. "We will use the week's end to prepare food for the journey. We meant to stay until mid-May, but we will depart after the May Day celebration."

After a pregnant pause, Darcy said, "I thought you had decided to remain in the area until details of your brother's death were disclosed."

Gry shrugged his shoulders noncommittally. "We Roma are accustomed to leaving before matters are settled. Overstaying our welcome in Wimborne will not bring my brother back to us, nor will it encourage justice."

Darcy wondered if the second part of the Rom's statement was not more important than the first.

Cowan asked, "I do not suppose you are familiar with either Reuben Hotchkiss or Bieder Bates?"

Silence reigned, as a cloud of confusion crossed the gypsy's countenance. Finally, Gry said, "I assume Hotchkiss and Bates have something to do with Mr. Samuel's death, and you wish to connect the mystery to my men; but I assure you we Roma have completed no business with either man."

Cowan said, "I did not ask if you conducted business with either Hotchkiss or Bates. I asked if you were familiar with either man."

The Rom sighed heavily. "I know nothing of Mr. Bates and only know of Mr. Hotchkiss by reputation. I have not had the acquaintance of either man." When no one else broke the tension, the gypsy leader stood. "If that is all, I will take my leave." Darcy and Edward followed the man to his feet. At the door, the gypsy paused. "It is with an honest regard that I say the loss of Samuel Darcy leaves a great hole in this community. Your cousin treated the Roma as friends." With that, Gry made his exit.

From where he remained seated behind them, Cowan said, "I still say Gry knows more than he pretends."

Darcy swallowed a deep cleansing breath. "Beside his likely knowledge of the horse, what other weakness did you note in Mr. Gry's tale?"

Cowan stretched out his legs and stood slowly. "I would think that if an outsider insinuated that I held knowledge of a confounding mystery that I would be curious regarding the crime which brought the accusation to my door. Although Gry repeated his claim of no knowledge of Hotchkiss or Bates, he never once expressed an interest in why we would inquire of two strangers."

Edward mused, "Perhaps the Rom prefers to keep his distance from controversy."

Cowan shook his head in denial. "No. My money says Gry has an informant under Woodvine's roof."

Cowan's words no longer surprised Darcy, and that fact shocked him more than did the possibility of a spy operating at Woodvine. "I certainly hope we resolve this mayhem soon. I would prefer to relax my guard and become a country gentleman again."

* * *

Over the evening meal, Mr. Cowan announced his intention of leaving Woodvine early the following day.

Elizabeth, who was seated beside the man, said with concern, "I hope it is nothing amiss that takes you from us, Mr. Cowan."

The Runner smiled easily at her, and despite knowing he had nothing to fear, the green-eyed monster rested on Darcy's shoulder. He wondered when this need for Elizabeth's exclusive attentions would fade. He had thought once he had won her heart that he would rest more easily, but even after six months of marriage, he could not quite accept the possibility that Elizabeth could love him as much as she professed. With such warm feelings and lively spirits housed in one woman, Darcy found it difficult to do justice to her affections.

"Nothing of a personal nature," Cowan confessed, "but I do have a possible lead that I should pursue."

The colonel inquired, "Might you share your suspicions?"

The Runner sent the colonel a quick look. "At this point, I think it best to investigate before I raise false hopes."

Darcy said, "As you wish, Cowan, but we charge you to take care."

Franklyn cleared his throat. "Might we retire to the late Mr. Darcy's library?"

As a group, they had decided that this would be the evening they would accidentally 'find' Samuel Darcy's secret room.

Before the servants' listening ears, Darcy said, "That sounds delightful. I imagine we might have a hearty discussion within Samuel's sanctuary."

When Mrs. Ridgeway appeared in the dining room door, Elizabeth asked with concern, "Mrs. Ridgeway, are you certain you should be from your bed?" The woman was paler than Darcy had recalled, and she wore a bandage on her left hand and forearm.

"Thank you, Ma'am." The housekeeper curtsied before grasping the door's frame to steady her stance. "It is time I return to my duties." The woman brushed an errant curl from her face. "Is there something particular you require this evening?"

It did not escape Darcy's attention how unusual it was for the housekeeper to appear in person to serve the guests. Elizabeth's eyebrow rose slightly, which indicated his wife had also taken note of the odd circumstances unfolding. "I believe the gentlemen prefer their port or brandy. I would enjoy another cup of tea."

"No Madeira, Ma'am?" the housekeeper insisted, which was also unusual.

Darcy said authoritatively, "Mrs. Darcy is not in the habit of repeating herself." The others might have lessened their suspicions regarding the woman, but he had not.

The housekeeper curtsied. "As you wish, Mr. Darcy." Her tone spoke of her exasperation.

Elizabeth stood, and the gentlemen rose. "I shall leave you to your cigars and port."

Darcy reached for her hand and brought the back of it to his lips. "We shan't tarry, Mrs. Darcy."

Elizabeth nodded and exited. She purposely closed the door behind her. With his wife's withdrawal, except for Murray, Darcy dismissed the attending footmen. "I suspect we have much to discuss, but let us enjoy the fine port and the imported cheroots first. I would not leave Mrs. Darcy to her own devices for long." As he said these words aloud, Cowan and the colonel reminded their tablemates not to speak of their mission before the servants.

Darcy turned to the scientist. "Tell me, Franklyn, have you learned anything of note from Cousin Samuel's journals?"

An array of emotions played across the man's countenance: Excitement. Anxiousness. Annoyance. Cynicism. "We have discovered some cryptic notes regarding a find your cousin was privy to when he traveled in America."

The colonel wondered aloud, "I thought the late Mr. Darcy sought ancient civilizations. Obviously, the Americas are but children in that matter."

"Not strictly true, Colonel," Sedgelock countered. "There are several ancient civilizations in the Southern Hemisphere. Likewise, one would suspect a period of advancements in the North."

Chetley explained, "Yet, it was not ancient peoples which the late Mr. Darcy sought. Your cousin was a scientist first, and he came across an invention that could solve an unusual problem plaguing mankind."

Darcy asked suspiciously, "A great treasure? Is there a hint as to what this discovery might be?"

"I fear not," Franklyn declared. "At least, not in what we have read to date. As I mentioned, Mr. Darcy chose to describe his find in some sort of code. We have yet to decipher it, but we have not relinquished our hopes. We suspect Samuel used some form of Egyptian or Indian notation. The question is which one."

Edward suggested, "Perhaps one of us should examine the documents."

Sedgelock said defiantly, "I assure you, Colonel, we are quite adept at deciphering languages. We are certain that Samuel used a code common to his studies."

Cowan said sagely, "I doubt if the late Mr. Darcy went to such lengths to conceal his secrets. From what little I have discovered of the man, Mr. Darcy would protect his treasure, but he would not go to such measures as to resort to an ancient language. Samuel Darcy would want his family to know what he knew."

Sedgelock asked skeptically, "And what makes you so certain, Mr. Cowan? By your own admission, you had no prior acquaintance with Samuel Darcy."

Cowan smiled amusedly, an expression Darcy had witnessed the man using previously when Cowan thought his opponent had overlooked the obvious. The Runner said, "Mr. Darcy left behind too many clues: his journals and the list of items to be donated to the Society, for example, were exactly calculated for that purpose. He wished for someone to recognize his genius. Samuel Darcy did enough to disguise his discovery from those who served him, but not from those who loved him."

Darcy mused, "An interesting theory, Cowan."

Sedgelock puffed up with self-importance, which Darcy recognized as a trait that would only harden Cowan's resolve. "I pray you speak the truth, Mr. Cowan. It will save us time in completing our tasks."

Edward observed, "Then perhaps my previous suggestion should be revisited. Might my cousin, Mr. Cowan, and I view Samuel Darcy's entries? I assure you that as a military commander I have encountered numerous coded messages, and I would venture that Mr. Cowan has seen a few in his professional life, and as for my cousin, few intellectual puzzles escape him."

Franklyn evidently recognized the slight, which Sedgelock had offered his host. He said with true regard, "I believe that an excellent idea, Colonel."

Darcy accepted the opportunity to change the subject. "If you gentlemen do not mind, I would seek my wife's company. I would not have Mrs. Darcy spend the evening in solitary pursuits." He stood to signal his intention. Cowan stepped to the door and opened it. "If you will follow Mr. Cowan and the colonel, I will have Murray deliver the port and the brandy to the library."

A few moments later, Darcy entered the library to find Elizabeth protectively situated beside his cousin. Part of him celebrated Edward's thoughtfulness and part of him knew disappointment. He glanced to his wife to capture her gaze before a slight nod released her to her conversation with his cousin. Darcy rubbed his hands together in anticipation. He and Franklyn had decided that they would stage a farce where they would "miraculously" discover Samuel's secret chamber. "We should locate the books my cousin wished to donate to the Society. I am assuming you brought the list with you, Franklyn."

The man fished in his inside jacket pocket to locate two sheets of paper. He unfolded them before spreading the papers on his lap. The archaeologist announced the first title: *The Manetho Dynasty*.

Darcy turned to the many shelves. "Fortunately, Cousin Samuel had the foresight to organize his shelves alphabetically." He reached for a thick, black leather-bound volume. "Here is the requested title." Darcy thumbed through the pages before setting the tome upon a side table. "Next."

Franklyn cleared his throat. "*The Mastaba and Abydos*."

Darcy smiled. "You are making it easy upon me, Franklyn. Two titles beginning with M." He quickly located the second title and placed it along side the first.

Elizabeth said, "Perhaps several of us should assist you, Mr. Darcy. The search would be more expeditious."

Darcy smiled warmly at her. "You were always one for a scavenger hunt, my dear."

Soon Darcy, Edward, Cowan, and Elizabeth sought the titles. They raced to be the first to spy the sought-after titles. Elizabeth laughed when she and Darcy placed books on the table together. "Thank you for being a gentleman, Mr. Darcy," she challenged. Her book rested below his in the stack.

Darcy caught her hand. "You would not think kindly of me if I treated you as a mere female, Mrs. Darcy. I learned long ago that you are not only a lovely opponent, but are also a worthy one."

Franklyn announced, "*The Demon Necromancer*."

Elizabeth squeezed Darcy's hand. "I believe it is your turn, Sir."

Darcy nodded his understanding. The others busied themselves as the backdrop to his "discovery." He said loudly enough for any eavesdropping servants to hear, "Ah, here it is." Although he knew the binding held the book in place, Darcy pretended not to understand the problem. Unsuccessful, as they each had anticipated, Darcy called for the same small stool he had used previously.

Elizabeth scrambled to retrieve it for him. "Thank you, my dear," he said with a conspiratorial wink. "I believe the binding may be damaged, Franklyn," Darcy said as part of his role. "It is evidently caught on some sort of nail." Darcy lifted the book from the shelf and handed it to Edward. Then he lifted the small lever to free the door. With a swoosh of cold air, the door opened a few inches. As before, Darcy stepped from the stool to wedge his fingers into the narrow opening. With a powerful tug, the wall shelf tilted inward and a gaping hole appeared.

"Dear Lord!" Edward expelled.

Sedgelock gasped, "My! My! What have we here?"

Behind them, a woman's voice rang out, "That secretive prat! I knew he lied about his discoveries."

Chapter 12

The Darcy party spun toward the sound to find Mrs. Ridgeway framed by the library's opened doors. Her hands rested on the teacart.

"I beg your pardon," Darcy said caustically. "Do you have an opinion you wish to share, Madam?"

Mrs. Ridgeway stiffened, but she did not divert her eyes from the dark opening. "No, Sir," she said grudgingly. "I have brought the tea Mrs. Darcy requested."

Darcy understood the ploy for what it was. "You have permitted my wife to remain without her required tea for nearly an hour?" Darcy asked as a reprimand. "I find that as a dereliction of your responsibilities, Madam. I am most displeased."

Mrs. Ridgeway's chin rose in defiance, but her words held the proper respect. "I apologize, Mr. Darcy. The tea kettle was dropped accidentally, and Mrs. Holbrook had to reset the service."

Darcy gritted his teeth with fury. "Mrs. Darcy will serve. You may be excused for the evening, but I will have a word with you tomorrow."

Mrs. Ridgeway's gaze finally fell on him. "Of course, Mr. Darcy." She curtsied and turned reluctantly for the door.

However, Darcy's words stayed her retreat. "You will instruct the staff, Mrs. Ridgeway, not to return to the insolence I found at Woodvine earlier. I shan't consider another opportunity for those who align themselves against my position as the heir to this property."

The housekeeper turned slowly to face him. "I shall relay your sentiments, Sir." Another curtsy signaled the woman's withdrawal.

Silence held the room for several elongated seconds before Sedgelock ventured, "Quite a cheeky female." The archaeologist straightened his waistcoat. "I am surprised Samuel Darcy tolerated the woman's impertinence."

One eyebrow went up. Darcy responded, "I am not certain my cousin was subjected to Mrs. Ridgeway's peevishness. I am of the persuasion that only I bring out her less than stellar temperament."

Elizabeth stepped around Darcy to retrieve the teacart. "I, too, have known the woman's rancor. The lady's slights have been most determined."

Darcy assisted her with the tray. "If I thought you had not meted out your own form of discipline, Mrs. Darcy, I would summon Mrs. Ridgeway before you for a proper apology. I will have no one abusing my wife."

Chetley asked, "Why not give the woman her walking ticket?"

Darcy growled, "Without a proper notice." He set the service on a low table. "As soon as there is a resolution to this folly, many on Woodvine's staff will know my discontentment."

Cowan suggested, "Perhaps I should ask Poore, McKye, and Maxton to join us."

"An excellent idea," Sedgelock said.

Edward instructed, "Close the door on your exit."

Cowan nodded his understanding and disappeared into the poorly lit passageway.

Elizabeth asked, "Would you gentlemen care for tea while we await Mr. Cowan's return?"

Edward accepted the cup Elizabeth extended in his direction. "I appreciate the fact, Mrs. Darcy, that I must never remind you of how to prepare my tea."

Darcy said affectionately, "It is one of Mrs. Darcy's more endearing talents, Cousin."

Elizabeth protested, "No talent required, Sir. I simply listen to what others say." She handed Mr. Franklyn a cup with two spoonfuls of sugar. Both Chetley and Sedgelock declined.

Edward seated himself beside Elizabeth again. "While we wait for Cowan, allow me to ask how we will proceed?"

Sedgelock responded first. "Obviously, the Society expects us three to catalog the late Mr. Darcy's collection."

"Have you an interest in the contents of the room beyond Samuel Darcy's finds?" Edward inquired.

Chetley shook his head in the negative. "Unless the late Mr. Darcy outlined a particular find as a donation to the Antiquarian Society, we have no claim to whatever else the room holds. Of course, that does not mean the Society would not negotiate with Mr. Darcy and with the Earl of Rardin for the more superb discoveries, which may pique our interest."

The door opened as Cowan ushered the three hired guards into the room. "Thank you, Mr. Cowan," Darcy said as he handed a lighted candle to the Runner. "You will join us below. You three will remain here," he instructed the men Cowan had secured through Tregonwell's contacts. "No one is to enter this room, and no one is to follow us into the passage."

All three said in unison. "Aye, Sir."

Elizabeth placed her cup on a side table as Edward stood. Darcy reached for his wife's hand. Holding a brace of candles high to illuminate their way, he led her into the room's damp darkness. The others formed a line behind the Darcys. Candlelight flickered off the brick and slate walls as they slowly edged their ways into the silent blackness.

They neared the bottom of the narrow stairs before Elizabeth jerked hard on his arm to halt Darcy's steps. Her fingers curled tightly about his sleeve. The others slammed into one another, and candlelight twisted and turned with their efforts to keep their balances. "What distraction holds your attention, Mrs. Darcy?" Darcy asked brusquely.

"Look, Fitzwilliam!" she said as she pointed to the dust-covered landing. "Someone else has been within."

Darcy's gaze followed the line of her arm. His stomach rolled with trepidation as his eyes fell on the outline of what appeared to be a woman's boot in the patina of dust covering everything in the room. "No one move!" he snapped as he bent to examine the numerous imprints. He lifted the brace higher.

"What have you discovered, Darcy?" Edward asked inquisitively.

Darcy ran his finger along a line to remove the dust. Deep in thought, he said, "When Mrs. Darcy and I discovered this room several evenings prior, every display case, as well as the floor, was covered in dust." He stood and showed the others the gray film covering his index finger. "We commented on how we were the only ones to have entered the room in some time because only our footprints covered the floor." The others surreptitiously noted the imprints left behind by the Darcys. "Now there is a third set of prints visible in the dust."

"But how?" Cowan asked suspiciously. "No one else knew of the secret lever."

Darcy corrected, "That was what we assumed because there were no other displayed prints when Mrs. Darcy and I were present previously."

Edward grumbled, "There is nothing easy about this mystery. I have never seen so many false clues."

Elizabeth shifted her weight where she might examine the prints. "It appears whoever else has been below ascended the steps but did not descend them." She pointed to where a distinctive footprint could be seen on the left hand side of the steps.

Cowan also knelt to examine the marks. "It is difficult to tell," he mused. "We have tracked the right hand side in our descent. Unknowingly, we could have destroyed the evidence."

Darcy concentrated on the multiple prints. "That may be true for the upper steps where Mr. Chetley waits, but not so on the lower steps where Mrs. Darcy stands. Without rotating or moving your feet, I would ask each of you to search for a similar shape to those to which Mrs. Darcy has indicated as distinct from her own. Notice my wife's print is significantly smaller than the fresher ones."

Cowan strained to see those prints closest to where he crouched. "There is a slight notch in the left heel of each of these new prints. As if the sole had taken on a small stone or had been cut on a sharp surface." The man's keen investigative skills never ceased to amaze Darcy.

Each member of the party craned his neck and bent in awkward positions to search the planks of wood upon which he stood; yet, none found any evidence to contradict what they had previously noted.

Darcy summarized, "Someone has been below, but he or she did not enter from the library. That means there is another entrance into Samuel's treasure room. Please step carefully. I would prefer to preserve several of these prints as evidence. I hope when we are within, there will be distinct markings indicating the other entrance."

Cowan noted, "We require lanterns rather than candles." The Runner instructed, "Chetley, please ask one of Tregonwell's men to retrieve several closed lanterns. No one else should move until we have more light."

Chetley, who brought up the rear and who rested on the top step, did not take offense. Instead, the archaeologist said, "I will retrieve them myself. Everyone stay put. I will return momentarily."

Franklyn asked anxiously, "Mr. Darcy, can you tell whether anything is missing?"

"I fear we must simply wait for Mr. Chetley's return. A single brace would do little to cut the darkness enveloping the interior room."

Silence fell over the group. It was several minutes before Mr. Chetley reappeared, but when he did he had managed to find three lanterns. He passed them forward to Darcy, the colonel, and Mr. Cowan. "Mrs. Holbrook says there are two more in the stables if we require them."

Darcy cautioned, "Again, take care with the placement of your steps. Once we have a better idea of what we have discovered, we may move about more freely." He steadied his wife's dismount from the last two steps, and then Darcy lifted the lantern high to illuminate the area.

Behind him, Elizabeth cupped her candle's flame with her hand. Darcy could feel her nervousness along his backside. His wife held her breath, but she did not turn her steps. Most women of his acquaintance would be in fits of vapors, but not *his* Elizabeth. She held an invincible spirit. Since Aunt Catherine's censorious disapproval of his proposal, Darcy had often considered how much he wished Her Ladyship had permitted Elizabeth her due. Despite Lady Catherine's societal prejudices, Darcy had always admired the woman's ability to survive in a man's world. Although neither woman would admit it, he had noted bits of his aunt's personality in Elizabeth.

"Easy," Cowan cautioned from somewhere behind him. "Do not rush."

Darcy stepped into the interior room. Although it had been but a matter of days since he had last ventured into Cousin Samuel's private treasure trove, the room possessed a different feel, as if it held something more sinister.

Elizabeth trailed close behind him. His wife's hand occasionally tugged at his coat. She steadied her stance, as well as sought his closeness, and Darcy experienced a rush of protectiveness again.

Edward's lantern flashed with light as his cousin shouldered his way into the room. "Much smaller than I expected," he muttered.

"Direct your lantern toward the far corner," Darcy instructed.

Edward lifted the lamp high to illuminate the area. "Nothing evident," Edward observed. "If there are prints, they rest along the aisle between the wooden cases."

Darcy sighed heavily, his countenance grim. "There are sconces with candles along the wall. Perhaps you could see to them, Colonel."

Edward turned to his right and gingerly stepped about the nearest display case. He retrieved a candle stub from his inside pocket. Setting the lantern on the nearest case, he lit the small piece of wax and used it to light several of the wall ornaments.

Cowan followed suit on the left-hand side of the room. The chamber would never know the light of day; therefore, the late Mr.

Darcy had placed numerous sconces at different levels to illuminate the room. "Whoever entered without your knowledge, Darcy, did not tarry," the Runner declared. "The footprints do not stray from the center aisle. He lifted his lantern high before motioning to the archaeologists to wait by the open threshold. "Let us trace the intruder's footsteps prior to our examining the cases. I am keen to locate the other entrance."

"The prints come this way from the upper left corner," Elizabeth observed. With her notice, it was easy for each of the men to see where the stranger's impressions hugged the side of the display cases. "One can see where the woman's dress trailed along behind her. Notice the swish of a curve across the heel print."

"Excellent eyes, Mrs. Darcy," Cowan said distractedly.

Darcy directed his words to the three scientists. "Enter carefully, Gentlemen, and permit Mr. Cowan his evidence. Join the colonel on the right if you will." The men followed his suggestion, and Darcy breathed a bit easier. Edward would rein in the archaeologists' enthusiasm for Samuel Darcy's many treasures. Darcy returned his attention to the Runner. "Do you require my assistance, Cowan?" he asked as he watched the man run his fingers over a section of wooden planks.

"Describe the lever you found in the library," Cowan said through gritted teeth as he tugged on each of the planks. "It is likely the late Mr. Darcy used a similar mechanism in this section of the room."

Darcy had not moved since entering the room. He and Elizabeth stood in the chamber's main aisle. They turned to the others, but neither he nor his wife had stepped into the display aisles. "The lever felt similar to a nail used by a farrier. Flatter than those used for wooden tables and flooring. Thicker head. Cut into the side of the wall with the lever inset."

Cowan continued systematically to check every inch of the wall. "How large of an opening?"

"Maybe two inches," Darcy confirmed. "The length of the first two knuckles of a person's index finger."

Cowan chuckled. "An interesting observation, Mr. Darcy." The man never removed his eyes from the section of wood planks which his fingers searched. He looked for imperfections and darkened indentations.

"Search lower," Elizabeth suggested.

The Runner straightened, but his hands remained flattened to the rough surface. "Explain, Mrs. Darcy," he instructed.

Elizabeth stammered, "By…by analogy, the device in the library is in the top corner of the highest shelf. This room is below the ground floor of the main house. Why should it not, therefore, have the lever near the skirting board?"

Cowan shrugged his shoulders in a "Why not?" gesture. He marked his place on the wooden slats with a small piece of chalk he had removed from a purse in his inside pocket. Then he bent low to examine the area below the wainscoting. On his knees, Cowan's fingers traced the baseboard. "Could you set your lantern on the floor, Mr. Darcy?" he asked in that tone Darcy now recognized as the man's being engrossed in his own thoughts.

Darcy was glad to have the excuse to move freely about the enclosure, but he was cognizant of his own cautions. He elongated his stride to step over the telltale trail of feminine footprints. Edging carefully about the corner of one of the storage cases, Darcy knelt beside the Runner and tilted the lantern to where it might shed light on the area.

"I may have something," Cowan said with a grunt. "What do you think?" The Runner indicated a recessed area directly below the seam of a corner where two walls met.

Aware of his clothing and of how Mr. Sheffield would react to yet another set of stained breeches, Darcy placed one knee on the floor and followed Cowan's lead. His fingers searched the indentation. Then he felt it. As his fingers grazed the metal bar, he said with true reverence, "Mrs. Darcy, you remain the most unrivaled woman of my acquaintance."

Elizabeth giggled with delight. "I was correct?"

"It appears so, my dear." Darcy adjusted his stance. He leaned an open palm against the wall and lifted up on the flat metal. Immediately, the wall groaned and separated along the corner. The wooden wall swiveled away from where Darcy knelt, and he and Cowan stood slowly. Through the small crack in the darkness, the muffled sounds of night could be heard at a distance. The chirp of insects. The hoot of an owl. Darcy lifted his lantern higher as Cowan reached for the light he had left on the cases.

"What do you see, Darcy?" Edward called. He could tell from his cousin's voice that the colonel had moved closer.

Darcy's eyes narrowed. "Steps. Ones made of bricks." He glanced to Cowan and asked the unspoken question. The Runner nodded his agreement, and together, they caught the partially opened crack in the wall with their free hands and pulled. The wall revolved, and the opening gaped before them. He said over his shoulder, "Cowan and I will return in a moment. Colonel, I charge you to protect Mrs. Darcy." He did not expect trouble, but he would anticipate it nonetheless.

"Be careful, Fitzwilliam," Elizabeth whispered from behind him.

He did not turn around, but a lift of his shoulders spoke the words of affection, which he could not say before the others. Instead, he spoke to the Runner, "As you have more experience than I in these matters, perhaps you should take the lead, Cowan."

The Runner set his lantern inside the space, but he did not retrieve it as he shouldered his way through the opening. Darcy followed suit, but he carried his light to the steps before he set it upon the ground. As he had come closer, he could see that the steps numbered but ten. Cautiously, he edged his way upward along the damp stairs. The passage was narrow, but solidly built. He would have expected nothing less of Samuel Darcy. His cousin Samuel was a man who tended to details.

"Give me your assistance, Darcy," Cowan said as he put his shoulder to a solid wall.

Darcy retreated a few steps to catch up the lantern. "Is there another lever?" he asked as he slid into place beside the Runner.

Cowan shook his head in the negative. "It does not appear so," he said abstractedly. His fingers searched the surface.

"There must be some sort of lock," Darcy insisted. He joined the Runner in seeking the slab's truth.

Edward called from the lower chamber, "The opening in Pater's wine cellar slides to the left. Perhaps this is similar. Lodge your fingers in the groove and give it a tug." Neither the colonel's curiosity nor his advice surprised either Darcy or Cowan. Instead, they followed his cousin's instructions. They found a slight indentation, and, using their fingertips, they whisked the hidden door from its place. On an unseen set of hinges, the once-immovable slab disappeared in a precut recess.

"Never seen anything like it," Cowan grumbled as he scrambled to his feet.

Darcy agreed, but he did not vocalize his wonder. "Let us discover where this passage leads."

Cowan took the last few steps into the open. "Just as I suspected," he said to the night. The Runner glanced to the darkened canvas. He said philosophically, "The night has rolled up its sleeves, but it has left its guard down nonetheless."

Darcy stood beside the man. They both straightened their shoulders after emerging from the low-ceilinged passage. "Mrs. Darcy will be beside herself with glee," he observed. "She has expertly forecasted our destination by reading my cousin's journals."

"Beyond the wall is the kitchen garden," Cowan noted. "To the right," he gestured, "is the sundial and the columns leading to the arbor."

Darcy stared into the blackness. Nothing moved. The night appeared calm and inviting, but he suspected that it held a great evil. He asked, "Could my cousin have left the door ajar on the evening he found the map?"

Cowan glanced about the area. "The opening could easily be concealed. Unless one was searching for it, a person would likely overlook the disguise."

Darcy, too, studied the area. "Then we cannot be certain whether our intruder meant to enter the passage or simply stumbled upon it by accident."

"Either way," the Runner noted, "the unknown woman has entered without permission. Perhaps it is best if we discover whether anything is missing." Cowan hesitated before adding, "We should have one of the men guard this entrance. Perhaps we should ask Captain Tregonwell to recommend one or two more."

Darcy roused himself from his own musings. "I will send Mr. Holbrook to Bournemouth in the morning." He glanced toward the opening. "We should return to where the others wait."

Cowan looked off to the lower garden. "If you can handle the door alone, Sir, I believe I will have a closer look around. I like being outside on a clear night."

"Now that I understand the how of it, I suspect I can manage. I will ask Mr. Poore to organize the men to secure the opening."

Cowan smiled easily. "I will wait close by until one of Tregonwell's men arrives." He said teasingly, "I might even try to operate the door from this side."

Darcy's gaze returned to the opening. "I suspect if a woman can manage the door's weight, neither of us will suffer unduly." He shook the Runner's hand. "Be safe."

Cowan stood silent for a moment. Finally, he said, "When the colonel and I were in Corunna…when we fought our way across Spain, your cousin often spoke of your close kinship, and I found myself wishing for the acquaintance." An awkward pause occurred. "I suppose the colonel has spoken of my irreverent disregard of most officers."

Darcy's slight smile of remembrance served as his response.

Cowan chuckled, "I thought as much." The man's lips twitched in mild disapproval. "I always respected the colonel, the captain then, because he spoke the truth. Yet, when he spoke of your friendship, I thought in that matter Captain Fitzwilliam had added appropriate embellishments. I am pleased to be found in error."

"I owe you a debt of honor, Cowan, but even if it were not so, I would be proud to have your acquaintance," Darcy said honestly. They separated with a new understanding.

Darcy slipped through the opening and slid the door into place. He had noted that on the outside, the opening appeared to be part of the wall separating the formal garden from the vegetable patch outside the kitchen's door. Only servants would use this part of the garden. Whoever had entered Samuel's hidden room was likely one of the Woodvine staff. The realization only added to his dread. He had suspected that the key to solving this mystery resided under Woodvine's roof. Now, he had proof of it.

Reentering Samuel's hidden room, he lifted both lanterns to set them upon the storage boxes. "Where is Cowan?" Edward asked.

"Mr. Cowan thought it best if he stood guard outside until one of Tregonwell's men assumes the duty." Darcy worked his way to Elizabeth's side.

Edward said, "Then I will send one of Tregonwell's former recruits to relieve Mr. Cowan." Darcy watched as his cousin cautiously made his exit toward the library and the waiting guards.

"What did you discover, Mr. Darcy?" Franklyn asked.

Darcy stood with his hands clasped behind him. "It is as Mrs. Darcy has indicated. The opening is at the rear of the garden. Near the columns and sundial."

Elizabeth said in a quiet voice, "Thank you, Fitzwilliam." Her eyes sparkled, and Darcy understood his wife's quiet pleasure at having been of service. Men, as a general rule, did not appreciate an intelligent woman, but he did, and Darcy would readily recognize Elizabeth's mindful insights with honest benevolence.

"Can you tell, Sir," Sedgelock interrupted their unspoken admiration, "from your last visit to this room, whether anything is amiss?"

Darcy glanced about the room. "Difficult to say from this position. Allow me a moment to examine the area." He retrieved his lantern before slowly circumambulating the room. "It does not appear as if the locks on the display cases have been breached." He gave a gentle tug on one of the hinged locks before moving on.

As he approached the corner where he and Elizabeth had found the documents of the possible coven, Elizabeth asked, "What of the maps?"

Darcy paused to peruse the items. "Someone has searched the documents on this table. Items have been moved." He picked up several stacks of papers and thumbed through them. "I see no evidence of the map."

Elizabeth said, "I had hoped to compare the map's features to that of Mr. Rupp's field."

Only Darcy realized how still she had become. In silence, Elizabeth came to his side. "We should have considered a second entrance," he said softly. Without a word, Elizabeth sorted the papers on the makeshift desk.

Meanwhile, Darcy finished his tour of the room. He lifted several pages from those scattered across another table's surface. "I see nothing that should affect your study of Cousin Samuel's archaeological finds," he said distractedly. Rolling the document to take it with him, he said, "I believe you can safely catalog Samuel's Egyptian and Persian treasures without further delay. I would simply ask that you remain cognizant of the intruder's footprints. I intend to send for the magistrate." He stacked his cousin's writings in a box. "I believe Mrs. Darcy and I will take these other papers above. If we discover anything of import, we will inform you immediately." He lifted the box. "By the way, Franklyn, I suppose my cousin's journals are under lock and key in your quarters." The statement was a question.

The man's voice betrayed his obvious second thoughts. "I fear the late Mr. Darcy's writings are on display on the desk in my chambers."

Chapter 13

Though he felt anything but indulgent, Darcy nodded his understanding. Despite his having cautioned the Society members of the need to safeguard Cousin Samuel's legacy, in his distraction Franklyn had left Samuel's personal papers open to scrutiny. "Mrs. Darcy and I will retrieve Samuel's journals, if you hold no objection."

A reluctant, self-conscious laugh surfaced. "Of course, Mr. Darcy." Franklyn inclined his head in agreement.

Feeling dreadful presentiments, he was annoyed by the error, but what could he do? It was not as if Darcy held the expertise to complete the Society's part of this venture. All he could do was to concentrate his efforts toward discovering the mystery of Samuel's death and disappearance. If worse became the standard, he could always turn the supervision of the Antiquarians' task over to Rardin. As if completing his own inventory, his gaze carefully examined the room. "We will leave you to it." He caught Elizabeth's elbow to lead her from the room. "Come along, Mrs. Darcy." He noted that she carried a sizable stack of bound documents and loose papers in her grasp.

On the steps, she whispered, "What do you make of this newest development?"

A brief shake of Darcy's head indicated he would prefer to wait before they discussed the events. "Just bear with me," he murmured softly as they reentered the library.

"Colonel," he directed his cousin. "I will require your services." Darcy strode to the bell cord and gave it a solid yank.

Within seconds, Mr. Barriton appeared at the door. "Yes, Sir?"

"Mr. Barriton, you will direct every female employee at Woodvine to appear in the drawing room across the hall within the next five minutes. None is first to return to her quarters before reporting to me. Wherever each is within the household, she should drop what she is doing and report directly to the Egyptian drawing room. If the person is already in her quarters, someone is to escort her. She may not tarry or seek sanctuary or be given an opportunity to rearrange her room. Mr. McKye will assist you."

The butler said shakily, "Immediately, Sir."

Both Barriton and McKye disappeared into the bowels of Woodvine's passageways. "What do you require of me, Darcy?" his cousin inquired.

"You will escort Mrs. Darcy on a search of the quarters and common places within Woodvine. Before the prints are accidentally destroyed by those below, I wish to locate the footwear that created the impressions."

Elizabeth placed her find from the secret room upon the cushioned wing chair. "In addition to my search, do you have other duties you wish me to perform, Mr. Darcy?"

"It is possible that the culprit still wears the offending boots. As a gentleman, I cannot search the women, and as I am well aware that you enjoy being avowedly useful, it will be your task to examine the footwear and to confiscate any that might fit the bill. I will remain in the hallway to guard against anyone leaving until you have completed your search. Meanwhile, I will send Jatson to ask Mr. Stowbridge to join us. I am not certain the magistrate will be of much use, but we will conduct this investigation under his oversight."

The colonel noted, "I will carry your instructions to Jatson." He bowed to Elizabeth. "I will return in a few moments to escort you to the servants' quarters."

Darcy placed the papers Elizabeth had carried from the room below into the box he had retrieved earlier. "We will review these later," he said distractedly. "Mr. Poore, beyond those from the Society, Mr. Cowan, the colonel, Mrs. Darcy, and me, no one is to enter the room below."

The hired guard bowed. "I understand, Mr. Darcy." He added quickly, "Mr. Maxton is outside. We will rotate the positions, but someone will remain on duty at both entrances at all times."

Darcy stressed, "Mr. Holbrook will secure the services of several others on the morrow. You will be certain that each man understands his first duty is to guard the room below. Even if there is a disturbance outside this room's door, you are not to seek out its source. I want no strangers to have access to my late cousin's archaeological finds."

"I understand, Sir."

The first of the servants to arrive at the drawing room could be heard in the hall. "Time to perform our roles," he said to his wife. Taking Elizabeth's hand, they stepped into the passageway together.

"Mr. Barriton, I do not understand," Mrs. Ridgeway pleaded as the two men ushered the women into the room.

The butler said, stone faced, "It is as Mr. Darcy has requested."

The housekeeper shot a defiant look in Darcy's direction, but she entered the drawing room without protest. The others appeared frightened by the unusual events.

"Do you still suspect Mrs. Ridgeway?" Elizabeth whispered.

Darcy spoke for her ears only. "It does not seem likely, especially after her remark upon viewing the open door; but for every revelation that seems to exclude the woman from some sort of perfidy, I cannot relinquish the feeling that Mrs. Ridgeway is not what she appears." He exhaled a sigh of exasperation.

Elizabeth observed, "The lady is insolent and unforgiving. Perhaps it is Mrs. Ridgeway's attitude to which you object rather than to her abilities to perform her duties. It is certain that at Pemberley the woman would not long retain her position."

"I have told myself repeatedly that Mrs. Ridgeway is as much a victim in this matter as are we, but my mind cannot convince my instincts," he confessed.

Edward reappeared. "Are you prepared for a bit of sleuthing, Mrs. Darcy?"

Elizabeth left Darcy's side, and immediately he felt deprived of her closeness. He watched her walk away with his cousin, the two of them sharing some teasing comment, which brought his wife's laughter echoing through the empty hallway. It was a foolish weakness—this sick, hollow gnawing in the pit of his stomach when he considered a future without her. He closed his eyes and sighed heavily. He could control only what was within his realm, and his obsession with Elizabeth Darcy had always been beyond his reason. With a shrug of resignation, Darcy stepped into the drawing room and closed the door behind him.

Surprisingly, Mrs. Ridgeway permitted Mrs. Holbrook to speak for the group. "Mr. Darcy, Sir? Have we done something to displease you? We kinnot fathom why the men be not with us."

Darcy appreciated the woman's honesty. The lady and her son were the only ones among his late cousin's staff for whom he held any respect. "The house has experienced another breach, Mrs. Holbrook. Fortunately for us, whoever executed the invasion was unaware that she left behind distinct footprints."

"She?" Several of the women gasped. They clutched at each other for comfort.

"The prints are smaller than a man's," Darcy explained.

"And you think one of us the culprit?" Mrs. Ridgeway had found her voice, and, as usual, her tone held contempt.

Darcy answered in a tone that dared the woman to defy him. "I have sent for Mr. Stowbridge and have secured the area. It would be to my deficit if I did not do all I could to learn if anyone at Woodvine is involved. As a group, you will remain in this room until the magistrate arrives."

"How be you knowing the person in question is someone employed at Woodvine?" Mrs. Holbrook asked calmly.

"As the intruder entered from the garden to the library, we have made the natural assumption that an employee would have noted a complete stranger casually making her way through Woodvine's passageways and would have either detained the person or would have alerted Mr. Barriton."

Mrs. Ridgeway asked, "Has your interloper stolen Mr. Samuel's great treasure?"

Darcy sneered, "I fear that information is family business and not available for the servants' rumor lines."

Mrs. Holbrook shushed two of the younger girls. "Then we best be making ourselves comfortable. If'n we have nothing to hide, then there be nothing to fear." Darcy nodded his exit. He placed Fletcher outside the door and returned to the library to sort through Samuel's papers. He was certain Stowbridge would want to know if anything other than a map was missing.

* * *

Elizabeth and Edward had methodically searched three of the servants' sleeping areas. From each, the colonel had removed shoes belonging to the female who had occupied the space. Elizabeth had attempted to convince him that not every pair of shoes fit the pattern, but the colonel had countered that Darcy would expect them to be thorough. Elizabeth suspected it was the colonel who preferred thoroughness rather than her husband.

As she fished another pair from under one of the scullery maids' cots, she said casually, "Fitzwilliam tells me we shall soon be bereft of your company. Your orders send you abroad." She handed him the shoes, which he placed in a box with the others.

The colonel frowned. "I have not shared the news with the Earl. I would not wish His Lordship to use his position to prevent me from being a part of the British force."

"I understand," Elizabeth said softly. "Yet, I must admit that I would be tempted to seek my father's influence if I were you."

Her assertion making the moment a trifle uncomfortable, Edward looked on with frank regard. "It is difficult to explain. Perhaps it is my unmitigating pride, but I hold the belief that my men—those such as Cowan—possess a healthier opportunity for survival if I place myself between them and those who wear the epaulets upon their shoulders." He laughed self-consciously. "I am vain to think myself essential." A shrug of his strong, broad shoulders announced how private his thoughts remained.

Bile rose in Elizabeth's throat. The thought of this fine and caring man purposely placing himself in danger's path jangled her nerves. "Pride is a common failing," Elizabeth observed. "By all that I have ever read, I am convinced that it is very common indeed; that human nature is particularly prone to it, and that there are very few of us who do not cherish a feeling of self-complacency on the score of some quality or other, real or imaginary." She paused to emphasize her point. "Early on in our relationship, I accused your cousin of misplaced pride," Elizabeth confessed.

The colonel laughed lightly, "I cannot imagine how you could have misjudged Darcy as such."

Elizabeth teased, "It was a leap of faith to change my opinion." Edward smiled warmly at her as he extended his hand to assist Elizabeth to her feet. "Yet, please permit me to finish my thought. In reality, it was my sister Mary who offered this sage advice: Vanity and pride are different things, though the words are used synonymously. A person may be proud without being vain. Pride relates more to our opinion of ourselves; vanity to what we would have others think of us."

"Miss Bennet speaks with the solidity of her reflections," the colonel observed.

Elizabeth privately considered his conclusion, but she could not merit Mary with too much sensibility. She smiled sheepishly. "If you had asked me at the time, I would have told you my sister was simply piqued because she had danced but one set at the assembly. Five sisters are often competitive in such matters. In hindsight, Mary had the right of it where Mr. Darcy was concerned. I had misjudged my dear husband."

A rather philosophical expression crossed the colonel's countenance. "Although my cousin suffered your initial rejection, Darcy has won the prize. I admit I am often envious of the happiness he has secured with your marriage."

Elizabeth said tentatively, "I held hopes that your relationship with Miss De Bourgh would bring you contentment."

He said with a shake of his head. "As did I." Edward paused before saying, "Anne has many fine qualities, but she lacks the maturity of her years. I offered her an escape from what my cousin termed as her isolation, but in the end, her affection came from gratitude."

"And you required more?" Elizabeth searched his countenance for the truth of his words.

Edward appeared discomfited, and she instantly regretted her inquisitiveness. "As a second son, I must marry an heiress; yet, I have hopes of discovering a woman who would return my affection."

Elizabeth laced her arm through his. "I am certain that you shall know both, Colonel."

He held the door for her. "Do you have personal knowledge of such a female, Mrs. Darcy?" he teased.

Elizabeth patted his cheek affectionately. "I have my suspicions, Colonel."

She led the way toward Mrs. Ridgeway's room while Edward hustled to keep pace with her. "Do you mean to tell me of whom you speak?" he asked as he juggled the box of shoes and half boots.

Elizabeth stopped suddenly. "I do not think so, Colonel. It is too soon. You must serve the King, and it would not be fair to begin a relationship only to have it interrupted by your career. And I do not believe you would betroth yourself to an innocent with the fear of war looming over your shoulder."

"'Tis true," he said begrudgingly. "Yet, I will charge you to speak of your suspicions upon my return." Edward's hope laced his words. "Of course, that is assuming that the lady has not been claimed by another in my absence."

Elizabeth cast a wary eye upon her husband's cousin. Their clasped hands were held at her heart. "I believe the lady in question is quite content with her current unmarried status. Yet, I must warn you, Colonel, I have not spoken of you to the young woman. It is purely my female intuition that permits me to venture a guess of the lady's true regard for you. I could be taken completely unawares in this matter. I would not wish to give you false expectations."

Edward held her gaze for several elongated seconds. The former aloofness receded from his face. "Mrs. Darcy, false hope or not, I will hang my hat upon your words. It may appear foolish, but a man facing death prefers to know that, if he can waltz with devastation and survive its wrath, a future awaits him."

Elizabeth eyed him cautiously. "While you dream of England in foreign lands, I shall bully my efforts to make your future a reality." She slipped her arms about his waist and rested her head on his chest. "Your heart is true, Colonel, and I shall take great pleasure in singing your praises."

* * *

Stowbridge strutted about the room like a peacock. The magistrate had arrived at Woodvine Hall as the colonel and Cowan had finished their attempt to match the gathered footwear to the imprints. Now, the squire had taken on the mantle of authority. Darcy watched with some amusement as Stowbridge stumbled through his official investigation. "The magistrate is certainly not of the caliber of Sir Phillip Spurlock," Edward had observed when no one was near. Darcy had agreed wholeheartedly. When Darcy returned to Derbyshire, he would make a point of expressing his personal appreciation for Sir Phillip's expertise in the law.

With his usual contempt worn comfortably about his shoulders, Stowbridge addressed Woodvine's female staff. "Mrs. Darcy has agreed to move among you and to collect your footwear. You will remove whatever boots or day shoes you currently wear. Mr. Darcy and I will step into the hall to provide you privacy."

Darcy thought it ironic it had been at Elizabeth's insistence that the magistrate had afforded the women any respect. His wife had placed her fists on her hips, and vocally charged into the fray. "Although it is likely that one of the women in the drawing room has committed a crime, there are ten others behind that door," she had gestured with an emphatic point of her finger, "that have done nothing other than their duties to this household. I shall not have the innocent vilified along with the guilty." And just like every man who ever crossed Elizabeth's path, Stowbridge had crumpled. Darcy chuckled with the memory of the magistrate's flushed face. He triumphantly held the door for the man as they exited the room.

When the gentlemen had departed, Elizabeth turned to the women. "If you would be so kind as to remove your footwear, this will be over soon."

"And what if we choose not to cooperate?" Mrs. Ridgeway asked with her usual defiance.

Elizabeth rolled her eyes in frustration. "Why would you wish to defy the magistrate unless you had something to hide?"

Mrs. Ridgeway stiffened with the accusation. "If you recall, Mrs. Darcy, I was astonished upon observing the late Mr. Darcy's secret chamber," the woman declared in her defense.

Elizabeth's jaw tightened. "One thing I have learned, Mrs. Ridgeway, is that men prefer to demonstrate their powers. If you choose to refuse my simple request, it is likely Mr. Stowbridge will use physical force to remove your boots. You will lose both the battle and your dignity."

"Is that it? Bend to the will of men?" the woman retorted.

"Women have their own powers, Mrs. Ridgeway. Our actions may be small on the scale of politics and law, but we have our ways of influencing the male species. Personally, I choose when to fight and when to bend to a man's will."

Mrs. Holbrook broke the tension by declaring, "I be not certain that me poor aching feet will fit back into these boots once I's take them off, but now is as good a time as any to let me old toes breathe." The woman bent to unlace the string holding her well-worn half boots on her feet. Automatically, the other women followed. Elizabeth was pleased to see that none of Samuel Darcy's workers still wore wooden clogs. She knew of landowners who, even in this age of great wealth and growth, did not pay their workers well enough for the women to own a decent pair of shoes. Her gaze purposely fell upon Mrs. Ridgeway, and the housekeeper reluctantly followed Mrs. Holbrook's example.

The elderly cook laughed. "I's a hole in me stocking." She wiggled the toe of her left foot.

The young scullery maid, a girl by the name of Moll, declared, "That be why I wears two pairs of stockings."

Elizabeth retrieved the box the colonel had employed earlier and passed it among the women. Each dropped her worn footwear into it. As she reached where the housekeeper sat in isolation from the others, she covertly leaned closer to the woman. "First, permit me to say that you have defied me for the last time. Consider this your notice, Ma'am. Your services shall no longer be required at Woodvine. I will have you gone by the first of the month." Elizabeth watched with satisfaction as the woman's eyes widened in disbelief and then in anger. "Bite your tongue, Mrs. Ridgeway, or you will find your feet on the road this very evening," she threatened. When the woman's lips thinned to a fine line, Elizabeth finished, "Your astonishment on discovering Samuel Darcy's chamber could have been true surprise, or it could just as easily have been a show to divert suspicion." With that, Elizabeth set the box on a nearby table. With a light tap on the door, she signaled the return of the magistrate and Mr. Cowan. Stowbridge acknowledged her efforts with a nod of his head, and then he and the Runner assumed possession of the box. As they strode from the room, she closed the door behind her and joined her husband in the hall.

"What is amiss?" Darcy murmured close to her ear. She motioned him away from the others. When they stood in the shadows, Darcy caught her hand. "Tell me," he encouraged.

Elizabeth growled in frustration. "That woman!" she hissed.

"Mrs. Ridgeway?"

Elizabeth wanted to howl at the moon in anger. Instead, she shook her head in disbelief. "I pray often for Jane's goodness, but never so much so as times such as these." She leaned into him, and Darcy encircled her in his embrace. "I have lost my temper and have given Mrs. Ridgeway her notice."

"Good," Darcy said dispassionately.

Elizabeth leaned heavily against him. "Yet, I had promised myself that I would rise above the woman's vituperation. Did I act with hasty indignation?"

Darcy chuckled, "Is your anger pointed toward Mrs. Ridgeway's obstinacy or toward your inability to convert the woman?"

Elizabeth frowned. She gave Darcy a serious look, but there was a bit of mischief in her eyes. "Why is it, my husband, that you recognize my faults and still offer me your regard?"

"Because you are my life, Elizabeth." He kissed her forehead. "Mrs. Ridgeway has set herself an impossible task. The woman has aligned herself against the Master and Mistress of Pemberley. Together, we are a formidable pair."

"Darcy?" Edward broke in with some urgency. "Cowan believes he has discovered a match to the prints."

Darcy looked from his cousin to Elizabeth. He hesitated, and she recognized that her husband held his own suspicions. "This is the first lead which may prove promising. Come along, my dear. We have a farce to play."

They joined Cowan and Stowbridge in the library. "Whose shoes fit the impressions in the dust?"

Cowan held the offending items by the heel. "These are the correct size for the prints. They also have a chip in the left heel's corner. They match the unusual pattern we noted earlier, Mr. Darcy."

"Are we certain to whom they belong?" Edward asked Elizabeth.

Elizabeth shook her head in the negative. "I suppose we should simply return the box to the room and observe who claims them."

"Allow me to mark them," Cowan said as he used his knife to make a small slit in the leather.

The matching boots were not placed on the top of the pile. "Too obvious," Elizabeth observed. "I do not want anyone to claim she had accidentally chosen the wrong pair."

"Then let us set our trap." Darcy hefted the box from the table. "Come, Mrs. Darcy. You must be our eyes once again."

Returning to the small drawing room, Darcy placed the box on a low table where Elizabeth might observe which woman chose the marked shoes. Then he exited the room. "The gentlemen have completed their tasks. After you have recovered your footwear, Mr. Stowbridge will return."

Mrs. Holbrook asked suspiciously, "Did Mr. Stowbridge discover anything significant?"

Elizabeth said with a straight face, "If so, I am not privy to the gentleman's investigation. While the magistrate and Mr. Cowan conducted the search, I spent my time in conference with Mr. Darcy." She purposely rested her gaze on Mrs. Ridgeway, but the woman kept her eyes on the moonlight streaming through the windows. In the beginning, Elizabeth had thought the woman all that was kind. Then the woman's caustic tongue had brought about Darcy's wrath. She had felt some sympathy for Mrs. Ridgeway when the woman had been injured: yet, Elizabeth would readily admit she held no inkling as to what motivated the housekeeper. With a deep sigh, she realized it was best for the estate to withdraw from an impossible situation.

The women rummaged through the box for their possessions. Elizabeth watched anxiously. First one, and then another, and another chose from the items, but still the marked shoe remained. Finally, only two pairs rested on the box's bottom. Mrs. Ridgeway stood, and for a brief moment, Elizabeth thought she would choose the ones in question; however, the housekeeper selected a similar pair, but not the marked shoe. Only one person remained: the maid known as Els. Somehow, Elizabeth could not believe the young girl wily enough to stage a theft. And if she were, it would make more sense if Els had stolen Samuel Darcy's rare coins or ancient jewels. Why would the girl steal a map of what may or may not be a witch's meeting place? Even if the girl actually dabbled in the black arts, assuming the young maid the culprit went against Elizabeth's logical side. "Does everyone have her own shoes?" she asked in hopes of a mistake. But the maid readily slipped on the offending pair and laced the ties through the loops. Perplexed, Elizabeth opened the door to the waiting magistrate.

"Do we have a match?" Stowbridge asked pompously.

Reluctantly, Elizabeth nodded her affirmation. "Els," she said softly. "But I…"

However, Stowbridge pushed past her, ignoring Elizabeth's protest. "Which of you is Els?" he demanded.

Elizabeth turned to see the girl flinch. "I be Els," she said through trembling lips.

Stowbridge, evidently prepared finally to put the blame for all the unusual events at Woodvine on someone's shoulders, scowled at the others. "You will remain, Girl. The rest of you may be about your duties."

Silently, the Woodvine staff filed past the young maid, and Elizabeth watched in sympathy as the girl's eyes widened and her face paled. She moved to steady the maid's composure. "Sit down," she encouraged as the girl swayed in place. "Fitzwilliam. A bit of sherry," she ordered.

Immediately, Darcy was beside her, glass in hand. He pressed it into the maid's unsteady grasp. "Drink," he encouraged as Elizabeth slid her arm about the girl's shoulders.

"Do not be frightened," Elizabeth whispered. "No one wishes to hurt you. Just speak the truth, and all shall be well."

The girl's eyes rose to meet Elizabeth's. "Yes, Ma'am. But I be doin' nothing wrong. I swear on me mother's grave."

Stowbridge cleared his throat. "Mrs. Darcy, I suggest you wait in the library."

Els clutched at Elizabeth's hand. "Oh, no, Ma'am. Ye kinnae leave me."

Elizabeth announced, "If Mr. Darcy holds no objections, I prefer to remain." She knew Stowbridge would not oppose a man of Darcy's consequence. Her husband's determinateness and his power seemed to make allies unnecessary.

Darcy said cautiously, "For the moment, I will tolerate your presence, but I would caution you, Mrs. Darcy, to permit Mr. Stowbridge and Mr. Cowan to conduct their investigation without interruption."

Elizabeth nodded mutely. Her husband rarely used his infamous authoritative tone with her. She had placed him in an awkward position, but Elizabeth could not shake the feeling that if she departed too quickly, poor Els would be on the first ship to Australia.

Edward closed the door to eliminate the possibility of eavesdropping servants. Stowbridge stood before the girl. "We have matched the shoes you wear with prints upon the floor in the late Mr. Darcy's chamber."

"I be knowin' nothing of any chamber until we be enterin' this room a few hours prior. Mrs. Ridgeway be tellin' us of the gaping hole in Mr. Darcy's library, but I's never seen any sich room," the girl protested.

Stowbridge stepped closer, and Elizabeth wished he would not lord his position over the girl. "Did you know there was an opening in the garden which leads to Samuel Darcy's treasure room?"

"I swears, Mr. Stowbridge, Sir, I be knowin' nothing of any openings or any secret rooms."

Cowan placed a hand on Stowbridge's shoulder, and the older man gave way. The former Runner knelt before Els, and Elizabeth appreciated Mr. Cowan's compassionate approach. "I will ask you specific questions, Els, and I require the truth."

"Yes, Sir," the maid said weakly. Elizabeth noted the tremor, which ran through the girl's body.

"First, I have often observed your comings and goings through the kitchen garden. The opening of which Mr. Stowbridge speaks is nearby. What do you do in the garden? You are not a kitchen maid."

The girl swallowed hard. "When I have a few minutes to meself, I like to go out in the fresh air. I miss me family and the farm," her voice quavered.

Cowan continued, "And what of when you go out late in the night? Where do you go then?" The Runner sat on a hammock at the girl's feet.

As if she were not certain how to answer, Els shot a glance to Elizabeth. Tears streamed down her cheeks.

Cowan encouraged, "You must speak the whole truth if you expect not to be charged with theft from your employer. Now, I will ask you again. Where do you go late at night? To a field by Mr. Rupp's farm, or to the forest?"

Elizabeth darted a quick glance at the young girl. Had it been Els Elizabeth had espied from her chamber window? The little maid shivered, and Elizabeth tightened her hold about the girl's shoulders. "No field and no forest," she declared adamantly. "I swear, Mr. Cowan. I go…I go to meet Toby…Toby Ritter from Mr. Skeet's farm. He be my friend since we be children in Crampmoor. We be happy to find one 'nother in Wimborne. We sits, and we talks about friends and home."

"So you have midnight assignations with this Toby character?" Stowbridge accused.

"Oh, no, Sir," the girl pleaded. "I be a good girl. I jist be so sick fer home, and Toby be too. We keep each other company, and it

224

don't seem so bad the next day. That be all we do. Jist sit and talk and dream of home."

Elizabeth declared, "I believe her."

"I appreciate your confidence in the young lady, Mrs. Darcy, but I think it best that Mr. Cowan and I continue our questioning at the gaol."

"Fitzwilliam, you cannot permit them to take Els away," Elizabeth pleaded.

Darcy reached for her, and Elizabeth reluctantly joined him. "It is best if we permit the gentlemen to execute their duties," he said solemnly.

"But Fitz…" Elizabeth began; however, one of Darcy's scowls stifled her protest.

Cowan assisted the maid to her feet. "I will protect Els, Mrs. Darcy," he said softly. "You have my word on it."

Chapter 14

The colonel said, "I believe I will accompany the magistrate. This may be one of those times when being an earl's son proves beneficial." Before he departed, Edward suggested, "It would be advisable if Mrs. Darcy conducted another search of the maid's quarters."

Darcy nodded his agreement as his cousin slipped from the room. Edward judiciously closed the door behind him. Darcy still held his wife's hand, but Elizabeth refused to look at him. Darcy said softly, "Perhaps it would be best if you retired, my dear."

"I would prefer to follow the colonel's suggestion, if you hold no objections," Elizabeth said obediently. His wife shifted her weight uneasily.

Darcy recognized how assuming a subordinate attitude would rub hard against Elizabeth's normally exuberant disposition. He certainly did not enjoy exerting his will over her, but Darcy could not permit Elizabeth to place herself in the middle of a never-ending mystery. It was too dangerous. There were too many unknowns. "Would you accept my assistance?"

Her eyes finally met his, and for once, Darcy could not read her thoughts, and that set his nerves on edge. "It would be best if I completed the task alone, and you oversaw the gentlemen from the Society," she said without emotion.

Darcy's mouth thinned as he chose his words carefully. "Elizabeth, I treasure your empathy for others—it is a quality which convinced me you would do well as Georgiana's sister—but I will not permit you to become the maid's advocate. *None of us*," and Darcy stressed the words, "know the depth of deception being practiced in this house."

Elizabeth nodded and turned her head away. "I know you mean well, Fitzwilliam," she said wearily.

"But…"

"But I am not a child." His wife lifted her chin in familiar defiance. It was his fault, this unusual gulf between them. Even when he held doubts of ever earning her love, he had not experienced the feeling of distance that he knew at this moment. Darcy had acted as a gentleman, so why did he feel so deeply disappointed in his performance? "If you will excuse me, I shall see to my duties." With that, his wife was gone. Darcy suspected he had not heard the end of the argument. Even Elizabeth's silence spoke volumes.

Well over three hours later, he entered her bedchamber to find his wife curled in a tight ball in the bed's middle. It had taken him some two hours to convince the Society members that they need not catalog all of Samuel's treasures in one sitting. To allay their concerns, Darcy had made a grand display of securing both entrances to the hidden chamber.

His cousin had returned from the village and had added his voice to Darcy's assurances that all would be well. Edward had reasoned, "The culprit has been apprehended. Besides, the girl made no effort to remove the late Mr. Darcy's archaeological finds."

Later, when Sedgelock had led Chetley and Franklyn away, the colonel explained how he had convinced Mr. Stowbridge to hold the maid under lock and key in the magistrate's root cellar rather than placing Els in the village gaol. "I saw no sense in tormenting the girl with more threats. I will speak to Mr. Ritter in the morning to confirm the maid's story." A long silence followed. Finally, his cousin asked, "Did you apologize to Mrs. Darcy?"

Darcy reacted immediately, "Why would I apologize? I did nothing to merit censure." He ignored the little voice which said, *but you accepted fault.*

Edward's lips turned up with amusement. "Will your bed be warmer if you claim righteousness, Cousin?"

Darcy felt the nuisance of the colonel's taunt. "I have never understood why a man must apologize to placate a woman's whims."

Edward stretched out his legs before him. "Consider it, Darcy. If you apologize in private to Mrs. Darcy, you lose no face among the Woodvine staff, and your wife will accept your offer of vulnerability as a balm to her romantic heart. Everything will return to normal. You will once again be the man of Mrs. Darcy's dreams. However, if you do not apologize…" Edward grimaced, and Darcy found himself wanting to know what he would face if he refused; yet, his cousin left the consequences to Darcy's imagination.

Darcy forced a casual laugh. "I would be a *poisson d'avril* to take marital advice from a confirmed bachelor." He did not wait for a response; instead, Darcy purposely changed the subject. "Please explain why you suggested that Mrs. Darcy reexamine the maid's quarters."

Edward prepared to stand. "Simple. When Mrs. Darcy and I searched for the boots to match the imprints, we also took the liberty of seeking out the missing map. We had thought the map the stronger proof. It would be possible for both the maid's and another person's boots to have similar imperfections, especially if the boots came from the same cobbler; however, only one map exists."

"I assume you discovered nothing unusual, or you and Mrs. Darcy would have mentioned it previously," Darcy remarked.

Edward said without artifice, "I suspect that knowledge was the basis of Mrs. Darcy's allegiance to the maid."

Darcy felt doubly wretched. "Then why instruct my wife to execute a second search?"

His cousin looked on in earnest sympathy. "First, it provided Mrs. Darcy with a diverting task. Your wife's objections could be proven legitimate if she recovered a map where one had not been previously."

"I see," Darcy said warily. "You would play Mrs. Darcy's hero?"

His cousin grinned. "If she required one, I would gladly play Elizabeth Darcy's hero, but not as you imply. I would serve any member of your family because you are my dearest friend." Edward stood to depart. "If Mrs. Darcy found a map, it would prove some-one else at Woodvine had decided to save herself by placing the blame on the maid." The colonel bowed. "As I expect more chaos tomorrow, I will seek my bed. I suggest, Cousin, you find yours only after extending an honest apology to your wife."

Darcy looked intently upon Elizabeth's small form. Sometimes he forgot how small she was. Her personality was so large that he often mistook her dominating individuality for her physical form. He placed the banyan he wore across the back of a chair and set the lamp he carried on the side table. It provided a mere trace of light and would quickly burn itself out. Darcy lifted the corner of the lightweight blanket and edged his way under the linens. The warmth of Elizabeth's body coated his chest as he inched her farther to her side of the bed.

She had not unfurled, but his wife huskily asked, "Fitzwilliam?"

He smiled at the familiar rasp in her voice as he answered her. "Yes, my love." Darcy kissed her temple. "I am here. I will protect you."

She rolled over in his embrace. Her silk gown felt cool along his skin. "I found it," she mumbled half asleep.

Darcy smiled easily. "The map?"

"Yes, the stolen map," she murmured against his chest. Her breath teased the line of hairs leading to his rapidly developing erection.

Darcy pushed his passion away. "We will discuss it in the morning. Sleep now, my love," he whispered.

Elizabeth snuggled closer to him. He never tired of the feel of her against him. He closed his eyes and inhaled the comforting scent of lavender in her hair. As the light dimmed in a wick drowned by hot wax, sleep crept across his countenance. He buried his nose in her auburn locks and relaxed against the woman who held his heart in the palm of her small hand. He murmured, "I love you, Elizabeth. I am infinitely sorry I hurt you earlier."

* * *

Darcy rose later than usual. Even though he had fallen asleep with Elizabeth in his arms, he had slept fretfully, with bizarre nightmares, none of which he could recall in the morning light. All that remained was the depressing feeling of dread pressing against his chest. His first thought was of his wife, and he had rolled over to reach for her, but Elizabeth's side of the bed was empty. He rubbed his palm across the linens. Cool. She had left the bed some time earlier.

Regretting having missed her, Darcy swung his long legs over the bed's edge. Scrubbing the sleep away with his knuckles, he glanced about the room. Nothing appeared out of place, and so he caught the banyan and made his way to his chambers. Sheffield had laid out his clothes and had delivered fresh water for Darcy's ablutions.

"Do you wish me to fetch your morning coffee, Sir?" his valet asked as he slipped into the chamber from Darcy's dressing room.

Darcy shook his head in the negative. He was anxious to see his wife. He and Elizabeth had never gone to bed in the midst of an argument. True, he had apologized, but Elizabeth had not actually said he was forgiven, and somehow that bothered him. The remnants of his dreams inspired him to settle the rift between them. "I should speak to Mrs. Darcy before the day becomes too hectic," he said in explanation.

Sheffield draped the shirt over Darcy's head. "Hannah has indicated that Mrs. Darcy has gone for a walk about the grounds, Sir."

Darcy frowned his disapproval. It was not unusual for Elizabeth to walk the grounds of Pemberley alone, but this was different. "Why did Hannah not accompany her mistress?" he demanded as Sheffield buttoned Darcy's waistcoat.

"I understood Mrs. Darcy had refused both Hannah's company and that of the colonel. The Mistress was heard to say she required privacy to consider the evening's events." His man set the jacket upon Darcy's shoulders and smoothed the seams.

His wife's continued disquiet bothered Darcy. It was not like Elizabeth to carry forward her anger. Normally, Elizabeth's natural contestations would flare hot and then fizzle just as quickly. She often thought herself right even when she had erred, but his wife was not an unreasonable woman. And even though Elizabeth had objected to Mr. Stowbridge's treatment of the maid, something deeper must be at the base of this sudden need for solitude. *Could it be our recent loss?* Despite the countenance she presented to the world, his wife had not taken well the loss of their child. "Hurry along, Sheffield," he said with a bit of irritation when his man fidgeted with Darcy's cravat.

* * *

Elizabeth had not meant to stray so far from the manor house when she had sought the outdoors to clear her thinking, but the waterfall had called to her. The steady flow of the water cascading over the jagged cliff spoke to the constancy of life, and she required that reassurance to fully understand her disquiet.

Her husband's obstinacy had been the plums in the Christmas pudding. She did not fault Darcy for his overprotective nature, but Elizabeth had found it ironic that the colonel had treated her with more respect for her intelligence than had Edward Fitzwilliam's illustrious cousin. "That is because you did not give your heart to the colonel," she argued aloud. Even with her condemnation of Darcy, he had sought to shelter her from Society's disdain. Yet, she still had felt the sting of her husband's autocratic attitude. A shrug of resignation shook Elizabeth's shoulders. "I knew the way of him when we married," she chastised her shadow. "And my husband's cousin is likely not to extend such tolerance to his own wife. As most women think to change a man's bad habits after they marry, so does a man lose his easy way with a woman when he perceives himself the Master of the house."

"So true," a deep voice said from behind her.

* * *

"Ah, there you are, Darcy," Edward remarked as Darcy entered the converted morning room. His cousin folded the newsprint to continue his reading. "I had thought to breakfast alone what with everyone late abed."

Darcy asked distractedly, "Has Cowan departed?"

The colonel frowned as he set his cup upon its saucer. "At the crack of dawn. A tap on my door and a note under the opening announced Cowan's withdrawal."

Darcy tore apart a hot roll as he strolled to a nearby window. "And the note?" He stuffed a wedge of the warm bread into his mouth.

"Not much. Said he expected to be gone several days. Said he would send word if he was delayed."

Darcy remained with his back to the room. His eyes searched the grounds for any sign of his wife. "Did Cowan disclose his destination?"

Edward chuckled. "It is not in Cowan's nature to reveal his sources or his suspicions. Yet, never question the man's integrity. I count him among my closest acquaintances."

"And the Society representatives?" Nothing moved outside the window. Even the breeze from overnight had ceased its ruffling of the young leaves of the nearby line of ash.

"Still abed," the colonel said with amusement. "For three men so intent on cataloging the late Mr. Darcy's ancient discoveries, the Society men love their slumber more. I have promised Mrs. Darcy that as soon as Mr. Franklyn rises I will secure your cousin's journals. In the uproar of last evening, we forgot to retrieve them from the gentleman's room."

Oblivious to the rise of the morning mist and the sun's hide-and-seek dance with a white, fluffy cloud, Darcy announced, "As my wife has not returned from her walk, I think it best that I seek her company."

Edward placed his serviette on the table. "Do you think something amiss?"

Darcy shook his head in the negative, but his body said otherwise. His anxiety could not be hidden. "Would you search the stables and the carriage house?"

"Certainly." Darcy followed his cousin from the room. They separated in the main vestibule. Darcy's steps quickened as he rushed toward the open courtyard entrance to the gardens.

* * *

Elizabeth spun around to find the face of danger. She automatically retreated two steps to the rear as the dark-skinned man stepped onto the cliff face before her. She surveyed the area. She had unknowingly fenced herself in. When Elizabeth had sought the waterfall's peace, she had chosen a complementary cliff face where she could watch the stream form high in the surrounding rock to slide over the jutting edge to a tranquil lake below.

Unfortunately, the space she occupied was not only solitary, but also very narrow. The stranger easily blocked her retreat. "Who are you?" Elizabeth caught her breath and defiantly challenged the man's gaze. She demanded and was pleasantly surprised that her voice did not betray her fear. "This is private property."

A bemused smirk turned up the man's lips. "I hold an invitation from the land's owner," he said in a highly accented speech.

Elizabeth knew without doubt that this stranger was one of the gypsy band. Suddenly, her earlier romantic musings regarding the Roma appeared quite foolish. It was clear that the man's presence spoke of danger. She worked hard to disguise her fears. "I understood your group planned to leave your camp behind."

He took a half step closer, and Elizabeth's back stiffened in response. "Not for three more days, Milady. Andrzej has spoken to the house's master regarding our departure."

"My husband," she said as a means to warn the man away.

He said with a sneer, "Then you are Mrs. Darcy." Elizabeth swallowed hard, fighting off the impending dread, which had crept along her spine. "Andrzej did not speak of your beauty."

If the situation had not been so frightening she might have enjoyed listening to the man speak. There was a soft roll of the 'r's and a growling hiss on each 's,' but she could find no thrill in the intended threat in the stranger's tone. "I think it best if I return to the house."

"You do not care for my company?" he asked as if she had disappointed him, but Elizabeth recognized the ruse.

She set her shoulders with a haughty slant and started around the man. "Mr. Darcy will be most displeased if you impede my return."

But the stranger did not withdraw. Instead, he caught her arm and forced Elizabeth to grasp his shirtsleeve to right her stance. "Do you think I care what will or will not please your husband?" he growled. He caught her chin in his large palm and shoved it upward. He said seductively, "I would give a care if I disappointed Mrs. Darcy, however."

Elizabeth jerked her head to the side. "Then you should know, Sir, I am greatly displeased. Unhand me immediately."

He laughed lightly. "Ah, my pet. You will not be so prickly when you know me better."

Elizabeth cringed. "If you persist in this folly, 'prickly' will be an understatement," she declared. "I have no desire to know you now or ever. I ask you once again to unhand me."

"And if I choose otherwise?" he asked in a sinisterly low tone. Elizabeth could smell the stink of his breath and the unusual spicy scent of his slicked-back hair.

"I shall fight you with every breath of my life. Whatever you plan shall not come easily," she said with conviction. And she would. Elizabeth would fight this man. Fight through the paralyzing fear, which had locked her knees into stone fortresses.

The man tightened his hold on her arm and pulled Elizabeth closer. He whispered into her ear. "Where is the amusement in such actions?"

Without considering the consequences, Elizabeth spun away from him. Jerking hard against his hold, she used a counterbalance move, which Darcy had showed her one evening when they had playfully wrestled before the fireplace in her sitting room. She jerked hard to throw her attacker off balance and followed that move with a firm shove against the man's chest. She turned to run, but the Rom caught her skirt to pull her toward him.

Elizabeth wound up her small fist and struck the interloper between the eyes, at the bridge of his nose. It hurt her hand more than she had anticipated, but she had no time to nurse the pain. The gypsy loosened his grasp as he automatically reached for his nose; therefore, she shoved hard and darted around him.

Unfortunately, her attacker recovered quickly. He caught her about the waist and jerked Elizabeth hard against him. Her back plastered his chest. The Rom viciously dragged her toward the tree line to the right. Soon he would have her under the cover of the bushes, and her chances of escape would decrease dramatically. She scratched at his hands and dug her nails into his wrist, but the man did not relent.

Panic had replaced determination in Elizabeth's veins. As a last effort, she twisted to elbow the Rom in his ribs. With all her strength, she hit him solidly in the side and was rewarded with a brief lessening of his hold on her. Elizabeth reacted immediately. She broke from his grasp to run, but there was no easy retreat. Her assailant remained between her and freedom. The cliff face and the lake lay at her back. It was a long way down, but she would take it if necessary. Her hands came up to ward off his next attack while she edged toward the drop.

"You do not want to jump," he placated, but she noticed how he leaned forward. He would pounce in a heartbeat if she allowed her guard to slacken.

Elizabeth's foot searched for solid ground as she widened the distance between them. "What I want and what I am willing to do are not necessarily in alignment," she said in warning. "I ask you again to walk away. To leave me be."

His eyes gleamed. A lock of damp hair fell across his forehead. He leaned close. Skeptical. "It is not so easy, my pet. The Roma are never seen to be in the right. Even if I leave, your husband will hunt me down."

Desperately, she pleaded, "I shall speak to Mr. Darcy. If you quit the area, Mr. Darcy will not pursue you."

The Rom smiled with regret. "Such a great man would bow to the wishes of a woman? You have married for love, Milady?"

Elizabeth nodded her hopes. "It is as I said. Mr. Darcy will listen to my pleas." Of course, it was only last evening that Darcy had ignored her wishes, but Elizabeth would never admit her reason for being alone on this cliff had been her irritation with Darcy for posturing before the Woodvine household. Her husband had chosen his pride over his loyalty to her.

She and the Rom stared at each other for a long time. Elizabeth watched a gamut of emotions cross her attacker's countenance. Finally, he said, "Mr. Darcy may wish to grant your request, but his conceit would never permit him to forget how a Rom had abused his wife. The stain would haunt him. Therefore, if I am to die at your husband's hands, it should be for more than a physical disagreement." A sadness crossed his countenance, and Elizabeth knew they were both doomed.

Without further ado, he lunged at her. Automatically, she braced herself for the blow. The impact knocked the air from her lungs as she fell backward into the open arms of sunlight and a sweet mist. The prism of light through the water was never more beautiful, and Elizabeth closed her eyes to forever cherish the image. Beside her, she heard the Rom say, "Forgive me," but she had no time to respond. Their combined weight had increased their velocity, and all she could do was to conjure up the image of her husband's handsome countenance before she hit the water and was dragged under by the gypsy's body.

Elizabeth had never swum in her gown and half boots, but she had swum before; therefore, she held hopes of surviving this encounter once she hit the water. One of her fears had been that they would crash onto the jagged rocks, but evidently, the gypsy's weight had carried them out over the lake's surface.

As they sank together, she turned from his grasp and kicked hard to surface for air. She broke the water and gulped in her first breath since the Rom had pounced. However, her efforts were short lived: her enemy had also surfaced. With flailing arms, he reached for her.

In a panic, the man fought to survive, but his fight would cost them both dearly if she could not calm him. "I have you," she shouted over the sound of water being slapped by her attacker. She trod water. Her gown floated upward and wrapped about her waist, but she still thought they could reach the shore if she could make him listen to her. "I have you," she screamed louder, but the man's shouts for assistance drowned her efforts.

She caught him about the neck to pull him through the water; yet, the Rom evidently thought she still fought him. An arm across her throat sent her backward and struggling to stay afloat. The Rom swallowed a mouthful of water and spit it out in a sputtering twirling motion, which caught Elizabeth in the side of the head. His loosely closed fist had stunned her, and she shook her head to clear it.

Again, the Rom reached for her, catching Elizabeth's shoulders and dragging them both below the surface. His grasp shoved her downward where the light did not reach, and the temperature was cool. The gypsy's grasp tightened as he realized his peril, and she was pushed deeper and deeper. Even in the murky water, she could see her attacker's eyes widen with the realization that he had breathed his last breath.

Yet, even then, the man did not release her. Instead, his fingers twisted into the material of her sleeve, and he tugged her closer. Still, she fought him, striking his face, his throat, his chest. But he held her tightly. Elizabeth struggled. She had held her breath for longer than she ever remembered doing previously. With one last effort, she brought her knees to her chest and kicked him as hard as she could. She slid farther from him, but still the gypsy clung to her gown. Her hair had come loose when he had struck her, and her bonnet's ribbons had twisted about her neck, making it harder to hold her breath. The Rom's grasp loosened when she used his chest as a footboard. A final kick to his throat sent her hurtling from him and slamming into a soft spongy object on the lake's bottom.

* * *

Darcy had circled the garden and had emerged in the small orchard at the back of the estate. He had walked this way with Elizabeth only yesterday when Cowan had uncovered Mr. Bates' shallow grave. Now, he retraced his steps. Darcy could not imagine his wife straying too far from the paths with which she was familiar. It was not in Elizabeth's nature to place herself in danger; yet, he could not abandon his feeling of doom.

Cutting through the glen, he turned his steps toward the waterfall, which had renewed his wife's spirits after the gruesome reminder of death's true power. An unusual noise caught his attention, and Darcy quickened his steps in hopes of finding her.

But those hopes soured when he cleared the tree line. His wife stood on the top of an overhang. Her stance told him she was in trouble. Elizabeth's arms were extended as if to ward off a menacing looking man. Darcy did not need to see more. He broke into a run.

"Elizabeth!" he called, but she did not turn her head. Standing so close to the waterfall, he suspected she heard little else but the thunder of the falling water.

Darcy climbed the rough rock face. He had considered the trail to the top, but it would take too long because the path was designed as part of a nature walk. Each step brought him closer, but the distance remaining seemed interminable. His fingers searched for purchase. Darcy could not believe that she was here and in danger. He was a man prepared for every contingency, but not today. Today, he had been totally unprepared to fight for his wife's honor. His whole focus was on reaching Elizabeth in time and placing himself between her and her attacker.

But, to his horror, Elizabeth's situation deteriorated. She had stepped rearward, dangerously close to the drop, and then her assailant charged. Before Darcy could react, she tumbled over backward. She seemed to float for a moment, a jonquil-clad bird riding the air, and then she fell. The man who had accosted her kicked out to send them over the water rather than the rocks. His wife had literally sailed over Darcy's head. "No!" he screamed to the heavens.

Chapter 15

Darcy scrambled to reach her. It would have been easier to dive in after her, but there was no way he could clear the sharp crags jutting outward from the rock face; therefore, he set his feet to slide down the way he had come.

The dirt streaked his face and temporarily blinded him. The rough surface tore at the fine cloth of his jacket. Sharp stones bruised and cut his flesh, but none of that mattered. Only his reaching Elizabeth in time would heal his anxious heart. "Please, God," he prayed repeatedly as he bumped his way toward the bottom. Pebbles preceded his descent in a rocky rain. Finally, he lay back and allowed his weight to carry him roughly along the last fifteen feet.

Landing hard on his side, Darcy rolled to all fours. Inhaling deeply, he cursed his clumsiness before springing forward. The earth beneath his feet was damp and muddy. It smelled musty and dank and filled with death's aroma. As he ran, he stripped away what remained of his shredded jacket and tore open his waistcoat, sending buttons flying in golden droplets along the shore. "Elizabeth!" he called to the woman struggling in the water beyond his reach. A sob caught in his throat.

His wife fought to stay afloat. As they had recently enjoyed a private swim in one of Pemberley's lakes after he had rowed them out to a small island for a romantic picnic, Darcy knew her to be an adequate swimmer, but Elizabeth did not possess the skill to both fight her attacker and save her own life. Darcy was thankful that Mr. Bennet had taught his two eldest daughters not to fear the water: It could be the difference in Elizabeth's chance of survival.

"I am coming, Elizabeth!" he shouted as he flopped down upon the damp bank to remove his boots. He prayed the time he spent in doing so would not affect his success in rescuing his wife. However, he recognized the fact the heavy boots would only weigh him down, and Darcy would likely need every advantage in this life-and-death struggle. His wife grasped her attacker about the neck, wrestling with him, while the man flailed and punched.

As Darcy stood once more to judge the conflict, the dark-skinned man caught Elizabeth about the waist and shoved her under the murky water. Darcy waded into the water, but his eyes never left the spot where she had disappeared. *How long could Elizabeth hold her breath?* He wondered as he lowered himself into the water. "One. Two. Three," he silently counted as he churned away the strokes. Could he reach her in time? "Dearest God?" his mind pleaded. "Do not take her from me." His eyes searched the water both above and below the lake's surface. "Seven. Eight…"

* * *

Elizabeth fought with the bonnet, which tugged her backward. It had caught on something on the lake's bottom, but she had no time to untangle it. The Rom drifted downward, her last thrust finishing the man's struggle against death. She yanked at the ribbons which had wrapped about her neck, but she could not free them, so instead she reached for the offending item that had caught the straw confection, which had once been her favorite bonnet. Elizabeth could not see what held her in place, but she could feel. Twisting at an awkward angle, she reached for the impediment. As

243

her feet fluttered in place, Elizabeth readily comprehended that she had but a few precious seconds remaining before she would join the Rom on the lake's bottom. Her fingers traced something she could not see. It was soft, yet coarse at the same time; then rough and spongy against her chilled fingertips. "Clothing!" Her mind shouted. "But not the Rom's. Another body!"

If she had had time, Elizabeth thought she would be sick, but time was her enemy. Somehow the body with which she fought had shifted in the water and now held her bonnet captive beneath its weight. Without time to reason her escape, Elizabeth used her shoulder and her numb hands to pry the unknown victim free from whatever held him in place. With each effort to loosen her trapped headwear, she silently said the one word that mattered: her husband's name. "Darcy."

With the last of her strength, she managed to rock the body to its side long enough to pull the remnants of her bonnet free. However, she was too weak to swim to the surface. All she could manage was one last kick and a prayer that God would protect her.

* * *

In his panic, Darcy had lost track of the number of seconds his wife had remained below the water's surface. He had reached the spot where he thought he had last seen Elizabeth alive, but Darcy was no longer certain he had chosen correctly. Repeatedly, he dived into the dark waters in search of any sign of his wife and her attacker. Each time he surfaced with nothing to show for his efforts, his heart seemed to die a slow death. The terror made it hard to breathe. He could see nothing of Elizabeth anywhere, and the dread of not finding her in time built in Darcy's chest.

A gulp of air was all he had permitted himself before Darcy dove again. His eyes searched for a bit of jonquil in the blues, greens, browns, and blacks of the water. Then he saw her floating, still in the water. Lifeless. Unmoving. The blood in his chest pounded as his heart lurched with the image. Darcy kicked hard to propel himself toward her. She was drifting downward. His mind demanded that she hear him. That Elizabeth's soul would answer his plea. "I love you. Do not leave me. You promised we would grow old together."

Darcy caught her about the waist and kicked against the water's resistance to haul their combined weights to the surface. Breaking the surface, Darcy sputtered and spat. He lifted Elizabeth's head above the water before he tossed her over his shoulders. "Lord in Heaven," he prayed aloud. "Permit this to work." Darcy realized she would never make it to the shoreline with a chance for survival if he did not do something drastic immediately. He struck her back hard with the palm of his hand, but his wife did not respond. Struggling to stay afloat, he lifted her higher above his head and let her drop again. This time, her weight hit him hard enough to drive Darcy under, but he kept Elizabeth supported above the water. Resurfacing again, he draped her limp body over his shoulder and slapped her hard across her back.

This time his efforts were rewarded with a weak whimper, but it was enough to give Darcy hope. He wrapped her safely under his arm and side-crawled his way to the shore. With each stroke, he pleaded with Elizabeth to return to him. "You are my indomitable Lizzy," he announced to the open water. "You can do anything. Set your mind to it, Lizzy. Return to me."

When he reached a depth where he could stand, Darcy swung her up into his arms to carry Elizabeth to safety. Finally reaching the grassy area, Darcy sank to his knees and lowered Elizabeth to the ground. Exhausted, he gulped for air and draped himself over her, but his wife was not safe; therefore, Darcy rolled her to her side. "Come on, Sweetheart," he coaxed as he pressed his knees against her back. He pulled her shoulders upward and backward to arch against his body. "Open your lungs, Lizzy. Permit the air to come in," he encouraged. His stomach clenched with anguish.

Darcy cupped her body with his. Elizabeth's back plastered against his chest, he bent her like a bow. Clasping his hands together across her abdomen, Darcy thrust upward. Once. Twice. On the third time, he heard a gurgle. Then a gasp. And finally Elizabeth spit out mouthfuls of dirty water. Quickly, he rolled her to her side so she would not strangle on what she brought up. "That is my beautiful warrior goddess," he professed as he stroked the hair from her face. As she opened her mouth to cough up more of what she had swallowed, Darcy's fingers worked to loosen the wet knot that choked her. "Damn this thing!" he cursed. "Do not move." He scrambled to retrieve his boots from the beach.

Rushing to where she laid hacking and coughing, Darcy dug the small knife from the secret compartment in the boot's side. Pulling the blade free, he knelt beside her again. Her fingers clawed at the twisted mass of ribbons as she fought for air. "Lie quietly," he whispered close to Elizabeth's ear, "and I shall have you free."

His wife opened her eyes, finally seeing him. Even drenched and lying in the mud, Darcy thought her the most beautiful woman he had ever beheld, a miracle. His fingers automatically cut the frayed ribbon, but Darcy saw none of it. White-faced and staring, Elizabeth's brilliant eyes shone wide with fright and wonder. "Thank God," he whispered as he freed the string from about her throat. Then he kissed her forehead. "I had thought I would lose you. Thank you for clawing your way back to me." Anger and relief churned madly within him.

"You…you were…my hope," she said through a hoarse rasp.

Darcy soothed her cheek with the back of his hand. Her face was pale, and her breathing remained uneven. Gently, he brushed away a strand of wet hair. "Shush now. Permit me to see you to safety. We can speak more when you recover. I am going nowhere without you. You are my soul."

Another round of watery coughing interrupted the tender moment, but Darcy smiled despite her retching. Each twist and distorted turn meant Elizabeth had survived death's grasp.

Darcy wrestled his boots on over his wet stockings and retrieved what remained of his waistcoat and jacket. For warmth, he wrapped both about Elizabeth's body before lifting her to him. "I have you, Darling," he whispered as her trembling body snuggled into his. Elizabeth's hand fluttered at the irritation at her throat, and then she laid her head to rest against Darcy's shoulder. Each step brought him closer to the manor. Darcy was exhausted, but he would not stop until Elizabeth was safe. Until she was free of danger.

"I…I love you," she sobbed against his shoulder. The warmth of her shallow breath spread hope through Darcy's veins.

By the time he had cleared the groves and had entered the lower gardens, Darcy's steps were heavy from the effort, but his purpose remained. He would see Elizabeth well before he rested. Dampness clung to every inch of his body: a mixture of his dip in the lake and the sweat running down his body from the exertion of carrying her over such a distance. He could feel his pulse pounding along the back of his neck where the muscles strained against the cut of his shirt. Twice, they had stopped for Elizabeth to empty her stomach. Each time, Darcy had held her on his lap and had soothed her brow with his damp handkerchief. He had praised her bravery and had promised his wife his undying love.

He looked up from the sweat dripping into his eyes to see his cousin racing to where Darcy stood. Despite his best efforts, he swayed in place.

"Permit me to take Mrs. Darcy," Edward ordered as his cousin released the sword from about his waist to unbutton his heavy military jacket. The colonel stripped the garment from his shoulders and dropped it across a low stone wall.

Reluctantly, Darcy's fingers uncurled. The colonel scooped Elizabeth into his waiting arms, and Darcy collapsed to his knees.

"Can you reach the house on your own?" Edward demanded.

On all fours, Darcy nodded. With great effort, he said, "See Mrs. Darcy to safety. I will follow in a moment."

Edward turned in place. "Put my coat about your shoulders. You are shivering."

Darcy looked up into his cousin's all-too-perceptive eyes. "From fear. I might still lose her. Carry my wife the rest of the way, and I will forever be in your debt."

Edward nodded curtly. "I will send someone to assist you." Then his cousin turned his steady steps toward the manor house. Willing the colonel to ferry Elizabeth to Hannah's safekeeping, Darcy watched Edward's retreat. His wife's maid held a strong allegiance to Elizabeth. The woman would see to Elizabeth's recovery.

Once Edward had disappeared on the other side of the arbor, with great difficulty Darcy rose. He caught up his cousin's jacket and sword where they lay upon the broken wall. A growl of determination escaped Darcy's lips as he set his feet in motion. His task was not complete. Only when the surgeon pronounced Elizabeth well would Darcy rest.

* * *

Edward kicked the partially closed courtyard door open, sending the door slamming against the Oriental wallpaper and leaving a gash in the design, but the colonel took little notice. Instead, he strode through the empty study to emerge into the main hall. "Barriton," he bellowed. "Hannah. Sheffield." Servants scrambled to respond.

"Yes, Colonel?" The butler responded from behind an ornate medieval shield.

Edward's temper flared. It was not as if he walked about every day with a limp woman in his arms. "Mrs. Darcy requires a physician," he barked. "Both she and Mr. Darcy will require hot baths."

"Oh, my!" Hannah squealed as she rushed to her mistress's side. "What happened?" she pleaded, as she gently touched Elizabeth's hand.

Edward frowned deeply. "I am not certain. Darcy found her. He had carried Mrs. Darcy from the vicinity of the orchard and the lake. She is soaked," he said as he climbed the stairs.

Hannah trailed behind him. "That be more than three quarters mile," she declared in amazement.

"Explains Darcy's complete exhaustion. I imagine it so. I have ordered a hot bath and have sent for Mr. Glover." He hefted Elizabeth higher in his arms. "Go before me and see to Mrs. Darcy's things." Hannah darted around him and disappeared into the upper passageway.

Above him, Sheffield's voice inquired, "You sought my services, Colonel?" Despite the valet's usual unflappable attitude, concern crossed the man's countenance.

"Mr. Darcy is injured. He is trailing me through the lower gardens. Your master requires your assistance immediately," the colonel said over his shoulder. Sheffield did not respond verbally. Instead, the man scurried past him to seek Darcy. "Thank God some of the servants in this house recognize their duties," he grumbled as he shouldered his way through the open door to Elizabeth's bedchamber.

"Set her down here," Hannah said as she draped a sheet over the small sofa.

"Do you require assistance?"

"I shall attend Mrs. Darcy." The maid patted Elizabeth's wrist. "The Mistress is so pale."

Edward simply nodded. What could he say? He had never seen Elizabeth look so, and it worried him as much as it did the lady's maid. "I will leave you to it. I will check on the warm water and assist Sheffield with Mr. Darcy. Knowing my cousin's devotion to his wife, Darcy will be in here before you make your mistress comfortable."

Elizabeth opened her eyes slowly. "Thank you…Colonel," she said with difficulty. "See to…Mr. Darcy…if you please."

"As always, my dear," he said gallantly. Edward bent to kiss Elizabeth's forehead. "Recover quickly, Mrs. Darcy. Your husband will be a bear until he knows no more worries over your health." With that, he exited and closed the door to her room.

Edward skidded to a halt when he discovered his cousin slumped over in a chair in the study. Sheffield had wrestled the swollen leather from Darcy's feet. Lacerations covered Darcy's lower legs and blood dotted his stockings. Although it was midmorning, Edward shoved a brandy into Darcy's hand. "My wife?" Darcy asked anxiously.

"Is in the capable hands of her maid," Edward assured. "Elizabeth spoke to me briefly before I left her room. As you worry for her health, your wife wished me to see to yours."

"Thank you…" Darcy leaned heavily into the chair's cushion. "For a time, I thought I had lost her. When I discovered Elizabeth, she was under water and not breathing." Darcy closed his eyes as if reliving that terrible moment. The realization of his cousin's words brought a shiver to the colonel's spine.

Sheffield motioned that he would prepare things above stairs, and Darcy weakly nodded his agreement. Edward pulled a chair closer to where Darcy sat. "How in the world did Mrs. Darcy end up in the lake? It is not like Elizabeth to chance such peril." Darcy could see his cousin's thoughts: *Had Mrs. Darcy attempted suicide?*

Darcy took a long draught from the brandy. Finally, he described the horrible tableau upon which he had stumbled. "It is not what it seems," Darcy assured. "Mrs. Darcy fought a man upon one of the overhanging cliffs above the lake. Before I could reach her, her attacker sent Elizabeth tumbling over my head into the water." Darcy's lips trembled. "I have never been more frightened in my life," he said while lost in his thoughts. "Nothing made sense. Elizabeth's body hung in the air like some sort of brightly clad angel, and then she crashed into the water below."

Edward's assessing eyes met Darcy's gaze. "I was some halfway up the rock face when Elizabeth went into the water." His cousin shook his head in disbelief. "How I reached her, I will never know."

Edward said softly, "Love gives a man a great strength." He placed his hand on Darcy's forearm. "What happened to Mrs. Darcy's attacker?"

The colonel watched as a chill stole down Darcy's spine, and his cousin's anger returned. "The bastard followed her into the water, and their fight continued. You should have seen her. Elizabeth was a vengeful Artemis, punching the man, but he struck her across the throat and dragged her under with him." Edward waited for the tale's end. "When I reached the spot where I had last seen Mrs. Darcy tussling with her attacker, I searched the murky depths in hopes of feeling her below me, but I was running out of time. Elizabeth had not resurfaced after the man had shoved her into the icy waters. Neither of them had. When I finally discovered her, Elizabeth's body was floating toward the darkest depths. She was lifeless."

Edward asked for no more details. Darcy had suffered enough for one day. "You did your best, Darcy," he insisted.

Darcy buried his head into his hands. "Yet, is it enough?"

Edward leaned over to lift Darcy to his feet. "Only time will tell." Darcy stood stiffly. "Let us see to your injuries and to some warm clothes. Then, along with Hannah, you may tend Mrs. Darcy."

With Edward's assistance, Darcy lumbered toward the open door, but suddenly he came to an abrupt halt. "As God is my witness," he swore. "The day Mrs. Darcy is well enough to travel, I will leave this cursed household behind. Woodvine's occupants may dance with the Devil in the moonlight, and I will not give a care. I will refuse to look back in regret. Woodvine will become Rardin's problem."

Edward asked cautiously, "Even if we have no answers to our questions?"

Darcy declared, "Even if the world tilts on its side sending parts of India and China tumbling off the end. I will never place Elizabeth in danger again."

* * *

Mr. Glover pronounced Elizabeth on her way to recovery. "Your wife will know more fine sunny days," the man insisted.

"How long before Mrs. Darcy can travel?" His earlier declaration still rang in Darcy's ears. He had not removed his eyes from Elizabeth's pale countenance. His wife had offered him a series of weak smiles, but Darcy was not convinced. Only when he could rid himself of the annoying surgeon and could speak privately to Elizabeth would Darcy know comfort.

"Likely a week. Maybe less. Mrs. Darcy appears to come from sturdy stock." The man good-naturedly slapped Darcy on the back. "Place your worry behind you, Mr. Darcy." The surgeon returned his instruments to a small bag. "I have given Hannah several salves and draughts for your wife's comfort." Darcy glanced to Elizabeth's loyal servant and smiled when Hannah rolled her eyes heavenward. Obviously, Elizabeth's lady's maid held similar opinions of the surgeon as did her mistress. "If you do not object, Sir," said Glover, "I would call on Mrs. Ridgeway while I am at Woodvine. I would reexamine the lady's injuries and spend time in conversation."

Darcy's mouth tightened into a thin line. He held no kind thoughts when it came to the housekeeper. "Mrs. Ridgeway is free to entertain whomever she pleases. After all, the lady's employment has been terminated."

Glover asked incredulously, "You have released Mrs. Ridgeway? May I ask the cause?"

Edward said from his place near the door. "I am certain the lady would prefer to explain the circumstances personally."

Glover frowned, but he kept his remarks to himself. Even in the most bizarre situations, manners required polite civility. "I suspect you are correct, Colonel."

After the man made his exit, Darcy sat on the bed's edge. Capturing Elizabeth's hand in his, he said affectionately, "I am pleased you are sitting up, Mrs. Darcy." He had rushed through his own ablutions so that he might assist Hannah in tending to Elizabeth. The maid had blushed thoroughly when he had insisted on lifting Elizabeth in and out of her tub and when Darcy had gently washed the dirt and film from his wife's skin and hair. The bruises on her arms, where her assailant had held her so tightly that the man's fingers had left an imprint on Elizabeth's fair skin, had come close to ripping Darcy's heart from his chest. He blamed himself for sending Elizabeth off in a bad humor. In the future, he would take Edward's advice: Even if he thought himself in the right, Darcy would apologize.

During her bath, Elizabeth had indicated how her retching and the lake water had irritated her throat. Darcy privately thought her discomfort had come from her assailant's violent attack upon Elizabeth's breathing. The attack and the fact that her bonnet had wrapped itself solidly about her neck likely led to her current physical discomfort. Realizing she would not easily give up her need to communicate, Darcy had gathered several sheets of foolscap from Samuel's desk, a serving tray, and two artist's pencils so that Elizabeth might write her responses. He read her sentiments as they skittered across Elizabeth's countenance, her gratitude went beyond the gift of the foolscap.

She brought his palm to her lips and kissed it. Despite the ghostlike sheen on her cheeks, Elizabeth's eyes sparkled with their customary mischief, and Darcy breathed easier for it.

He motioned his cousin to sit on the other side of the bed, and a bit of jealousy resurfaced when Elizabeth intertwined her fingers with Edward's. "What can you tell us about your attacker?" the colonel encouraged.

Elizabeth's face contorted in fear. Panic crossed her expression. "Do not fret," Darcy assured her. "The man did not resurface after the two of you went under."

"Are you certain?" she scribbled quickly on the paper's middle.

Darcy's thumb traced the blue-black bruise on the inside of her wrist. "Absolutely. I was there. Searching for you," he explained. "Only you floated toward the light."

Edward asked again, "Had you seen your assailant previously?"

She shook her head in the negative, but Elizabeth reached for the paper. In the upper corner, Elizabeth wrote a single word: *Roma*.

Darcy's temper flared. Not only had he allowed his wife to leave Woodvine unchaperoned and in an agitated state, but he had permitted the man who had assaulted her to live on Woodvine land. Fault was his newest companion. Darcy would blame himself forever. "One of the gypsies attacked you?" he demanded.

Elizabeth nodded in the affirmative, and then she ducked her eyes. She wrote: *I killed him*.

"No," Darcy said immediately. "The man set his own course. You did nothing more than to survive, which was God's plan for you."

A tear crawled down Elizabeth's cheek. Her shoulders shook with true sorrow. It would be a long time before she could reconcile her actions to the end result, but Darcy would be beside her on the journey. His cousin's eyes said that they would pay a visit to the gypsy camp, and the result would not be a pretty sight.

Edward said without emotion, "I will see to recovering the Rom's body. It will resurface in the next few days. It is the way of nature."

Elizabeth shook her head violently. *NO!* she wrote, in large letters.

Edward patted the back of her hand. "It is true, my dear. I have seen it often. The time varies a bit depending on the water's temperature, but whether the person died from drowning or died on land and was placed in the water, the body rises to the surface in somewhere between two and five days."

Until recently, Darcy had never thought about how quickly a body decomposed after death. He supposed his cousin had come to look upon death as commonplace. The thought grieved him dearly.

Elizabeth jerked on Edward's jacket sleeve for his attention. *More than one.* She had written the words and underlined them twice.

"What do you mean by 'more than one'?" Edward asked curiously. "You had more than one attacker?"

Again, she denied his words. Writing frantically, she scribbled, *More than one body.*

Edward asked, "How can that be? Darcy observed only one attacker. If another is on the lake's bottom, he would have to have been placed there within the last few days," he reasoned.

"Another witch's sacrifice?" Darcy asked. He said to Elizabeth, "Perhaps it was Els you followed into the night, after all. Could she and her followers or she and this man she calls 'Toby' have done away with another from the community? Is it possible you over-looked the stolen map when you initially searched the maid's room?"

Edward answered for her, "Definitely not. None of Samuel's servants have extensive quarters: a small bed, a chest, and an area to store one's clothes. Mrs. Darcy and I searched under mattresses and inside drawers."

Darcy summarized, "Then there are two bodies to recover: those of Elizabeth's attacker, and of a stranger, who has likely disappeared in the past week."

Elizabeth scrawled, *Mr. Crescent?*

Darcy looked from his wife to his cousin. "Is that possible? No one has heard of Crescent for nearly a fortnight."

Edward asked gently, "Could you see anything of the person?"

Elizabeth shook her head in the negative. Her fingers stroked the slender column of her neck, and with great effort, she said on a throaty rasp, "Could not see. Too deep. Felt his hand. Trapped my bonnet. No escape. Rolled him. But no more air. Cannot remember…anything after I kicked…away from him."

"That is enough," Darcy ordered. "Glover said no talking until, at earliest, tomorrow. Hannah, would you bring Mrs. Darcy some more lemon tea?"

"Aye, Sir."

Edward said cautiously, "If it is Crescent, then someone must have killed the man."

"How so?" Darcy asked as he stood.

Edward followed him to his feet. They had another mystery to solve. "The only way a body would stay under water for that long would be if someone had weighed it down."

Chapter 16

In their own world and ignoring everyone around them, Darcy and the colonel were nearly to the door when Darcy heard his wife snort and knew to duck before the wooden tray came sailing in their direction. His cousin was less experienced in the ways of married women. The tray hit the back of Edward's left shoulder.

Darcy laughed as he turned to observe his wife's confrontational posture. True, she remained propped up on the bed's many pillows, but his wife's arms were crossed stiffly across her chest. Her eyes flared with a warning Darcy recognized, and a tight-lipped scowl marred Elizabeth's handsome countenance. "Did you require something to relieve your discomfort, my dear?" he asked in a mock-solemn tone, which brought a mischievous grin to his wife's lips.

Edward rubbed his arm briskly before he retrieved the tray from the floor. "I say, Darcy," he said with a bittersweet taunt, "you did not warn me you had married a shrew."

Darcy's lips twitched in amusement when he noted Elizabeth picking up the empty teacup and testing its weight in her hand. "Be cautious, Colonel. My wife has a deadly aim when she requires one. You are about to be introduced to the pleasures of wedded bliss."

Edward leaned easily against one of the four posts of Elizabeth's bed. "In that case, perhaps I have been too eager to place my head in the parson's noose." He flipped a small pillow in Elizabeth's direction.

At least her testiness had brought a flush to Elizabeth's pale cheeks. For that, Darcy said a private prayer of thanksgiving. In her frustration, his wife snapped her fingers at Edward. Emphatically, she pointed to him and then motioned to the door with a jerky movement that required no words to relay her meaning. Elizabeth had ordered Edward from her room.

His cousin chuckled. He said as he strode toward the door, "I do not know which is worse: being profoundly dismissed by a lovely lady or being dutifully retained to face her wrath."

Darcy said to his cousin's retreating form, "Being profoundly dismissed. Without complaint, I would dutifully stay by the lovely lady's side."

With an elegant bow, Edward dramatically closed the door before Darcy sat beside Elizabeth again. "I apologize," he said automatically. "The colonel and I fell into a familiar pattern. My cousin requires little encouragement to rush off to save the world."

Even without the words, Darcy knew his wife's sentiments. He wondered how it could be so—how after so short an acquaintance had they given themselves so completely to one another. Normally, a couple spent years together before they knew each other so well. If ever. In Society, a man and wife often lived apart. The gentleman's mistress likely knew more of the man's preferences than did the woman he had married.

Darcy gathered Elizabeth into his arms. Her curves fit snugly against his hard angles. His cheek was pressed to her hair. "I promise not to go into the lake again," he assured her. She relaxed against him. "And I will see that the colonel takes care if he should venture forth." He stroked the back of Elizabeth's head. "You must know, however, that my cousin and I must discover the truth of this madness." She nodded against Darcy's chest. "If you wish, I will tell you what we uncover." He gently kissed the top of her head. "Yet, I will take the information to my grave if it disturbs you in any way. I will not see you hurt by this mayhem."

Elizabeth tightened her arms about his waist and pressed closer. "And?" she whispered.

"Do not ask it of me, Lizzy. I cannot promise you I will not seek revenge upon the gypsies." Darcy closed his eyes to force away the image of Elizabeth fighting for her life. She squeezed harder and began to sob. "I am sorry, Lizzy, truly sorry. I will promise not to attack the innocent, but I cannot simply look away."

"Your heart," she rasped.

Darcy sighed deeply. "You wonder if I can continue to love if I lose my honor?" He lifted her chin with his fingertips. "When did you become my conscience?" His wife's lips turned up in a smile. "You think that amusing, do you?" He kissed the tip of Elizabeth's nose. She shrugged heavily. "I will have time to consider all the possibilities before I will visit the gypsy camp. That is the extent of my promise."

Elizabeth pulled herself to him, lacing her hands about Darcy's neck. "Kiss," she said on an exhale. Darcy needed no prompting. He had come close to losing her on this day; he would claim Elizabeth as the love of his life. Elizabeth automatically opened her mouth; he no longer needed to urge her along. His tongue swept in to tantalize the depth of her affections. Elizabeth arched into his body, and Darcy meant to brand her as his own.

A quarter hour later, he found the colonel and Glover waiting on him in the main foyer. "I thought we might require the surgeon's expertise," Edward explained with a knowing look. Evidently, his cousin had something of import to share with Darcy regarding the surgeon.

"It is an excellent idea," Darcy said wisely. "Have you found someone willing to assist us at the lake?"

"Mr. McKye claims expertise at both swimming and diving, and Holbrook has taken a flat wagon to the site."

Darcy chuckled. His cousin was a man built to make decisions, to organize and to order. "Then I suppose we should be about it."

"I will take my curricle," Glover said as Darcy and Edward mounted the waiting horses.

Within a mere matter of minutes, they had outstripped the surgeon. "What might you wish to share regarding Glover?" Darcy asked as he glanced over his shoulder to where the surgeon deftly maneuvered the curricle around yet another rut in the road.

The colonel followed Darcy's inquiring gaze with one of his own. "When I sought the surgeon's assistance in recovering the bodies, I overheard an interesting bit of information of which you should be made aware."

Darcy kept his eyes on Glover. "Go on."

"First, it seems Mrs. Ridgeway has sent word to Mr. Stowbridge that she will accept employment in the magistrate's household."

"That makes little sense," Darcy said. "When Mrs. Darcy and I first came to Dorset a little over a week prior, it was quite obvious that Mrs. Ridgeway wanted nothing to do with Stowbridge and the magistrate desired a relationship beyond the woman's being his servant."

Edward said softly, "The surgeon is aware of the oddity of the lady's change of heart, and Glover is most displeased. Their conversation had reached a heated impasse by the time of my appearance."

Darcy observed, "I do not doubt it. Mr. Glover holds a strong *tendre* for the woman."

They neared the lake. Darcy could see Mr. Holbrook climbing down from the wagon in the distance. "One thing more," Edward cautioned. "The good doctor said the oddest thing."

"Yes?"

"Glover asked Mrs. Ridgeway if she knew which of the gypsies might have attacked Mrs. Darcy."

The hollow feeling of uncertainty had returned to Darcy's chest. He looked to his cousin inquiringly. "Did the lady have a response?"

Appearing a good deal perplexed, his cousin shook his head in the negative. "I am afraid the couple became aware of my presence and did not finish their conversation."

Darcy bit his bottom lip in frustration. The action reminded him of Elizabeth, and he could not resist smiling. He and his wife were assuming each other's mannerisms. "I suspect at the end of the day we should add a few more details to Mrs. Darcy's list of what we know and what we have yet to discover. Mayhap, this day will even out the lists."

* * *

McKye had proved a more than able swimmer. Before he had been pressed into service under Captain Tregonwell, the man had spent several years upon fishing boats. It had taken but three attempts to locate the first body. As Darcy looked on, he had relived every harrowing moment of his wife's rescue: the strong, determined stroke as Elizabeth fought with the gypsy; his heart pounding a staccato; the dizzying terror; wishing away the nausea. "The man who attacked your wife, Sir, is still below," McKye explained. "He will be the easy one to bring up. He is floating along the bottom head down."

Darcy frowned and looked to Glover for an explanation.

"No one knows why what McKye describes is true, but 'tis so. Most of the uninformed assume that somehow the blood gathers in the head because those who drown can no longer breathe. Yet, that makes little sense to a man who has studied the human body to discover the truths of nature and God," the surgeon disclosed. "Submersion causes the skin to turn blue."

McKye dried his face and arms with the towel Holbrook handed him before asking, "Do you wish me to bring up the gypsy first, or one of the others?"

Edward demanded, "*One* of the others? What mean you by this?"

McKye leaned easily against a large boulder along the shoreline. "I spied two others in the same vicinity as the gypsy. Likely all went under from the same spot. No way to tell until we finish our search as to whether that is the extent of the lake's secrets."

"Dear God," Darcy groaned. "I feel I am in one of those Gothic novels of which Mrs. Darcy is so fond. We have three dead at last count and now some three more. Is this estate cursed?"

Edward caught Darcy's shoulder. "I will assist McKye," his cousin declared. "The fewer who know of this tragedy the better."

Darcy reluctantly agreed. "Mrs. Darcy has charged me with your protection. Do not make me disappoint my wife."

A little over an hour later, four bodies were stretched out upon the shore. Glover examined each carefully.

"Can you tell how these men died?" Darcy asked cautiously. "Is it possible they were struck in a manner similar to Cousin Samuel?"

Glover's fingers had prodded the distorted skin of each victim. "It would be difficult at this point. When the body sinks, it skims the bottom, often suffering a series of abrasions. Small fish attack the soft tissue of the face. Any head injuries I could identify could have come before the man was submerged, or it could be the result of the shifting waters and the rocks on the lake's bottom."

In the background, Darcy could hear Holbrook relieving himself of his earlier meal. Three of the bodies resembled no human Darcy had ever seen: Each was a greenish brown, excepting the gypsy, who had already taken a *tête de nègre* appearance. The bodies had swollen and just touching the gooselike skin caused a soft soaplike material to squirt from beneath Glover's fingers.

"These bodies have been below for several months. It will be difficult to identify them," Glover concluded. "I see no reason to cut upon what remains. Leave these men a bit of dignity."

Edward straightened the line of his coat. "We cannot simply bury these men as if they never existed," he declared. "They must have names and families."

Holbrook, who had recovered somewhat, said, "I will search the clothing, Mr. Darcy."

Noticing the tenuous steps of the groom, Darcy suggested, "Perhaps Mr. Glover might assist you. I believe the good doctor has more experience in such matters." In comparison to Holbrook, Glover held a fascination with the decomposing body.

Holbrook's tongue licked away the dryness from his lips. "It be odd. I can look upon birth but not death."

Darcy said, "My cousin and I will return the Rom to the camp."

Darcy noted the guarded look in Holbrook's eyes. "Be wary, Mr. Darcy. There be danger and menace among that one's people." The groom gestured to where Elizabeth's attacker lay.

Darcy and Edward had hoisted the gypsy's body upon the back of Darcy's horse. They had loosely tied the man across the horse's rump and had purposely not covered the body with a blanket or a rug. "We will announce our disdain by treating their dead with our utter disregard," Edward had said.

For Darcy, it was more than that. The gypsy's death had cheated him of revenge for the interloper's actions against Elizabeth. His total disregard for the dead would be a salve for his hard resolve. As they rode into the camp, nausea roiled his stomach. In all his years, Darcy had never faced an evil such as the one he had found at Woodvine. In Derbyshire and London, he had dealt quickly and decisively with those who would have cheated him of his family's fortune, but he had no experience with those who would manipulate and murder with such ease.

"Follow my lead," Edward cautioned under his breath. "And do not permit any Rom to tarry behind you. They are known to be deadly accurate with a knife."

Darcy nodded his understanding, for the truth was unavoidable: He operated under the impediment of principles and good manners. Darcy feared he possessed no skills to defend his wife's honor under these bizarre circumstances. A duel would have easily expressed the contempt he felt, but men of breeding dealt differently with honor than did these men. Yet, he held the responsibility to right the wrong exacted against his wife, even if Elizabeth had told him in her indomitable manner that she required no such revenge.

Gry met them when they entered the gypsy camp. As they had done the previous time, several of the band gathered behind their leader. "Mr. Darcy? Colonel?" the gypsy asked tentatively. "To what do we owe the pleasure?"

Gry glanced to the corpse. Intent crossed his countenance, and Edward warned menacingly, "Do not mistake our purpose, Gry."

The gypsy asked stiffly, "Of what is my cousin accused that he would deserve such disrespect? Or is his only crime that of being a Rom?"

"Your cousin," Darcy growled, "had the audacity to insert himself into the life at Woodvine."

"And for that crime Vandlo Pias met his death?" Gry accused. "I would know Vandlo's offense. What did my cousin do? Flirt with one of Mr. Samuel's servants?"

Edward nudged his horse between Darcy and the gypsy leader. He swore beneath his breath when he noticed the dark-skinned youth stepping from the clearing. Darcy purposely planted his heel in the horse's side, and the animal dutifully kicked his hind legs. "Best not to stand too close," Darcy said blandly. "I do not know this mount." He motioned with the gun he had produced prior to their riding into the camp. "I suggest you join your family."

With a knife he had palmed for protection, Edward leaned over to cut the two ropes securing the corpse to the horse's hindquarters. The one Gry called *Vandlo Pias* unceremoniously slammed into the dirt. His distorted features told part of the tale.

Gry's expression changed instantly from his usual feigned respect to one of pure hatred.

Darcy could almost feel the gypsy plunging his knife into Darcy's chest. "*Desperate situations*," he heard his father's voice as a warning. Darcy said indignantly, "Despite my better judgment, I have returned your cousin's body."

Gry hissed, "I have yet to hear of Vandlo's crime."

Before the gypsy leader's words died in the late spring breeze, Darcy was off his horse and striding toward the man. He caught

Gry up by the man's open-necked shirt. Behind him, he heard Edward's horse whinny sharply, and he knew his cousin had, literally, protected Darcy's back. "Your filthy cousin placed his bloody hands on my wife," he growled within inches of Gry's face. "Left his fingerprints on Mrs. Darcy's wrists. I watched in horror as my wife fought the bloody bastard. As he attempted to drown her. You speak of injustice, Gry. Where was the justice when your cousin attacked an innocent woman? If he held me at fault for some matter, then I should have been his target. Instead, the bloody coward looked for a victim."

Gry's eyes betrayed guilt's edge. "A woman brought about Vandlo's end?"

The thought made Darcy smile. "Not just any woman, Gry, but my woman. Why do you think I rushed to make Mrs. Darcy my wife? Elizabeth Darcy is as magnificent as she is invincible. Your cousin was no match for her."

Gry asked defiantly, "Then why are you here?"

Darcy shoved Gry from him. "I want you and yours gone from this place within the hour. If you ever come near Dorset again, I will see your family brought up on charges for assault and for horse theft. And Heaven help you if you think of entering Derbyshire during my lifetime."

"An hour?" Gry repeated incredulously.

Darcy strode to his horse. He easily swung into the saddle. "Would you care to vie for half that time?" he growled. "At one minute past the hour, my men and the local magistrate will take anyone remaining on Woodvine land to gaol." With that, he turned his horse and swiftly rode away from the scene. His anger had transformed into cold wrath. He had erred in permitting the gypsies to remain on Woodvine land. He vividly recalled Elizabeth's self-imposed silence and her vulnerability. He had hoped never to taste such fear again. Fear that he had utterly failed her. He bestowed such very disrespectful reflections on his accountability. Darcy slowed his horse's pace as Edward came abreast of him. He could no longer afford to cherish pride or resentment. He required a large glass of his cousin Samuel's best brandy and the presence of the one woman whose spell had captured him some nineteen months prior. The soft certainty of Elizabeth's love was Darcy's only reason to live, or to seek honor.

* * *

Within the half hour, they rode into Woodvine's stable yard. Seeing Holbrook scrubbing the planks of the flat wagon to remove the stench of the bodies surprised them. "What happened to the other three?" Edward inquired.

Holbrook wiped the sweat from his brow. "Glover went for the curate while Mr. McKye and I brung the bodies around. Once Mr. Williamson arrived to claim the deceased, the curate thought it best to git the deceased in the ground as soon as possible. By and by, the gentleman be recalling the clothing of one of our discoveries and the gold watch we found on another."

"Did you recognize the names Williamson provided?" Darcy asked as he dismounted.

"No, Sir, but Mr. Williamson seemed to know enough of each to think that he could contact those the man left behind."

"Where is McKye? Glover?" Darcy glanced to his cousin, who was patiently watching and waiting.

"Dun't know 'bout Glover. Supposin' he had others to tend to. Said something about having to git home to wash up after his examination. Didn't look so good if'n you ask me. Looked as pale as I did earlier." The man wiped his neck with a large handkerchief. "Seeing how three more of Tregonwell's men arrived while we be at the lake, McKye assisted the curate with transporting the bodies to the church."

Darcy desperately wished to see to his wife's recovery, but as the afternoon had gotten away from him, he said, "We should speak to the curate before dusk." He caught the saddle and mounted once again.

His cousin's brow gathered in deep thought. "We might wish to send Holbrook and a couple of Tregonwell's men to be certain the gypsies have departed."

Darcy glanced to the house. "Take Murray and Jatson also," he instructed the groom. "I have told Gry that I want him and his family off Darcy land within the hour. If he has not obeyed me, send for Stowbridge."

"Aye, Sir. I be glad to see that lot gone. Never understood why the late Mr. Darcy be tolerating them such about." Holbrook dropped the brush he had been using on the wooden slats into a bucket of water. "I be bringing me gun."

"No one is to use force unless the gypsies initiate a confrontation," the colonel cautioned.

"Does no harm to be prepared," Holbrook assured as he walked away.

Darcy might have once cared for the outcome of the ejection of the gypsies from Woodvine land, but his interest in the result had died the moment Vandlo Pias had touched Elizabeth Darcy. Instead, he turned his head, his mount, and his heart from the possibility.

Without discussion, he and his cousin set a comfortable pace. It was not far to the village. Darcy doubted that Edward approved of

Darcy's actions in dealing with the gypsies. The colonel was a man of diplomacy; yet, his cousin would think differently once Edward married. Even if the colonel settled for a marriage of convenience, rather than one based on true affections, a married Edward Fitzwilliam would have sought revenge on the gypsy camp, likely exacting a more violent response than had Darcy. Edward was slow to rile, but he was dangerous once he was. "The curacy is just ahead," Darcy said as he dismounted outside the entrance gate.

"Mr. Williamson and his sexton have been kept busy this past week," Edward observed as they let the knocker drop on the weathered door.

"Much to my chagrin," Darcy remarked. "We have uncovered five bodies in less than a week. How will this community ever recover?"

Edward said seriously, "By uncovering the perpetrator."

The door opened upon the normally jovial curate on the other side. Darcy noted how the dark eyes acknowledged them grudgingly. His cousin's affairs had introduced deceit into the society of this country. "We had thought to speak to you before the additional deaths become common knowledge."

The curate stepped aside to admit them to his austere quarters. "I have asked Mr. Sharp to hire additional diggers, and I will conduct the ceremony tomorrow," Williamson explained. "Mr. Glover assures me the bodies will decompose quicker once they have been brought to the surface. I thought to keep the services very private. It requires a delicacy of feeling."

Darcy nodded his agreement. "I trust your judgment on such matters, Williamson. I will see to the costs if you will send me a tally of the expenses."

Williamson gestured to a cluster of chairs. "You are everything that is generous and considerate, Mr. Darcy. The church members will be glad to know that charity will not be necessary."

Edward expressed his regret at the sudden intrusion of death upon the village.

The curate's dark eyebrows drew together in a pronounced frown. "One does not anticipate so much devastation in the space of days, but I suppose I should have expected something would go amiss. Our little village has known God's benevolence for too long not to face the world's worst as a test of its worthiness." Williamson paused before saying, "I have failed to recognize the obvious, Mr. Darcy."

Darcy leaned forward with interest. "Would you care to explain?"

In an attempt to clear his thinking, the curate scrubbed his face with his dry hands. "In this matter, I have sought similarities, as I am certain have you, Mr. Darcy."

Darcy inclined his head aristocratically. "You perhaps have the better of me in that matter. I have no knowledge of the relationships that bind Wimborne's residents to one another."

The curate offered tea, which both Darcy and his cousin declined. Finally, the man said, "From what I know of three of the victims, they each planned to marry."

"I am not certain I understand," Edward interrupted.

The curate explained, "As I am the vicar's representative in this village, those who plan to marry often call upon me for advice and to arrange for a calling of the banns." He paused as if to gather his thoughts. "As such, some time last autumn, Mr. Meurig Pugh called upon the curacy. I recall most vividly how Mr. Pugh extolled his future wife's many fine qualities, which I thought quite amusing because the gentleman had yet to meet the woman. A friend of an acquaintance had suggested a correspondence between Pugh and his lady, and they had regularly written for nearly a year before Pugh had decided that they should meet and marry. As his home parish was in the western reaches of Wales, I suggested that Pugh establish a residence in the area while the banns were called.

"He left my parlor on that day with a promise to return once he had earned the lady's hand. Unfortunately, I never saw the man again. I made the assumption that the woman had sent Pugh packing."

"What did Pugh say of the lady?" the colonel inquired.

"The Welshman spoke of a woman I could not envision. At the time, I had thought that perhaps the lady resided in another parish. He spoke of a woman who had known something of the world. One who had earned her living as a governess before arriving in Dorset to tend to her brother's household."

"Anything else of significance?"

"I have studied upon it, but I cannot recall any other details," the curate assured.

"How did you recognize the man?" Darcy asked.

Williamson smiled easily. "That atrocious waistcoat. Purple and green and yellow. I have seen nothing to compare in the country. Perhaps in some of London's ballrooms. I thought it quite comical that Pugh believed it appropriate for wooing his ladylove. There was little of the man's clothing remaining intact, but the waistcoat announced Pugh's identity."

"Then we speak of the one with the darker hair." Suspended only by intervals of astonishment, Darcy spoke his thoughts aloud.

"Did Pugh ever mention the lady's name?" he asked as an after-thought.

Williamson shook his head in the negative. "As I said earlier, I could not think of any among my congregation who fit the man's description, nor one who would write to a stranger in another land. When I asked of the lady's identity, Pugh said he would prefer to wait until he had spoken to the woman before sharing her name. For all I know, Pugh could have had the directions in error, or he could have overestimated the lady's interest. Some men take words spoken in kindness as being deeper than they are meant."

"Who else thought of marriage?" Edward asked in a tone of great amazement.

"The slim man with the dark blond hair," Williamson confided. "A Norwegian with an English mother by the name of Cawley Falstad. He arrived in Wimborne in November of last year with a tale similar to Pugh's but different enough that I took no note at the time."

Darcy asked, "How so?"

"Falstad claimed his mother had wanted to return to England after her husband's passing, but she feared her son's lack of understanding of English society would prove a detriment to their remaining in the country. In addition, Mrs. Falstad reasoned a man married to an English-born wife would fare better than a foreign-born country gentleman. Falstad was to inherit a small estate from his mother's family.

"Falstad's mother made inquiries and found a woman who had reportedly lost her bloom and was willing to marry a man wealthy enough to provide her a suitable home. They were to marry in his mother's home shire of Lincolnshire. I thought nothing amiss when Falstad did not return to Wimborne. I assumed he was successful. I had thought to hear of how one of the local beauties had chosen to marry, but when I considered my conversation with Falstad, in hindsight, the man had not said the woman was from Wimborne, only that she resided in Dorset."

"And I am to understand you know something of Mr. Falstad's watch?" Darcy inquired.

Williamson nodded miserably. "The Norwegian checked his watch several times in my presence: I assumed him eager to meet his betrothed. I noted the watch's unusual carving: a lightning bolt. Mr. Falstad placed the watch in an interior pocket in his jacket. He claimed it a family heirloom—one passed to his father from a great-grandfather."

Darcy was stung into practicality by Williamson's position as Wimborne's advisor, spiritual leader, and confidant. He supposed even complete strangers would readily trust in a man who followed God. "Which of our two previous finds also spoke of marriage?"

"Mr. Bates," Williamson disclosed. "I returned home one day from sitting with the Widow Leonard to find Bieder Bates on my doorstep. He was ecstatic with the news that he intended to marry; however, when I asked the name of his intended, Bates became quite tight-lipped. Bates said he planned to marry an older woman, and the community would not approve, but his heart was engaged. His business with me included his request that I speak to his family on the merits of marrying for love."

The colonel's brow pinched in frustration. "The idea of marriage linking our victims is tenuous at best. If all of our would-be lovers sought the same woman then perhaps we could pin our hopes of solving this mystery on the lady, but the descriptions you have provided us are of three different women."

The curate's expression fell. "I realize my suspicions lack depth; yet, I fear if we do not resolve this mystery soon my services will be required again, and I would find that most disconcerting."

Chapter 17

Immediately upon returning to the manor, Darcy sought news of his wife's recovery. According to Hannah, Elizabeth had slept fitfully. "Has Mrs. Darcy found any rest?"

"Not much, Sir. Mrs. Darcy dreams of her ordeal," Hannah whispered.

Darcy frowned. "You will remain by my wife's side," he ordered. "Send for me if Mrs. Darcy knows no peace."

The maid curtsied. "Yes, Sir."

"And, Hannah," he added as he made his way to the door. "I do not wish Mrs. Darcy to be left alone. If you must step away, then I want either Sheffield or Mr. Fletcher outside my wife's door. The Woodvine staff is not to have admittance to Mrs. Darcy's room." He reached for the door latch. He said cautiously, "There is an evil practicing its art under this roof. I find it hard to believe that all these bizarre events are not connected. Remember your first and only duty is to protect Mrs. Darcy."

"Is the Mistress in danger?" The maid's eyes widened.

Darcy offered an encouraging smile. "I am likely being overprotective, but humor me. Mrs. Darcy will not approve of my measures, but a husband's duty is to his wife."

Hannah's expression said she understood his obsession. Women of all classes approved of a man's romantic gestures. "Mrs. Darcy shall be well watched, Sir. Have no fear in that matter."

* * *

He and his cousin had separated upon leaving the curate's cottage. With the earlier chaos associated with Elizabeth's rescue, Edward had yet to call upon Mr. Ritter to verify the maid's tale. Of course, his wife's having located the missing map had made a prosecution of the girl null. Therefore, he and Edward had constructed a plan to flesh out the person who had planted the map in Els's quarters.

"I think it advisable that no one other than the three of us have knowledge of the map's recovery," the colonel had reasoned. "If whoever placed the map in the maid's belongings believes we have yet to discover it, then he or she will likely bring our attention to it by suggesting that we search the girl's quarters."

Darcy suggested, "We should remove the maid from Mr. Stowbridge's house. If the magistrate has offered Mrs. Ridgeway sanctuary, the maid is not safe under the man's roof."

"Do you have a place in mind?"

"I despise imposing on Tregonwell's acquaintance again, but the captain is one of the few we can trust in the area," Darcy insisted.

The colonel took a deep breath and blew it out. "Time to play the part of the Earl of Matlock's son again. To dare any person to deny my orders. I will retrieve the girl and Ritter and then see them to Bournemouth. Probably best not to leave the Hampshire youth at Skeet's farm. He could be in danger and not know it."

Darcy was quiet for several seconds before he said, "I had not considered the question of Ritter's safety. Can you see the couple to Tregonwell's care before nightfall?"

His cousin shook his head. "Not likely, but I will return to Woodvine this evening. Meanwhile, you should check on the Society members, secure the map, and begin a perusal of Samuel Darcy's journals."

Darcy's lips twitched. "In other words, you will see to the physical duties, and I the mental ones."

Edward smiled easily. "They are the roles to which life has assigned us."

"Yet, they fall short of describing either of us, Cousin," Darcy declared.

The colonel shrugged. "Perhaps if I had been the Earl's heir rather than the spare…"

Darcy noted his cousin's pained expression. Not for the first time of late, Darcy wondered what troubled his cousin so deeply that he allowed his customary guard to slip. Edward was so much more than his older brother Rowland. The colonel had depth to his character. It was not as if Rowland were a poor Viscount Lindale. Darcy's older cousin honorably saw to his duties; however, Darcy could not help but think if Edward had been the future earl, rather than Rowland, that Matlock could have become a dominant force in England's future. "True. Then you would have developed a more legible scrawl," Darcy teased.

"And you would have spent more hours in the saddle." His cousin's countenance resumed its habitual expression of authority, but Darcy noted that the deep sadness in the colonel's eyes remained.

* * *

Before Darcy could complete any of his tasks, Mr. Holbrook returned with news of the gypsy camp. "Trailed them into the next shire," the groom announced without prompting. "They be met by an unwelcoming crowd so I be doubting they stay more than a couple nights. Likely will leave after they bury their dead."

Darcy had no care for the grief of the gypsy's family. Vandlo Pias had purposely hurt Elizabeth. No forgiveness could be found in Darcy's heart. "Then we are rid of the Roma?" he said solemnly.

Holbrook dug into his pocket. "This were nailed to a tree in the clearing. It has your name on it, Sir." The groom handed Darcy a single sheet of paper.

Darcy unfolded it. "Thank you, Mr. Holbrook. I release you to your duties."

The man appeared disappointed that he would not be privy to what the note held. "Aye, Sir."

"And, Holbrook, please be advised that the colonel will return late. Have someone waiting for my cousin's appearance at the stables."

"I'll see to it meself, Sir."

With the groom's withdrawal, Darcy returned to the note. Reluctantly, Darcy admitted whatever Gry wished to tell him was likely something he did not wish to consider. The note was short, but certainly not simple: "Mr. Darcy, your anger is directed at the wrong target. Ask yourself why Vandlo made your wife his victim, and who told my cousin where Mrs. Darcy might be found."

Darcy reread the note several times, but the gypsy's intent remained unclear. "My anger," he growled, "knows but one target. Unfortunately, Vandlo Pias died before he could know my wrath." Yet, the remainder of Gry's message was what concerned him. What was Elizabeth's gypsy attacker doing so far from the Roma camp? Had Pias trailed Elizabeth to the site? And Heaven forbid that someone had employed Pias in such perfidy! "Bloody hell," Darcy hissed.

However, the truth of Gry's words rang all too clear. The gypsy leader had no reason to offer Darcy a reason for the attack. If the assault had been one of opportunity, the truth would have died along with Pias. But if the attack had been planned, others might know Pias's motivations and who instigated the assault on Elizabeth.

Immediately, Darcy wanted to chase after the gypsy band to discover what Gry meant by his riddle, but he instinctively knew even if he gave pursuit, he had learned all he would from the Roma leader.

Another mystery. His mind raced with the possibilities. Part of him wanted to order his coaches and to be as far from Dorset as his horses could carry him; yet, a part of him knew that to leave all the unexplained pieces to a gigantic puzzle behind would drive him insane. "Perhaps I should send Elizabeth to Hertfordshire until this is over," he mused. However, the thought of spending even one day apart rubbed raw his selfish need for his wife. "I am a pathetic romantic," he confessed to the empty room.

As he could not think until he assured himself of his wife's safety, Darcy made his way to her quarters.

* * *

Darcy had not taken his meal with the Society's members and Captain Tregonwell's men. Instead, he had sent word to Mrs. Holbrook that he and his cousin would partake of a late supper upon the colonel's return. Elizabeth's continued recovery had thoroughly pleased him. Contrary to Hannah's report of her mistress's agitated dreams, his wife's physical appearance had improved: She showed more color in her cheeks and a sparkle in her eyes. However, because of her raspy voice, her frustration remained high.

For his part, Darcy enjoyed the irony of having a woman known for her vocal opinions unable to hold a conversation. Darcy kissed the tip of Elizabeth's nose in a teasing manner when she openly pouted over her dilemma. Leaning close to whisper in her ear, he said, "If I did not crave hearing you call my name when we know our personal intimacies, I would ravish you this instant."

His wife had blushed, as Darcy had expected, but he should have recalled that Elizabeth usually gave as good as she received. His wife had tugged him closer. She licked his ear lobe and feathered kisses across Darcy's cheek. Then she nibbled on his lips. When he could resist her no longer, Darcy claimed his wife's mouth. He felt Elizabeth's body flash with anticipation. Darcy directed the slant of her head where he might taste her completely. Finally, he reluctantly dragged his mouth from hers. Abandoning the headiness, he cupped Elizabeth's chin tenderly. "I should allow you to rest."

Elizabeth turned her head to kiss his palm. The pulse in her neck beat twice as hard. "Tonight," she mouthed. Darcy blinked slowly. His wife was a drug of which he could not have enough. Darcy nodded, but, in reality, he would take his cue from her when he returned to her chamber in the evening.

He told her of the curate's theory regarding the bodies discovered in the lake. Elizabeth shed tears for the men who had come to Wimborne with high hopes only to meet their deaths. Darcy had explained how the colonel had escorted the maid and her Hampshire friend to Bournemouth. "We thought it best to remove the girl from Stowbridge's care, especially as the magistrate has offered Mrs. Ridgeway a position in his household."

That news had surprised his wife. She scribbled on the fresh sheets of foolscap. "Mrs. Ridgeway spoke poorly of Stowbridge, and he disparaged her influence in Samuel Darcy's life."

Darcy said grimly. "It is just another piece in this ongoing mystery."

"Soon," she said on a breathy exhale and smiled softly.

Darcy kissed her fingertips. "I pray for a quick conclusion. Then we will be free of my obligations to my father's cousin."

She traced his profile in a lingering caress, then Elizabeth wrote in bold letters: *You are the best of men.* He tenderly kissed her again.

A soft sigh brought him from their embrace. Reluctantly, Darcy stood to depart. "You are to permit Hannah to tend to your every need." He lovingly squeezed the back of Elizabeth's hand. "I will hear no objections from your pretty mouth," he teased with an ironic chuckle.

Elizabeth swatted at Darcy's arm in an affectionate chastisement.

He motioned Hannah's return before saying, "I have sent the gypsy band away. Mr. Holbrook and our men have followed the Roma's retreat into a neighboring shire." He had not wanted to speak of the gypsies to his wife, but he recognized that she would discover the truth through the servants' gossiping. It was better if Elizabeth heard it from him. "Murray reports that he spoke discreetly to the local magistrate in the village. The man will permit Gry to bury his family and then the magistrate will see the band on its way."

Despite his own misgivings regarding showing any kindness toward the gypsy troop, Darcy realized his wife would have a concern for her attacker's soul. Elizabeth would grieve for her part in the man's demise. "No one will hurt you again," he whispered as he leaned over her. Darcy kissed her forehead. "I will not tolerate it." A tear slid slowly down her cheek. He used his thumb to flick it away. "None of what happened was your fault. The blame lies elsewhere." He would not speak to her of Gry's note, at least not at this time. His wife's emotions teetered, and Darcy would not tilt the balance against her.

* * *

For some three hours, he had surveyed the pages of Samuel Darcy's journals and compared the passages to the personal papers he and Elizabeth had removed from the treasure room. He skipped the sections from Samuel's time abroad; Darcy would read those later. To solve the many facets of the Woodvine mystery, Darcy thought it best to focus on what Samuel had discovered upon his return to Dorset.

"Deep in thought?" Edward's voice broke Darcy's concentration.

Darcy looked up and smiled. "Did the good captain accept the refugees graciously?"

Edward sighed in exhaustion. "The '*good captain*' would never refuse a request from a colonel in the regulars," he said as he sat heavily in a nearby chair.

Darcy stood to summon a servant. "I have asked Mrs. Holbrook to save us portions of the evening meal."

"Bless you," Edward said with a not very convincing show of enthusiasm. "Yet, I am nearly too fatigued to eat."

"Yes, Sir?" A footman appeared at the open door.

"Ask Mrs. Holbrook to send up a meal for the colonel and for me. Then she may retire for the evening." The servant nodded and then disappeared into Woodvine's many passages. Darcy closed the door behind him. "I pray you are not too bone-tired to assist me with several new clues in our mystery."

The colonel groaned, "Another clue? Is there no end to this poser?"

Darcy sat across from his cousin. "Unfortunately, no." He said with their normal teasing smirk, "And they are *clues*, not clue."

Edward rolled his eyes in supplication. "Why did I ever permit you to talk me into joining you on this adventure?"

Darcy countered, "Because you have sworn an allegiance to my family."

Edward asked with some asperity, "Have you ever considered that my mental acuity may not be all it should be?"

Darcy leaned comfortably into the chair's cushions. "You will feel more of yourself once you have tasted Mrs. Holbrook mutton cutlets."

Edward stretched his neck and shoulders. "While we wait, tell me what else I am to know."

Darcy reached into his inside pocket to remove the gypsy's note. "Gry left this behind."

Edward reached for the note. He unfolded it and read it carefully. Well aware of his cousin's propensity for details, Darcy studied the colonel's thoughtful expression. "So, what do you make of this turn of the story?"

Darcy's stillness intensified. "I have known a gamut of emotions since first reading the gypsy's words. I originally thought it a perverted means to claim Vandlo Pias's innocence."

Edward remained deep in thought, as was characteristic of Edward Fitzwilliam. The colonel rarely made a rash decision. "You have experienced second thoughts?"

Darcy pursed his lips. "It appears reasonable to assume that Elizabeth's attacker had sought her out. That he trailed her to the waterfall. That the Rom sought some sort of revenge on me. Even Cowan thought the killing of the horse a private warning. And what better means to have retribution on me than to hurt Elizabeth?"

"If we accept your conjecture as the truth, then we must assume someone at Woodvine arranged for your wife's demise," Edward concluded.

Darcy's frown lines met. "Perhaps not. What little Mrs. Darcy has shared of the incident says that the Rom spoke as if he possessed no other choice."

"Then who do you suspect as our informant?"

Darcy scrubbed his face with his hands to clear his thinking. "God, I wish I knew. Every time I have an inkling into the perfidy practiced at Woodvine, I am thrown into another vat of hot oil." He shrugged heavily. "Now that Els is at Bournemouth, the most obvious suspect is no longer under Woodvine's roof."

"What of the housekeeper?"

"Mrs. Darcy has regularly reminded me the woman has done nothing amiss beside speaking her mind, and although I detest the lady's attitude, I must grudgingly agree with my wife. I can only condemn the woman for gross ignorance, some meanness of opinions, and very distressing vulgarity of manner. The worst suspicion I can lay at the woman's feet is she had a heated argument with the gypsy leader," Darcy confessed.

Edward reasoned, "Which was likely over the illegal selling of Samuel Darcy's stable. Do not forget the lady held responsibility in that transaction."

Darcy sucked in a deep breath. "I have not forgotten; yet, I am unclear on the woman's motives. Was she ignorant of her position's limitations? Mrs. Ridgeway has proclaimed to others that Cousin Samuel had given her permission to act in his stead after his death. Or was the woman's motivation of a devious nature?"

"If not the housekeeper, then to whom do we look?"

"I cannot imagine any of Samuel's footmen to have the guile to perpetuate a crime. Carry one out? Definitely. But to design thefts, to arrange attacks, and to orchestrate murders, I cannot conceive it."

Edward agreed. "What of Barriton?"

"I would put the butler in the same boat as Mrs. Ridgeway," Darcy insisted. "Again, we must wonder whether Barriton has simply been given too much liberty. Without Samuel's oversight, the servants have made their own decisions."

Edward refolded the note and returned it to Darcy's care.

"According to Samuel's journal, Mr. Hotchkiss thought many of Woodvine's employees had seen themselves as above their station. Hotchkiss wrote to my cousin regarding his concerns."

Edward summarized, "No butler. No footmen. No housekeeper. Then who? The Holbrooks? The maids?"

Darcy's lips thinned into a firm line. "I doubt the maids are any more culpable than the footmen, and neither of the Holbrooks has done anything to trigger my suspicion."

Edward noted, "Some of the most nefarious in history have appeared the most innocent."

Darcy ventured cautiously, "What of Franklyn? The scientist is intelligent enough to orchestrate the crimes, and he was at Woodvine in January when Samuel returned to England."

"You think this is about your cousin's treasures?"

Darcy conceded, "How do we know the list Franklyn provided us represents to what Samuel agreed? From the beginning, we have taken the man's word. Think how often Franklyn has not responded to the chaos operating at Woodvine. Is that because he is the distracted scientist we assume or does Franklyn not respond because he has previous knowledge of the events? And we must not forget that Sedgelock and Chetley were among those sent to

Dorset previously by the Society. Is it by guile or coincidence that Franklyn, Sedgelock, and Chetley have reunited at Woodvine?"

"Damn!" Edward expelled breathlessly. "I had never considered the possibility."

Darcy confessed, "Neither had I until this afternoon."

The footman returned with their meals, and they paused until they were alone. With the servant's withdrawal, Edward said, "I hate to admit it, but Franklyn could be our culprit. We have taken the man into our confidence and have given him full rein over your cousin's archaeological finds. Could we have misjudged the Society or the man?"

"Or both?" Darcy asked.

Edward sliced the cutlet. "That possibility makes a great deal of sense. Do you suppose the Earl might have some insights into those who oversee the Society? Father is in London for the Season; the Countess has promised her niece, my cousin, that she would sponsor Miss Topping for the girl's Presentation. I could send a note to London."

Darcy wiped his mouth with the serviette. "It would be to our benefit to have the Earl's opinions. In the meantime, we should become more tight lipped around the others. You, Elizabeth, Cowan, our trusted servants, and I should be the extent of our circle until we know otherwise."

Edward looked up from his meal. "Agreed." He took a sip of his wine. "We will consider our options more carefully and see what develops. Now, what of your second mystery?"

Darcy said equably, "Let us finish our meals. Then we will wrestle with the next item on my list."

"That bad, eh?" Edward asked inexorably.

After a moment, Darcy responded, "I believe I have deciphered Samuel's code, and what I have discovered has me puzzled."

Edward said earnestly, "That spells trouble."

They finished their meal in silence, each man considering the situation in which he found himself. Eventually, Darcy said, "I do not intend to share this information with any of the others."

"Not even Mrs. Darcy?"

Darcy shook his head. "At least, not initially. My wife's dreams are filled with personal horrors. Once I hold a better understanding of what we face, then I will make Elizabeth aware of what I have discovered. In fact, I plan to share the code with Mrs. Darcy. While she is abed, it will prove well for my wife to have something productive to do with her time. If truth be told, Elizabeth has bemoaned the fact that she had to skip several passages in the journals she read previously."

"If you knew how to decipher the code, why did you not share the knowledge with Mrs. Darcy?" Edward inquired.

Darcy chuckled. "I held no memory of my cousin's cryptic ways until I set myself the task of determining Samuel's hidden meaning. As I played with the passage, I looked for patterns. The letters 'e' and 'a' are found in many words. The idea of starting with the words 'the' and 'and' seemed most logical. Many people, as you are aware, will use every third letter of the alphabet as a simple code, but not Samuel."

Finished with the meal, Edward and Darcy moved to the desk, with the colonel seating himself with a look of great vexation. "If you will note," Darcy pointed to the page where he had worked on the code, "I attempted many combinations before one fell into place."

Darcy shifted through the papers, finally choosing one. "When my father passed, Samuel arrived at Pemberley to counsel me in my transition as the estate's master, but he also spent valuable time with Georgiana. I was deep in grief and overwhelmed by my new responsibilities, and poor Georgiana was so young, I knew not how to meet her needs. But Samuel had his ways, and one of Georgie's favorites was an enigmatic treasure map. Samuel would hide a special treat for Georgiana, and my sister would set about to solve the mystery. Her laughter returned because Samuel found time for her childhood fears. If Georgiana had had to depend purely on my efforts, she might never have learned to smile again."

Edward assured, "You would have found a means to bring Georgiana pleasure. You have never neglected your responsibilities to your sister."

Complacently, Darcy said, "I would like to think so, but I have my doubts. Sometimes, I wonder if my father recognized my deficiencies and, therefore, added you to Georgiana's guardianship to safeguard his daughter's future."

Edward said bluntly, "That is ridiculous. Your father simply followed the standard of the day. If something happened to you, I would stand between Georgiana and the more infamous members of both the Darcy and the Fitzwilliam branches of your family."

The truth was, he would never know George Darcy's reasons, and automatically, a crease formed on Darcy's brow. "It is an argument for another time," he said prudently. "For now, we will concentrate on Samuel's coded messages. Something must be fixed on."

Edward accepted Darcy's change of subject, and Darcy reached for a blank sheet of paper. He wrote the six and twenty letters of the alphabet upon the page, carefully spacing them where he might write a number above each.

"Samuel and Georgiana developed a special coding system. They played this game so often my sister became quite adept at deciphering Samuel's puzzles at a glance. If Georgie had come to Dorset with us, Samuel's textual messages would have been easier to interpret."

"Tell me the secret," Edward said with admiration.

"Samuel would choose a date. Perhaps the current date or a birth date or even a date of historical importance. He would provide clues to the date because it was the key to the hidden message. For example, this is one of his later entries. I determined the code by how Samuel recorded the date. Note on all the previous pages, my cousin simply wrote the day and the month: 2 March, 3 March, 4 March, and so forth. On this page, he has written 5 March 1813. It is not noteworthy, and most would consider the change simply a matter of Samuel's rush to record his thoughts for the day; yet, if one thumbs through the journal, the only pages, which record the year, are those for the first day of each calendar month. The change in Samuel's pattern was the clue."

"Amazing," Edward murmured as he perused the journal's many entries.

Darcy, too, had grown more excited. "So the pattern for this page is 5, three for the third month, and then 1, 8, 1, 3. To understand the code, one must assign the numbers from one to six and twenty to the alphabetic equivalents. Count the letters. The fifth one is *E* so it receives a 1. Count three letters, and *H* is assigned a 2. *I* becomes 3; *Q* is 4; *R* is 5, etc. One continues the pattern: 5, 3, 1, 8, 1, and 3. If one lands on a letter already given a numeric value, one skips over the letter and continues on until all letters are assigned a number." He demonstrated by placing a small number above each letter.

Edward drew his own conclusion. "The phrase 'God Save the King' becomes 15, 24, 9 … 18, 26, 25, 1 … 19, 2, 1 … 17, 2, 23, 15." He scratched out the code on the foolscap. "Seems simple enough."

"What makes Samuel's messages difficult to interpret is my cousin never uses the same date for any of them. He has an infinite supply of codes. So, if a person manages to break the code of one passage, he cannot use the same numeric translation for the others. It is really quite ingenious."

The colonel nodded his agreement. "Then tell me something of this passage."

Darcy pulled a straight-backed chair closer. "Samuel writes of meeting an inventor when he traveled to America some years prior. Notice the sketches my cousin makes in the margins."

Edward turned the journal this way and that. "What is it exactly?"

Darcy pointed to the translated passage. "Samuel refers to it as a 'torpedo.'"

"Do you mean like the ones the American, Robert Fulton, attempted to sell the British government back in '05?" Edward flipped the page to examine more closely the other sketches in the late Mr. Darcy's journal. "These images display nothing of what I recall of Fulton purporting. The American's device floated behind his ship, the *Nautilus*. It was to explode upon contact with an enemy vessel. Of course, Fulton's work was more successful than that of Britain's *Turtle* back in 1800. Truthfully, I barely remember those attempts. Only what the newspapers reported. I had not entered the service in 1800. Not until '02. But I recall Father's contempt for the government for wasting money on the project."

Darcy shook his head in denial. "I do not think Cousin Samuel would be interested in a device that could cause mass destruction. He was more of a man of peace. A man who thought of personal comforts and advancements or how a civilization faced life's discord and successes."

"If not a military weapon, then what other use is there for a torpedo?" Edward asked in concern.

"That is part of what I have yet to uncover," Darcy confessed.

Edward continued to study the drawings carefully. "I cannot wrap my mind about these sketches. Each has an additional element not shown in the previous one. I wonder what the late Mr. Darcy had in mind."

Darcy's eyes traced the drawings; he absorbed each detail as if committing it to memory. "There is one passage for which I have not discovered the key," he admitted.

Edward looked up in surprise. "That is the mystery, is it not? You believe something in that particular numeric passage holds the key to quieting the drama found under Woodvine's roof."

Darcy swallowed hard. "In the passage marked for 10 March, Samuel speaks of receiving a copy of the plans for this device from his American friend and of his desire to make a prototype."

Edward's frown lines deepened. "I realize I have not searched Samuel Darcy's quarters, nor have I spent much time examining the contents of the man's formerly secret chamber, but I recall no detailed plans for such a contrivance, nor a model that matches a description similar to these sketches."

Darcy admitted, "When I read Samuel's passages, I searched his quarters again. There is neither among my cousin's belongings; however, I seem to recall shoving aside a parchment which held sketches and measurements when Mrs. Darcy and I first discovered Samuel's chamber. We examined the display cases, and I put the diagrams from my view."

"Was there such a document in Samuel's personal papers in the chamber?"

Darcy shook his head in denial. "Not among the items I removed the night we uncovered the additional entrance. Nor are there such documents among those remaining in the chamber. I looked."

Edward's attention returned to the journal's marginal sketches. "The late Mr. Darcy devoted page after page of his last journal to drawings of this item and to a description of its construction," the colonel reasoned. "Your cousin appears quite obsessed with this torpedo. So much so that it would make little sense for his not to have pursued the making of a model or even a working prototype."

Darcy asked ominously, "I had come to the same conclusion, but if it is as you say, who has Samuel's torpedo and what does he plan to do with it?"

Chapter 18

He and the colonel had decided to mount an extensive search of the house on the following morning. Every room. Every corner. As Darcy slid into the bed beside his wife, he wearily shook his head. There were so many variables he could not control, and the thought of his weakness frustrated Darcy to no end. He despised weakness in any man, and especially in himself.

Elizabeth rolled comfortably into his arms. She kissed his chest, and Darcy smiled for the first time in hours, perhaps all day. "I am here, my Lizzy," he whispered as he gathered her closer. Only in moments such as these did Darcy feel complete. Had he not been a successful and respected gentleman before he had encountered Elizabeth Bennet? Had he not known the praise and admiration of all he had encountered? Then why had it never been enough? Why had he only felt his own greatness whenever he had pleased *his* Elizabeth? Why had God designed this one woman for him alone? Such thoughts often baffled Darcy. "Ah, my love," he said tenderly as he brushed the hair from her eyes. "Without you I am nothing."

Elizabeth twisted a curl of hair from his chest about her finger. "Shush," she said in a throaty whisper. "Sleep."

Darcy kissed her forehead. "As you wish, Mrs. Darcy." He rested his chin on the top of his wife's head. For more than an hour, Darcy listened to the steady breath of life sliding in and out of her chest. He offered a string of prayers to God for sparing Elizabeth's life.

With a deep sigh, Darcy closed his eyes to the world. He would dream of knowing Elizabeth intimately. Of her scent. Her laugh. The desire in her eyes. Darcy would dream of the future.

* * *

"Nothing!" Edward grumbled for the tenth time. They were both covered in dust from crawling along the floor and from climbing upon chairs and ladders to reach the tops of wardrobes and chests. "No torpedo. No plans. Nothing unusual."

"That is what truly is unusual," Darcy declared. "We easily discovered the map showing Mr. Rupp's fields, but we can find no evidence of a copy of the Lemegeton, of the American's plans for some sort of explosive, nor of the model Samuel Darcy had thought to construct. It is as if we were offered the map to pacify us. To make us say, 'I have done my best. It is another's duty to finish what I began.'"

Edward leaned heavily against the doorframe. "To distract us from what is really important."

"Exactly," Darcy said enthusiastically.

Edward strode confidently into the room. "I do not know your mind, Darcy, but playing the defensive is not to my liking; I have spent too many years on the line to turn tail and retreat."

Darcy understood immediately. "We require a plan where we are in charge. Where we determine what is and is not important."

However, before they could set their new resolve into action, a knock at the door interrupted their conversation. "What is it, Barriton?" Darcy asked tersely.

"Mr. Holbrook, Sir. He awaits you in the kitchen. The groom says it is most important that he speak to you," the butler said apologetically.

The colonel said softly, "Holbrook would not lightly make such a request."

Darcy nodded his agreement. "I will go. You may return to your post, Barriton." The butler bowed and made his exit.

Edward asked, "What do you think this turn could mean?"

"Nothing good."

A few moments later, they entered the well-stocked kitchen. The groom bowed as soon as he saw them. "Thank ye, Sir, fer agreeing to see me."

Darcy glanced about the room. Of the busy kitchen staff, only the man's mother remained. Evidently, the elderly cook had sent her assistants on an errand until after her son could speak to Mr. Darcy privately. "I assume the news you have brought me speaks of exigency."

"Aye, Sir." The groom ran his fingers through his thinning hair. His weather-beaten face displayed the man's concern. "I found something unusual in the wooded area close to the lake."

Edward gestured the man to a straight-backed chair. "What were you doing by the lake?"

"Took several of the horses out for some exercise," the groom explained. "Chose the lake because I heard Mr. Darcy's man bemoaning his master's losing the gold buttons from his waistcoat when Mr. Darcy saved Mrs. Darcy's life. Mr. Sheffield be saying them buttons came from the late Mr. George Darcy's favorite jacket. So, I thought I might see if'n I could find them. Mr. Sheffield appeared most concerned for the loss."

Edward observed, "That was kind of you."

Darcy sat across from the groom at the roughly hewn table. "I pray another body has not washed ashore," he said earnestly.

The groom stared at Darcy and shook and his head. "No bodies from the lake, Sir."

Edward asked perceptively, "Bodies elsewhere?"

"Aye, Sir."

Darcy groaned in frustration. "One body? Or more than one victim?"

The groom scrubbed his jaw with the back of his worn gloves. "More than one."

Those words ricocheted through Darcy's bones. "My God!" he said on a raspy exhale. "Counting my cousin, we already have seven."

"I be certain of one, but I be thinking three," Holbrook confessed.

Darcy took a deep steadying breath. His chair scraped against the wood as he pushed away from the table. "What I would not give to have traveled to Derbyshire's lakes rather than to Dorset's."

"It be the Devil's work," the groom lamented. "I never thought to see the day."

The colonel addressed Mrs. Holbrook. "You are not to speak of this to the others."

The woman nodded. "What of Mr. Barriton?"

"Tell the man your son had heard a rumor regarding the two missing horses and the possible return of the gypsies, so we rode over to a neighboring village to determine if the rumor was true," the colonel instructed.

As they waited for Holbrook to saddle two of the horses the groom had exercised earlier in the day, Darcy confided in his cousin, "This is more than I could ever have envisioned. I am uncertain whether I am capable of solving this mystery."

The colonel's countenance revealed his own uncertainty. "We must return to our earlier decision: We must take charge of the investigation instead of permitting it to lead us about by our noses."

A spark of defiance appeared in Darcy's eyes. "I agree. Therefore, let us begin with what we know regarding the victims."

"We are certain two of those from the lake thought to marry a woman they had never met." The colonel ran his fingers through his hair. The ends curled easily, indicating Edward was overdue for a cut.

"Is it possible that Hotchkiss and our unknown victim had similar thoughts?" Darcy mused.

The colonel observed, "As all our victims are males, I suppose it possible. I had not thought so previously; yet, we have no other clues."

Darcy exhaled slowly. "Is our murderer a woman?"

Edward denied the probability. His stance said a mad run of emotions had settled on the colonel's shoulders. "How could a woman have buried a man? Or have moved a body to the lake and weighed it down? Have killed seven others?"

Darcy asked, "What if the lady in question had an admirer who efficiently eliminated his competition?"

"Would the woman not notice? Even though it is difficult to determine the exact date of each death, we can assume they occurred within the last year. How could one woman have so many gentleman callers?"

Darcy watched Holbrook tighten the straps about the first horse. "Could we have more than one woman and only one desperate man?"

"If we consider Mr. Williamson's descriptions of the potential brides, your idea makes sense." The colonel tapped his gloves against his thigh. "Somehow, I do not see either Samuel Darcy or Mr. Hotchkiss as being lovesick swains."

Darcy was quiet for several seconds before he said, "From what we know of Mr. Hotchkiss from Samuel's journal, I would agree with your assumption about the steward, and as to my cousin, he kept a mistress in London, but I have never known him to have a serious relationship. My father once spoke of a woman who Samuel had loved, but she married another, his elder brother, Stewart."

"That explains Samuel Darcy's strong affection for Lady Cynthia."

Darcy confided, "There were rumors of indiscretions, but no one spoke openly of the possibilities of Cynthia's parentage, and Samuel always treated his brother and Perdita Darcy with great reverence. Samuel *married* his work. He spent his life discovering the ancient loves of other people."

Edward nodded to where Holbrook had finished saddling the second horse. "One thing is certain. I plan to examine the countenance of each woman at services tomorrow. Surely there must be a Helen of Troy hiding among the country folk of the shire. I do not understand how I could have not heard of such an angel previously," he teased.

"Nor I," Darcy said ironically. "Would not one expect the news to have reached every corner of England?"

Edward slapped Darcy on the back. "I feel much relieved when your humor returns, Cousin."

"Either laugh or cry. There are no shades of gray at Woodvine. Evil or goodness is all we know."

* * *

A half hour later, they knelt beside a shallow grave. There were no markings, as there had been with Bates' grave, but the evidence remained. "The ground be recently turned," Holbrook noted as he crumbled a clod of dirt in his hand.

"Could a woman dig such a grave?" Darcy asked as his eyes searched the area for any clues to the crimes.

"Aye, Sir." Holbrook stood. "The ground be soft here. So many leaves making it rich. Little sun reaches through these trees; therefore, nothing to dry it out and make the land hard."

The colonel tossed his hat to the side. "Let us see if our suspicions hold true." He reached for a shovel from those they had stacked against a nearby tree.

Darcy tugged his coat from his shoulders. He folded it and placed the cloth beside his cousin's uniform jacket, which was draped across a felled tree. "Shall we have a contest?" he challenged. "If we must dig a grave, allow us to do so with speed."

Edward shook his head in amusement. "You are too soft, Cousin, to win a physical challenge. Married life does that to a man."

Darcy had no idea why he had issued such an asinine test. He certainly did not see the loss of life as a form of entertainment. He was far from being a barbarian. Yet, so many deaths had set his impudicity into action. Darcy doubted his ability to cope with one more mystery or one more body. "You are correct, Colonel. I withdraw my dare. Whoever lies below deserves our respect." With that, Darcy placed his shovel's tip into the soft dirt, rested his booted foot on the edge, and pressed his weight into the effort. Along the outlined gravesite, his cousin did the same.

Within a quarter hour, they had uncovered enough of the body to know Holbrook's instincts had been correct.

"He be wrapped in some sort of blanket," Holbrook noted.

Darcy wiped his brow with his handkerchief. "I care not to look upon death's face again so soon. Leave the blanket in place."

His cousin suggested, "Why do you not start on the site behind the line of ash? Holbrook and I will see to this victim."

Darcy swallowed hard. He shook his head in disbelief before stumbling off toward the second possible gravesite. If not for the shovel, he would have likely tumbled over, head first. His legs suddenly felt old and his footing unsteady. Never in the scope of his understanding had Darcy met so much death and destruction in one place. Certainly, the colonel would have seen much more, but Darcy could not comprehend how so many had lost their lives. Dorset was not the West Indies, nor was it the Continental front. This was a quiet country shire, not a battlefield.

Automatically, he set himself the task of removing the loosely packed dirt of the second grave. Soon Edward joined him.

As his cousin set a shovel full of dirt to the side, he said, "You should know, Darcy, that the blanket has an embroidered emblem in the corner. Holbrook says Samuel Darcy had previously ordered the maids to place three symbols—a triangle, a small square, and two parallel lines—on all the bedclothing being used within Woodvine's walls. The blanket ties the murder to someone in your cousin's employ."

* * *

Darcy comforted Elizabeth as he explained their latest discoveries. Although he and Hannah had forbidden Elizabeth from leaving her quarters, his wife had insisted upon rising from her bed. "I will escort you to services on the morrow," he had said in dutiful conciliatory tones. "But I will not have you rush your recovery. I do not often have the opportunity to tend to my beautiful wife's needs. Do not rob me of the pleasure of playing the role of doting husband. I will use such moments as a reminder of my loving devotion when next we disagree on some minor inconvenience."

Elizabeth chuckled lightly. "We have never disagreed on issues of a minor nature," she said with a rasp. Although she sounded better, Darcy would see that she did not overuse her damaged larynx. Twice during the night, Elizabeth had cried out in remembrance of her ordeal. Both times, Darcy had reassured her with words of endearment and his closeness, and Elizabeth had clung to him until he managed to woo his wife to return to her sleep. "In most instances, we are of a like mind, my husband."

Darcy stroked her arm, while Elizabeth rested her head on his shoulder. "Yet, when we differ," he teased, "I am held accountable; therefore, I will bank your gratitude and use it when next you turn a disdainful eye upon me."

"I shall grant you the use of your manipulations, Mr. Darcy." Elizabeth expelled a quick sigh. "Tell me more of what happened in the woodland," she pleaded.

Darcy had difficulty dismissing his forebodings, and he took the opportunity to express them to the one person who truly had a measure of his personality. "I cannot explain my fears, Elizabeth. And they are truly fears. Other than the gypsy, I have looked upon death eight times in less than a week, and in each case, the victim appears to be an innocent. It is not as if any of these men were an armed enemy. From those we have identified, they were hardworking country gentlemen."

"And?" Elizabeth asked softly. "You feel yourself unequal to it?"

Darcy said tightly, "I have known great grief in the matter. When one buries a loved one, he imagines his family member meets his divine reincarnation, as he was when he left this world. Yet, I am reminded with each of our discoveries how fragile the shell we call a body really is. It disintegrates into nothingness. When I consider my beautiful mother and my distinguished looking father so, it is enough to drive me to distraction." Darcy shivered in disgust.

"It is the person's soul which matters," Elizabeth assured.

Though he would not have owned it, Darcy was profoundly shaken. "If I had held any doubts previously, I would be a believer now."

"Then it is quite beyond the unthinkable?" Elizabeth ventured.

"It is not a sight I would ever wish upon another, and especially never for your eyes. I could not bear for you to know the depth of our vulnerabilities firsthand. I would slay dragons for you, Lizzy. I would protect you from the worst this world offers." He took a deep steadying breath as he lifted her chin. He noted the pale tissue of her cheeks. His wife was, obviously, frightened by his words and his somber tone; yet, even as Darcy looked upon her countenance, Elizabeth braced herself against any signs of weakness. It was a gesture which had once stirred Darcy's soul; however, today, he found it sorrowful. Darcy knew, against hope, Elizabeth would place herself in danger in order to protect him.

As if she read Darcy's thoughts, Elizabeth said defiantly, "I would stand in your stead, Fitzwilliam."

He kissed her tenderly. Darcy found her gloom less impenetrable on any topic than that of his regret at her secession from the life they had begun together. "I know your heart, my love, and I am blessed by your goodness."

"Yet…?" she whispered.

"Yet, you must promise me, Mrs. Darcy, that you will do nothing to endanger the future of Pemberley. Even now, you could be carrying our child." He paused to swallow the weight of responsibility pressing against his chest. "I made a sacred vow to my father that I would secure Pemberley's future. If for any reason I am not with you, you must promise to carry on my trust."

Elizabeth said boldly, "If some unforgivable act takes you from my side, I shall guard any child I may carry. However, if no child exists, I shall follow you into eternity. I should not wish to know this world without you."

"You will not bring shame to the family name by doing yourself harm!" Darcy demanded.

"I shall do nothing to which you would object, my husband," Elizabeth said obediently. However, Darcy knew her stubbornness. His wife would not disgrace either the Bennet family or his with her actions. She would simply give up living to life's fullest.

Darcy gathered her closer. He would not argue with her over this matter, but he would leave her a personal note among his last papers, one which would charge Elizabeth to live a full and happy life. It would be a part of his last testament. Despite her earlier words, Darcy understood that his wife would do his bidding: Elizabeth would honor his last wishes.

* * *

Darcy had returned below stairs, but he had left Elizabeth a task to keep her busy. In her special form of self-indulgence, Elizabeth despised how well he knew her. Darcy had wrapped his request in pretty ribbons—words of how valuable the yet-to-be-deciphered passages from Samuel Darcy's diary were to their solving the house's mystery, but she had recognized her husband's maneuverings. With nothing more to entertain her than a few historical accounts of earlier civilizations, which she had discovered in

Cousin Samuel's library, he feared Elizabeth would soon not only leave her bed, but her quarters, as well.

Darcy had shown her Samuel's convoluted code and had told her the passages he had not interpreted were ones for which he had yet to discover the date combination Samuel Darcy had chosen. Darcy had trusted her to finish his work.

"Hannah, I wonder if I might impose on you to retrieve the late Mr. Darcy's family Bible from the display table in the library?" After reading each of the previous passages carefully, Elizabeth had attempted several combinations, but none had proved true.

Hannah folded Elizabeth's freshly washed linens. "Aye, Ma'am, but I must wait for either Mr. Sheffield or Mr. Fletcher to return to the floor."

Elizabeth placed her pen within its holder. Turning to her maid, she asked suspiciously, "And why must you ignore my orders?"

"It is the Master's wishes, Ma'am. Mr. Darcy be saying I am not to leave you alone in this house. That it be too dangerous," the maid explained. "And truthfully, Mrs. Darcy, I am of a like mind."

Despite her instant disapproval of Darcy's edicts, Elizabeth maintained a rigid calm. "I can understand Mr. Darcy's concerns, but I cannot imagine in the midmorning hours that I should not be safe while you retrieved a book." Elizabeth would speak privately to Darcy over his setting the servants' orders contrary to her nature. "*My husband shall not shield me in a golden cage,*" she promised herself. Hannah appeared conflicted, and Elizabeth abhorred placing her loyal servant in such a situation. "Very well, Hannah, if you must wait, I hold no objection."

Hannah glanced to the door and back to where Elizabeth waited. "It should not take me long. I know of the Bible. I seen it when I assisted Mrs. Jacobs after her accident with the tea service."

Elizabeth said judiciously, "I would not set you against Mr. Darcy, Hannah."

"But it would be to your advantage to have the book," the maid reasoned.

"I know so little of Samuel Darcy's life. I had hoped the late Mr. Darcy recorded important family events in the Bible."

The maid hesitated before saying, "I shall return momentarily." With a quick curtsy, Hannah disappeared into Woodvine's passages.

With a smile of satisfaction, Elizabeth returned to her work. She looked for common phrases and words of similar lengths, comparing the ones Darcy had managed to decipher with the ones in the yet-to-be-translated passages. "Could Cousin Samuel have replicated the code in later passages?" she mused aloud. Looking through several of the entries, Elizabeth played with the possibilities. "If this word is '*about*,'" she mused aloud, "then every 8 would be an '*a*.'"

A quick rap at the open door brought Elizabeth's attention to the figure framed by the light from the window at the end of the hall.

"Mrs. Ridgeway," Elizabeth said cautiously. "You required something?"

The housekeeper gave her a satirical smile. "I thought perhaps you would care for fresh tea." The woman entered the room uninvited. "I am pleased you are recovering so quickly, Mrs. Darcy. I cannot imagine the extent of the ordeal you have experienced."

Elizabeth kept the frown from her lips. "That is kind of you." She aristocratically gestured to the tray Hannah had yet to remove. The thought of how easily she had assumed Darcy's mannerisms both pleased and amused her. She watched the woman place the teapot and fresh cup upon the tray. "Is there anything else, Mrs. Ridgeway?"

The housekeeper took a step in her direction, and Elizabeth immediately stood to block the woman's view of the desk at which she worked. She would not permit the housekeeper any additional information into Darcy's investigation. "I thought it best to inform you I have accepted a position in Mr. Stowbridge's household."

Elizabeth hid her relief. "Several of the servants had apprised Hannah of your decision. I pray it is a more satisfying position."

The woman said readily, "Mr. Samuel treated me well. I hold no ill memories of my service at Woodvine."

She observed the lady archly and after a short pause, Elizabeth said, "Then you hold no regrets. That is best when parting ways."

Mrs. Ridgeway sighed deeply. "I cannot say no regrets, but I have come to terms with my future." An awkward pause filled the room. "Mr. Stowbridge has asked that I join his staff sooner rather than later."

Elizabeth had not expected the woman to take a quick step to the left, and she was a heartbeat behind Mrs. Ridgeway's maneuver; but Elizabeth managed to counter the housekeeper's sudden move. She moistened her lips and took a steadying breath. "I see," she said cautiously. "When shall you leave us?" With a hand behind her, Elizabeth surreptitiously closed Samuel's journal.

The housekeeper hesitated. "I have told the magistrate that I could not leave before this coming Monday."

"In three days time?" Elizabeth did not hide her surprise well.

"Of course, that is if you and Mr. Darcy hold no objection," Mrs. Ridgeway said with some satisfaction. "After all, Saturday next is the first of the month: your deadline for my removal."

Her temper spiked, but Elizabeth quickly masked her thoughts. She straightened her shoulders. She stood tall, but she still felt dwarfed by the housekeeper's majestic presence. "We should be honest, Mrs. Ridgeway. Our relationship began cordially enough, but we hold different opinions on a servant's position within a household. Perhaps the difference comes from the years you spent in America. I understand those in the former colonies have less stringent class structures."

"Perhaps," the woman murmured enigmatically.

Elizabeth continued in her best Mistress of Pemberley voice. "Whatever the cause, our time together has proven ill. It is best if we part ways with as little ceremony as possible. When Mr. Darcy and I quit Woodvine, you shall wish to continue a relationship with those with whom you have served. You may make your proper farewells, but I would caution you to show diplomacy in your leaving. My husband is not normally a vengeful man, but never doubt that he is a man of great influence."

"And Mr. Darcy would turn that influence against a woman attempting to make an honest living?" The housekeeper and Elizabeth exchanged assessing glances.

All of her emotions condensed into this moment. They were done with useless words. Elizabeth managed to ignore the woman's tartness. "Mr. Darcy would do whatever is necessary to maintain the respect accorded his family name."

"I found it, Mrs. Darcy," Hannah called as she bounded into the room. Elizabeth's maid came to a stumbling halt when she saw the housekeeper. Hannah said cautiously, "I pray I did not keep you waiting, Ma'am."

Elizabeth gave her maid a thankful smile. "Mrs. Ridgeway brought me a pot of fresh tea. She was just leaving."

"I see, Ma'am." Hannah moved between Elizabeth and the housekeeper. "I think it best, Ma'am, if you return to your bed. I promised Mr. Darcy that I would not permit you to overextend yourself."

Elizabeth smiled tenderly at her maid. In the short time they had been together, Hannah had learned the art of deflection well. "I would not have my husband cross with you." Elizabeth accepted Hannah's arm about her waist. They moved across the room as one—as if Elizabeth were an invalid.

Hannah glanced to where Mrs. Ridgeway stood watching the interplay. "If there is nothing more, Mrs. Ridgeway, please close the door upon your exit. I shall return the tea tray to the kitchen."

The housekeeper hesitated, but the woman finally bestowed a curt nod upon Hannah and a brief curtsy in Elizabeth's direction. "With your permission, I shall send Mr. Stowbridge a note regarding my arrival."

Elizabeth said without rancor, "Go with God, Mrs. Ridgeway."

"God has never seen fit to guide my steps previously, Mrs. Darcy. He has left me to find my way alone."

Elizabeth scowled. "I have found that those who doubt God in their lives often ignore God's direction, especially if His wishes are contrary to theirs."

A deep red color came immediately to the woman's cheeks. The housekeeper said brusquely, "Again, we shall agree to remain in disagreement, Mrs. Darcy."

When the door closed behind the lady, Elizabeth and Hannah caught each other up in a companionable embrace. "I do not trust that woman," Hannah declared.

The ruse of additional bed rest over, Elizabeth sat at the desk again. "On many levels, Mrs. Ridgeway destroys my best efforts to remain congenial; yet, in reality, the lady has done nothing more than to show poor judgment. She has overstepped her authority, but does that make her evil or just an opportunist?"

Hannah picked up the fresh teapot. "Say what you wish, Mrs. Darcy, but I shall be glad when we leave this place." Hannah marched purposely toward the open window.

"Hannah?" Elizabeth asked with a burst of laughter that instantly irritated her throat. A coughing fit followed before she managed to ask, "What are you about?"

Hannah turned from the window from which she poured the tea to the ground below. "You will not be drinking any tea prepared by that woman's hands, Mrs. Darcy. Not as long as I am alive."

Chapter 19

With no new upheavals, Darcy spent the remainder of the day with the archaeologists and the evening with cards and port and the company of the colonel and Tregonwell's men. Mr. Franklyn had praised the caliber of Samuel's finds and the care with which Darcy's cousin had treated the most delicate discoveries. "We expect it will require another fortnight to catalog everything in your cousin's collection, Mr. Darcy."

Darcy thought it very unlikely he would be at Woodvine as long as another fortnight, but he did not share that information with Franklyn. He would secure the services of Mr. Cowan, or Darcy would send word to Rardin for the earl's man to oversee the collection until its removal to the Society's headquarters. "I am certain Cousin Samuel's excellent eye for detail held no bounds. What little I have seen of the displays was quite impressive."

"Indeed they are," Sedgelock said with admiration.

Darcy said in his own inimitable style, "Do not hesitate to call on me if you require my assistance." He returned the Egyptian bracelet to a display cloth. "I have other pressing responsibilities, but do not doubt that I review the detailed list of Cousin Samuel's treasures that you provide me each evening." Because the Society men held an advantage due to their knowledge of the items displayed in his cousin's "hidden" room, Darcy assured the Society men that he took an active interest in their studies. "Your diligence in your duties is admirable," he added as a balm to the men's egos.

In the evening, after he had assured himself Elizabeth had not overextended her energies or her voice on her first day from her bed, Darcy had remained below stairs, enjoying his cousin's company. "I understand you heard from Cowan," he said as he smoked a cheroot after the meal.

The colonel blew a twisting puff of smoke through his tight lips. The ends of the smoke curled in on themselves. "Arrived about three." Edward inhaled again and attempted a different design in the smoke. "The Runner has asked me to join him in Manchester. Cowan says it is important."

Darcy's countenance hardened. He did not approve of the idea of Edward's withdrawal, even for a few days. As the death toll had risen, Darcy had come to depend heavily on his cousin's reason. "Do you know any of the details of Cowan's task?"

Edward shook his head. "I have no guess as to Cowan's intentions, but what I do know is he requires my influence as a colonel in the King's service, and likely as Matlock's son. Trust me. Cowan is never one to seek another man's assistance unless he holds no other alternative."

"When will you depart?" Darcy conceded the inevitable.

"I thought shortly after services tomorrow. It is not ideal to travel on the Sabbath, but if I avoid the turnpike roads, I could be in Manchester by late Monday," Edward reasoned.

Darcy calculated. "Then you could return to Dorset by Thursday next."

"You do not intend for me to know any rest from the saddle, Cousin." Edward chuckled good-naturedly.

The colonel's jest had caused some smarting of Darcy's principles, but he placed his qualms aside. "You prefer to be of use,"

Darcy countered. "And you are well aware of my dependence on your logical mind and your most excellent company."

"Of course, I will speed my return, and if I am to be delayed, I will send word."

* * *

"Mr. Williamson appears quite pale," Elizabeth observed as Darcy had escorted her to his cousin Samuel's family pew.

He spoke for her ears only. "The curate has such a strict sense of propriety, so much of that true delicacy of spirit, which one seldom meets with nowadays, and, unfortunately, we have given the man more work than is normally within his realm of duties."

Elizabeth looked up at him lovingly. "*We* have done no such thing. The deaths we have uncovered took place long before we arrived in Dorsetshire. If the citizens of this village had kept their houses in order, we would have come and gone by now."

Darcy smiled easily. "I am addicted to your loyalty, my love."

Edward joined them. "The word has spread of the additional gravesites in the church's cemetery," he said quietly.

Darcy nodded to Elizabeth. "Mrs. Darcy refuses any blame on our part," he teased with a bit of left over admiration.

The colonel leaned closer. "Your wife's opinion, Cousin, is the only one which truly matters." A short parley of compliments ensued.

Darcy seated Elizabeth between them. "Do not forget to survey the congregation," Darcy whispered.

"Whatever for?" Elizabeth looked at him inquiringly.

Edward was all honey. "Do not fret yourself, Mrs. Darcy. My cousin only has eyes for his wife." Elizabeth rapped Edward's arm with her fan, while Darcy enjoyed the flush on his wife's cheeks. It had driven away the pasty color across Elizabeth's cheekbones.

"It is true," Darcy readily admitted.

His cousin ignored Darcy's profession of affection for his wife. Instead, Edward explained, "We are looking for a woman."

Elizabeth's eyebrow rose in anticipation. "For you, Colonel?" she asked playfully.

Edward's smile widened. "If only, Mrs. Darcy," he feigned solemnity. In reality, Darcy saw the familiar agreeableness return to his cousin's countenance as he looked upon Elizabeth. As usual, Darcy found a twinge of jealousy resting upon his shoulders. Edward continued as he glanced about those already seated, "We search for any woman who resembles the description Mr. Williamson provided us."

"One woman?" Elizabeth asked curiously.

Edward said, "We had wished for one, but it appears there are multiple ladies of interest in the community."

Elizabeth caught Darcy's eye. "You, Mr. Darcy, have my permission to look upon other women, but only just this once, Sir. Mind you that my confidence would be destroyed if you took too much pleasure in the process."

A crack of laughter escaped Darcy's lips before he could stifle the sound. "You are incomparable, Mrs. Darcy." He brought the back of her gloved hand to his lips.

After the service, Mr. Williamson motioned Darcy away from the others in the congregation. "I thought you should know, Sir, one of the local families has claimed a victim from Mr. Holbrook's wooded find."

"How so?" Darcy asked discreetly. He held his breath as he waited for the clergyman to deliver his latest revelation.

Regina Jeffers

Williamson's eyes scanned the milling churchgoers. "I sent word to the Clarkson family. Old Mr. Clarkson has spent many hours and more money than the family can afford in a search for his eldest son Robert."

Darcy watched Edward lead Elizabeth toward the waiting carriage. "What happened to Robert Clarkson?" he asked privately.

"Young Clarkson had been hiring himself out for day work on the adjoining farms. One day, he departed his family home with word that he had found a multiple-day position. He reportedly planned to be gone a week. When Robert did not return after a sennight, Aron Clarkson set out to visit all the local farms and estates, seeking word of his eldest child's fate." An expression of satisfaction settled on the curate's countenance.

"How long ago did Robert Clarkson go missing?"

"During the Festive Days."

Darcy immediately thought of his time with Elizabeth at Pemberley and how gloriously happy he had been. Whilst he was cozy with his new wife, Robert Clarkson had been lying in a shallow grave upon Samuel Darcy's property. "Some six months," he mused. "How did the elder Mr. Clarkson recognize his son?" Darcy recalled how quickly the body decomposed, and he grieved for a father who had to look upon his eldest son in such a state.

"The elder Clarkson had given his son five pence which Mrs. Clarkson had sewn into the lining of Robert's jacket. He had told Robbie that no matter where he found himself, the boy could come home."

Darcy thanked the curate for his diligence in bringing a resolution to some part of the insanity in which they found themselves. He said honestly, "Your dedication to your congregation is duly noted, Mr. Williamson. I will share my praise with the Bishop when next I see him."

With a heavy heart, Darcy said his farewells to his cousin. "Ride safely," he admonished.

Edward glanced to the window where Darcy knew Elizabeth stood, observing his cousin's departure. The colonel raised his hand in an abbreviated wave. "Your blessings are numerous, Cousin. Do not doubt your wealth."

Darcy's eyes followed his cousin's. As he expected, Elizabeth was turning away. "My life began the day I stepped foot in Hertfordshire."

Edward chuckled as he reached for his horse's reins. "You give the woman too much domain over you. I never thought to see the day, Darcy," the colonel teased.

"Some day I expect to hear you praise your own wife."

Edward shook his head in denial. "I hold misgivings." An unknowingly sad smile turned up his cousin's lips. "Yet, even with my doubts, I have placed my hopes in Mrs. Darcy's most capable hands."

"Then you will know success. Whatever Mrs. Darcy touches turns to gold."

With a brief handshake, the colonel was gone. Darcy returned to the house. He would spend the day proving his love to his wife with a walk about the grounds, a few stolen kisses, perhaps a highly contested game of chess, a few more kisses, a relaxing meal with good conversation, and a night of passion. It would be the perfect end to a very harrowing week.

* * *

Somehow, Sunday foreshadowed the upcoming week. The five days which followed the colonel's departure, had proved productive and lacking in drama. Yet, try as he might to enjoy this long-hoped-for normalcy, Darcy kept waiting for the other shoe to fall.

He had ordered wooden crates constructed to protect Samuel's treasures, and he and the three Antiquarians had transferred the first of the Darcy donations to the crates for shipment to London. As he examined each of the pieces of Samuel's collection, Darcy's enthusiasm grew by leagues. He had always held a deep-seated interest in the past, but this was different. His family—the Darcys—would present England with a grand gift from a man who Darcy revered. People would look upon Samuel's donation with awe. "Perhaps some day I can escort my son into the Society's museum and show him the greatness of his family's name," Darcy had told Elizabeth as they cuddled late into the night. He had regaled his wife with praise for his cousin's intelligence and the magnificence of Samuel's collection.

"Shall the Antiquarians finish before the Earl of Rardin's arrival?" On Tuesday, Darcy had received word of Rardin's and the Countess's intended journey. The Rardins, with three children in tow, were expected by the end of the following week.

Darcy's lips grazed his wife's ear. "Personally, I believe Franklyn, Sedgelock, and Chetley are of the mind of an adventurous boy who has been presented with every toy of his imagination. They admire first one item and then another and another before returning to the original find. Then they start again."

Elizabeth smiled into his chest. Darcy could feel her lips part and her light breath on his skin. A hot palm grazed his hipbone. "You paint a lovely picture, my husband. Shall our children be spoiled so?" Her voice was slowly recovering, and Darcy had thanked God it was so.

"Our children, Elizabeth, will be taught what is right. They will be given good principles, but unlike my parents, we will not leave them to follow those principles in pride and conceit."

After a breathy hesitation, Elizabeth said, "You are too severe on your perceived flaws, Fitzwilliam." Before he could respond, she silenced him with a touch of her fingers to his lips. "Mr. Darcy, we have agreed not to dwell in the past. What I would prefer to hear from your lips is how we shall spoil our children with books and toys and dogs and…"

"Horses," he said into her hair. "Oh, Lizzy, how much I desire the world you describe. Before we departed Derbyshire, Sir Phillip's best filly came to foal, and I thought, if only…"

She kissed his neck and embraced him tighter. "I promise you," she said on a sob. "I promise there shall be other foals, and our children will enjoy having their magnificent father teach them to ride. You will know such pleasures, Fitzwilliam Darcy. You were born to father a gaggle of children."

Darcy chuckled. A teasing glint entered his eyes. "A gaggle?" He paused dramatically as if considering her words. "I shall know contentment with each one with which we are blessed." He kissed the top of her head. "How many is a gaggle exactly?"

Elizabeth crawled up the length of his body. Propped up on one arm, she draped herself across Darcy. "I thought we might create a strong son, one who resembles his very handsome father."

Darcy thoroughly enjoyed these private bantering moments. He would cherish them always. Darcy kissed her long and hard, with a need he could not quench. "Let us create a thoroughly independent daughter, who wraps her father about her small finger," he said as he kissed the column of Elizabeth's neck.

Elizabeth brushed her lips across his palm before guiding Darcy's hand along her hip. "May we begin our journey, Mr. Darcy?" she murmured.

"Oh, my dearest Lizzy…"

* * *

As the woman had declared previously, Mrs. Ridgeway made her exit on Monday. The fact only Mrs. Holbrook had seen the housekeeper off spoke loudly of the lack of respect the woman had engendered in those within the household. From his chamber window, Darcy had observed the interchange between the cook and the former housekeeper. Evidently, Mr. Stowbridge had sent a small coach for the woman. "Quite luxurious for a servant—even an upper one," Mr. Sheffield said derisively from behind Darcy.

In the privacy of his quarters, Darcy permitted Mr. Sheffield latitude in his opinions. After all, Sheffield had been with him since before the passing of Darcy's mother. In fact, it had been Sheffield to whom a distraught boy of sixteen had turned to make sense of losing a beloved parent.

"We both understand the situation the lady has accepted," Darcy said honestly.

"I have never cared for the woman's sharp tongue," Sheffield shared. Something in the man's tone caused Darcy to regard him closely. "Yet, no female should be made into a whore," his valet said bluntly. Darcy gazed at his long-time companion in shock; Sheffield rarely used crude language.

"Perhaps Stowbridge means to make Mrs. Ridgeway an honest woman." Darcy turned away as Stowbridge's servant assisted the housekeeper into the carriage.

Sheffield returned to his duties. "The woman possessed other options. It is not as if Mrs. Darcy turned the lady out without notice."

Darcy silently agreed. When he had learned of Mrs. Ridgeway's plans, Darcy had searched for some sense behind the housekeeper's decision. The woman could have gone to London or one of the more productive centers, such as Bath or Brighton or Liverpool, and easily found employment. Even without a reference, the housekeeper could have pretended a recent arrival from the Americas and have secured a position. Or Mrs. Ridgeway could have accepted Mr. Glover. Darcy was relatively certain the surgeon possessed an affection for the woman. Instead, she had accepted a tenuous situation under the magistrate's roof. "No. Mrs. Darcy would never purposely send any woman into dire straits. My wife has a kind heart."

"She has at that, Sir. The Mistress is of the first order."

* * *

On Wednesday, Darcy had received an unusual message from his cousin, which stated that even his position as Matlock's son had not resolved the situation in which Cowan had placed them. Edward had sent for his brother Viscount Lindale, as well as dispatching a message to the Archbishop. Unfortunately, the colonel had offered no explanation for this unusual twist, only confiding that he and Cowan would return by week's end. "It must be of great importance for the colonel to seek the assistance of his brother," Darcy told Elizabeth as they prepared for bed. "The only higher indignity that Edward would suffer would be if he sought the Earl's assistance."

"Perhaps Mr. Cowan has located Mr. Crescent," Elizabeth ventured.

Darcy's eyebrow rose in curiosity. "What is it about Mr. Crescent that has you searching for Cousin Samuel's valet at every turn?"

Elizabeth slid a gown of satin over her head, and Darcy watched as the silky fabric slid over her full curves. "Mayhap it is the man's name, which I find so fascinating. Perhaps it is that Mr. Crescent was willing to go against his Christian beliefs to prepare your cousin's body for burial. I cannot say for certain as I have never held the man's acquaintance."

"Then I will hope Mr. Cowan has successfully found Samuel's valet and the man is safe," Darcy declared.

From either side of the four-poster, they crawled into the bed. Darcy extinguished the last candle and then moved to embrace his wife. The calm found at Woodvine for the past three days had gone a long way in settling his nerves. Although no resolution to the mystery of the deaths associated with Woodvine Hall had been discovered, Darcy felt strangely optimistic. The house ran more efficiently without Mrs. Ridgeway's influence. Mr. Barriton had assumed several of the housekeeper's duties, and Mrs. Holbrook the others.

Elizabeth had suggested that the earl should consider replacing the cook with one accustomed to more fashionable dishes and promote Mrs. Holbrook to the housekeeper's position. "It seems Mrs. Ridgeway frequently consulted with Mrs. Holbrook regarding household duties. Mrs. Holbrook's mother was a maid-of-all-work for a local family, and the Woodvine cook assisted her parent with the household duties before assuming the position of cook for Samuel Darcy. The late Mr. Holbrook held his son's present position. He brought his young wife to Woodvine some thirty years prior."

Darcy promised to speak to Rardin on Mrs. Holbrook's behalf. He also would speak to the earl about the possibility of Rardin purchasing Darcy's share of the property. Lord Rardin and his countess could then designate Woodvine as an inheritance for one of the minor children, and Darcy could use the funds from the sale as an investment for his own future family.

With the lights extinguished and his wife close, Darcy ventured, "Mrs. Darcy, we came to Dorset with two purposes in mind. However, having to put Samuel's affairs in order, one goal has superseded the other. Unfortunately, in the chaos in which we arrived, I have neglected a promise to see my wife enjoying Dorset's societal pleasures."

As she walked her fingers across Darcy's bare chest, Elizabeth asked playfully. "What did you have in mind, Sir?"

"Sea bathing." Darcy steeled himself for her reaction. He had considered his suggestion for the past several days and had come to the conclusion that it was best for his wife to return to the water soon. If not, she might never swim again.

Elizabeth shoved hard against his chest. "Sea bathing!" She spit the word into the empty room. "Do not ask it of me, Fitzwilliam. I am not certain I can bear even to walk along the shore."

Elizabeth made an anguished, barely audible sound as Darcy sat beside her. He eased his wife to a reclining situation. "Listen to my reason, Lizzy," he said calmly. When his wife did not respond, Darcy continued cautiously. "Although I did not experience what you did, I was there—at the lake—and I knew my own horror. But throughout your ordeal, I thanked God Mr. Bennet had seen fit to teach both you and Mrs. Bingley to swim. If he had not, we might not be sharing this moment."

Darcy could hear her soft sobs. He knew them as tears of healing so he purposely did not rush to shush them away. "Someday, if God wills it, we will have our own children. You have seen the number of lakes on our property. I cannot believe you would wish to spend a lifetime in fear that one of our children had wandered into the waters and was in danger."

She rasped, "You could teach them to swim."

Darcy stroked the hair from her cheeks. "I could, and I will. Yet, that pleasure would be easier if their mother could sanction the skill as necessary, and it would be a pleasurable activity on a hot summer afternoon."

"I promise to encourage them," Elizabeth declared.

"Children know the truth of false platitudes, Lizzy. They will sense your fear and make it their own." He brought her cold fingers to his lips and kissed them tenderly. "Is that what you wish for our children? To know fear in one area is to practice it in another." He felt his wife's body stiffen in disapproval. Darcy offered his final persuasion, "And Heaven forbid any of our children would wander in too far, and have no one to save him but his mother, a woman afraid of going into the water's depths."

"If my child needed me, I would be able to reach him," she said defiantly.

Darcy said, "I am certain you would attempt it, but I would prefer for you to have the confidence to know success. I hold no desire to bury my wife and my child."

Hope laced Elizabeth's tone. "Could we not wait a bit longer?"

Darcy kissed her palm and pressed her hand to his heart. "The longer you delay…"

Her voice caught on a sob. "Mr. Darcy, you do not play fair."

"True, my Lizzy," he said sympathetically. "Yet, as you are a sensible woman, I place the decision in your hands."

Irritation had arrived, and despite the fact Elizabeth had given an angry tug on his chest hair, Darcy smiled. She would concede. "Do not present me that hackneyed speech about a horse throwing a person," she protested.

Darcy rubbed where her anger still stung his chest. "Then I will bow to your wishes and say no more. Just think on it, Lizzy."

* * *

She had complained of every rut in the road, the possibility of rain in a cloudless sky, and the lack of summer flowers on the new bonnet Darcy had purchased for her at the village's millinery and dress shop. However, none of those were at fault, and Elizabeth knew it as truly as did he: His wife questioned her sanity for agreeing to his previous argument. Keeping his eyes on the passing scenery, Darcy judiciously did not comment.

He would have liked to be the one to coax Elizabeth into the water, but Darcy realized his wife must face her worst nightmares without his assistance, so he would leave Elizabeth in Hannah's capable hands. Besides bringing a towel and a dry chemise for her mistress, the maid would take every opportunity to minister to Elizabeth's frayed nerves.

When they debarked close to the shore, Darcy breathed in the clean sea air. He loved the feel of the salt on his cheeks, and the sound of the gulls as they circled overhead. As an untested youth, Darcy had dreamed of living like Defoe's Crusoe on his own small island. The idea was quite impractical, but an unspoken reality for a boy with a very large imagination. Mudeford was no Bath, but there were still many couples promenading along the narrow streets, while vendors hocked meat pies and pastries. "Would you care to walk along the shore, Mrs. Darcy?" he asked politely.

Her mutinous expression spoke volumes. "Do not Mrs. Darcy me," she said tersely. "You brought me to this place," Elizabeth gestured wildly, "to bury my fears. Let me be about it." His wife's choice of the word *bury* did not escape Darcy's notice. The gypsy's death would haunt Elizabeth forever.

Darcy bowed elegantly. There would be no point arguing over something in which they were essentially in agreement. Elizabeth was an intelligent woman. She would see the reason behind his insistence. "As you wish, my dear." He pointed off to the right. "The gentlemen's beach is farther on. I will await you at the carriage. Say in an hour."

"One hour." Elizabeth grumbled and started across the sand, with Hannah on her heels. Darcy smiled at the determination in his wife's steps. She would know success today.

* * *

Knowing she could return to the coach and Darcy would never criticize her decision, Elizabeth counted each step and each breath that accompanied it. The brightly colored bathing machine reminded her of the ribbons and paint she had observed upon the gypsy wagons in the Woodvine clearing. All of which reminded Elizabeth of her gypsy attacker and made this task more difficult than it was. The image of Vandlo Pias's countenance brought her steps up short. Hannah skidded to a stop beside her. "No one would think poorly of you, Mistress, if you decided not to do this," the maid whispered.

"I would," Elizabeth admitted. She waited for the skittish beat of her heart to settle before she replied, "I would question my abilities for the remainder of my days." The wind dried her lips further. "I would give my assailant domain over every breath I take in the future."

Hannah caught Elizabeth's elbow. "Pardon my saying so, Ma'am, but you must have your freedom." The maid gave a little tug, and Elizabeth's feet moved forward. "I have always admired your spirit, Mrs. Darcy, and I shan't have you forfeit it to the likes of Mr. Gry's family."

Despite the terror clutching her chest, Elizabeth chuckled. Her instincts had proved sound when she had asked the young maid from the Lambton inn to join her at Pemberley. "Your loyalty honors me, Hannah."

Wooden huts with tented sides, each painted with the colors of the British flag and emblems of the sovereignty, rested upon large wheels. A huge horse was hitched to the wagon's tongue, with a pixie-sized urchin upon his back.

Hannah approached the owner of one of the smaller machines and made arrangements for Elizabeth to use it. With a deep sigh of resignation, Elizabeth climbed the steps and entered through the draped opening.

The carriage was larger than she expected. A wooden seat ran along each side of the wagon. Hannah assisted Elizabeth from her gown and corset. Dejectedly, Elizabeth sat on the bench to remove her stockings and slippers. "Would you care to join me?" she asked Hannah. A thread of desperation laced her words.

"Oh, no, Ma'am," the maid protested. "It would not be correct as I'm no lady. Besides, you must recognize your demons alone."

"You sound very much like Mr. Darcy," Elizabeth hissed.

The maid stored Elizabeth's clothing in an overhead box. She laughed familiarly. "Himself be correct in this matter."

Elizabeth shooed Hannah from the space. Her maid would wait obediently on the beach until Elizabeth's wagon returned to shore. With a lurch and a shriek she could not stifle, the machine rolled forward across the shale and into the water.

Her white knuckles gripped the bench as she fought to keep her balance. The wagon rolled deeper into the water, and the sea began to seep though the tied-down cloth of the tented side and the slats between the boards.

Elizabeth purposely blew out short *whoot*'s of air to steady her breathing. The wagon made its required turn in the water so the door would face the open sea and her presence would be blocked from prying eyes on the shore by the wagon itself. Finally, the movement ceased.

She released the breath she had held for what seemed forever, but, in reality, had been only several elongated seconds. She waited in the silence. Her stomach pitched. The sea gently slapped the wagon's sides, but Elizabeth did not move. Could not move. Outside the wagon, someone splashed and grunted, but Elizabeth remained on the hard bench. Shivering from the cold water, which splashed about her ankles, she stared at the closed door and wondered how she was to make her way to the stairs and the water on legs as stiff as the concrete pond on Pemberley's land.

Someone called from the other side of the portal, "The umbrella and tent are in place, Ma'am. Do ye require me hep?"

Elizabeth's mind searched for the identity of the voice before settling on the idea that it was the dipper, a woman who would dip her in the cold water. It could be that easy. She could open the door, and the stranger would assist her on the steps and into the water. Then it would be over, and she could return to the shore. Yet, Elizabeth could not permit herself to know such manipulations. Instead, she said, "I shall tend to my own needs. I shall raise the flag when I am prepared to return to shore."

"As ye wish, Ma'am." Then the stranger withdrew.

Elizabeth was alone with her anxiety, and she had yet to move. Swallowing hard, she pushed against the bench and stood in the wagon's center. Still staring at the door, which led to the sea, Elizabeth reached for it, but her feet remained locked in place. The cold water sloshed against her ankles and calves, but, other than her hand, nothing moved. She was caught by her inability to will her legs to freedom. She was just about to reject her attempts and order the wagon to shore when the door was pulled from its closed position to frame her husband's fine form with daylight.

"Fitzwilliam?" her trembling lips formed the word, but no sound filled the air.

Like a guardian angel, he extended his hand to her. "Come, Lizzy. I will protect you." With his dark gaze penetrating hers, Elizabeth felt warmth spread through her veins.

Elizabeth's eyes drifted over his body. Rivulets of water trailed down his chest and arms from where Darcy had brushed his hair from his face. If the gods had seen her husband, they would consider him the male equivalent of Aphrodite rising from the sea foam. He wore nothing but a smile, and suddenly Elizabeth's mouth was dry for another reason. "How did you come to be here?" she rasped.

"You did not think I would abandon you when you most needed my assistance, did you?" he asked soothingly. She shook her head in the negative, but her heart had held such thoughts. She had wondered if Darcy had realized how hard this need to prove her determination really was. "Come, Sweetheart," he coaxed. "I have paid the wagon owner not to bring anyone near, but the man can only stall for so long. I assume you would not wish for another lady to see me dressed thus." Darcy's smile widened as he gestured to his state of undress.

With some feelings of resentment and mortification, Elizabeth rolled her eyes in supplication. "How did I not recognize how incorrigible you truly were, Sir? And here I had thought you the model of propriety." As if they had a mind of their own, her feet, surprisingly, moved toward him. Elizabeth shrugged her shoulders and followed.

Darcy caught her close. "My lack of attire is model propriety for gentlemen when they sea bathe," he teased. Darcy braced her steps as Elizabeth weakly descended toward the dark liquid death.

She gave a restless wave of her trembling hands. "It is cold," she protested weakly.

Darcy assured, "Your body will become accustomed to it." Elizabeth remained unimpressed by Darcy's guarantees. On the last step, her husband turned to her. "Do you trust me?" he demanded.

Elizabeth looked deeply into his eyes. "With my life," she murmured.

Darcy kissed her then. Kissed her long and hard. Kissed her until Elizabeth slumped heavily against his strong body. His tongue claimed hers, and she gave herself up to the passion they shared.

Darcy adjusted his mouth against hers before stepping backward into the water, taking her with him. Warmed by his hands upon her curves, it took Elizabeth's mind several additional seconds before it realized she was under the water. Instantly, she thought to fight him, to free herself from the all-encompassing fear, which coursed through her veins. Yet, her husband held her close. They shared the same breath. Darcy's arms tightened about her as he kicked hard to bring them to the surface.

Elizabeth sputtered and spit as her husband released her; but her instincts took hold, and her feet fluttered to keep her afloat. She spun around to face her husband. "You are beyond irredeemable, Sir," she accused.

Darcy remained near, and she realized he would protect her. With a sheepish grin, he said, "My means may lack finesse, Lizzy, but they obviously proved true."

"I shall never hear the end of this, shall I?" she asked brusquely, but her condemnation had little effect on her husband. "You shall take great pleasure in reminding me of your dominance in this matter."

Darcy caught her about the waist. No one could see them under the umbrella tent, so Elizabeth went willingly into his arms. They kicked together to stay afloat. "I could be persuaded," he said as he lifted her braid across Elizabeth's shoulder, "to forget your weakness in this matter, if we replace it with a more memorable one." He kissed Elizabeth's ear. "I have never known a woman in the water," he said seductively.

Her body reflexively pushed against him. "We were intimate at the lake when we picnicked at Pemberley," she countered. "Beside, I do not care to dwell on the thought of you with another." In the modesty of her nature, Elizabeth immediately felt she had been unreasonable for expecting Darcy to never have known another, but her heart and her mind showed themselves independent of this great irreconcilable difference. She frowned deeply before pushing against his chest to free herself.

Darcy towed her closer to the wagon's steps. "You know I meant no offense. I never knew my heart until you entered my life, Lizzy."

She stepped upon the lowest step. He reached for her, but she avoided his touch. "The moment has passed, Mr. Darcy," she said softly. Elizabeth could not look at him. She was being foolish, but the pain she always experienced when she imagined Darcy enjoying intimacies—the same type of intimacies they shared—with another had taken hold of her heart. "I suspect it is past time for your return to the men's beach. I shall wait five minutes before I raise the flag." She took another step away from him. "I shall meet you at the carriage." Her slight had been most determined.

Darcy reached for her. "Do not do this, Lizzy. You knew I came to our marriage bed having known others. Most men have."

"Yet, you are not most men, Fitzwilliam. You are the man I have married."

Chapter 20

They had gone to bed with the remnants of a silent argument hanging over their heads, and Darcy had regretted how his slip of tongue had ruined a perfectly beautiful day. He had almost wished they had had a "heated discourse"; at least then the words would be out, and he could deal with them. Elizabeth's cold exchanges were far from rude or demanding; in fact, they were almost subservient in nature. All of which frustrated Darcy to no end.

"Elizabeth?" he whispered to the darkened room. She lay on her side facing away from him, and Darcy gritted his teeth to keep from commenting on her act of defiance. "We must resolve this."

Her voice held no emotion. "There is nothing for us two to resolve. I cannot control my abhorrence at considering you with another. I do understand what happened before we met has nothing to do with our future. I am being unreasonable. I do not deny the state of my reaction."

"How long?" he pleaded. "I cannot bear this chasm between us."

A long silence ensued. Finally, she said, "It shall pass, Fitzwilliam, but not tonight. The emotional chaos of the past week has me at wit's end. I shall be my former self soon, but for this night, I can make no such promise. Tonight, I must nurse my bruised ego. I must taste the bile in my mouth. Women are foolishly insensible of their uncommon good fortune."

He had hurt her. Despite every promise Darcy had made to shelter her, it was he who had brought pain to Elizabeth's door.

First, Darcy had infuriated the gypsies, which had likely precipitated Pias's attack, and then he had negligently made a glib comment that had wounded Elizabeth a second time. In his estimation, his words had caused the deeper wound. "I admit that in my youth I was guilty of entering into a life full of spirits and with all the liberal dispositions of an eldest son. However, with my father's sage advice, I soon discovered it was a shameful insensibility. Now, I take a prodigious delight in only one thing—one person. You, Lizzy."

She said stoically, "I possess no doubt of your current affections, my husband. Yet, all your protestations will not serve as a salve to my disapprobation."

Darcy turned on his side facing away from her. "As you wish, Lizzy. Good night."

* * *

Needless to say, he had slept very little, and his disposition had not improved with the light of day. He felt a surge of frustration with the continuing conflict with his wife, and as quickly as he could, Darcy had finished his ablutions and then retreated to Samuel's study to take up the journals again. Over the past few days, Elizabeth had attempted to insert every date recorded in Samuel's Bible to the pattern Darcy had shown her, but to no avail.

He certainly was not in the mood for company, but when Mr. Williamson called, Darcy accepted the curate's interruption with more grace than he felt. "What brings you to Woodvine Hall?" Darcy asked once they were settled and tea had been served.

"I have news of the identity of one of your other victims," the curate said gravely.

Darcy sat forward in the chair. "How is that possible? I thought all had been given a proper burial."

Williamson quickly assured, "Each man has received a proper funeral, but I took precautions, especially regarding those for whom we possessed no identities. I have hired two widows to prepare each body with as much reverence as possible. The condition of each man has created its own issues, but I have approved the purchase of simple clothes for the men's burials and the wrapping of each in blankets to disguise the level of decay present. It would not do for the public to view the changes. Certainly, it would be too much for our female congregation."

Darcy had always thought it ironic that men questioned a woman's sensibilities in regards to attending a funeral, but those same men thought nothing of a woman preparing the body for burial. "Your decision appears most prudent. I assume you have included the cost of the clothing and the women's efforts in your accounting."

Williamson sighed with relief. "I have, Mr. Darcy, and I thank you for supporting my efforts in bringing dignity to these men as a viable expense."

Darcy assured, "I recognize an honest endeavor, Mr. Williamson. Now, tell me what I should know."

Williamson swallowed hard. "Needless to say, word of so many fresh graves in our little parish has spread." Darcy had hoped such tales had not escaped into the community, but he had known it an inevitable reality. He nodded for the curate to continue. "Mr. and Mrs. Lawson from over near Upton called at the curacy this morning. A relative in the neighborhood had sent for the Lawsons after he heard of the deaths. Mr. McGinnis is Mrs. Lawson's younger brother, and he had offered his nephew a place to stay while Felix

Lawson found employment on one of the farms in the area. The younger Lawson left home in February, but he never arrived in Wimborne. Or so the Lawsons believed. The couple had prayed their son had changed his mind and had followed his dream to join the British Navy."

Darcy knew the life of a sailor held its own dangers. "How did the Lawsons identify their son?"

"The clothing, Sir. Mrs. Lawson had given her eldest son a red scarf she had knitted from scraps of wool. It was a bitterly cold day when young Lawson departed. Plus, the youth carried his grand-father's purse."

"Did Felix Lawson have any funds in his possession?"

"None in the man's purse or pockets. Likely, whoever killed him robbed Lawson first," Williamson reasoned.

Darcy could not imagine a common thief or a highwayman committing the crimes. Those who took to the road to procure their living did not stop to dispose of their victims. "Would not our unknown assailant have taken Lawson's purse along with his money? I cannot image a robber taking the time to empty a man's purse and then return the item to his pockets." He mused, "Were there any funds found upon the other victims?"

Williamson's face brightened. He had an inquisitive mind, and Darcy had just placed another piece of the puzzle in the man's lap. "There was no jewelry, other than Mr. Falstad's watch, and no money in the pockets. I have placed each man's belongings in separate boxes if anyone cares to search through them. Of course, I have given the Lawsons their son's personal items, and I plan to post the items we retrieved from Pugh and Falstad to their families once we have a confirmation of their proper directions."

"What of Mr. Bates?"

"Bates came to the area alone and kept much to himself. I will ask about if anyone knows something of the man's family."

Darcy suspected their conversation had come to an end. "I appreciate your efforts, Williamson. You have acted admirably in this matter. If you learn anything more of value, do not hesitate to call upon Woodvine."

With the curate's withdrawal, instead of applying his distracted efforts to his cousin's journals, Darcy turned to Samuel Darcy's household ledgers. He thought it best to have a full accounting of all the expenses he had accepted against the estate. Rardin would expect as much. Darcy recognized Barth Sanderson as an astute estate manager. In addition to the usual expenses for food and staff, Darcy had sanctioned the hiring of Tregonwell's men, the letting of the captain's horses, and the burial expenses of eight men.

He retrieved the pen and ink, but an item of interest among those Samuel had posted caught Darcy's notice. Another notation brought his full attention. Then another. "What is this?" he mumbled as his finger traced the column. "Supplies for some sort of explosive: gunpowder, stand pipe, cork, a funnel, thin metal sheets. Our mysterious torpedo! It appears Samuel meant to make more than one of these devices." He studied his cousin's notations before gathering his gloves from a nearby table. The evidence of what he and the colonel had suspected lay in his cousin's estate books. "Yet, I have seen none of these supplies. I should speak to Mr. Holbrook. See if the groom knows of Samuel's experiments."

* * *

Two hours later, Darcy knew no more than he had when he had started. He and Holbrook had searched the stables, the barn, and two small outbuildings on his cousin's property. Other than a layer of dust on his shoulders and a patina of sweat across his forehead, Darcy had returned to the manor house having gained nothing. "Another trail which leads nowhere," he grumbled. He sat heavily in his cousin's chair. "Why would Samuel make drawings in his journal if he had no intention of recreating some sort of device?" He leaned backward into the chair's cushions and closed his eyes. All he required was to solve one of the house's mysteries, for Darcy was certain if he solved one, the others would follow. "Unravel the threads," he murmured. None of the deaths made sense. "No connections," he declared.

"Fitzwilliam?" his wife's voice was a welcome diversion.

He opened his eyes to discover Elizabeth standing before the desk. How had she entered without his hearing her? Automatically, he smiled. "Yes, my dear?" He stood to circle the desk to capture her hand.

"A message arrived while you were out." Her tone remained uninviting, but Elizabeth's expression had softened. She would forgive him soon, and they would go forward with their relationship.

Darcy grabbed at the opportunity to kiss her fingertips. He held her hand to his heart. "What do you know of it?"

Elizabeth recovered her hand from his grasp to reach into a pocket of the apron she had donned to protect the pale green day dress she wore. "It is from Mr. Drewe. The gentleman wishes to speak to you immediately upon your receiving this note. I took the liberty of sending Mr. Drewe a message that you were out but expected soon."

"Mr. Drewe?" Darcy's frown lines deepened in concentration. "I thought my business with the gentleman at an end." He accepted the note from his wife to read: "I have called upon Mr. Glover. It is of great import that you come to the surgeon's cottage. Drewe."

Elizabeth continued, "I also took the liberty to ask the lower groom to saddle a horse in anticipation of your response to Mr. Drewe's request."

"I should go," he murmured as he reread the note.

Elizabeth nodded curtly. She had latched onto the opportunity not to ignore his pride of duty by saying, "I have considered your remark regarding Samuel's former relationship with Perdita Darcy. I have attempted to use both the date of Perdita's birth, as well as that of her joining to Stewart Darcy. However, I did not use significant dates for Lady Cynthia. I thought to apply those to Samuel's journals."

Darcy gathered the stack of thin journals. The vulnerability, which had been plainly visible in his wife's eyes only moments earlier, had disappeared. Guilt slapped him hard, but Darcy said evenly, "I have made no progress. I was out of doors because there were unusual purchases recorded in Samuel's ledgers. Mr. Holbrook and I searched for the purchased items, but to no avail."

Quite unexpectedly, Elizabeth said, "Fitzwilliam, I want this madness to end. I want to return to the bliss we knew at Pemberley." Her chin rose in that adorable defiance of which he had become so enamored while they shared Charles Bingley's company at Netherfield.

He said honestly, "If you feel that strongly, we will depart tomorrow."

Elizabeth's eyes stung with tears, and she blinked hard to keep them away. "Mr. Cowan and the colonel are due tomorrow. And then there are Sunday services," she protested.

"Then Monday. Whether we have a resolution or not..." Darcy declared.

Elizabeth reminded him, "Samuel Darcy's will is to be read on the seventh."

Darcy reached for her, and his wife came willingly. "Elizabeth, if you wish to leave, we will. I promise."

She buried her head in his chest. Several minutes passed before she sobbed, "I do not know what I want. All I know is that we have been out of sorts with each other since we arrived in Dorset. I despise finding fault with you, and I do not wish to be the reason you do not see these matters through to a conclusion."

"Then we will leave Woodvine. We can remove to Christ-church, or, better yet, to Lyme. You wished to walk along the Cobb, and I promised you a stroll along the shale beach. We can return for Mr. Peiffer's reading of the will. By then, Rardin and Cynthia will have arrived."

Elizabeth's arms came about his waist. "You are the most gener-ous of men."

Darcy lifted a hand to cup her chin. "I am simply a man who places his wife's happiness above all else."

Elizabeth sighed heavily before she released him. His wife closed her eyes and fought for some semblance of control. "You should see to Mr. Drewe's request." Straightening the line of her dress, she continued, "Might we dine in chambers this evening? I do not rel-ish facing the Antiquarians and Captain Tregonwell's men. Being the only lady in the party has become quite distressful."

"Certainly." Darcy kissed her forehead. "I will be pleased for Cynthia's arrival. The Countess's company will do you well."

Elizabeth gathered the journals. "I look forward to holding Lord Rardin's newest heir."

Darcy noted the longing in his wife's eyes. *Soon*, he thought; yet, their future was in God's hands. "It has taken Rardin three attempts to have his son. I imagine the Earl to be quite beside himself."

Elizabeth mused, "Do you happen to know the birthdates for Rardin's two daughters?"

Darcy understood immediately. "I recall both girls were born in the same month. They celebrate before Michaelmas, although I cannot recall the exact dates."

"And their ages?"

"Margaret will be eight in the fall, and Perdita will turn four."

"There is a child named for Samuel's great love?" Elizabeth asked curiously.

Darcy shrugged. "It is a possibility, but do not set your hopes too high, Lizzy."

* * *

Darcy had asked Mr. Holbrook for directions to Glover's cottage. The surgeon's small house sat upon the village's outskirts. Both a well-tended vegetable garden and an exquisite rose garden spoke of the surgeon's many interests, and Darcy was ashamed to admit he had not thought of Glover in that manner. As he dismounted before the main door, Darcy considered how uncharacteristic the very straight rows of the garden were in comparison to the often-disheveled appearance of the village's physician.

"Thank God!" Drewe expelled as he jerked open the door. "You have come at last. I knew not who else to contact."

"My goodness, man." Darcy followed the author into Glover's main foyer. "Has something amiss happened to Mr. Glover?"

Drewe's voice arched in agitation. "Amiss?" The man paced the hall. "*Amiss* does not come close to defining what has happened in this house." Drewe gestured wildly.

Darcy used his best Master of Pemberley voice. "Where is Glover?"

"Dead!" Drewe said in disturbance, as his pacing came to a sudden halt.

There was no avoiding the truth: The impossible had occurred once more. "Where?" Darcy demanded. "Where is the surgeon's body?" Darcy prayed he would not have to unearth yet another corpse. An unconscious hand rose to soothe his furrowed brow.

Drewe pointed toward the back of the house. "Through there!" The man's voice squeaked with edginess.

Darcy pushed past Drewe and trailed his way through the shadowed hallway. Other than the telltale tick of a clock, no other sound could be heard. *The passage of time*, he thought as the possibility of yet another murder loomed. He entered the kitchen and came up short. The surgeon's body sat slumped over a roughly hewn table, almost as if the man had fallen asleep; but nothing moved. No breath seeped in and out of Glover's lungs.

Darcy circled the table, where he might look upon the scene. Glover's head rested in a pool of tea, which slowly dripped from an overturned cup sitting precariously on a saucer's edge.

"What you see is how I found him," Drewe said from the still-open door.

Darcy looked about the well-ordered kitchen. "You did not move him?"

Drewe shuddered violently in denial. "I shook his shoulder. I thought Glover asleep. I had come to see the surgeon about a personal matter, but Glover did not respond to my knock; and neither did the woman the surgeon hires to clean for him. Thinking he might not have heard my entreaty, I called at the kitchen door. That is when I saw him lying over the table. I tried the handle, and when it turned, I let myself in. I discovered Glover just as you see him. I did not know what else to do. There have been so many deaths of late. What if someone accuses me of Glover's death?"

Darcy glanced at Drewe, and his brow creased in consideration of the young poet. He was likely no more than three and twenty, a man with a softer side, who dabbled in poetry, probably modeling himself after Byron and praying for the same success as the English Barony of Byron of Rochdale had achieved with *Childe Harold's Pilgrimage.* "We do not know whether Glover's passing was an accident or something more sinister. I observe no obvious wounds upon the man's body."

Drewe latched onto a string of hope. An expression of genuine relief crossed the young man's countenance. "Could Glover have passed naturally?"

"The stress of the last few weeks," Darcy suggested.

"Of course," Drewe declared. "Why did I not consider such?"

Darcy sighed in exasperation. "First, we will require someone who can identify the cause of death. I know of no other surgeons in the village."

Drewe pounced on the suggestion. "I know of two in Christchurch. I could ride for one."

Darcy nodded his agreement. "I will send for the magistrate, as well as the curate, and I will guarantee no one will touch the body until you return with a man of medical expertise."

Drewe shot a quick glance to Glover's silent repose. Darcy wondered if the man's nature gave the poet permission to believe in ghosts and apparitions. "I will ride with all speed, Mr. Darcy," the young man declared, and then he was gone.

Ironic, Darcy thought. A man frightened by his own shadow. In contrast, when Darcy was Drewe's age, he had held the running of Pemberley and his father's vast holdings for more than a year. Darcy had come into his majority as Pemberley's Master. "Let us see if there are other clues to Mr. Glover's demise."

Darcy gingerly lifted each of Glover's arms to search for wounds and then replaced them in the same position. It seemed important to maintain the scene until the authorities had reviewed the evidence. He next lifted the surgeon's head, but there was no sign of bruising, only a bluing of the lips and the small veins about Glover's nose. He replaced Glover's cheek into the pool of tea. It bothered Darcy to do so, for Glover did not deserve such degradation. Despite the man's affinity for Mrs. Ridgeway, Darcy could not speak ill of the surgeon. Glover had served the community well.

Then he noticed something unusual: Glover had used crumbled bits of beet sugar to sweeten his tea. Darcy had seen many of his tenants do so. The mixture was cheaper than the sugar loaves used in Darcy's kitchens. The spilled tea had left a sweet paste behind on the table's surface. Upon closer inspection, Darcy could make out a few letters scrawled in the paste. He set the teacup aright before he leaned over Glover's body for a closer look. "A," he murmured. "R." He thought the third letter was an "E" or an "S." The sugary paste had obscured the bottom half. The final letter was another "E." Darcy muttered, "A, R, E, E." It made no sense. "A, R, S, E." His first thought was the surgeon had thought himself an *arse*, but the beginning of the fifth letter proved that premise incorrect. "Arsenic," Darcy announced to the empty room. "Someone has given the surgeon arsenic. There is no other explanation," Darcy reasoned aloud. "A man does not commit suicide and then leave a note written in sugar on a table top. It makes little sense."

* * *

A little over an hour later, he stood in the same cramped kitchen, along with Mr. Williamson and Mr. Stowbridge. Other than an exceedingly well-equipped room for a country surgeon to use to treat his patients, they had taken no note of the unusual. The curate and the magistrate had quickly come to the same conclusions as had Darcy: Arsenic was the source of the surgeon's demise. In reality, Williamson had made the logical connections, and Stowbridge had concurred. The magistrate's concentration had been sorely absent, and Darcy held his suspicions as to the right of it. Mr. Stowbridge had brought Mrs. Ridgeway along in his coach.

"Why do you not send the lady home while we deal with this tragedy?" Darcy had suggested diplomatically. "This is no place for a woman."

Stowbridge waved away Darcy's objections. "Mrs. Ridgeway insisted on accompanying me. The lady and Mr. Glover were once dear friends." Darcy regarded the magistrate with scathing incredulity.

Darcy found it telling that Stowbridge had thought it appropriate for Mrs. Ridgeway to be exposed to Glover's death, but the man had thought Elizabeth's "feminine frailties" too pronounced to hear of Samuel Darcy's death. Perhaps it was how Stowbridge thought of women: Elizabeth was a lady to be protected and patronized, whereas Mrs. Ridgeway was the magistrate's property. Although he knew her current residence had been the housekeeper's choice, Darcy experienced a twinge of self-reproach upon the woman's behalf, which he purposely ignored. "The lady could have turned to Mr. Glover," he warned his self-blaming thoughts. "Then perhaps we would not be making arrangements for the surgeon's passing."

Secondly, Darcy could not justify Stowbridge's benevolence in allowing Mrs. Ridgeway to express her grief over Glover's passing. He could understand if Stowbridge had brought the woman along to bolster his own self-importance in the lady's eyes, but if Mrs. Ridgeway was the man's property, he would not normally wish to share her with the memory of Geoffrey Glover.

"In that case, I must insist the lady remain in the drawing room. We must preserve the scene for the surgeon," Darcy declared.

"I will speak to her," Stowbridge assured. The magistrate's smile remained; yet, Darcy held the clear impression that Stowbridge had made a shift from indolent to watchful.

Before they could reexamine the scene for additional clues, Mr. Drewe returned with a young surgeon by the name of Michael Newby. "I cannot believe Mr. Glover is gone," Newby spoke confidentially to Darcy. "I trained under him at a private medical school in the North."

"That is odd," Darcy said as he assisted Newby with Glover's already-stiffening body. "I had thought Mr. Glover had spent a good number of years in this community."

"Oh, he has, Sir. In fact, Mr. Glover is the reason I chose to set up my practice in Dorset. He convinced several in my college to follow him. Mr. Glover was a dynamic instructor." The young surgeon's praise rubbed against Darcy's early opinion of Glover. "I must say, Mr. Darcy, there will be more than a few fellows who will see Glover's passing as a great loss."

Darcy examined Mr. Newby's composure. The man appeared competent in a youthful sort of way. "If it would not be importuning you, I would be obliged if you would consider remaining in Wimborne; at least, until another surgeon can be enticed to the community. You might even use Mr. Glover's quarters. I am certain no one would object."

Newby paused as in contemplation. "There are several more experienced surgeons than I in Christchurch. I might find my calling in a community which possessed a need for my services, and I would be honored to serve in Mr. Glover's stead."

Darcy nodded his approval. "Perhaps a period of transition would serve the good people of Wimborne, as well as you. It appears prudent that such a relationship be mutually acceptable." Darcy knew better than to speak for the villagers, but he observed nothing out of the ordinary in the young surgeon.

Newby swallowed his anticipation. "Such appears logical," he said softly.

Judiciously, Darcy changed the subject. "What do you suspect for the cause of death?"

"That is a simple diagnosis." The surgeon pried Glover's lips apart. "Can you smell the odor coming from Mr. Glover?"

Darcy fought the gagging reflex. He had purposely opened doors and windows and had waited outside for Williamson's and Stowbridge's appearances. "Quite pungent." He could not understand a man who would choose to perform these tasks for a living.

"Your assumption of arsenic is accurate," Newby assured. "The strong smell of garlic. The regurgitated remnants in Glover's throat." The surgeon rested Glover's body against the back of the chair. He lifted Glover's hand. "Notice the change in the color of Mr. Glover's fingernails." After Darcy's quick perusal, Newby returned Glover's hand to the older man's lap. "Likely, Mr. Glover has been receiving small doses of arsenic over several weeks."

"How is that possible? Would not a surgeon recognize the symptoms?" Darcy asked skeptically.

Newby shook his head in the negative. "A bit of arsenic would cause Glover stomach cramps. It might cause him to drink more water. Those are common symptoms, along with a few less savory possibilities." Newby washed his hands in a nearby basin. "The arsenic could be in the water Glover used to make his tea. It is common in the wells in the North."

Darcy pressed, "It appears you have determined the source of Mr. Glover's demise, but not how the surgeon came to have the arsenic in his system."

Newby explained, "If you are asking me if Mr. Glover was murdered, I cannot swear to it. Arsenic caused Mr. Glover's passing; yet, I cannot say in all honesty how he came to have ingested the poison.

Darcy nearly groaned aloud with frustration. "Another unsolved death."

* * *

"How did Mrs. Ridgeway react to Mr. Glover's passing?" Elizabeth asked as they dressed for bed. Darcy sat behind his wife as she brushed her long hair. He preferred it when Elizabeth left her auburn locks free of her nightly braid. It was glorious to have the opportunity to run his fingers through the length of it, to feel the silky strands surrounding her shoulders.

Darcy tore his attention from the auburn strands. "The lady shed what appeared to be genuine tears."

"If that is so, then why did Mrs. Ridgeway choose to accept Mr. Stowbridge's veiled invitation?" She turned on the small padded stool to face Darcy. "Mr. Glover demonstrated an affection for the woman. I am certain the surgeon would have extended a legitimate offer."

Darcy smiled easily at her. His beautiful wife possessed a sentimental heart. "I have thought long on just that question," Darcy assured. "You noted Mr. Glover's overt affection for Mrs. Ridgeway, but did the woman ever display a like interest in Glover?"

Elizabeth paused in concentration. "None I might name," she confessed. "But surely you are not suggesting that Mrs. Ridgeway affects Mr. Stowbridge?"

Darcy shook his head in denial. "Hardly. What I suspect is Mrs. Ridgeway has an inflated opinion of her worth, and the lady thought being a surgeon's wife below her."

Elizabeth's features twisted in disapproval. "What Mr. Glover offered was a sensible choice for a woman with no family of which to speak. I possess no knowledge of Mr. Glover's family, but the surgeon operated as a gentleman." She came to sit beside Darcy, and he thanked his stars his wife's hair remained unbound. Her long locks were a delicious distraction from the worries of late, and Darcy wrapped one curl about his finger. "A surgeon's wife in a small rural community could wield great influence."

"Yet, not as much power as a squire's wife. A husband who is also the local magistrate," Darcy countered.

Elizabeth appeared shocked by the possibility. "Could Mrs. Ridgeway believe that she can bring Mr. Stowbridge to the altar?"

Darcy said sarcastically, "First, the woman would be required to enter the church." He brought a strand of his wife's hair to his nose to sniff the lavender oil she used to scent it. He said abstractedly, "I suspect Mrs. Ridgeway intends to withhold what Mr. Stowbridge most requires of her, using her person as an enticement for his making an honest woman of her."

"What a tangled web you weave, my husband," Elizabeth accused.

He required no reminders of the aggravating control this mystery had over Darcy's life. He slid an arm about her shoulders. "Not everyone marries for love," he said in firm tones. "We are the fortunate ones."

Elizabeth snuggled closer. "We stumbled into the best of worlds."

Darcy chuckled, "*Stumbled* is an appropriate word for our courtship." He set her from him before standing. "I admit needing to know my bed." He stretched his arms to the sides, and then overhead. "Would you mind if I turn in before you?"

"Of course not." Elizabeth immediately caught his hand to lead Darcy to the turned-down bed. "I would very much like to return to Cousin Samuel's journals. I believe I am close to deciphering the passages."

Darcy yawned deeply. "Do not tire yourself with your efforts." He kissed the top of her head before crawling under the sheets. "I would not have you exhaust your energies."

Elizabeth released the ties for the draped four-poster. Before closing the heavy material to block the light, she bent over him, and Darcy accepted the kiss his wife offered. "Rest, my husband," Elizabeth said softly as she brushed a strand of hair from his forehead. "I shall serve as your sentry while you sleep."

Darcy's eyes scanned her lovely countenance and the room's décor before drifting closed. Unfortunately, reality invaded. His eyes shot open to attend to a most unusual object resting on the top of the wardrobe behind where his wife stood. He pushed himself to his elbows. "Please tell me that is not what it appears to be." He nodded to the object.

Elizabeth's eyes followed Darcy's gaze. She laughed lightly. "A gift from one of the maids," she confessed.

"It is a Sheela na gig," Darcy said incredulously. "Why would a Woodvine maid present a fertility symbol to my wife?"

"Oh," Elizabeth said in shocked surprise. "I suppose the carving could certainly represent a woman." His wife giggled self-consciously. "Yet, I believe the wooden symbol is meant to protect us from evil, as are the painted eyes, the witch balls, the overuse of mirrors throughout the house, and the small gorgon figurines."

Darcy collapsed against the pillows and rolled his eyes in exasperation. He brushed his initial thoughts away. "At least, your explanation adds light to what I perceived to be my cousin's sudden vanity in his declining years." He glanced to the wooden symbol again. "Could we not turn the figure to face the wall, Lizzy? I am not certain I care to wake in the night's middle to have that creature staring down at me."

Elizabeth's smile turned up the corners of her mouth, and Darcy knew his wife bit back any condemning remark, which had crossed her mind. "Certainly, Mr. Darcy." She reached for the three-inch carved symbol. "However, I accept no blame if the Sheela na gig's powers are less effective because of your peculiar beliefs." She giggled as she replaced the figure on the wardrobe's top shelf.

Darcy settled deeper into the bedding. "I absolve you of any fault, Wife," he said dutifully.

* * *

The urgent tapping on the door roused Darcy from a deep sleep. Darkness had filled the room, and he was slow to respond. A fog of exhaustion remained, and Darcy groaned as he rolled to his side and swung his legs over the bed's edge. "Yes," he said snappishly as he reached for his shirt. He had actually fallen asleep wearing his breeches, something he had not done since his wedding night.

He staggered from the bed and stubbed his toe against a chair; a curse slipped from Darcy's lips. He tottered toward the sound that had ruined his slumber: a tattoo against the wooden panel.

"Mr. Darcy," came a pleading female voice.

He adjusted himself in the tight fit of the breeches before he jerked open the door to put an end to the annoying racket. From beside him Elizabeth slipped his robe into Darcy's hand.

"Thank God!" Mrs. Holbrook declared when the door opened. One of the cook's hands held a fresh candle while the other was raised to knock again.

"What is amiss?" Darcy demanded. He slipped the robe over his clothes. The sight of the distraught countenance of the manor's cook brought him fully awake. Behind him, he could hear Elizabeth moving efficiently about the room. One light after another invaded the room's darkness.

"Oh, Mr. Darcy!" The cook swayed in place, and Darcy reached to steady her. "You must stop him, Sir."

"Stop whom?" he demanded. The sleep had retreated, but the need for a restorative rest had not, and Darcy's tone held his frustration.

The cook shivered visibly. "Mr. Barriton, Sir. He has taken Mrs. Jacobs."

"Barriton?" Darcy looked to Elizabeth for an explanation, but his wife's shrug said she was as badly informed as he. "What has Mr. Barriton to do with Mrs. Jacobs?"

As if the woman expected someone to stop her from carrying her tale to the manor's master, the cook looked off toward the servants' stairs. "She meant no harm," Mrs. Holbrook explained. "Mrs. Jacobs be of the old sect, those who believe in fairies and familiars and omens. There be no mischief in a few figurines scattered about the house. The late Mr. Darcy housed enough bits of ancient superstition on every surface of this house—what be the difference if there be a few English ones mixed in?"

Darcy considered how England had imported from Germanic peoples many of the superstitions the cook described as English, but rather than comment, he repeated his earlier request. "Tell me about Barriton."

The woman's weight sagged heavily against the doorframe. She sighed deeply. "Millie Jacobs thought Mrs. Ridgeway be a witch, so Millie be hiding her witch bottles about the house to prevent the housekeeper from doing her evil."

Darcy glanced knowingly at his wife. They had held similar qualms regarding the housekeeper. Clarifying what Mrs. Holbrook was attempting to explain, he asked, "As Mrs. Ridgeway has taken herself off to Stowe Hall, what business does Mr. Barriton have in this madness? Did Barriton think to punish the maid for bringing her superstitions into this household?"

Mrs. Holbrook paled. "Oh, aye, Sir, but not as ye think. Mrs. Ridgeway not be practicing witchcraft under Mr. Darcy's roof, but Mr. Barriton has. He has taken Millie to the stones, Mr. Darcy. I fear he means to kill her."

Chapter 21

They had left their horses in the wooded area and had approached the field on foot. In addition to Holbrook, Darcy had recruited Mr. McKye, for the man was well versed in the local traditions, and Mr. Castle, who, according to McKye, had been the best shot in Tregonwell's former command. Castle was one of the men Darcy had hired as reinforcements. Over his wife's objections, Darcy had brought several guns with him. He would not use them unless necessary, but he had argued, "I know not what I may encounter, Elizabeth. Mrs. Holbrook's concerns were real, and I would be sore to ignore the strange world into which we have tumbled."

His wife had begged to accompany him, but Darcy would have none of it. "It is too dangerous," he had insisted. "I will not permit it, Elizabeth, so place your arguments on the shelf. I will not be swayed." He had quickly dressed to join the others.

"I shall not sleep a wink until you return." Elizabeth had followed him about the room as if she were his shadow. "Promise that you shall know care, Fitzwilliam."

Darcy gathered her quickly in his embrace. "On our wedding day, I made a sacred vow to see you through a long life and to provide you a family. I have not met those obligations. I will return, Elizabeth." Darcy kissed her tenderly.

"I swear, Fitzwilliam…" she began with tears in her eyes.

"I know, Lizzy," Darcy said softly. He caressed her cheek. "I give you my word I will do nothing foolish." With that, he had left her with tears streaming down her cheeks.

"There!" McKye whispered close to Darcy's ear. "See the fire."

Darcy's mind had not understood the strange glow on the horizon until the man had brought it to his attention. "A fire?" His voice held a bit of awe.

"Aye, Sir. I have seen it before, when my family lived near Edinburgh. Part of the Beltane festival. To mark the blossoming of spring. It is a beautiful celebration of life," McKye explained. "The relighting of the world from the Need Fire. The purifying of the herd." The man nodded toward the lighted field. "That be the way of my home, but what we are likely to find beyond those stones will bear little resemblance to what I have known." Darcy leaned closer to hear the man's tale. "There are rumors of the Wita calling upon the strength of the Celtic god Cernunnos to bring destruction to their neighbors. We know much of these tales, but we refuse to recognize the roots of such paganism within our souls. Have you not loved the stories of Sir Gawain and of Lincolnshire's Robin, Mr. Darcy?"

"Of course," Darcy murmured softly.

"Yet, you never considered how closely related are the tales of Shakespeare's Robin Goodfellow to those of Viridios or Odin. The stories are connected, Mr. Darcy," McKye said honestly. The former fisherman had the soul of a scholar.

Darcy pressed, "I am familiar with the stories, McKye, but I am ignorant of how those tales affect what is occurring in Mr. Rupp's field."

The man continued, "Beltane is a celebration of fertility and of life's cycle: of birth, death, and rebirth. The Celts honored the cycle with offerings and sacrifices." He nodded toward the brightly glowing spectacle.

As if he wished to hold onto his sanity, Darcy curled his fingers into a tight fist. "Could Mrs. Jacobs be a sacrifice?" His voice sounded strangely detached. The grim visage of a funeral pyre rose in his mind. Darcy rose on unsteady legs to stare off at the strangely lit horizon.

Beside him, McKye ran his fingers through his blond hair. "There be no way of knowing until we enter that circle, Sir."

Darcy's heart lurched. The ramifications of their words lay heavy on his soul. "We must make haste." Without considering how they would survive this encounter, he was on a run. The others followed closely. They crossed the road and easily vaulted the fence's stile, which marked Rupp's land. As he and Holbrook knew the path, they took the lead. The field had been recently tilled and planted, and the way was rough going.

When he and his cousin and Elizabeth had viewed the fields a week past, they had stayed to the lanes between each of Rupp's straight rows, but tonight Darcy led a diagonal charge across the field. Reaching the three trees which had marked Mr. Hotchkiss's grave, Darcy stopped to assess the situation. McKye crouched beside him, with Holbrook and Castle taking cover behind a nearby hedgerow.

"What do you think?" he asked softly. They looked upon a sight Darcy had never thought to see. He strained to discern what occurred in the confines of the oddly shaped circle defined by the heavy stones in the field's center.

Several revelers carried torches as they wove in and out among a dozen others. Most swayed from side to side and twitched to a low hum that filled the air. Two small bonfires highlighted the movements of those milling about the circle.

In his youth, when Darcy had first read the witches' scenes from Shakespeare's *Macbeth*, he had envisioned creatures of the night, and when he had told Georgiana tales of wee folks and ogres and wicked witches, Darcy had enjoyed the excitement the tales engendered. However, he possessed no point of reference in reality for what to expect when he looked upon those gathered in Rupp's field.

McKye leaned closer. "Mr. Rupp has turned a blind eye to the comings and goings of those in the field. I would wager Rupp has a stuffed bullock's heart studded with thorns and nails hidden up his chimney."

"The man appeared ignorant of our purpose when the colonel and I viewed the fields previously," Darcy protested.

McKye countered, "If Rupp had tilled the fields beforehand, how had the man overlooked Mr. Hotchkiss's grave? Surely, Rupp knows every inch of his land as well as he knows all the freckles peppering his arms. More likely, Rupp and his missus fear the authority of the witches. Many believe in the power of those who dance with the Devil to make a woman barren or to deliver storms that will destroy a man's crops."

Darcy swallowed his fears. "Do you recognize any of those in the group?" It was a foolish question, but Darcy's sensibilities lay raw.

McKye denied knowledge of any in the fairy circle.

As if he were an apparition of the night—a figure forged from fire—an undefined shape stepped through a narrow path between the two fires.

Holbrook moved up behind Darcy. "I think it best if I take Mr. Castle to the other side where he might observe the entire show."

Darcy nodded his agreement. "Tell Castle to be prepared for all contingencies." He returned his attentions to the circle. "What should we do, McKye?" he asked, feeling quite disjointed.

The man kept his eyes on the merry-making group. "We watch," McKye said definitively. "And learn." He braced himself against the tree and hunkered down for a better view. "If those in the circle have nefarious plans, they be showing themselves soon. It be nigh onto three of the clock. Those who dance beyond will leave before the dawn brings recognition."

Darcy settled nervously beside the man. He was characteristically a patient person, but he seriously wished to be anywhere but in this field. Darcy watched as the hooded figure, who had cleverly "appeared" from the fire, circled each of those in the ring, wrapping the revelers who swayed to the growing rhythm in leafy vines. Darcy assumed the hooded figure to be a man for he was taller and broader of shoulder than many of the others, and if what Mrs. Holbrook had relayed held true, the hooded apparition was none other than Mr. Barriton. The question remaining was whether Mrs. Jacobs was among the revelers, or had the maid met another fate?

For a quarter hour, they watched in silence. Darcy half expected to see the revelers break into some sort of Bacchanalian rout. While on his Grand Tour, he had studied Italian folktales of how the goddess Diana had seduced her brother Lucifer, and how their daughter Aradia had taught the world magic and had given witches and gypsies special spells and charms. "Gypsies?" he mouthed the word. "Could the man in the hood be Gry, and not Barriton?" he wondered. Darcy peered closer—looking for any distinctive movements which would identify the group's leader. Yet, before he could draw a conclusion, the situation changed drastically.

McKye straightened as the "hum" died. The flesh at the back of Darcy's neck tingled as he stood and prepared to approach the group. He palmed a pistol in one hand and an unsheathed knife in another.

"It is time," the hooded figure announced in a smoothly masculine voice of authority. Immediately, those who had been milling about the open area ceased their dance of freedom and gathered about their leader.

The cloaked figure raised his arms, and silence fell upon those assembled before him. Darcy caught McKye's eye, and although Darcy's nerves pleaded for action, the guard motioned for Darcy's tolerance. They would have difficulty catching anyone in the darkness, and other than a possible trespassing violation, the people gathered before the bonfire had committed no crime. And if McKye was correct and the group had intimidated Rupp, Darcy doubted the farmer would press charges against these intruders. With that assumption in mind, Darcy reluctantly nodded his agreement.

"Who has spoken against us?" the hooded man demanded of the group.

Those within the circle parted and a woman wearing a black cloak was ushered forward by two younger women in deep-green gowns. "This one," an attractive blonde, who Darcy recognized as the daughter of one of the shopkeepers, declared aloud.

The girl stripped the cloak from the shoulders of the accused to reveal Mrs. Jacobs. *So, Mrs. Holbrook had the right of it*, he thought as he waited for McKye's signal. Although decidedly outnumbered, the elderly maid did not cower. Instead, she raised her chin and straightened her shoulders. The woman began to recite in a surprisingly clear voice from the Book of Common Prayer, "Our Father, which art in heaven, Hallowed be thy name."

Those around Mrs. Jacobs struck out at her and hissed their threats, but the elderly maid did not recoil. She shouted above the melee, "Thy Kingdom come. Thy will be done in Earth as it is in Heaven." Those about the woman increased their efforts to silence Mrs. Jacobs; yet, their efforts knew little success. First, one blow and then another landed about the woman's head, and the maid dropped her chin, but not her voice. "Forgive us our trespasses, as we forgive them that trespass against us. And lead us not into temptation, but deliver us from evil."

Darcy started forward to stop the abuse, but McKye stayed his step. "One moment more," McKye cautioned.

"Silence!" the hooded figure's voice boomed from a place of prominence before the bonfire. Those gathered about the maid ceased their caterwauling, and Mrs. Jacobs staggered to a swaying halt. "Announce the charges," the man ordered as he removed the hood. It was the distorted countenance of Woodvine's butler, which looked out over those gathered before him. *Grotesque*, thought Darcy. Painted green and marked with belladonna to exaggerate the man's wrinkly eyes. It was as McKye had said. The look of Cernunnos showed forth in Dorset's darkness. It would be enough to frighten even the bravest of men, but the elderly maid did not react. Darcy could see the woman's lips moving, and he imagined Mrs. Jacobs continued her prayers to ward off the impending evil.

"A direct attack on all we hold dear," the shopkeeper's daughter charged.

Barriton concurred, "I bear witness to the truth." The man's voice spoke with confidence. "To those who speak out against us there is but one possible punishment."

McKye's fingers released his grip on Darcy's arm. "Move forward quietly," he ordered.

"Death!" was the instant chant to Barriton's assertion. "Death! Death!" The group's voices combined.

"Death by fire in celebration of Beltane," Barriton declared as a hum of discontent lifted the flames higher. "*Bel* means fire," he announced. "And the fire demands a death and a rebirth."

The butler caught the elderly maid in a rough grasp to shove the woman toward the fire just as Darcy and McKye stepped into the ring of light. "The lady comes with me," Darcy shouted about the melee. Everything came to a complete halt. Even the fire seemed to retreat into itself.

"Your domain holds no preference in this most sacred place," Barriton declared boldly.

Holbrook and Castle joined Darcy and McKye within the light. Each man held a gun pointed upon those who now huddled together. Surprisingly, neither the butler nor the shopkeeper's daughter retreated. They held Mrs. Jacobs' arms pinned behind the woman's back.

McKye said, "We wish no trouble; yet, we cannot permit you to take vengeance on this woman."

The pretty blonde's countenance hardened into tight lines, which reflected the harshness of the slowly dying fire. "You will know my vengeance, Sir," she said ominously.

"You only have province if I permit it," McKye said simply. "And I have seen evils worse than any you can concoct. I am not easily persuaded."

Darcy motioned Holbrook to the other side of the circle. "No one is to leave the ring of light. Use your weapon if necessary."

"Aye, Sir." The groom assumed a place of prominence in the shadows surrounding the odd-shaped ring formed by the large stones.

Darcy ordered, "If you wish to return to your homes when this madness is over, sit quietly upon the ground where you are."

McKye cautioned, "Make no false moves. Mr. Castle is known for his accuracy with a variety of weapons." Darcy noted how the marksman shifted to raise the gun higher.

Barriton, meanwhile, tightened his hold on Mrs. Jacobs, placing the woman between himself and Mr. Castle.

A sharp breath rushed past his lips. "You must release Mrs. Jacobs," Darcy insisted.

Barriton shook his head in a sharp denial. The butler replied in a clipped manner, "Releasing Mrs. Jacobs earns me nothing. I die either way."

Darcy glanced about the circle. The fire was dying, but the sky showed signs of an early dawn. The blackness had receded to a dark gray. "We can wait as long as necessary," he warned. "Would you deny the others the right to return to their homes before they are discovered? If the approaching dawn brings them recognition, they each will know censure and punishment. And what of their families? Of those innocent in this matter?" He gestured to the dozen figures huddled together in a tight knot before him. Only Barriton, Mrs. Jacobs, and the blonde boldly stood together in defiance.

"You shall pay for your insolence," the young woman threatened.

Darcy's eyebrow shot high enough to meet the hair framing his brow. "What will you do to me?" he taunted. "A charm or a magic spell?" He desperately attempted to maintain his composure. "I make my own magic through the knowledge of a forgiving God, through hard work, and with the love of an excellent woman."

The woman spit on the ground at Darcy's feet. "That is my opinion of your God and your magic," she snarled.

Darcy would not argue with a spiteful female. Instead, he increased his efforts to reason with Barriton. He took a half step forward. "What is Mrs. Jacobs' offense?" He stifled the blonde's likely reply with a dismissive gesture.

Barriton said bitterly, "You have seen the lady's work: miniature gorgons, witch's balls and bottles, and painted eyes." Something in the butler's tone had Darcy regarding the man with a probing gaze.

Darcy spoke to the elderly maid. "These talismans were at your hands?"

"Aye, Sir. I do my best to protect those at Woodvine, including yer wife," she admitted.

Barriton gave the woman a hearty shake. "Mrs. Jacobs thinks herself a witch hunter." The butler's voice held pure contempt.

This situation had proved itself another in which Darcy recognized his vulnerability. Since entering Dorset, his sense of right and wrong had remained off kilter. Forcing the thought away, Darcy's hands flexed at his side. He did not acknowledge the butler's assertion; instead, he asked Barriton to clarify what the man hoped to accomplish by holding Mrs. Jacobs hostage. "Surely, you recognize the futility of this stance. You have no weapons and are surrounded by those who do. You have been seen by four who would testify against you if you managed to briefly escape."

Barriton reached into his robe and brought forth a ceremonial knife. "You err, Mr. Darcy. I do have the means to protect myself." The man placed the point against Mrs. Jacobs' throat. "Or to take another's life."

Darcy's heart flinched with horror. A savage smile twisted his lips. He could not permit Barriton to harm the elderly maid. The woman was blameless in this madness. Darcy softened his voice. "The maid is insignificant in these circumstances. Mrs. Jacobs's superstitious nature is no cause for murder. Release the woman. As it stands, you will be prosecuted as a vagrant, and know a fine and some time in gaol, but if you hurt Mrs. Jacobs, you will hang." The butler's eyes darted to and fro in a frenzied manner, and Darcy suspected this would not end well.

Barriton asked with contempt, "Will you forget Mr. Hotchkiss, Mr. Darcy? I think not." Darcy had not put Hotchkiss's death from his mind; yet, he had hoped to negotiate with the butler for the release of the maid before facing the issue of the Woodvine steward's death. "I have no options before me," Barriton declared.

Darcy edged closer. With a slight flick of his wrist, he motioned the others to remain alert. He carefully considered his words. "These are not incurable faults. I have no proof of Hotchkiss's demise. Unless you speak otherwise, the steward's death cannot be laid at your feet." He stepped boldly into the realm of the butler's reach.

Barriton laughed without humor. "I chose my path years ago. I cannot look back with regret." With those words, the butler took a retreating step toward the fire. He dragged Mrs. Jacobs with him, and Darcy hesitated long enough to give Barriton the advantage. Deceptively quick for a man of his build, Barriton lifted the maid's fragile form from the ground and flung the woman into the fire.

"McKye!" Darcy yelled to the man who had already hurtled several of those on the ground to charge into the midst of the fire. A blood-chilling scream said the woman suffered, but Darcy would not turn his head to view McKye's success or failure. Instead, he slowly stalked the butler.

The man's boot searched for solid footing before he took each retreating step. Darcy watched carefully as the butler brandished the jewel-encrusted knife. He towered over the man by some four inches, but that fact provided no comfort. Barriton's demeanor spoke of one who acted in desperation, like a rabid animal; therefore, Darcy practiced caution.

He could have simply shot the butler, but Darcy suspected the man held answers to so many of Woodvine's mysteries that he held hopes of apprehending the man alive. "Do not make matters worse, Barriton," he warned. From his eye's corner he could see McKye rolling the body of Mrs. Jacobs in the dirt to smother the fire. He heard Holbrook order the dozen or so women who sat upon the ground to remain where they were.

The butler maintained his steady retreat, and they were soon covered by the shadows. "You realize I cannot permit you to simply walk away," Darcy declared.

Barriton snarled, "And I cannot permit you to place me in custody."

Darcy steeled his resolve. He brought the gun into position. He had hunted grouse and rabbits, had fished, had even killed the occasional fox, but Darcy had never shot a man. He wondered how many times Edward had looked into another's countenance and pulled the trigger. Darcy swallowed hard against the roll of his stomach. Determinedly, he lifted his hand and was surprised to observe that it did not shake. "I will ask you once more to surrender."

Yet, before he could act, someone hit him from behind, a mighty blow across his shoulder blades. Darcy pitched forward and staggered to keep his balance. "Bloody hell..." he growled through tightly clenched teeth. Bent over and gasping for breath, Darcy glanced up to see a tree branch. "Run, Jacks," his attacker yelled to the butler, and Darcy was sore to react before the man's footsteps announced his escape.

Darcy dropped to his knees He shook his head in desperate denial as his vision blurred. From behind him, those in pursuit breezed past him. The woman who had struck him darted around him, but Darcy had the forethought to catch the female's long flowing robe and to give it a hard yank, pulling her backwards to land less than a foot from where he staggered to his feet. "I am a gentleman," he growled, "but if you move one hair, I will cuff you."

Holbrook was at his side. "Mrs. Jacobs has several burns, but she will survive." The groom braced Darcy to a steadier stance. "McKye and Castle have gone after Barriton."

"Can you manage this alone?" Darcy was anxious to see an end to this badly staged burlesque.

"Aye, Sir."

"Beware of this one," he cautioned as the blonde pulled herself to a seated position.

Holbrook grinned wryly. "Like taming a headstrong horse, Sir."

Darcy nodded his gratitude before trailing after the sound of shouting and hurried steps. He slowed his pace when he overtook Tregonwell's men. "To the left," McKye whispered. Darcy's breathing had not fully recovered, but he managed to follow McKye's command and move off to the left to circle the trees where they had taken cover earlier. McKye took the right and Castle the middle. Both men moved stealthily through the vegetation to emerge on the other side, and Darcy mimicked their moves.

He stepped gingerly over a fallen branch from the tallest of the three trees, only to be taken down by an uncloaked Barriton lying on the ground. Tumbling forward, Darcy encountered a fist to the side of his head that snapped his jaw to the right before he smacked the hard earth face first. Rolling to his knees, he lunged at the man, who had scrambled to his feet. His momentum carried them both backward, where Darcy pressed Barriton over the rotted wood. The punches and jabs came short and hard. He had often wrestled with Edward as a youth, but Darcy had only once used his knuckles on a man. Well, actually twice. But both times it had been the same man: George Wickham. Once when they were at university and Wickham had openly defamed Darcy's father, the man who had treated Wickham as a beloved godson. The second time he had used his fists on the man was when Darcy had interrupted Mr. Wickham's attempted elopement with Georgiana.

Now, he rolled and kicked and punched a man for whom he held no rancor, just disgust. He landed an uppercut on the point of Barriton's chin and prepared to strike again, but the wily butler had his own designs. Barriton's fingers caught the handle of the once-forgotten ceremonial knife, and the butler thrust upward to catch Darcy across his ribs. The knife cut through his waistcoat and shirt and left a three-inch gash across Darcy's side.

Instinctively, Darcy reached for the wound. In doing so, he released his hold on Barriton's lapels. The butler bolted away, and then a shot rang out. "No!" Darcy groaned as he staggered to his feet.

The butler lay face down on the grassy patch under the trees. The moon had lost its luster, but the sky held streaks of the morning sun. Bent over, Darcy half crawled to where Barriton rested; he rolled the butler to his back. "Barriton, Barriton," he pleaded. "Speak to me."

Slowly, the man opened his eyes. "Better than Jack Ketch," he gritted through clenched teeth.

Darcy leaned closer. "Tell me the truth. Did you kill Hotchkiss, Bates, and the others?"

Barriton gurgled, and a stream of blood dribbled from the corner of the man's mouth. McKye and Castle knelt beside him, but

Darcy did not turn his head. He needed to hear the butler's final words. Barriton's eyes rolled Heavenward. He said through tight lips, "Yes, Hotchkiss discovered my secret. He followed me here."

Darcy pressed his hand to his wound, but the blood seeped through his fingers. Ignoring the pain, he insisted, "And Bieder Bates? And Clarkson? And Falstad?"

"That is where you err." The butler gasped for air. "Only Hotchkiss." Barriton's voice was barely a whisper. "There is more than one evil at Woodvine."

Chapter 22

"His answers only leave more questions," Darcy said in frustration as the butler released his last breath in a shuddering exhale.

Castle's face paled. "I meant only to still his steps. I feared if he escaped that Barriton would attack you again." Darcy knew real regret: Despite Mr. Barriton's past crimes, Darcy had seen enough of death.

"We should see to the others," he said as he stood.

McKye caught Darcy when he stumbled forward. "You are hurt, Sir?"

Darcy murmured, "A flesh wound."

Castle braced Darcy's right shoulder and McKye the left. Tregonwell's men half dragged him to where the fire would provide them additional light. "Permit me to have a look," McKye said as the men lowered Darcy to the ground. McKye ripped open Darcy's waistcoat and tugged his shirt from his breeches. Then gently the man probed the area with his fingertips. "The wound does not appear deep, but it is bleeding quite heavily." McKye pulled a small knife from an inside pocket. "Permit me to cut a strip from your shirt to bind the wound. Then I will send for the magistrate. With Glover's passing, there is no surgeon in the area. I will return you to the care of Mrs. Darcy." McKye tore several strips from the bottom of Darcy's fine lawn shirt. He placed a clean linen against the wound before wrapping the strips about Darcy's waist, and tied them tightly in place."

As he sucked in a sharp breath, Darcy said, "Mr. Newby remains in Mr. Glover's stead. Mrs. Jacobs will require his care. Send Holbrook for Newby and Stowbridge." From where he rested against one of the large stones, which had brought him to this field, Darcy surveyed the circle. Women wept and clung to each other in misery. Holbrook and Castle secured the blonde by tying her hands behind the girl's back, and Mrs. Jacobs rested on the ground. One of the dark capes served as a blanket. She moaned in pain. "So much mayhem," he said sagely.

"At least, you have an answer to Mr. Hotchkiss's death."

Darcy's gaze remained on the oddly expressed scene. "Yet, I fear it will not be enough."

* * *

Stowbridge arrived before the surgeon. The magistrate had brought several of his servants with him to take possession of the prisoners. "Hell of a story," Stowbridge said as he sat upon the ground beside Darcy. The man wore no cravat or waistcoat.

Darcy said solemnly, "The day we discovered his body, I retrieved several gold threads from Mr. Hotchkiss's grasp. They are in my quarters at Woodvine. I believe you will find they match those on Mr. Barriton's cloak."

"The Thigpen girl triumphantly told me how Hotchkiss had followed Barriton when the butler came to the stone for the Oimelc celebration. Miss Thigpen says no one else was in attendance. Barriton meant to leave Mr. Rupp a warning sign, but the butler and Hotchkiss argued. Barriton hid Hotchkiss's body behind the hedgerow until he could retrieve a shovel from Rupp's barn. According to the girl, Barriton thought the steward was dead when he buried him, but evidently, the butler erred. The stone on Hotchkiss's chest kept the steward from escaping the shallow grave."

Darcy could do little but listen to the magistrate's retelling. "Oimelc?" Darcy asked.

"It is a celebration of spring, right before our Candlemas. The Irish 'imbolc' is sometimes rendered as 'Candlemas,'" Stowbridge explained.

Darcy did not understand the connection between a pagan celebration and an ecclesiastical one, but he kept his comments to himself. "What of Mrs. Jacobs?"

"The young surgeon says the woman will have a time of much discomfort, but Mrs. Jacobs will recover. I will have Holbrook see her to Woodvine. For now, Mrs. Rupp tends the maid in her home."

Darcy had always found Stowbridge more than a bit incompetent, but in this matter, the magistrate had acted honorably. "I appreciate the speed at which you have responded to this matter."

Stowbridge managed a warm smile of utter insincerity. Darcy had to work to keep his composure against a most untoward gravity of deportment. "It is but a token to what I owe Samuel Darcy's memory." The magistrate stood and stretched. "Will you be able to sit a horse, Darcy?"

Darcy rose slowly to stand beside the magistrate. "Although Newby has pronounced me in fair condition, I believe I will return to Woodvine and seek Mrs. Darcy's tender care."

Stowbridge brushed the dirt from his coat, his countenance a perfect study in stone. The early rays of sun had lightened the sky. "A woman can bring a man comfort," the magistrate said confidently. "Your wife would not suit every man, but Mrs. Darcy appears to complement you." Darcy felt he should take the man to task for disparaging Elizabeth's personality, but he considered it an act of futility. Stowbridge would never change his opinions of the fairer sex, nor would the magistrate learn to address women with more than an injudicious particularity, and the argument would delay Darcy's return to Elizabeth's side.

"By the way," the magistrate continued, ignorant of Darcy's earlier objection. "Mrs. Jacobs admitted that the footprints in Samuel's hidden room were hers. She borrowed the younger maid's shoes because Mrs. Jacobs' pair had a hole in them, and the elder woman was to walk to the village to purchase several items for Mrs. Holbrook. Els knew nothing of the exchange, for Mrs. Ridgeway had given the girl some time off as Els suffered with her womanly woes. While Els slept, Mrs. Jacobs borrowed the girl's shoes for her journey.

"Upon her return to Woodvine, Mrs. Jacobs came across a partially open passage leading to Samuel's private room. The woman swears she knew nothing of the treasure room until that day. Mrs. Jacobs admitted to removing the map of this field and the Lemegeton."

Darcy ran his fingers through his hair. "Mrs. Jacobs' explanation sheds light on why the maid dropped the tea kettle when she overheard Mrs. Darcy and the Society men discussing the document. Mrs. Jacobs likely thought someone would discover her presence in Samuel's private room," he reasoned. "But where did the woman hide the papers? Mrs. Darcy and the colonel searched each servant's quarters."

"Evidently, when Mrs. Darcy excused Mrs. Jacobs to her quarters to tend the burn on her hand, Mrs. Jacobs hid the map and document behind several loose boards in the wall behind her bed."

Darcy nodded his gratitude for the explanation. "If you require nothing else from me at this time, I will return to Woodvine. I am certain Mrs. Darcy has known no sleep in my absence."

"You are very weak," Stowbridge said with concern.

"I require my wife's presence if I am to know peace. I must go."

* * *

Elizabeth had finally fallen asleep with her head resting on her folded arms on the small escritoire in her chambers. In Darcy's absence, she had removed Samuel Darcy's journals from the hiding place among her most intimate wear to return to the coded passages. With Darcy searching for Mr. Barriton, it became more vital for her to solve the mystery of his cousin's words. Steadfastly, she had manipulated the possible dates for Perdita Sanderson's birthday, for Elizabeth was certain, after learning something of Samuel Darcy's history with the child's grandmother, that it seemed only natural for Darcy's cousin to hold a heightened interest in the girl named for Samuel's great love.

It had taken Elizabeth thirteen attempts before she had come across the correct combination. "14 September 1808," she had announced to the empty room. "Fitzwilliam shall be surprised to learn that Perdita Sanderson is a year older than my dear husband recalled."

Diligently, she had translated several related passages. She found with gratitude that Samuel had used the same coded pattern for the entries. In his own words, Samuel Darcy had spoken of contacting a gentleman in a newly minted state in what was once known as the Northwest Territory in America. According to the late Mr. Darcy, Ohio had become a state in 1803. Surprisingly, Samuel spoke of having explored several sections of the land beyond the mountains of Virginia some fifteen years prior, and having made the acquaintance of a Giles O'Grady. The gentleman of Samuel's acquaintance had passed some ten years prior, but Samuel had encouraged the acquaintance of Mr. O'Grady's son, Peter.

Three years ago, the younger O'Grady had contacted Samuel Darcy with news of an invention, which Peter thought would awaken Samuel's scientific hunger. Samuel and the younger O'Grady had corresponded regularly, and Darcy's cousin Samuel had offered financial support for the man's efforts.

Samuel Darcy had traveled to America twice in the past eight years. The earlier of the journeys had served as a duty call on the O'Gradys, for Cousin Samuel had held a great affection for the elder. Samuel had written, "Giles O'Grady saved my life when I foolishly stumbled into a bear trap. Giles nursed me to health over a six-week period. In gratitude, I made O'Grady a loan so Giles could purchase his homestead. A proud one, Giles refused my thanks, but I finally convinced O'Grady to accept the money. I held no doubts of Giles' success. As expected, my friend repaid me every penny."

Elizabeth enjoyed reading of the O'Grady family, but when Samuel Darcy began to speak of the likelihood of the young O'Grady's creation exploding if not handled properly, she had ceased her translation and had studied the sketches Samuel had made in the margins. "Fitzwilliam referred to this device as some sort of torpedo." Elizabeth turned the sketch on its side, and upside down. "I have not the right of it," she grumbled as she compared one sketch to another. Each drawing displayed more details than the previous one. "It is as if Cousin Samuel meant to construct his own explosive. I can give no account of what I have read," Elizabeth said in frustration. "Perhaps Fitzwilliam or the colonel will understand these notations."

She had left the pages resting on the small desk to stand and stare out the window. Heavily, she leaned against the frame. Elizabeth's cheek rested against the cool pane. "Protect him, God," she whispered to the night sky. She said no more. God would know her sentiments regarding the probability of Darcy's demise.

There she had stood from three to five of the clock, staring out the window, gazing at the road, but seeing nothing. She had kept an anxious vigil awaiting Darcy's return. As dawn's fingers broke through the blackness, her anxiety increased. "Where is he?" she whispered as she searched the outline of trees and shrubbery on the horizon. Elizabeth reasoned, "If he were injured, Mr. Holbrook would have brought word." For a brief moment, she felt the satisfaction of Darcy's continued health, but the dread Elizabeth had forcibly placed aside returned. "But if Fitzwilliam were dead..." She stared intently at the narrow path leading to the main road, the same road her husband would ride upon his return. Hot tears pricked her eyes, and Elizabeth could not catch her breath. "Would they not inform me?" she sobbed. "Would they not permit me to comfort my husband in his last hours? His last minutes?"

A figure appeared at the far end of the path, and for the pause of three heartbeats, hope swelled in Elizabeth's chest. She clung to the sash and watched as the figure moved closer. Her heart lurched. "Not Darcy," she whispered. The figure belonged to a woman. "Too spry for Mrs. Jacobs," she speculated.

Whoever it was, Woodvine was the female's destination. Elizabeth turned from the window. She quickly gathered Samuel's journals and shoved them from view between the mattresses of her bed. She would hide them more carefully upon her return. Elizabeth shed the satin robe she had worn over a simple chocolate-brown day dress to ward off the night's chill. She had chosen the brown dress for its warmth when she had hoped to accompany Darcy to the field. When her husband had refused, Elizabeth had remained dressed for an impending emergency.

Now, she caught up a heavy wool shawl before rushing toward the servants' stairs. Elizabeth meant to meet their visitor and learn news of her husband. Surely, a woman would not be on the road at this hour without words of pressing importance.

Elizabeth burst into the kitchen just as the door opened quietly upon the room. Few servants were about at this hour, and other than a scullery maid filling a kettle with water at the well, no one stirred. The familiarity of the visitor's countenance subtracted from the surprise Elizabeth might have felt otherwise.

"Mrs. Ridgeway?" Elizabeth hissed. "What has brought you to Woodvine at this hour?"

The woman glanced to where the door to Mrs. Holbrook's small room was propped open with a broom. She stilled, her features, initially, going flat. With a grimace, the housekeeper caught Elizabeth's arm and tugged her in the direction of an alcove, which served as a stillroom. "I came to fetch you, Mrs. Darcy," she whispered.

"Why all the secrecy?" Elizabeth asked.

"Mr. Stowbridge did not want the others to know what happened in Mr. Rupp's field."

Elizabeth's breath caught in her throat. She let out a long exhale. It was her impatience showing, but Mrs. Ridgeway appeared to ignore Elizabeth's exigency. "You have word of my husband." The housekeeper nodded curtly. "Is Mr. Darcy in health?" Elizabeth asked through trembling lips.

Mrs. Ridgeway tugged Elizabeth along a passage to a side entrance. "I cannot say for certain," she said seriously. "For I have not seen Mr. Darcy personally. Mr. Stowbridge thinks such matters are not in the realm of a lady's disposition."

Elizabeth could hear the strained words, a sound of contention between the housekeeper and the woman's new employer, but she had more pressing concerns. "Speak to me of Mr. Darcy." She rushed to keep pace with the housekeeper. They had exited Woodvine and had set off across the well-tended lawns.

Mrs. Ridgeway spoke over her shoulder at the trailing Elizabeth. "I possess only the knowledge of second tongue in what I overheard Mr. Holbrook tell Mr. Stowbridge."

Elizabeth caught the housekeeper's arm and dragged the woman to a halt. For a discomfiting moment, neither of them moved. "I understand," she said with more calm than she possessed, "that Mr. Stowbridge did not confide in you. Yet, if you possess any knowledge of Mr. Darcy, I demand you speak of it immediately."

Mrs. Ridgeway's eyes appeared distant, and Elizabeth could not read the woman's true intentions; yet, she would let nothing stand between her and her husband. The lady paused for what seemed forever, but was likely only a handful of seconds. Finally, Mrs. Ridgeway said, "If you will accompany me, I shall explain what I have learned. I think it best if we speak while we walk. It will save time, and, as I am certain you will wish to reach Mr. Darcy's side as soon as possible, we should hurry our steps."

Elizabeth offered, "Should I have someone saddle horses or bring around a gig?"

Mrs. Ridgeway tutted her disapproval. "In the time it would take to rouse one of Captain Tregonwell's men to assist us, and then have the gentleman find us appropriate transportation, you could be reunited with your husband. That is assuming you do not mind a walk across a country lane."

Elizabeth despised the challenging tone in the woman's voice, but she hesitated only a moment to glance toward the house before making her decision. "Lead on, Mrs. Ridgeway," she said with determination.

The housekeeper strode toward the line of trees, and Elizabeth quickened her step to keep abreast of the woman. They entered the shadowy overhang before the woman spoke again. "This is what I overheard when Mr. Holbrook came to Stowe Hall in the early hours." Their pace slowed when they reached the rough terrain of the wooded area. "Mr. Samuel's groom called at the squire's house at a little past four of the clock. He told Mr. Stowbridge a most astounding tale."

They climbed a stile and descended the other side. Mrs. Ridgeway set a diagonal path across the field. "Mr. Holbrook spoke of discovering a coven celebrating Beltane under the stars where the old monoliths are found. Do you know the field, Mrs. Darcy?"

Elizabeth wished the woman would speak of Darcy's condition, but she understood the housekeeper's perverseness. Mrs. Ridgeway held all the high cards, and Elizabeth was a mere player. She said encouragingly, "I am familiar with Mr. Rupp's land."

The housekeeper continued her tale and the punishing exercise. When they exited the field over a like stile, Elizabeth realized this was a part of the Darcy estate with which she was unfamiliar, but she brushed the thought aside as she hiked her skirt to maintain her gait. If Mrs. Ridgeway thought her a pampered lady of the *ton*, the housekeeper was in for a surprise. Elizabeth was not afraid of a long walk or a steady stride.

"Apparently, Mr. Barriton had taken Mrs. Jacobs prisoner and threatened to kill the woman."

Elizabeth heard the derision in Mrs. Ridgeway's voice. She supposed the housekeeper thought Mrs. Jacobs deserved part of her punishment. Elizabeth said cautiously, "Mr. Darcy and Mr. McKye journeyed to Mr. Rupp's field to stop Mr. Barriton."

"Well, they certainly managed to accomplish their task," the housekeeper declared. "One of Mr. Tregonwell's men shot Mr. Barriton after the man shoved Mrs. Jacobs into the fire the coven had built in Mr. Rupp's field."

Fear skated along Elizabeth's spine. She offered up a silent prayer that it had not been Darcy who had dispatched Mr. Barriton. She thought such an act would lie heavily on her husband's conscience. "Was Mrs. Jacobs badly injured?"

The housekeeper led Elizabeth deeper into the woods. Elizabeth supposed this was the shortcut to Stowe Hall, which Samuel Darcy had traversed the night he died. The thought of how easily someone had overcome the trusting archaeologist sent a shiver of dread down Elizabeth's spine. She glanced around to learn her bearings.

"According to Mr. Holbrook, he was to seek the services of the junior surgeon Mr. Glover had once trained," Mrs. Ridgeway shared.

"Mr. Newby." Elizabeth provided the name.

Mrs. Ridgeway confided, "If Geoffrey Glover trained the man, Mr. Newby will serve this community well. Mr. Glover was a man of science."

Elizabeth's patience had worn thin. She had thought to permit Mrs. Ridgeway her moment. In some ways, she supposed she owed the housekeeper that much, for Mrs. Ridgeway's forced exit from Woodvine had placed the woman in an untenable position. In truth, Elizabeth harbored a bit of guilt for having dismissed the woman, but she could no longer tolerate the lack of news of her husband. "Please," she said as she came to a halt. "I beg of you; speak to me of Mr. Darcy. I cannot bear not knowing."

The housekeeper came to an abrupt standstill. She turned to Elizabeth, and with a smile of what appeared to be satisfaction, she said, "Mr. Holbrook was to fetch the surgeon to tend your husband. It appears Mr. Darcy fought with the butler. Your husband was stabbed with some sort of ceremonial knife. Mr. Holbrook says Mr. Darcy has lost a sizeable quantity of blood."

Elizabeth felt her legs buckle, and she could do little to prevent herself from sinking to her knees. Darcy had been seriously injured. While she slept at her small desk, her husband had lain in a field, possibly bleeding to death. "Dear God," her trembling lips offered in supplication. "Do not take him from me." She swayed in place as the darkness rushed in.

"Mrs. Darcy," the housekeeper said brusquely. "We have no time for histrionics."

Despite wishing to rock herself for comfort, Elizabeth gave herself a sound mental shake. She bit her lip to prevent the cry of anguish on the tip of her tongue. She looked up into the disapproving countenance of the housekeeper. However, Elizabeth did not apologize; instead she managed to stagger to her feet. "What else should I know?" Elizabeth asked fearfully.

"Mr. Stowbridge sent word of his late return to Stowe Hall. In the message, he indicated that the surgeon had seen to your husband and had advised Mr. Darcy to permit Mrs. Rupp to nurse him until a coach could be sent from Woodvine. However, Mr. Darcy insisted on returning to your side."

Elizabeth thought how like Darcy it was to recognize her concern and, therefore, place himself in danger in order to relieve Elizabeth's anxiety. "Where is my husband now? At Stowe Hall?"

"They found him on the road after he could not sit his horse. Mr. Newby is treating Mr. Darcy in a small tenants' cottage while Mr. Holbrook escorts Mrs. Jacobs to Woodvine and returns with a wagon. Tregonwell's men assist Mr. Stowbridge with the investigation and the prisoners." The woman turned back to the path, and Elizabeth fell in step beside her. "It was thought that Mr. Darcy would prove a better patient with you in attendance."

Despite the seriousness of the situation, a smile shaped Elizabeth's lips. She could easily imagine an aristocratic Darcy barking orders to the young surgeon. *That is if he were able*, Elizabeth cautioned the knot lodged firmly in her chest. "Where is this cottage?" she asked in concern.

"One more field to cross," Mrs. Ridgeway said confidently. "See." The woman pointed to where a thatched roof could be seen behind an overgrown hedgerow.

Elizabeth quickened her stride. "Why in the world would they have taken shelter in such a deserted area?"

The housekeeper shrugged her shoulders. "It is the way of men to make women's lives complicated."

Elizabeth rushed across the field, which now stood fallow. Her heart pounded in her ears from the speed of their journey and from the all-encompassing fear that surrounded her. Would she be in time? *Mr. Holbrook had said Mr. Darcy had lost a sizeable quantity of blood.* Men did not normally worry so unless danger existed. Was Mr. Newby skilled enough to stop the bleeding? What of infection? She lifted her skirts higher and quickened her pace. Soon she was running, needing to reach Darcy before it was too late.

Gasping for air, Elizabeth burst into the small cottage, nothing more than a one-room sanctuary from the cold, to discover a profound silence. Nothing moved within. Her chest heaved from her run and from the heart-stopping realization that Mrs. Ridgeway had erred somehow. She caught at the stitch of pain in her side. "Where is he? Where is my husband?" she croaked.

An arm caught her across the neck while another hand placed a large damp handkerchief over her mouth and nose. From behind her, Mrs. Ridgeway's harsh words stung her ear. "Dead. Mr. Darcy is dead."

For a brief second, Elizabeth's mind forgot to fight. She slumped heavily against the woman who had easily manipulated her into this trap. Heaven above, she had been such a fool. If Darcy were dead, she would have no reason to live, but a small voice said clearly, *"If Darcy were dead, you would have known the instant he died."* And Elizabeth knew it was true. Her heart would have stopped at the same instant as did his. She had felt no such doom; therefore, Darcy was alive. With the realization, Elizabeth turned her efforts toward freeing herself from Mrs. Ridgeway's hold. She knew not what the woman planned, but whatever it was, Elizabeth would have none of it.

She kicked at the housekeeper's legs, but her efforts did little to allay the woman's attack. Mrs. Ridgeway's hold tightened across Elizabeth's neck, and Elizabeth's ability to breathe lessened with each second. She had always felt at a disadvantage physically when she had confronted Mrs. Ridgeway. The woman towered over her by several inches.

She twisted against the housekeeper's powerful hold, but it was fruitless. The realization arrived: She would die, and Darcy would survive. She had rushed to save him and found her own demise awaiting her. The handkerchief across her mouth and nose reeked of a sweet apple scent. *Satan's apple. Mandragora,* she thought. At Longbourn, they had often boiled the root in milk to make a poultice for her father's indolent ulcers, but she had always heeded her mother's warnings regarding the temptation to taste the mixture. "You girls are never to act so foolishly," Mrs. Bennet had warned the inquisitive Elizabeth and the compassionate Jane Bennet. "Mandragora can excite delirium and madness. It can put a grown man into a deep sleep, one which mirrors death." *Will sleep be my only circumstance?* Elizabeth wondered. *And what does the housekeeper have planned for me?*

Elizabeth felt the blackness creeping across her mind. Mandragora; yet, something more. The damp cloth tasted of something sweet. Mrs. Ridgeway pressed the cloth into Elizabeth's mouth as the woman jerked upward on the arm which lay across Elizabeth's windpipe. With a powerful grip, one well beyond that of most women, the housekeeper spun Elizabeth about before delivering an elbow across her cheek. Elizabeth's head snapped to the right, and she felt herself teetering on the brink of an unknown land. Elizabeth instinctively fought to keep her balance, to maintain her mental clarity, and to fend off Mrs. Ridgeway's attack. However, winning any of those battles was not in her power. As she spun to the dirt floor, like a leaf floating on an autumn breeze, Elizabeth wondered if she would ever see Darcy again in this world.

Chapter 23

Darcy reined in the horse before Woodvine's main entrance. There was not a muscle in his body which did not scream out in protest, and the knife wound had opened again to burn with hell's fire. It could not be more than eight of the clock, but Darcy desperately required a bath and his bed, preferably with his wife within his arms. The young groom, whom Mr. Holbrook had described as an orphan, scrambled to catch up the horse. "Holbrook will be bringing in a wagon. I came ahead." The head groom had secured a flat wagon in which to escort Mrs. Jacobs to Woodvine.

"Aye, Sir."

Darcy wearily made his way up the main steps. Without the butler, there would be no one to greet him, so Darcy let himself into the manor house. The halls were deathly silent. "Anyone about?" he bellowed. Despite the fact his wife's chambers faced the rear gardens, Darcy half expected her to scramble down the stairs to launch herself into his embrace.

Unsurprisingly, Mr. Sheffield appeared on the landing. "My goodness," his man gasped before the valet regained his composure. "Allow me, Sir." Sheffield rushed to assist Darcy with his filthy, blood-stained jacket.

Darcy braced his arms about Sheffield's shoulder. "Where is my wife?" he groaned as they negotiated the steps.

"I have not seen the Mistress nor Hannah this morning, Sir." Sheffield shoved upward on his master's arm, and Darcy hissed with pain. "How bad is it, Sir?" the valet asked softly.

Tightening his jaw, Darcy murmured, "Worse than I care to mention."

Sheffield tightened his hold about Darcy's waist. "Permit me to assist you to your quarters; then I will seek out Mrs. Darcy."

Exhausted, Darcy leaned heavily on his valet. His only thought throughout the three-mile return to Woodvine had been that he had witnessed another man die, and the smell of death clung to him. It was in his nostrils and the pores of his skin. He was not certain he would ever escape the odor.

"Did you find the butler?" Sheffield asked cautiously.

Darcy shook his head in disbelief. "Barriton is dead, and Mrs. Jacobs is badly injured. I am weary of this madness."

His valet remained silent until they reached Darcy's private quarters. He assisted Darcy to a nearby chair. "Perhaps we should return to Pemberley, Sir."

Darcy sighed heavily. "I am of a like opinion." He lazily tugged at what remained of his shirt. "I will undress myself if you will arrange a hot bath and send my wife to me."

His man bowed politely. "Immediately, Sir."

Alone in a room he had rarely used since coming to Woodvine, Darcy wrestled the remnants of his shirt over his head before dropping it on the floor beside his chair. He glanced at the furnishings, which should have become familiar in the short time of his residence, but which suddenly felt foreign and uninviting. He had decided after his first joining with Elizabeth that he could consider any place his wife resided as 'home'; however, Woodvine Hall had defied that concept. From the moment Darcy had entered his cousin's province, nothing of normalcy had survived. "Witchcraft and sacrifices and Egyptian treasures and murder. How can such things coexist without one seeking dominance over the other?"

He loosened the makeshift bandage Newby had wrapped about his waist to examine the jagged opening in his side. Reluctantly, he struggled to his feet to make his way to the washstand. Pouring fresh water into the basin, Darcy wet a cloth and purposely scrubbed his face with a healthy dose of soap. He badly required a shave, but he would wait until after his bath. Rinsing the cloth clean, he soaped it again. This time he dabbed at the dry blood and the rough edges of the opening of the cut. In the back of his mind, Darcy could hear his mother's voice warning him to keep an open wound clean. Once, he and Edward had climbed the old oak tree behind Pemberley, but upon their descent, Darcy had slipped to land on a sharp branch. A rip in his new breeches had earned him a swat of a switch from his stern-faced father, while the jagged cut across his thigh had brought the tender care of Lady Anne Darcy. His mother had succumbed to her illness by that time, but Lady Anne had left her bed to tend to her only son. The tiny scar on Darcy's leg was a reminder of the love he had shared with both his parents.

He looked up in anticipation at the sound of Mr. Sheffield's entrance, to be disappointed not to see Elizabeth in his valet's wake. "Do not tell me that my wife is still abed?" Darcy asked as he reached for a towel.

His man grimaced. "No, Sir." When Sheffield swallowed hard, dread returned to Darcy's chest. "Mrs. Darcy was seen leaving the manor on foot early this morning."

He rubbed his tired eyes as his impatience increased. Darcy warned, "Do not coddle me, Sheffield. Tell me the whole of it."

The valet nodded curtly. "Hannah woke to find her mistress not in Mrs. Darcy's chambers. When she checked, no one reported seeing Mrs. Darcy leave the estate. Hannah assumed her mistress had stepped out for a walk."

Darcy spoke through tight lips. "There is no need for you to invent an excuse for Hannah. I am not seeking to place blame. I simply desire word of Mrs. Darcy's whereabouts."

Sheffield shifted his weight nervously. "Of course, Mr. Darcy." The man's Adam's apple worked hard. "Hearing Hannah's tale, I questioned the staff below stairs. The scullery maid was the only one with news of Mrs. Darcy. The girl claims to have seen the Mistress leave Woodvine with Mrs. Ridgeway."

"Ridgeway!" the word exploded into the room. "What the hell was this house's former housekeeper doing at Woodvine?"

Sheffield's eyes stared at a point past Darcy's shoulder, and it irritated Darcy beyond reason. "The scullery maid is distraught. She realizes she should have questioned the situation, but the girl did not think it her place."

Darcy hissed, "What time was this? Did it appear that Mrs. Darcy accompanied the woman willingly?"

"The incident occurred when the girl first came to her duties. The maid speaks of filling the morning kettles at the well. Therefore, it must have been sometime after five of the clock." Sheffield hesitated before adding, "I did ask the girl of Mrs. Darcy's disposition, asked her if the Mistress was upset or angry or acting oddly. From her position, the girl could not see Mrs. Darcy's countenance, but the maid reports that Mrs. Ridgeway was in the lead, and Mrs. Darcy scurried to keep apace of the woman."

Darcy distractedly ran his fingers through his hair. "Damn! This makes little sense. Elizabeth would not leave with a woman for whom she held no respect unless it was an emergency. Where could they have gone?" He glanced to the mantel clock. "It has been more than three hours!"

Sheffield offered, "In anticipation of your injuries, perhaps Mr. Stowbridge sent the lady to find Mrs. Darcy."

Darcy asked incredulously, "On foot and in the nighttime hours? Even though the squire holds little respect for womankind, he would act the role of a gentleman."

His valet finally met Darcy's gaze. "Is it possible that Mrs. Ridgeway learned of the confrontation with Mr. Barriton second-hand and took it upon herself to seek out Mrs. Darcy?"

Darcy considered the scenario. "With what I know of the housekeeper's character, I cannot reconcile such benevolence. Besides, Mrs. Darcy would have returned to Woodvine once she became aware of the truth of the situation." He heaved an exasperated sigh. "We must assume something devious has occurred. Please tell Captain Tregonwell's men that I require their assistance immediately. Mr. McKye and Mr. Castle are likely following the magistrate's orders, but I can use Mr. Poore, Mr. Maxton, and Mr. Douglas. Inform Mr. Franklyn that no guards are available for Samuel's treasure room until I return, and send Hannah to me." Sheffield raised an eyebrow. "I require your skills elsewhere, and someone must bandage this wound." Sheffield bowed and turned on his heels to exit. "Sheffield, tell the young groom I require a fresh horse."

The valet paused by the dressing room door. "You also require a fresh shirt, Sir." His man caught up a crisply pressed shirt and pressed it into Darcy's grasp. "I insist, Sir."

Despite the madness, Darcy reverently accepted the fine lawn garment. He recognized his valet's efforts to place order into Darcy's hands. "Be on your way," Darcy said politely.

"Yes, Sir." A quick bow announced his man's withdrawal.

Darcy's steps drifted to the window. He looked out over the gardens. His eyes searched for any sign of his wife. "Where are you, Elizabeth?" he murmured.

* * *

Elizabeth's eyes fluttered open before drifting closed once more. She had no idea how long she had slept, but the sun's rays caressed her cheek. It was comforting in its warmth, for if she could still feel the sun on her face, then Mrs. Ridgeway had failed to dispatch her to Heaven. The thought pleased Elizabeth, and she smiled.

"You find your situation amusing, Mrs. Darcy?" The housekeeper's breath brushed across Elizabeth's ear, but Elizabeth could not actually see the woman.

Elizabeth did not answer. Instead, she concentrated on opening her eyes fully. The dizzying blackness called to her conscious mind, but she made herself search for the light. Slowly and purposely, Elizabeth lifted her lids, but the light she had doggedly sought caused her to blink and to tear. Droplets seeped from the corners of her eyes, and she made to wipe them away, but her arms would not move.

Dreamily, she turned her head to the right to discern the difficulty, only to discover her hand tied to some sort of post. She twisted her hand, but the ruby-colored binding held. "You will find the one on the left is equally secure." There was a note of satisfaction in the housekeeper's tone.

Elizabeth's eyes closed of their own volition; however, she made the effort to remain conscious. "Why?" her dry lips formed the single word.

The housekeeper laughed sadistically. "Why have I taken you prisoner? Simple, Mrs. Darcy. Eliminating you will destroy your husband." With that announcement, the woman covered Elizabeth's mouth and nose again with a cloth dipped in the same sweetly sickening mixture as before. Elizabeth concentrated on not breathing in the fumes, but it was impossible for her to hold her breath forever, and Mrs. Ridgeway was determined to do her worst. Finally, she could offer no resistance. With a quick inhale, Elizabeth relaxed into the hard mattress upon which she rested.

"Fitzwilliam." Her thoughts latched onto the one word which made sense in this chaos.

* * *

He had personally questioned the maid before setting out for Stowe Hall. The young girl had repeatedly sworn that the woman she had seen with Elizabeth had been Mrs. Ridgeway. "I swears it to be as true as the morning sun, Sir. I should be asking questions, but it be early, and I not be thinkin' proper."

Mrs. Holbrook snorted, "As if ye ever think proper."

Darcy had left the woman to prepare a salve for Mrs. Jacobs's burns, and went to meet with Tregonwell's men. He had sent Douglas into the village with instructions to call at the church, the shops, Mr. Newby's cottage, and the posting inn. He sent Poore and Maxton on similar tasks, asking the men to examine the lower third of the estate and the neighboring villages. Darcy was cognizant of the possibility that the housekeeper and Elizabeth had transportation waiting beyond the view of the household, but he had set Stowe Hall as his destination.

"Mr. Darcy," Stowbridge said with surprise when he entered the room. "I had thought you had retired to Woodvine. I have just returned to Stowe this minute. Is there another matter in which I may be of service?"

The skin of the magistrate's cheeks had become suddenly pinched and tight looking. "I had hoped to speak to Mrs. Ridgeway."

Stowbridge's brow dipped into a scowl. "I will not entertain the possibility of Mrs. Ridgeway returning to Woodvine."

Darcy schooled the grimace from his countenance. "I hold no such motive for this visit. I simply possess several questions for which I hope the lady has answers."

The older man's gaze sharpened, but the magistrate reached for the bell cord. When a servant appeared, Stowbridge gave the order for Mrs. Ridgeway to attend him. Darcy was not certain whether he preferred the woman to respond to the request or to prove herself absent from the manor house. The first would provide him the opportunity to question the woman's motives for calling on Woodvine and to learn something of Elizabeth's whereabouts. The second would prove what Darcy had known from the beginning: Mrs. Ridgeway had brought evil to Samuel Darcy's door.

"You sent for me?" Mrs. Ridgeway appeared in the open doorway.

Stowbridge turned toward the sound of the lady's voice. "Ah, yes." Darcy half expected the man to finish his welcome with a "my dear," but the magistrate cut his remarks short. "Mr. Darcy wishes to speak with you."

"Yes, Sir." The housekeeper's gaze finally met Darcy's. "May I be of service, Mr. Darcy?"

Darcy's frown lines deepened. "I returned to Woodvine to the news that you had called upon the manor very early this morning. I thought perhaps you might enlighten me as to the purpose of your visit."

The woman's countenance portrayed mild surprise, but her eyes shuttered an obvious secret. "At Woodvine, Sir?" she protested. "Why would I call on my former employer without notice? I assure you, Mr. Darcy, I hold no desire to experience further abuse at your hands, or those of Mrs. Darcy."

Darcy's ire reached an immediate boiling point, but he bit back the desire to shake the truth from the woman's lips. "I have not called at Stowe for an attack on your professionalism or for a confrontation. One of the Woodvine staff reports your presence in the manor's kitchen at nearly five of the clock." He thought to ask of Elizabeth, but Darcy kept his wife's absence a secret from Stowbridge and the housekeeper until he ascertained what deception Mrs. Ridgeway practiced. It was difficult to believe he would ever meet another woman so entirely deficient in the less common acquirements of self-knowledge, generosity, and humility.

"Why would I take such privilege? I have no reason to do so. Five of the clock?" She turned to the squire. "You must surely see, Sir, that what I have said of the degradation practiced at Woodvine is true." Stowbridge nodded his agreement. The housekeeper said disdainfully, "You may examine the squire's stables. Other than the horse Mr. Stowbridge rode to your rescue, no animals have been used."

Darcy said, "I never spoke of your arrival, Ma'am." He watched the woman carefully. Mrs. Ridgeway expected him to refute her twisting of the truth, but Darcy would not play into her game. He reached for his gloves. "I will take no more of your time, Madam. I had thought to clarify a most unusual report, but we obviously have no further business. Good day, Squire. Ma'am." Darcy offered Stowbridge an aristocratic nod of his head before making his exit.

Stepping into the light, he cursed his foolishness for coming to Stowe Hall, and, more importantly, to Dorset. He would return to Woodvine and pray Elizabeth would greet him, but somehow he thought it would not be that easy.

Accepting the reins from Stowbridge's groom, he asked casually, "Have there been visitors at Stowe this morning beyond the lady who called upon Mrs. Ridgeway?"

The groom accepted the coin Darcy pressed into the man's gloved hand. "There be no one, Sir, but yer groom and you, Sir. Mrs. Ridgeway had no visitors either. The lady only returned to the hall some half hour prior."

"On horseback?" Darcy asked softly.

The groom glanced toward the house. "No, Sir. On foot."

Darcy nodded his gratitude before turning the horse toward a road he had hoped never to ride again. At the fork leading to Wimborne, he met McKye and Castle returning from the village. "Might I importune upon one of you to watch Stowe Hall from a distance?"

"What is amiss?" McKye asked.

"The young scullery maid reports that Mrs. Ridgeway called upon Woodvine at dawn, but the housekeeper denies any knowledge of the event."

McKye's eyes narrowed. "I do not trust the woman. In fact, there are several at Woodvine who would be seeking employment elsewhere if I had the say." The man blushed at having criticized Darcy's management of the estate.

Darcy admitted, "We are of a like mind, Sir; however, I am not the sole owner." He looked backward to where the roof of Stowe Hall could be seen over the treetops. "I fear Mrs. Ridgeway has lured Mrs. Darcy from the estate. When I questioned the housekeeper regarding these charges, the woman staged a confrontation for the squire's benefit. For now, I want to know if Mrs. Ridgeway leaves Stowe Hall, and where she goes."

McKye nodded. "I know the area better than does Castle. I will see to it."

Darcy shook the man's hand. "I will send someone to relieve you. I suspect Mrs. Ridgeway will not venture forth until she has the cover of darkness."

"Just ask Mrs. Holbrook to send over some of her roast chicken, and I will be satisfied."

Darcy turned his horse in place. "It will be my pleasure."

Less than a half hour later, he dismounted before Woodvine. "Keep the horse close," he told the young groom. He glanced toward the manor house. When Elizabeth had not opened the door immediately and bounded into his embrace, he instinctively knew his wife had not returned to the estate. Upon entering the main hall, Darcy noted how Mrs. Holbrook had set the remaining servants to very specific tasks, and Darcy silently applauded the woman's initiative.

"Any news of the Mistress?" Hannah asked as soon as Darcy closed the door.

Darcy shook his head. "Mrs. Ridgeway claims no knowledge of the actions which the maid described."

Hannah bristled. "Heaven help that woman if she is ever in my presence again."

Darcy smiled. His wife's lady's maid was the perfect complement to Elizabeth Darcy's spirit. "I plan to return to the search, but I wish to speak to the young maid again. Might you send her to me?"

"Immediately, Mr. Darcy."

With Hannah's exit, Darcy entered his cousin's study. He carried the guns he had brought with him from Pemberley, but he knew Samuel stored several others in a locked desk drawer. Finding the key, he bent to the task. Retrieving the first, he was pleased to see it clean and loaded. A timid knock at the open door announced the maid's arrival.

"Ye wished to see me, Sir."

Darcy forced a smile to his lips. He would not purposely intimidate the girl. "Yes. I had hoped you might show me the exact spot where you observed Mrs. Ridgeway and Mrs. Darcy."

"I'd be 'onored, Sir."

Darcy nodded. "If you will meet me in the vegetable garden in five minutes, I will be in your debt."

His request must have appeared a sensible one, for the girl's countenance lit with pride. She nodded several times, executed a clumsy curtsy, and disappeared. If the situation with Elizabeth had not taken on such dire overtones, he would have found it amusing how much the atmosphere of the household had changed with the departure of Mrs. Ridgeway, combined with Mr. Barriton's passing.

Grabbing a second gun, Darcy strode through Woodvine's halls to emerge in the kitchen garden. He found the young maid waiting for him. A few questions, a few more clarifications, and he was on the move. Darcy had discovered a set of two prints beyond where the groomed lawns gave way to forest. The marks were most definitely female in nature, and Darcy quickened his pace. His eyes searched for torn threads and bent branches, but nothing appeared unusual until he reached an open field.

A clearly marked print upon a stile mixed with muddy smears indicated that Elizabeth had crossed the field. He spent several minutes examining the area before determining the direction his wife had gone. There was a smoothed-over diagonal trail crossing the field. Darcy imagined the housekeeper triumphantly leading his wife farther and farther from the estate. Their skirt tails had left a telltale sign of their progress.

Exiting the field, it took Darcy several minutes to discover which way his wife had gone. Surprisingly, the chosen path circled in upon itself some one hundred yards from where he had crossed the stile only moments earlier.

Darcy wondered if his wife had been aware of Mrs. Ridgeway's deception. Somehow, he doubted it. Elizabeth acted from emotion; despite the fact his wife possessed a logical mind, first and foremost, she wore her heart upon her sleeve. If she thought him in danger, Elizabeth would walk through hell's fire to reach him.

The soft soil finally provided him another clear print, which led into the thicker woods—to the same trail upon which his cousin's body had been found. The thought of rounding a curve and finding Elizabeth's lying prostrate quickened Darcy's step; so much so, that he nearly missed the narrow path, which jutted off to the right. The heavy bramble had been trod upon recently. Pushing aside the overhanging branches, Darcy plunged deeper into the woods.

Surprisingly, the restricted path opened to another unseeded field. Darcy was not certain whether he was on Darcy land or land belonging to Stowbridge. Either way, he meant to explore. On his many excursions of late, he had not observed this area.

Again, he looked for a clue. He walked the combination fence and hedgerow line until he found an indentation in the soft grass. Darcy closed his eyes to imagine what his wife had been thinking, in how much distress Elizabeth must have been.

Early on, he had thought Mrs. Ridgeway had forced Elizabeth to leave the manor with her, as Elizabeth would never have done so willingly. His wife would have put up a fight. No, Elizabeth would only have blindly followed the woman if she believed he was in danger.

A few feet from the soft indentation, Darcy discovered another print, and then another. As he looked up, the tip of a thatched roof caught his attention. Vaulting over the low fence, he was running across the open field before he had time to consider his actions. With each stride, Darcy's heart pounded harder. Despite the odds against his finding his wife in this secluded cottage, he held no doubt she was there. His heart told him it was so. For the past several hours, his heart had ceased its steady call, but the moment he had spotted the cottage's roof, every nerve in Darcy's body had called him to her.

Breaking through the surrounding vegetation, Darcy skidded to a halt. He knew Mrs. Ridgeway had returned to Stowe Hall, but had the woman an accomplice? Slowing his approach, Darcy carefully placed each step to avoid signaling his presence. Circling the area, he hunkered down to peer into a small window.

Inside, deep shadows filled every corner, and nothing moved within. Darcy used his forearm to shade his eyes as he examined the small room for any sign of his wife. He had thought it impossible that Elizabeth could not be within, for his stretched-taut emotions had declared it to be so. However, Darcy made the effort to enter the cottage nonetheless. "Perhaps I have placed my hopes too high," he said as he turned the door's latch.

Darcy allowed the door to swing wide. Several seconds passed as his eyes adjusted to the darkness and he saw her. Two long strides brought him to her side. His wife lay lifeless on an undressed mattress. "My God, Lizzy," he gasped.

Leaning over her, Darcy worked frantically to loosen the bindings, which held her. He kissed each wrist as he freed it. He could not believe Elizabeth had experienced such humiliation. Once he had his wife safely at Woodvine, Darcy would take great pleasure in escorting Mrs. Ridgeway to the nearest gaol. He lightly slapped Elizabeth's cheeks, but his wife did not respond. "Speak to me, Lizzy," he demanded as he gave her a strong shake of her shoulders. "Come on, Darling. You must assist me. It is some two miles to Woodvine." He cursed himself for leaving the horse behind.

He looked for a pitcher of water but found none. "Lizzy. You know the way back to me," he insisted. A powdery mixture covered his wife's mouth and cheeks, and Darcy touched a damp finger to it to taste the concoction. He had no difficulty identifying one of the ingredients. "Opium." He had tasted it only once, in his university days. Another fellow in his college had slipped a small amount into Darcy's food as a poor joke. He always suspected George Wickham had egged on the son of a baronet, but the young man had refused to name others in the prank. Darcy had spent three days in his bed, while the other youth had been sent down for his participation.

"If Elizabeth has ingested opium, it will be a long while before she can think straight. Her small frame will make her susceptible to the plant's potency," he reasoned aloud.

Darcy stripped the jacket from his shoulders to wrap about his wife. "Allow me to warm you, Lizzy," he said as he slid her arms into the sleeves. They hung well beyond the tips of Elizabeth's fingers, and Darcy used the extra length to help wrap the garment about her chest. "There. That should feel better." He easily recalled how cold he had felt during those hours the opium had played havoc with his body.

He dug a handkerchief from the inside pocket of his jacket, and his knuckles brushed against Elizabeth's breast. Even under these conditions, his wife remained the most desirable woman of his acquaintance. His hand lifted, brushing back a lock of hair from her forehead. Darcy placed his errant thoughts aside. With the cloth, Darcy brushed the powder from her mouth. At least, Elizabeth breathed steadily, and for that he was thankful. Darcy shook his head in disbelief. He smiled, the grin loose and easy. "You are determined that I will carry you again," he said with a bit of irony. "Therefore, I will prove myself your hero," he declared as he lifted his wife's small form to his lap. "This time I have not been thrashed about by a rock face nor have I swum the length of a lake to pull you from its depths." He would not consider the tear in his side as a trial he must overcome. Standing with her cradled in his arms, Darcy kissed Elizabeth's forehead. "Slow and steady, my love."

Darcy had taken but two less-than-perfect steps before he stopped to adjust his hold about his wife and before he felt the shock of a blow to his upper back. His head was turned, but even if he had been expecting an attack, with Elizabeth in his arms, he could have done nothing more than absorb the impact. The force drove him to his knees, but he had the presence of mind to support Elizabeth close to him. His wife's chest lifted on a heavy, serrated breath beneath him. He would protect her with his last breath.

As the shadows consumed him, he heard the ominous whisper, "Welcome, Mr. Darcy. I wondered when you would find us."

Chapter 24

The darkness came and went, but one thing remained the same: Darcy still cradled Elizabeth in his arms, and he would do so for as long as it took to see her to safety. He would place his body between his wife and whatever evil had followed them to this place.

A booted foot nudged his side, but Darcy did not open his eyes. Instead, he concentrated on breathing the sweet scent of lavender, which clung to his wife's hair. Although Elizabeth's breath came shallowly, Darcy thought of all of God's miracles. His wife had survived the gypsy's attack, and with both God's will and Darcy's assistance, she would survive this latest disaster.

"I know you hear me, Mr. Darcy." A swish of skirts identified his assailant. Another nudge—this one sharper—landed close to where the blood seeped from his earlier wound. Despite his resolve not to react, he flinched. "Ahh, movement at last." The woman's voice held bitterness. "And here I had thought you so all-powerful."

Darcy would gladly relinquish any power he held if he could discover a means to see Elizabeth to freedom.

"Nothing to say for yourself?"

Darcy reluctantly opened his eyes. They rested on the smooth curve of his wife's cheek. He asked wearily, "Of what do you wish me to speak, Madam?" His tormentor kicked at him again, and Darcy dropped his elbow to protect his ribs.

"I prefer to look a person in the eye when we converse." She stepped away from him and sat in a nearby chair. "I assume that even with all your unsocial and taciturn ways that you understand the dictates of good manners."

He had mistrusted the woman immediately and for no reason other than the lady's impertinence. Grudgingly, Darcy grumbled, "In my social circle, one is not forced to converse." He readjusted Elizabeth in his arms. He was on his knees, and he sheltered his wife with his body.

Mrs. Ridgeway feigned a jovial laugh. "Delightful repartee."

She struck a table with the highly polished cane she carried. Darcy flinched again. From his eye's corner, he could see Mrs. Ridgeway tap her foot in frustration, and he made himself concentrate on the other little nuances of the lady's presence, such as the boot heel bearing a small indentation, and the dust and cobwebs on her skirt's hem. Behind her, the door remained open. *"Damn,"* he cursed internally. *Could the housekeeper have manipulated Els's arrest and Mrs. Jacobs's confession?*

When he refused to respond, the lady stood over him again. "You have a choice, Mr. Darcy," she said menacingly. "You may sit and converse, or…" She paused pointedly. "Or this cane will come down upon your back again and again until you acquiesce." The shadows along the wall indicated the woman had lifted the cane above her head, and Darcy braced himself for the blow.

When she hesitated, Darcy said, "Be on with it if that is your purpose."

The laughter came again, but it was laced with irony this time. "Do you not wish knowledge of my true purpose, Mr. Darcy?" She took a step to the other side of where he knelt. Turning the cane to hold it as if she carried a paille-maille mallet, Mrs. Ridgeway lined it up to a position from which she could strike Elizabeth solidly in the head.

Darcy scrambled to cover his wife's body, to shield Elizabeth from the woman's vengeance.

"Are you truly willing to die protecting Mrs. Darcy?" the house-keeper asked with disbelief.

Darcy caressed his wife's cheek as he curled himself about her. "It would be no sacrifice," he said earnestly.

A long pause ensued. Finally, the housekeeper leaned heavily on the cane. "An aristocrat in love with his wife? I thought never to see the day." She returned to her seat.

Darcy wondered if he could reach the gun in his jacket pocket without exposing Elizabeth to more danger. He gently stroked the back of her head and murmured words of devotion. "What did you give her?" he asked through gritted teeth.

Mrs. Ridgeway responded in her customarily conceited tone. "Just a mixture, which I learned from a Scottish medicine woman. The lady swore it would put the strongest of men to sleep for hours." Again, she paused in that sickeningly sweet way which Darcy had come to despise. "Hemlock and a bit of mandragora, along with a touch of opium."

Darcy raised his head to glare at the woman. "My God! You meant to kill her!"

Mrs. Ridgeway tutted her disapproval. "I have no desire to kill Mrs. Darcy," she stated baldly. "Your wife, Sir, is as much a victim as every other woman. Mrs. Darcy holds no rights. Your lady oper-ates under your instructions."

Darcy thought of the woman he cradled in his arms. True, in the law's eyes, Elizabeth was his possession, but, in reality, the opposite applied. However, he would not argue with Mrs. Ridge-way, especially if in not doing so, he could negotiate Elizabeth's release. "Mrs. Darcy performs her duties as my wife," he said with a bit of false pride.

"What say you, Mr. Darcy? Does the lady affect you to the same degree as you do her?" the housekeeper asked suspiciously.

Darcy glanced to the woman in his arms. He did not doubt Elizabeth's love; yet, he hoped to keep Mrs. Ridgeway talking by offering the woman half truths. Perhaps by doing so, he could devise a means to rescue his wife from this perilous situation. "Mrs. Darcy is the second of five daughters, and her father's land is entailed upon a distant cousin. Mrs. Bennet was ecstatic for such a smart connection and all I could offer her daughter. My heart was engaged long before I was aware of what idiocy had overtaken me."

"You avoid my question, Mr. Darcy."

Darcy shifted Elizabeth to a more comfortable position. "Do I?" He worked hard to remove the contempt from his tone. "Mayhap, I meant only to avoid the truth," he said with as much self-pity as he could muster. "I suppose that comes with the realization that Mrs. Darcy always held objections to our joining. In fact, when I offered Miss Elizabeth my hand, she said that from the beginning, from the first moment of our acquaintance, my arrogance and conceit had convinced my lady that I could not have made the offer of my hand in any possible way that would have attempted her to accept it." It was odd how remembrance of those words no longer tore his heart to shreds.

"Yet, Mrs. Darcy succumbed to your charms," Mrs. Ridgeway taunted.

"I possess an income of ten thousand per year. I can bring Mrs. Darcy's family comfort and connections. And we have gotten on well together. Mrs. Darcy is a sensible woman. My 'charms' are considerable in comparison to her other choices."

Mrs. Ridgeway's disdain had returned. "Perhaps I would be doing Mrs. Darcy a favor by releasing her into widowhood."

Darcy wished to beg for Elizabeth's life, but showing too much preference for his wife could be detrimental in this matter. He asked in an icy temper, "What have you planned for me?"

The housekeeper reached inside her cloak to remove a gun. She pointed it at Darcy's head. At this short distance, her aim would not need to be accurate to do him severe harm. Darcy eyed the woman cautiously. "First, you will make your wife comfortable on the bed."

Darcy swallowed his fear. He held no doubt Mrs. Ridgeway would shoot him. With arms and legs stiff from the protective position he had held for so long, Darcy staggered to his feet. Elizabeth had lain heavily against him. He closed his eyes to drive away the swirling blackness that his efforts had produced and made his feet cover the short distance to the bed. He lovingly placed Elizabeth's limp body on the bed's middle and then stood shakily beside the raised mattress. He silently waited for the housekeeper's next order. He hoped to convince the woman to take him elsewhere and to leave Elizabeth behind.

"Sit, Mr. Darcy," she ordered. "On the floor beside the bed." Darcy's knees ached with the effort, but he followed the woman's instructions. When he was settled uncomfortably against the bed's wooden frame, she said ominously, "From this angle, Mrs. Darcy rests within my view."

Darcy realized the woman had outmaneuvered him. His initial response was to jump between the housekeeper and Elizabeth, but something in the woman's countenance said she had expected him to act so. Therefore, he sat very still, his lack of movement holding the woman's attention.

"Are you interested in how I came upon this place, Mr. Darcy?" she asked mysteriously.

Darcy glanced about the room, seeing it for the first time. Despite the dirt floor, the place was tidier than he would have expected. Little feminine touches—a bit of frilly lace, a vase with fresh flowers, a set of lemon-yellow drapes—all gave the room a cozy feel. Only the bed stood unadorned.

"I assume you wish to tell me, and I hold no objection to hearing," he said blandly.

"Your cousin," came her flippant remark. "Mr. Samuel planned to offer it to Mrs. Holbrook when he pensioned Sarah off. Can you imagine?" The woman narrowed her gaze. "Of course, you can. In your conceit, you would think this an appropriate reward for all the years Mrs. Holbrook has served this estate, and, of course, the sorrowful excuse for a woman believes she deserves nothing better. She is quite content with the notice Mr. Samuel had paid her." She gestured with the cane. "Sarah brought me to this cottage to show me her future home. Every few months or so, she brings another bit of herself here and puts it on display."

The woman's words explained everything except the fresh flowers. Darcy suspected Mrs. Ridgeway had treated Mrs. Holbrook's future cottage as her own. He remained unmoving. His silence encouraged the housekeeper to continue her tale.

"I wondered to what I might have to look forward," she said honestly. "If this simple room was the reward for more than twenty years of service, what might be my reward for less than ten? Half of this luxury?" she said with true contempt.

God, he hoped all this misery had roots deeper than simple greed. "How often do you make use of Mrs. Holbrook's cottage?"

Mrs. Ridgeway's eyes narrowed. "Sometimes I come here for the solitude, to be alone with my thoughts. I do not imagine Sarah would mind awfully so."

As he had assumed from the beginning of their acquaintance, Darcy recognized the housekeeper as the key to Woodvine's evil. "And other times?" he urged.

The woman snarled, "I suppose you think I arranged trysts…"

Darcy thought something of that nature happened within these walls, but he said, "My mind was more seriously engaged."

He watched carefully. The lady's eyes had taken on a dazed look, and the housekeeper began to preen. "I was raised as a lady," she announced without preamble. "I am the daughter of a Spanish *Conde*, a pompous man who thought so little of his own flesh that he would sell his child to a vagrant for some fifteen doubloons and two horses. Less than a pound of gold! A fortune for the man to whom I was sold, but a pittance to my father."

Darcy shivered involuntarily. He could not imagine an insult so dire as to force a man to part freely with his children. "Your offense?" he whispered softly into the empty room.

"Against my father's wishes, I thought to choose my husband." A single tear escaped the woman's eye before she blinked those that would follow away. Darcy's first thought was of Elizabeth. He had always assumed his parents would have wished him the happiness Darcy had found with the former Elizabeth Bennet; yet, in reality, Darcy held no way of knowing for certain. Unfortunately, as the only son, for many years an only child, he was spoiled by his parents, who, though good themselves, had allowed, encouraged, almost taught him to be selfish and overbearing; to care for none beyond his own family circle; to think meanly of all the rest of the world; to wish, at least to think meanly of their sense and worth compared with his own. It was likely his parents would have forbidden him to pursue a joining with the one woman who completed him. If they had objected to Elizabeth, as had his aunt, Lady Catherine De Bourgh, would he have had the strength to oppose his parents? Darcy would like to think he possessed such good principles, but he feared that in such circumstances his cousin, Anne De Bourgh, would be the reigning Mistress of Pemberley.

"A woman born to the Spanish aristocracy," Mrs. Ridgeway said bitterly, "is not equipped to become the wife of a man little more than a peddler. My father closed the door to my family home, and I never looked back."

"How did you fare?"

She laughed sarcastically. "Not well. A woman who has known luxury finds it difficult to accept a running river as her toilette, but I refused to permit either my husband or my father dominion over me. I bore Merripen two sons, and then I left him."

Darcy did not readily respond. The tension in the room was thick with uncertainty. "I had thought you a widow," he said cautiously. A light flick of the hairs on the back of his neck made him wish to slap a stubborn fly away, but he would not risk a sudden movement.

Mrs. Ridgeway smiled knowingly. "I am. Several times over."

Darcy concentrated on what the woman did not say. Had Mrs. Ridgeway assisted her husband to his grave? He opened his mouth to ask of the source of her husband's passing, but he bit back his foolish question. Instead, he asked, "And your sons?"

Before the woman could respond, the "fly" had returned, but this time the pesky insect drew a line up and down Darcy's neck. Elizabeth was awake! Darcy wished he could turn to take her in his arms, but neither of them was safe. As an alternative, he casually leaned into her touch to tell Elizabeth he was aware of her presence.

"One lives. My youngest has recently passed. But the elder is a strong leader of my former husband's family."

Darcy tilted his head as if he meant to stretch his neck. He hoped Elizabeth was listening carefully to the housekeeper's tale. "And how did you come to travel to America?"

"My second husband meant to earn his fortune in the former colonies." Another sarcastic laugh followed. "I have never chosen well, Mr. Darcy."

He possessed many more questions regarding the woman's personal life, but Darcy tempered his curiosity. He licked his dry lips and swallowed hard before saying, "Then you made the acquaintance of my cousin?"

She glanced briefly to the open door. "Mr. Samuel offered me a position of authority within his household." She sighed. "Your cousin spoke to me as a lady; we would drink our tea and converse of an evening. Mr. Samuel thought me intelligent enough to share his work."

His brows lifted, knowing that feigned wistful tone all too well. Darcy ventured, "But something changed with my cousin's return to England in February?"

The lady scowled. "The fault lay at Mr. Hotchkiss's feet. The steward had written repeatedly to Mr. Samuel of his outrageous suspicions. I attempted to assuage Reuben's fears, but he was unreasonably set in his opinions. By the time Mr. Samuel had returned to Dorset, his mind had taken a distrustful turn. Mr. Samuel saw evil where none existed."

Darcy considered what perfidy Samuel likely met upon his return: his most trusted servants missing or released to other employment. Rumors of a witch's coven. All this led to a desperate need to secure his most precious treasures before someone could spirit them away.

"As if Mr. Samuel had lost all hope, your cousin roamed Woodvine's passages. Who would have known the late Mr. Darcy felt such a strong sense of loyalty to a man of Mr. Hotchkiss's lineage?" The woman was a walking juxtaposition: a gun-wielding tigress and a stunningly vulnerable innocent.

"Samuel held a great affinity for those who came within his protective realm," Darcy declared baldly.

Mrs. Ridgeway snarled, "Mr. Samuel held an affection for you, Mr. Darcy. That is infinite proof of your cousin's great heart." A strange sadness crossed the woman's countenance. She stood with determination. "It is best if we finish this." The housekeeper took a step in Elizabeth's direction.

Darcy instinctively scrambled to his feet to shelter his wife. "I will not permit you to hurt her," he hissed.

The housekeeper chuckled ironically. "And how shall you prevent me?"

"You will need to kill me first." Darcy's eyes searched the room for a weapon. "Saving Elizabeth is no encumbrance."

The housekeeper raised the gun she held. "To kill you would be of little consequence," she said bitterly.

"It does not have to be as such," Darcy coaxed. He edged farther to the left. Mrs. Ridgeway's mouth set at a tight downward slant, and her eyes narrowed. Any beauty the woman had once possessed had faded to hard lines. Darcy watched her closely. Surprisingly, the woman handled the gun with an impressive level of expertise. She motioned him to the right, but he shook off her silent request with a tilt of his head. His refusal appeared to frustrate her. "I will not make this easy," he warned.

She smiled harshly. "I expected as much when I discovered you here."

The sound of the shot filled the room. The exploding gunpowder spread like an encroaching fog. As Darcy spun to the right, the bullet entered his arm, but he quickly straightened his stance before springing forward. In the tight quarters of the room, his weight drove the housekeeper to the floor; however, the woman was not so easily defeated. Mrs. Ridgeway fought like one of the legendary ghostly black dogs of the British countryside. She bit and snapped at his hands and scratched her nails across his face. Finally, Darcy managed to wrestle the woman to a halt. "I swear if you do more than bat an eyelid, I will forget that I was raised as a gentleman," he hissed.

Ejected with the vengeance of those of the lower classes, Mrs. Ridgeway's spittle covered Darcy's face. "I do not fear you," she growled. "Men stronger than you have attempted to tame me."

Darcy dared not to release the woman's pinned hands, so he turned his cheek into his sleeve to wipe away the foul liquid. He pressed his weight harder against her. "I do not wish to tame you, Madam. I simply want you out of my life."

A struggle of wills ensued, but finally the housekeeper nodded her agreement. Darcy eased his weight from her and backed away. His arm burned with the fire of a thousand flames, but he refused to remove his eyes from the woman who lay flat on her back on the dirt floor. He sidestepped to where the gun rested under the chair.

Cautiously aware of the woman, Darcy bent stiffly at the knees to catch the gun between his fingers. The housekeeper pushed upward to her elbows. "Do not move," he warned.

"You are bleeding heavily, Mr. Darcy," she said with satisfaction.

He looked directly and intently into her eyes. "It is nothing," he assured her. "A flesh wound." However, Darcy knew the woman had the right of it. He must secure Elizabeth's safety before he succumbed to the pains in his arm and side. Even now, his vision had taken on a dizzying swirl. With his booted foot, Darcy shoved the straight-backed chair in her direction. Surprisingly, it slid close to where the woman sat upon the floor before it tilted on its side. "Sit," he ordered.

The housekeeper slowly rolled to her knees and then stood stiffly. She caught the chair's back and righted it before sitting. "Now what?" she asked, judgingly.

A long silent moment passed between them. Darcy kept the gun pointed at her. It was a single-shot volley, but he would use the useless gun as a club against the woman if necessary. He circled the chair where she sat. Reaching the window, Darcy jerked the yellow muslin curtains from the hooks, which held them.

"Mrs. Holbrook will not appreciate your destroying her efforts." Mrs. Ridgeway's sarcastic response filled the small space between them."

"I will purchase better for the lady." Darcy could feel the storm rise in his stomach. He carefully breathed his way through the pain. Ripping the cloth over a nail protruding from the window frame, Darcy tore strips of yellow to bind the woman. He was not certain how long the thin cloth might restrain her, but if it were long enough for him to see Elizabeth to safety, Darcy would be satisfied.

He knelt behind Mrs. Ridgeway. "Give me your hands," he ordered. She resisted, but Darcy managed to capture her two hands into his one. He laced the strips through and around the housekeeper's wrists and pulled them tight. He then threaded additional strips through the runnels of the chair's back to secure Mrs. Ridgeway's hands behind her. The pain of using his arm was great, but Darcy simply repeated his wife's name over and over in his head. '*Elizabeth*' would keep him sound.

Standing slowly, he announced, "I will send someone to release you once I return Mrs. Darcy to safety."

"Then I will die in this chair," the woman said bitterly, "for there is no possibility that you and your wife will ever reach Woodvine."

Darcy stumbled toward the bed. "God will show me the way," he declared baldly. He bent to lift Elizabeth to him. "Come, Sweet-heart," he said tenderly to her. "I will have you well in no time."

It took all of Darcy's strength to gather Elizabeth's limp body into his arms. With every ounce of awareness his body possessed, Darcy had thought her awake when he and Mrs. Ridgeway had argued, but Elizabeth did not respond to his touch. However, his wife breathed the breath of life, and that fact was all which mattered. The mixture the housekeeper had given her would work its way through Elizabeth's body, and she would wake up as he had awakened after the school prank.

Darcy brushed his lips across Elizabeth's forehead. "One step at a time. We will be at Woodvine soon, my Lizzy." With a fortifying gulp of air in his lungs, he started for the door.

"You truly mean to leave me behind?" Mrs. Ridgeway accused.

Darcy paused beside the open door. "I do."

A heavy enveloping silence wedged itself between them. He pivoted to carry his bundle through the opening. It was late after-noon. By the time he reached Woodvine, it would be dark. Darcy wondered if his cousin and Cowan had returned to the manor house and what news they had brought. With each step, he felt the blood dripping from his arm. He feared to turn his head to see the droplets in the dirt. Did he have enough blood flowing through his veins to leave a trail to Woodvine?

"I love you," he whispered to the woman he carried like a sacrificial lamb. Elizabeth's arms and legs dangled about his thighs, but Darcy had no strength to correct his hold on his wife. He focused on the stile so he might cross the field. From the stile, he would choose a new goal, then another and another until he crossed Woodvine's threshold.

"Fitz…" she murmured, and Darcy halted his weary steps to lean against a tree. Darcy refused to place his wife down for fear he might not have the strength to gather her to him again.

"Shush, Sweetheart. I am here." With his back against the tree for support, Darcy managed to lift Elizabeth higher in his arms.

"Alive," she whispered.

"Yes, my Lizzy. We are both alive, and soon we will be at Woodvine. You and I are meant to be together." He kissed her hair where it draped across his shoulder. Reinvigorated by her two simple words, Darcy started again on his journey. "Just a few steps, Darling."

However, the crack of a crushed branch told him they were no longer alone. Darcy turned slowly in a circle, attempting to discover what or who watched them. His eyes fell on movement behind a low-lying bush. "Whoever is there, show yourself," he challenged. The gun rested against his waist, but without ammunition, it was useless.

Sweat poured into his eyes and exhaustion burned his chest, but Darcy stood strong. As he blinked away the darkness, time crawled. Finally, a familiar figure pushed through the vegetation to step into the clearing. Darcy's breath caught in his throat. "My God, Stowbridge, you frightened me," he expelled in relief. "I have never been so happy to see anyone in my life."

"Where is Areej?" the magistrate demanded.

"Areej?" A grimace crossed Darcy's countenance. "I do not understand."

"Mrs. Ridgeway. Areej. My wife."

Chapter 25

"Your wife?" Disbelief clouded Darcy's words. His heart faltered with false hope. "When did you make the woman your wife?" he demanded. "There has been no reading of the banns while I have resided in Dorset. How can it be?"

The magistrate stepped to where he might have the advantage. Stowbridge smiled with condescension. "Actually, I married Areej some thirty years ago. It was only with your cousin's offer of a position within his household that we were reunited. In fact, my Areej spent some ten months under Samuel's roof before I discovered her again."

Darcy adjusted Elizabeth in his hold. He no longer possessed feeling in his arms and shoulders. Even his wounds had ceased their throbbing. "You are a country gentleman. Your wife…Mrs. Stowbridge spoke of a forced marriage."

For a brief second the magistrate tossed him a confused glance, but then Stowbridge laughed sarcastically. "Has my dear Areej told the old tale of a vagrant and a pound of gold? My wife does love to twist the truth. It gives her a reason to blame her trials upon others."

Darcy staggered as he shifted his weight. He did not think he could carry Elizabeth much farther.

As if he read Darcy's mind, the magistrate said, "Place Mrs. Darcy on the ground, and come with me."

"I will not abandon my wife," Darcy declared boldly.

The magistrate scowled, as if he were uncertain whether Darcy spoke the truth. "Under the current circumstances, the choice does not rest in your hands. Carefully place Mrs. Darcy where she might rest easily. I assume Mrs. Stowbridge has used her '*healing*' powders for evil. You will learn, Darcy, that the longer you know Areej, the more you will swear never to trust her."

"That is an easy assumption," Darcy hissed. Unable to support Elizabeth's weight any longer, he reluctantly bent to place his wife gently on a grassy patch. As he adjusted his coat about her, he managed to palm the small pistol he kept in his inside pocket. Hiding it in the fullness of his shirtsleeve, Darcy rose to face the magistrate. "What I do not understand, Stowbridge, is why you would wish to claim a woman whom you willingly admit breathes deceit."

The man smiled wistfully. "I have held a tender spot for my darling Areej since I first laid eyes upon her. My wife reminds me of a horse of fine lineage, but one which possesses a wild streak. The lady wishes to roam free with the rest of the herd rather than enjoy the luxury of a clean stall and plenty of oats." The magistrate's posture indicated a loss of any amiability. "You will accompany me to the house, Mr. Darcy," Stowbridge said darkly.

"And if I refuse?"

The magistrate's chest puffed out in self-importance. "Then I will be persuaded to shoot you where you stand."

The detachment with which Stowbridge pronounced the words was in sharp contrast to his earlier demeanor. The difference played to the building dread which Darcy fought hard to control. A quick glance at his wife in repose permitted Darcy to acquiesce. He turned his feet toward the cottage's still-open door. "What do you hope to accomplish?" he asked carefully.

Stowbridge trailed some five feet behind him. "I will rescue Areej from whatever torment you have wreaked upon her being, then I will devise a means to rid myself of your interference in Wimborne affairs."

Darcy paused briefly. "I would gladly fade from your memory if you will permit me to remove Mrs. Darcy to safety."

Stowbridge drew in air sharply. "If I could but trust you, Mr. Darcy, both of our lives would turn for the better; yet, I am aware of your honor. It is the salt of your soul, and you could no more look away from what has occurred here than you could to stop yourself from loving Mrs. Darcy."

Darcy declared, "Surely a man who speaks kindly of a woman who has left him alone for more than twenty years should understand. For my wife, I would do the impossible."

"And I would do likewise for mine," Stowbridge baldly responded. He gestured with the gun for Darcy to precede him into the cottage.

The housekeeper looked up upon their entrance. Darcy noticed that she had managed to manipulate her position on the chair to where her arm hung over the back, and her tied wrists were contorted painfully. "It is kind of you to make an appearance, Loiza," the lady said sarcastically.

Despite his wife's testy attitude, Stowbridge smiled kindly. "If you expected me to rescue you, my dear, then you should have informed me of your whereabouts." He motioned Darcy to step aside so he might kneel at the lady's side. "Do not move, my darling," he said as he used a small knife he had retrieved from his pocket to cut away what remained of the frayed muslin strips.

"I have asked for no endearments." Her voice held more irritation than Darcy thought necessary. She rubbed away the pain where the material had left red welts on her skin.

"Then who would speak the truth, *mí amor?*" he asked softly.

Heaven forbid! Darcy thought. The squire truly held an affection for his wife. The thought of loving such a woman sent shivers down Darcy's spine. He did not know whether to pity Stowbridge or to fear him. The man's blindness to Mrs. Stowbridge's true nature made the squire a dangerous foe.

Surprisingly, the housekeeper's countenance softened. "You are an excellent man, Loiza," she murmured, "but I refuse to permit you to own my soul."

Stowbridge stiffened. He stood quickly to glare down at his wife. "No, I suppose not," he said coldly. "The only one you ever allowed to know that part of you was that bastard Merripen, the one to whom you bore two sons. My sons, Areej," he hissed. "You presented your lover with my rightful children!" His accusations stung Darcy's compassion, but Mrs. Stowbridge appeared unmoved. The lady's countenance showed no signs that she had behaved in a shameful manner.

"I could never have lived the life you wished of me, Loiza," she said matter-of-factly. There was no sadness. No guilt. The woman had left Stowbridge in limbo. He had married Mrs. Ridgeway, or whatever she had once been called. The magistrate must have been a man in his prime when they had wed. Even if Stowbridge could have divorced the woman and have taken another wife, the man would have been too old to sire an heir. "I was but fifteen." It was the woman's only attempt at a defense, and Darcy felt consideration for both. They had made each other miserable.

Mrs. Stowbridge glanced to where Darcy watched their interchange. "What have you done with Mrs. Darcy?" she demanded.

"Nothing more than to leave the lady upon the ground outside," her husband reported.

Mrs. Stowbridge sighed heavily. "We have another quandary, Loiza." Her voice had changed to one of business. She gestured toward where Darcy waited. Darcy considered making a run for safety. But even if he were not weak from his injuries, Darcy would never leave Elizabeth behind.

Stowbridge straightened his shoulders. "You promised that Glover would be the last of them." Darcy's full being had come alert. The couple spoke openly of what Darcy had long suspected.

"I thought Geoffrey's passing would have been the milk which spilled from the jug," she reasoned. "Would not reasonable people walk away after so much heartache?"

Stowbridge observed, "You have never understood *pride*, Areej. A man's pride and his honor encourage him to do the impossible."

"We shall go away this night," the lady coaxed. "To America or home to Spain. You would love to see Corunna again, would you not, Loiza?"

"And if I refuse?" Stowbridge tested his wife's words.

The housekeeper reasoned, "We have little choice, Mr. Stowbridge. The Darcys know too much of what has occurred here."

Darcy certainly did not enjoy being spoken of as if he were not present, and he disliked the gist of this conversation even more. "You could still leave without harming Mrs. Darcy or me," he suggested. "Leave us in the cottage. It will take several hours before anyone mounts a search and several more before anyone comes across us. As a payment for my wife's life, I will give you my word as a gentleman that I will not send anyone after you." Darcy would bargain with the Devil to keep Elizabeth alive. He still had the small pistol in his possession, and he could use it against Stowbridge or the man's wife and then fight off the other of the pair.

The woman tilted her head as if considering Darcy's proposal, and for a few brief seconds, he thought the couple would acquiesce. However, when the lady pointedly turned her back on him, Darcy knew he had failed; he would require a different plan to free his wife. The lady glowered at him, her scorn showing.

Mrs. Stowbridge said, "Mr. Darcy's words would make one believe that he could turn his head and pretend not to see what is obvious; yet, you have just spoken of a man's pride. Tell me, Loiza, is it possible that Mr. Darcy possesses no pride?"

Stowbridge stared long and hard at Darcy. Finally, he said grudgingly, "No, Mr. Darcy is eaten up with pride." He shrugged his shoulders in defeat. "Could we not simply give both Darcys a dose of your healing powders? There has been enough bloodshed."

Darcy pounced on the idea. It enflamed his hope of seeing Elizabeth safe. "I have an idea that may ensure the security you seek. Give my wife another of your powders, but leave Mrs. Darcy here. She can be no threat to you. If you agree, I will willingly leave with you. I will see you to a ship in Portsmouth," Darcy said readily. He cursed himself for not bringing Mr. Castle with him. The sharpshooter could have protected Darcy's retreat.

Before the woman could respond, the magistrate caught his wife's arm. "I believe him," he announced baldly. "Despite the man's conceit, Mr. Darcy loves his wife to distraction." The man's glance shifted toward the window. "It is coming on to night. We must hurry, Areej." From her posture, it was evident the woman did not agree with her husband's decision, but she allowed him to direct her to her task. "Prepare one of your sleeping draughts."

Darcy gestured to the door. "May I retrieve my wife from where she lies? Mrs. Darcy would be safer inside the cottage." He carefully eyed Mrs. Stowbridge's efforts at the small table. She had withdrawn several vials from the shelves and mixed the powders liberally. He must find a means to protect Elizabeth from receiving a dose from which his wife could not recover.

Stowbridge raised the gun he still held. "I will tolerate no tomfoolery," the magistrate warned.

Darcy nodded his understanding. He stood stiffly. His eyes never left Mrs. Stowbridge. The lady sprinkled the powder over a doubled-over cloth. So, Elizabeth had not ingested the powder. The idea pleased him. "You have my word," he said as he made his way to the door. "I mean only to protect my wife."

The magistrate smiled sadly. "It is a man's fate." He noticed how the squire looked on lovingly as his wife created her concoction. Darcy understood how love could twist a man's heart, but not how that same love could make a man blind to evil. How could Stowbridge condone what his wife had done? How much betrayal would one man tolerate?

Stowbridge had followed closely on Darcy's heels, so Darcy made no effort to speak to Elizabeth. He simply gathered her to him. Standing slowly, he focused on their return to the cottage. Stepping into the darkening shadows, he reverently carried his wife to the undressed mattress. Tenderly, he placed Elizabeth on the thin padding and straightened her clothing. He draped her braid over Elizabeth's shoulder. "I love you," he whispered as he kissed her forehead.

Mrs. Stowbridge leaned across the bed. "Move away, Mr. Darcy," she ordered.

Darcy refused to retreat. "I will administer the mixture. I agreed to permit you to place my wife under a deep sleep, but there is a fine line between sleep and death when one mixes such potent ingredients. I will not stand by and permit you to kill my wife." He extended his hand for what the woman carried, and a battle of wills ensued.

After several elongated seconds, Stowbridge ordered, "Give the man the cloth, Areej. You may supervise."

The woman shot her husband a look of pure contempt, but she pointedly dumped the damp cloth into Darcy's outstretched palm. "Place the cloth over Mrs. Darcy's mouth and nose," she said testily. "You must hold it tightly against your wife's face. Mrs. Darcy must inhale the powder." Her explanation brought clarity as to how Elizabeth had come to have the powder upon her lovely face. Darcy shifted the small pistol under his bent knee, where it rested on the bed. He leaned over Elizabeth to mask his efforts. Darcy straightened the cloth and palmed it in his right hand. The slight movement set his teeth on edge as pain ricocheted down his arm.

Determined to finish this idiocy, Darcy spread the cloth across the flat of his palm; then he cupped his hand slightly to protect his wife from the full impact of the mixture. With a sigh of reluctance, Darcy placed the cloth across Elizabeth's nose and mouth. With his upper arm, he blocked Mrs. Stowbridge's sight enough that he could slip his thumb under the cloth's edge. He pressed his thumb against Elizabeth's lips to prevent them from parting. That bit of manipulation would keep his wife from ingesting the mixture through her mouth.

Almost immediately Elizabeth's mind registered his presence as another attack, and she instinctively fought him. Darcy quickly realized if he had permitted Mrs. Stowbridge to deliver the concoction, Elizabeth would have suffered. Therefore, he kept the cloth across his wife's mouth and nose, but Darcy leaned over Elizabeth to whisper in her ear. "Shush, my Lizzy. I mean you no harm. Shush, Darling."

Elizabeth ceased her struggle. She gasped for a breath, and, slowly, her eyes opened. At first, her gaze remained clouded, but *his* Elizabeth fought her way to consciousness. Darcy cherished the moment. If harm came to him, it would be the last one they would share. "I am here, Elizabeth." He kept his right hand pressed across her mouth, but with his left, Darcy caressed the side of her head. "You must rest again," he said encouragingly. Darcy prayed his wife's lucid thoughts would understand that he meant for her to pretend to sleep. Elizabeth blinked twice and then inhaled deeply. Darcy prayed her breath had not been too deep. He did not want her haunted by hallucinations.

"I have agreed to go with the Stowbridges." Darcy placed a slight emphasis on the last word to convey important information. "Do not fight me, Lizzy. I mean for you to survive." He used his pet name for her to soften what Darcy meant for her to understand. "Do your duty as my wife," he instructed. Elizabeth blinked her understanding, and Darcy noted the panic, which crossed her expression before his wife valiantly chased it away with an unwavering resolve. "Breathe in the mixture, Elizabeth. It is my wish." A single tear escaped her eye, and Darcy kissed it away. "I have always loved you."

Mrs. Stowbridge scoffed with disgust. "Enough sentimentality," she growled. "Give me the cloth."

The woman planned to replace him as the powder's administrator, but Darcy violently shoved her away. "If you touch her,

422

I will kill you," he hissed. "My wife has known enough of your perfidy, Madam." Darcy's chest heaved with anger. "I promised to accompany you and Mr. Stowbridge without incident, but only if you exact no harm upon my wife."

"Leave the man to say his farewells, Areej," Stowbridge encouraged.

Darcy ignored the interplay between husband and wife. Instead, he concentrated on giving his wife to understand that he would save her no matter the cost to himself. Anxiety tautened the lines of his wife's muscles. "Should I not return, I charge you with Georgiana's care and the future of Pemberley. You know my wish in this matter," he said with a slight emphasis. "Now, close your eyes and breathe deeply." Subtly, he had managed to slip his smallest finger under the cloth without Mrs. Stowbridge's notice. He partially blocked the openings to Elizabeth's nostrils. When his wife's lungs expanded, Darcy noted how she purposely created the illusion of her chest rising and falling. He breathed easier: She would follow his instructions. Elizabeth had understood his urgency.

Darcy continued to study her face, memorizing each line and that one small dimple, which deepened when she smiled at him. Darcy knew exactly how much of the powder his wife inhaled. He could feel what did not reach her lungs accumulate on his finger and thumb. Elizabeth was a wonderful actress. She stared into his eyes, and Darcy saw his love returned. Periodically, his wife would slowly blink, as if she fought the inevitable sleep. Finally, she released him by closing her eyes and leaving them so. Her breathing shallowed.

Reluctantly, Darcy kissed Elizabeth's forehead. Removing his hand from her mouth, he surreptitiously wiped the excess powder from his fingers onto the cloth before he returned it to Mrs. Stowbridge. Before he rose to stand beside the bed, Darcy attempted to retrieve the small gun, but Mrs. Ridgeway watched him too closely. Refusing to place Elizabeth in more danger, he left it beside where his wife's body rested on the mattress. He edged it under the folds of his jacket before setting his shoulders against the inevitable.

"We should depart," Stowbridge declared.

Her chin rose as if the lady meant to verbally attack her husband's character. Instead, she swallowed her retort, and despite her pronounced frown, she asked, "How shall we proceed?"

"I must return to Stowe Hall to gather my papers before we may leave." Stowbridge motioned Darcy toward the door. With one longing look at his wife, Darcy exited the small cottage, likely for the last time. He prayed he had made the correct decision.

Mrs. Stowbridge followed her husband into the quickening evening shadows. Darcy noticed the woman carried the last of the vials in one hand. "We cannot simply march Mr. Darcy into Stowe Hall and expect the servants to look the other way," she said challengingly.

Stowbridge's patience with the woman was inexhaustible. "What do you suggest?"

"I will take Mr. Darcy with me to await your arrival," she declared.

The magistrate's lips flattened into a thin line. "Do you think that best?" he asked cautiously. "After all, I found you tied to a chair less than an hour prior." Darcy suspected the magistrate wondered if the woman had an alternate plan. After all, the lady had, obviously, practiced her perfidy often.

The man's wife sighed in exasperation. "I made a mistake. It shall not occur again."

"But, still…" the squire began.

However, the former housekeeper allowed her husband no sway. "It is as you have said: Mr. Darcy's honor shall keep me safe." She caressed the squire's arm. "It would be best if we traveled by night. Please hurry your errand."

The magistrate's features softened. "We will meet at the customary place." With that, the squire pressed the gun into her hand before disappearing into the brush.

"Where to?" Darcy asked sarcastically.

In the fading light, he saw a smile of satisfaction shape the woman's lips. "To my favorite place in Wimborne: the village church."

Chapter 26

"I apologize, Colonel," Ian McKye said for what must have been the twentieth time in the past hour. "I had thought I observed all the entrances and exits of Stowe Hall."

Edward Fitzwilliam did not blame the man. To date, McKye had proved a most valuable asset in the investigation, but the colonel's frustration had reached its breaking point. He and Thomas Cowan had returned to Woodvine Hall to discover both Darcy and Elizabeth missing. "I understand," Edward said evenly, "but I require more information. Question each of Stowbridge's servants. I want answers."

"Aye, Sir." The man disappeared into the bowels of Stowe Hall.

Edward stared out the window of Stowbridge's study on the rapidly encroaching shadows of nightfall. How was he to find his cousin and Elizabeth if he possessed no idea where to begin? "Damn," the colonel growled. "Where are you, Darcy?"

He and Cowan had just begun to make sense of Holbrook's tale of Barriton's stabbing Darcy and of Mrs. Darcy's early morning departure with Mrs. Ridgeway when McKye had ridden into Woodvine's circle to report that both Mrs. Ridgeway and Mr. Stowbridge were missing from Stowe Hall. The magistrate and the housekeeper had slipped from the main house through a root cellar tunnel leading to the wooded area surrounding the house. Unfortunately, McKye had not discovered their exits in time to detain the couple. "Are they a couple?" Edward wondered aloud.

"Or had the magistrate attempted to curtail Mrs. Ridgeway's plans for Elizabeth?"

Immediately, he and Cowan had rushed to the magistrate's house to confirm what McKye had reported. They had taken over the squire's home and demanded to know the truth.

Edward looked up at the sound of hurried footsteps. McKye's head appeared around the door's frame. "Mr. Cowan reports that the squire has reentered the tunnel through the opening in the woods. Cowan has secured the exit against escape."

Immediately, Edward was on the move. "I want the man alive so I might question him."

McKye followed on the colonel's heels. "I have Castle and Douglas waiting in the kitchen, Sir."

Edward took several steps together to skid to a stop on the threshold of the cellar's door just as it opened to reveal the worn countenance of the magistrate. Behind him, the colonel heard the click of a gun. "Welcome, Stowbridge."

The magistrate shot a quick glance about the room. Edward had vast experience in reading a man's countenance, but Stow-bridge's face held nothing but shock at finding himself prisoner in his own house. "What is the meaning of this?" the squire asked angrily. "You have entered my home uninvited."

"You will come with me," Edward ordered.

The man's cheeks reddened. "I will not be importuned by your actions, Sir," Stowbridge declared. "Instead, you and your men will leave my house immediately. Your status as an earl's son will not serve you in this matter."

Edward caught the man by the lapels to jerk him to within an inch of the colonel's scowling countenance. "Listen to me, Stow-bridge, I am not a patient man. I want information regarding Mr.

and Mrs. Darcy's disappearances, and you will tell me what you know," he hissed.

The magistrate spit out the words. "And if I choose otherwise?"

Edward smiled wickedly. "I hope you refuse," he said flatly. "My ire has had several hours to stew, and I am prepared to introduce you to the more creative means I have learned of forcing a man to spill his most private secrets."

Evidently, Cowan had followed the squire through the tunnel, for he appeared behind the man. He whispered ominously, "In the Army, a man learns many ways to kill another. To kill him quickly or slowly. To feel no compunctions about laying a hot iron across a man's chest until his enemy's skin sizzles with the smell of burning flesh. Or to place that same iron upon a person's manhood. To watch it shrivel to nothing; yet, the pain does not go away."

Edward added, "Or to cut a man over and over. Little pricks that permit him to bleed to death slowly. One drop at a time." He tightened his grip on Stowbridge's lapels. "As I said previously, I can be quite creative with my options."

For several elongated seconds, Stowbridge resisted, but his composure crumpled when Cowan placed a knife's point above the squire's kidneys. "Say the word, Colonel," Cowan threatened.

"What will it be, Stowbridge?" Edward asked coldly.

The magistrate straightened his shoulders. "Not before the servants. In my study."

The colonel reluctantly released the man. "If you think to stall, you will regret your choice." With a simple nod of agreement, Edward turned on his heels to lead the way to the room. Behind him, he heard Cowan giving orders for Castle to station himself outside the tunnel and Douglas inside. The former Runner placed

McKye outside the study's door and then joined Edward in the room with the magistrate.

Upon reaching the room, Stowbridge sat heavily. He dropped his head into his hands. "What do you wish of me?" he asked dejectedly.

"The truth."

The magistrate snorted his disbelief. "It has been some five and twenty years since I have spoken the truth. I am uncertain whether I would recognize it."

Edward sat across from the man. "Do you know the whereabouts of Mr. Darcy and his wife?" He would not permit the squire's fallen countenance any compassion.

The magistrate rested his head against the chair's cushions. He squeezed his eyes closed, and Edward noted that the man's hands trembled. "Mrs. Darcy is in a cottage on the border of Woodvine's land," he said in defeat. "It is the one Samuel promised to Sarah Holbrook."

Edward spoke to his former recruit. "Send McKye to the stable for the horses. Ask him to have Holbrook available to lead us to this cottage."

Cowan disappeared into the hall, but returned before Edward could ask his next question. "And my cousin?"

"I am not certain," the magistrate said without affect. "Mr. Darcy left with Areej. Your cousin has used his life as security for Mrs. Darcy's."

"Areej?" Edward demanded. "Who the hell is Areej?"

Stowbridge opened his eyes, but he did not look at the colonel. "My wife of a little less than three decades."

Edward did a poor job of hiding his surprise. "You are married?"

Cowan finished Edward's question. "To Mrs. Ridgeway?" As usual, the Runner's quick mind had leapt over Edward's to reach the crux of the situation.

Stowbridge swallowed hard. "Yes to both questions. I am a man with a wife who has never loved nor respected him. A man whose wife preferred a simple vagrant with not a penny to his name to the life I could have provided her as my Baronesa."

"Who are you?" Edward demanded.

The magistrate's shoulders straightened and his chin lifted. "Barón Loiza Puente de Stowe."

"A Spanish baron?" Edward's wary tone betrayed his surprise.

"In truth, Aragonese." Sadly, the man's former stature returned. "Long ago, prior to more wars than I can recall, I left my country behind to seek freedom in your great land. For a quarter century, I have been Mr. Louis Stowbridge. I purchased this land's connections, along with the manor house. For nearly twenty years, I have been Squire Stowbridge. Not as important as a baron, but quite satisfying nonetheless."

"And where has Mrs. Stowbridge resided?" Cowan coaxed.

The squire turned his head in the Runner's direction. "Areej despised being told that she could not marry as her heart chose. At her father's insistence, we spoke our vows, but within a month of our joining, she was gone, off with her lover. I searched for my wife, but in 1779, the war came to Corunna, where I had taken up residence." The colonel and Cowan exchanged a knowing look. They had experienced Corunna in '09, and they knew northwest Spain well. It was a quirk of Fate that they had encountered a man from the infamous Spanish corridor here in Dorset. "The French brought scurvy and typhus and smallpox to the area while they waited for the Spanish fleet to arrive. The illnesses and the lack of a timely joining of their forces cost the French a victory. The disease spread to those on land, and, eventually, I fled with what remained of my family, first to Italy, and later to England."

"You have not answered my question," Cowan observed.

Stowbridge shrugged noncommittally. "I cannot speak to Areej's early years. I worked to salvage my fortune. To tend my aging parents. I knew nothing of Areej until one day I called upon my dear friend Samuel, only to discover that my wife had served as Samuel's housekeeper for some ten months. Ten months she could have lived as my wife, in my home."

Characteristically, the Runner ignored the magistrate's sentimentality. Instead, he asked, "And you are to meet Mrs. Stowbridge where?"

"At the customary place."

"Which is?" Cowan persisted.

"In the assembly hall's lowest level."

Edward thought that an odd rendezvous place, but before he could question Stowbridge further, a knock at the door signaled Mr. Holbrook's arrival. "I have more questions, but I must see to Mrs. Darcy." The colonel retrieved his gloves. "I will leave two guards with you."

Stowbridge raised his head to speak to the colonel. "Give Mrs. Darcy my deepest apologies."

"For what offense?" Edward insisted.

The magistrate's expression fell. "Areej had given Mrs. Darcy a heady mixture prior to my arrival. The lady suffers the degradation."

"And you call yourself a gentleman?" Edward accused.

Stowbridge sighed deeply. "I call myself a husband."

Cowan said caustically, "A husband without a wife."

"My fate." Those two words fell into the silence. Finally, the man's chin dropped to rest on his chest. He said morosely, "If you discover my wife in time, tell Areej that I am grieved to have failed her the one time she trusted me."

Edward demanded, "What do you mean by *in time?*"

The squire had closed his eyes again.

"Speak to me, damn you." The colonel shook the man violently.

A tear ran down the magistrate's wrinkled cheek. "Mr. Darcy is bleeding from both his shoulder and his side. He has lost much blood."

* * *

Elizabeth struggled to roll from the bed. Darcy had meant to protect her by drawing the magistrate and Mrs. Ridgeway from the cottage, but she would not permit her husband to leave her behind. He could not sacrifice himself to save her. Whatever happened to Darcy would be her fate also. She would not live without him.

"Fitz…william." Her lips formed his name as she reached for the chair to support her weight. She rubbed the back of her hand across her dry lips. The sweet taste of apples remained but was not as strong as previously.

Through the still-open door, Elizabeth could see Darcy's strong back muscles clench in pain as he trudged along the narrow path. Stowbridge had left them, but Mrs. Ridgeway now held the gun on Darcy. If she did not hurry, the pair would leave her in this cottage alone.

Although her legs felt as limber as one of Mrs. Holbrook's jellies, Elizabeth lunged for the door. She overheard Darcy and the housekeeper arguing over what to expect next. Supporting herself against the doorframe, Elizabeth listened with her complete self.

"Where to?" Darcy had asked sarcastically. Elizabeth wished he would look her way so her husband would know that she would follow him anywhere, but Darcy's attention remained on the woman with the gun.

In the fading light, Elizabeth noted the smile of satisfaction, which crossed the housekeeper's lips. The woman meant to kill Darcy, and it would be Elizabeth's responsibility to stop her. "To my favorite place in Wimborne: the village church." The woman, who had created havoc in their lives, walked away into the night. Unfortunately for Elizabeth, Darcy followed.

Determined to reach him in time, Elizabeth forced her feet forward. *One step at a time*. Her dear husband had said those words when he had carried her to safety. "I will follow you, my husband."

Unfortunately, she had taken no more than a half dozen steps before her vision swirled with an array of colors, and the ground rose up to slap her hard across her cheek.

* * *

"My God!" Edward gasped as he slid to the ground. He threw his reins at Holbrook as he rushed to Elizabeth's side. He rolled her gently to her back. "Elizabeth!" he pleaded. He slapped her cheeks, but his cousin's wife did not awaken.

"Here." Cowan shoved a small leather flask filled with water into Edward's hand.

The colonel fished a handkerchief from his pocket and wet it. The excess water formed a muddy outline along Elizabeth's shoulder, but Edward ignored the dirty smudge on Darcy's jacket, which was wrapped tightly about Elizabeth's frame. Instead, he wiped her face over and over. "Please, Elizabeth," Edward spoke with urgency. "I require your assistance to locate Darcy."

Somehow his cousin's name reached through her unconscious state, for the lady's lids slowly opened. Edward felt instant relief. He knew Darcy's temperament. If Edward managed to save Darcy, but not Elizabeth, his cousin would not be long for this world.

"Colonel." Her lips formed the word, but no sound escaped.

Edward placed the handkerchief to her lips. "Suck the water from this." At first, Elizabeth meant to shove his hand away, but Edward insisted, and she finally succumbed to his strength. "That is better." He handed the cloth to Cowan. "A bit more water, if you please, Thomas." Never once did Edward remove his eyes from Elizabeth's countenance. Someone had struck her, for a bruise was prominent even in the moonlit shadows. "Once more," he encouraged when the Runner returned the cloth. "Allow the water to trickle down your throat."

Finally, he lifted her to a reclining position. "Can you tell me what happened?"

Immediately, Elizabeth clawed at Edward's hand. "Fitz…will…iam," she whined.

"Is my cousin alive?" He motioned Cowan toward the cottage.

Elizabeth slumped against his shoulder. "No idea," she whispered on a rasp. "Was shot."

"I know," Edward saved her from straining her voice. "We caught Stowbridge. The magistrate told us where to find you. Did Darcy leave with Mrs. Stowbridge?"

Elizabeth's eyes widened in shock. "Mrs. Ridge…way?"

"Yes. The housekeeper is the magistrate's wife of some thirty years. Stowbridge is a former Aragonese baron."

Elizabeth shook her head in denial or disbelief. Edward was uncertain which—perhaps a bit of both. "She has…a gun." His cousin's wife shoved herself to a fully seated position. "Must stop

434

her," Elizabeth insisted. Despite Edward's best efforts to restrain her, Elizabeth struggled to stand.

"I mean to do just that." He supported Elizabeth to her feet. "But first I will see you on your way to Woodvine and Hannah's tender care."

Elizabeth caught his arm in a surprisingly tight grip. "No," she said adamantly. "I will travel with you."

"You are too weak," Edward argued. "And it is too dangerous."

Although her voice lacked its usual soprano tones, Elizabeth spoke with force. "If you ferry me against my will to Woodvine…I shall trail after you."

Edward had never met a woman like his cousin's wife. Elizabeth Darcy had a spirit which surpassed words. If he could find such a woman, Edward would marry her in a heartbeat—fortune or no. He caught her chin where he might see her features clearly. "If we encounter difficulties, you must promise to remain out of danger and to allow Cowan and me to rescue Darcy." She bit her bottom lip as if to argue, but Edward tipped Elizabeth's chin higher. "I mean what I say, Mrs. Darcy. Either you act responsibly or I leave you behind; locked in your room, if necessary."

She shifted her shoulders to a defiant slant before saying, "There is not a servant at Woodvine who would dare lock Mr. Darcy's wife in her room. And even if they would resist my protests, I would find a means of escape." She smiled in challenge. "However, as it would expedite Mr. Darcy's liberation if I acquiesce, I shall follow your instructions, Colonel."

At that moment, Edward regretted the fact he had never stolen a kiss from the former Elizabeth Bennet. Only her lack of fortune had kept him from acting upon his initial attraction to the woman. *Her fortune and Darcy's obvious infatuation with Elizabeth Bennet,* he thought. Would that not have been a jump into the hornet's nest? Edward would have lost his cousin's friendship if Miss Elizabeth had chosen him over Darcy. Or worse, his wife would have belatedly discovered how much she respected Fitzwilliam Darcy. Then they would all have spent a lifetime of misery, each knowing unrequited love.

"Good. You will ride with me." He caught Elizabeth up in his arms and carried her to the waiting horse. Edward set her upon the saddle before turning to the approaching Runner. "Anything?"

"Signs of a struggle. Some powdery mixture on the table. Found this small gun under the bed." He extended his hand to the colonel. "The cottage will require a thorough cleaning, but no sign of where the housekeeper has taken Mr. Darcy. We should set our steps for…"

"The assembly hall."

"The village church," Cowan and Elizabeth said concurrently.

Edward turned curiously to his cousin's wife. "What makes you believe the housekeeper would take Darcy to the church?"

"I overheard her. Mrs. Ridge…I mean, Mrs. Stowbridge, said she meant to see Fitzwilliam to her favorite place in the area: the village church."

"Are you certain?" Cowan asked from a respectful distance. "The powder on the table tasted of opium."

Elizabeth's small hands fisted in her lap, and Edward found it amusing that the strapping Thomas Cowan took another step backward. "It is true…that the housekeeper covered my mouth and nose…with an intoxicating mixture, but that was early this morning. Am I prepared to climb Derbyshire's peaks? No. But did I hear Mrs. Stowbridge's response to my husband's question?

Definitely. The woman said that she meant to travel to the village church."

Edward ventured, "Yet, the magistrate has assured us he was to meet his wife at the assembly hall."

Elizabeth grasped the saddle horn with a tight grip, which spoke of her anger. "Mr. Stowbridge means to make it easier for his wife to escape, or the magistrate deludes himself into thinking the woman means finally to remain true to her vows."

She meant to slide to the ground, but Edward caught her and pointedly returned Elizabeth to the seat. "Holbrook and I will escort Mrs. Darcy to the church to ease my cousin's concern for her husband. Cowan, you are to ride for the assembly hall. Whichever of us finds his search fruitless will join the other."

Cowan nodded curtly. "Be safe, Colonel." The investigator strode toward the waiting horse.

Edward knew enough of the man to realize Cowan thought Edward had allowed a mere woman to manipulate him. However, the colonel had witnessed the connection between Darcy and his wife. If Elizabeth was convinced that Darcy was at Wimborne church, he would follow her instincts. "And you, Cowan. No heroics," Edward cautioned.

Cowan smiled knowingly. "I leave those to the commanding officers, Sir."

Chapter 27

Darcy had initially wondered if he would make it to the church or not, but if today was his day to die, doing so in a church would be an appropriate statement to the world. He wished he had kept the small pistol to use against Mrs. Stowbridge, but Darcy knew he was not of the nature to kill someone in *sangfroid*. And even if he could manage to overpower the woman, his fever and his pain told Darcy he would likely not see the light of a new day.

"We will rest," the woman announced. She seated herself on the stump leading to the back of the church.

Darcy frowned. He had hoped to lie upon one of the wooden benches or even the floor of the private pews. "Do you hold a reluctance against crossing over the church's threshold?" He leaned over at the waist. His exhaustion screamed for him to lie upon the cold earth, but as their position looked out over the church's cemetery, Darcy ignored the impulse.

The woman glanced behind her to the small stained-glass window. She said, "God turned his back on me the day I walked away from Loiza. It seemed heretical to seek sanctuary in God's house." She patted the cold brink. "Come sit. We have some time before Mr. Stowbridge returns."

Reluctantly, Darcy stumbled forward. Catching the brick wall, he lowered his weight upon the cool stone step. Instinctively, Darcy sighed audibly. He leaned against the step above and closed his eyes to the world. He heard her moving about, but Darcy was too exhausted to care for the woman's manipulations.

"Here." Mrs. Stowbridge shoved a jar containing some sort of liquid into his hand.

Darcy lifted the jar to examine it in the moonlight. "Whence did this come?"

"From under the steps. I keep a few essentials hidden about the grounds. No one steals from the church," she said in explanation. Mrs. Stowbridge sounded almost normal, and Darcy considered himself quite delusional for even thinking of trusting the woman who had caused him so much grief.

"What else might be in your secret cache?" he asked as he set the jar on the step beside him.

The woman glared at the unopened jar, but she made no reference to it. "Dry clothes hidden under the floorboards of the alcove, along with a box of coins I earned in America. Some day, I shall return to my homeland and claim my heritage." She drank from the glass jar she held.

Darcy watched her quench her thirst. He would love to wash away the dry film coating his tongue, but he could not afford to relax his guard. The lady was too eager for him to partake of her offering. "Would not Stowbridge have aided your ambitions? The magistrate appears to hold you in affection."

A long silence followed. Finally, she said, "Loiza deserved better than he received in our joining. My husband entered our marriage with the intention to make us both comfortable, but I was too young to see anything beyond the heat of desire. By the time I matured enough to appreciate Loiza's steady regard, I could not turn from the course I had chosen."

Darcy no longer knew what to think of Areej Stowbridge. The woman exuded evil, but there was an air of vulnerability about her. "How long must we wait?" he asked cautiously.

"I suspect another hour, maybe two."

"Do you not fear discovery?" It seemed only reasonable that a speedy retreat would be in order.

Mrs. Stowbridge chuckled. "Few are comfortable in such close proximity to a church's cemetery at night. Mr. Williamson goes home to his small cottage, and the church remains unused for a large portion of each day." Darcy had never considered the truth of what the woman said. A church always appeared an integral part of a community. "Along with Mrs. Holbrook's cottage, the church yard is one of the few places I claim as my own when I require solitude."

Darcy permitted the conversation to dwindle. What was there to say: Soon the Stowbridges would either kill him, or he would be the victor. He stared off over the lawn marking the entrance to the village cemetery. It was serene in its own way, composed and inviting. Darcy would enjoy the opportunity to explore the gravesites in the daylight—not because he feared being alone with the dead, but because he found reading gravestones an amusing pastime. Some stones simply announced the person's name and the dates marking the deceased's lifespan. Others were more prophetic epitaphs: A Good Life Is Rather to Be Chosen Than Great Riches; Be Kind to the Old, They Are Not Long with Us; and Sunshine Fades and Shadows Fall But Love and Memories Outlast All.

When he had read these words on the stones in a Lincolnshire cemetery shortly after calling upon the family of yet another of his father's boyhood friends to pay the Darcys' respects, Darcy had considered his short life and what he had wanted his own marker to say of him. Naturally, his first thoughts were to choose an appropriate verse that would reflect his life, but Darcy quickly rejected such superficial sentiment. Instead, he had chosen something simpler: Fitzwilliam Darcy ~ Son ~ Brother ~ Husband ~ Father ~ Master of Pemberley.

Only one of those appellations remained unfulfilled, and Darcy sadly realized he might never look upon the angelic countenances of his children. The thought brought a deep sadness, so he closed his eyes to summon forth Elizabeth's image. He prayed that someone had discovered her or that his wife had managed to make her way to safety on her own. If so, anything he suffered would be worthwhile.

"You are early," the woman's voice broke the silence.

Expecting to see Stowbridge, Darcy opened his eyes to find another familiar face.

"You said nine of the clock," Merrick Gaylord said without emotion. "Did all go as you planned?"

Mrs. Stowbridge stood on the highest level of the stump. "Everything except the fact that Loiza discovered me at the cottage before I could finish with Mrs. Darcy. My husband expects me to meet him at the assembly hall."

"The man has never truly understood you, Areej." It had not slipped Darcy's notice that Gaylord held an unusual-looking gun pointed at Darcy's chest. He automatically thought of the gun his cousin had described when the gelding had died. Had he accused the gypsy band in error?

Darcy was careful to make no rash moves. He knew little of Gaylord's personality, other than to know from the beginning that he did not trust the man. Obviously, his instincts had been accurate.

"Is there enough in the box for us to leave?" Gaylord asked as he watched Darcy carefully.

The woman descended slowly. "The money is no longer relevant," she announced. "Within hours, all lanes of escape will be closed to us." She stopped beside where Darcy remained seated upon one of the lower steps. "Drink the water, Mr. Darcy," she instructed.

"What happens if I refuse?" Darcy asked suspiciously.

The woman snorted her contempt. "You will die. Your only chance to survive this ordeal is to drink the water and hope your friends discover you in time to save you."

He shook his head in denial. "I think I would prefer to have Mr. Gaylord shoot me. A substantial portion of arsenic would bring me a long, agonizing death. I choose the quicker method."

An ironic laugh filled the air. "Who says the water contains arsenic?" Mrs. Stowbridge picked up the jar, removed the cork, and thrust it under Darcy's nose. "Do you smell arsenic, Mr. Darcy?"

Despite his best efforts to remain unaffected by the woman's taunt, Darcy sniffed at the jar's opening. He had expected no odor and found none, but his action had proved his fear to the satisfaction of Mrs. Stowbridge. "I refuse the offer just the same," he said without emotion.

Mrs. Stowbridge knelt beside him. She touched the jar's lip to his. The woman whispered bitterly. "We could bind you and pour the liquid down your throat, Mr. Darcy."

"You could," he responded matter-of-factly. A brittle silence descended.

The woman smiled wickedly. "Permit me to explain the situation so you might comprehend the extent of your choice. If you choose not to comply, I will send Gaylord to the cottage. He will kill Mrs. Darcy before your wife can recover from the opiate you administered to her. Of course, he will enjoy himself with Mrs. Darcy prior to seeing your wife to her grave." Darcy's gut twisted with the woman's direct threat.

His mind raced. What was the possibility that Elizabeth had found her escape? Could his wife remain unconscious upon the undressed mattress? Could they both lose their lives on the same day? Could he knowingly permit his wife to be exposed to danger? Yet, if he drank the arsenic, Darcy would hold no hope of escaping this quandary.

"As you wish, Mr. Darcy." The woman had taken his indecision as a refusal. She stood to address her accomplice. "Mrs. Darcy is not to leave the cottage," she ordered. "And Merrick," she added, "when the lady protests, inform Mrs. Darcy that her torment is courtesy of her husband's cowardice."

The steward nodded his understanding. He strode toward his waiting horse. Darcy's heart clenched with panic. "Wait!" he yelled. To Mrs. Stowbridge, he asked, "How do I know you will not execute your threat after I drink the poison?"

"You do not," she said coldly. "You must pray that your friends will pursue us before Mr. Gaylord can act. Or you must trust my word when I say I hold no desire to see Mrs. Darcy suffer on your behalf."

With a hand which trembled despite his best efforts, Darcy reached for the dark, irregularly shaped jar. He closed his eyes to murmur a simple prayer, asking God to protect Elizabeth and Georgiana and his tenants at Pemberley. He thanked his Maker for his many blessings. With a throat-clearing swallow, Darcy pressed the jar to his lips, tilted it to release the liquid, and drank deeply of the mixture.

* * *

The ride to the village church had taken longer than Edward Fitzwilliam would have liked, but it was more important to have Elizabeth Darcy arrive in one piece than to know speed. In the beginning, Edward held her loosely before him, but when Elizabeth had slipped for the third time, the colonel had placed her tightly in his embrace.

Despite the innocent way Darcy's wife trustingly wrapped her arms about Edward's waist, his thoughts drifted to the sweet smell of lavender in her hair and the warmth of Elizabeth Darcy's frame along his chest. He was uncomfortably aware of his treacherous thoughts. It had been months since he had known a woman intimately and a lifetime since he had felt this "clean." At times, Edward could smell the stench of death emanating from his pores. He had experienced death and dying and fear for nearly a decade, and Edward was sorely tired of feeling Death's arm about his shoulder. This moment of normalcy had been his long-time dream: one where he embraced a woman he held in such high regard as he did Elizabeth Darcy.

He had never dreamed a dream of knowing his cousin's wife, and certainly not a dream of chasing after a badly wounded Darcy in order to save his cousin's life, but definitely he held a dream of a woman clinging to him for protection, a dream of a wife and family—all the things which were lacking in his life.

"Colonel?" Elizabeth said softly against his chest. The warmth of her breath filtered through the fine lawn of his shirt to warm him in a comforting way.

He had slowed the horse as they reached the village. "Yes?" Suddenly, Edward did not know what to call his cousin's wife.

"Mrs. Darcy" appeared too formal for the situation, and "Elizabeth" was too intimate.

"Shall we find Mr. Darcy in time?" Her voice trembled with the possibility of their failure.

Edward instinctively lifted her closer to him. "I pray for our success, but we must recognize our fallibility."

Her arms instinctively tightened about him, and Edward found it sorely hard to remember why he should not turn his horse for Woodvine and his chambers. To remove Elizabeth from danger and to protect her with his life. Mr. Holbrook's horse came abreast of his, and Edward was jarred into reality. "Do we call upon the curate?" the groom asked.

"We may require the man's assistance in searching the church," Edward reasoned. "I will escort Mrs. Darcy about the grounds while you seek Mr. Williamson's support."

"Aye, Sir." Holbrook turned his horse aside.

Meanwhile, Edward slowed his horse to a walk. "When we reach the church, I expect you to remain with the horse, Elizabeth."

"I understand," Elizabeth said as she raised her head from where it had rested on his chest. "You will exercise care, Colonel."

Edward swallowed his loneliness. The woman cared for him, but not in the manner he required. It was the story of his life. The dream remained beyond his reach. "I will heed your caution, my dear."

Silently, he reined in the horse before they reached the open square upon which the church sat. Sliding from the saddle, Edward turned to lift Elizabeth to the ground. "Take Major to wait behind those trees," he instructed.

"Major?" she asked teasingly.

He grinned. "It is really Major General," Edward confessed. "A man can hope that the epaulets on his shoulders match the name of his horse."

Elizabeth patted Edward's cheek. "I shall add your desire to my prayers, Colonel."

He retrieved a pistol from an inside pocket. "If something happens which places me in danger, you are to take Major and ride for Mr. Holbrook. The groom and Mr. Williamson should arrive shortly." When she did not respond, Edward demanded, "Agree with me, Elizabeth, or I will refuse to leave you here alone."

Even through the dark shadows, Edward could see her indecision. Finally, she said, "Fitzwilliam requires your assistance. I shall do whatever is necessary to save my husband."

Edward hesitated before giving her a curt nod. "I suppose that is as close to a concession as I will receive from you." With that, he darted away into the night.

Behind him, the colonel did not hear her whisper, "And to save Fitzwilliam's favorite cousin."

* * *

The bitter taste of the laudanum remained on his lips, and Darcy meant to wipe his mouth with the back of his hand; but his arms appeared locked to his side, wedged in beside his body. When the first taste of laudanum crossed his tongue, Darcy had spit the liquid into the smirking face of Mrs. Stowbridge. Immediately, the bitter taste of the opium derivative had signaled the perfidy practiced by the pair. He had expected the odorless and tasteless freedom of arsenic and had not found it, but had discovered another danger.

Before he could respond, the housekeeper and Gaylord had overwhelmed him. He had fought them with all the energy remaining in his frame only to succumb to an uppercut on the square of his chin from the butt of the rifle the steward carried. Darcy had hung on for a few seconds longer before the blackness had taken him.

"Where am I?" he asked aloud to test his voice, and the echo returned in a hollow discord. Darcy wiggled from side to side to free one of his hands. He skimmed it across his body to assure himself he had sustained no further injuries.

The blackness encompassed all, and Darcy had difficulty in determining his bearings. He struggled to rein in the gathering panic. "It is as dark as a grave," he said before the reality of his words slammed into the lid over his head. The woman and Gaylord had locked him in a box, and Darcy feared he knew where he rested.

* * *

Edward had circled the building to emerge on the far side of the space, which opened onto the adjoining village hall and main street. The church sat upon a cleared section of land, which slanted away from the main road. Not even half as grand as Minster Monastery, this simple church served those on the far side of Wimborne, those closest to the Roman Road.

He edged from the shadows to stand in a shaft of moonlight. Despite Elizabeth's insistence, Edward had discovered nothing unusual. "Bloody hell," he growled. "I pray Cowan is more successful." With urgency, he crossed the open plain to reach his cousin's wife. The colonel worried for Thomas Cowan's safety.

* * *

Elizabeth had watched her husband's cousin disappear into the night. She held tightly to the reins of the horse, keeping the animal close in case she must seek assistance. The drugs still coursed through her veins, and Elizabeth fought for clarity. She would not succumb to the dizzying blackness. Her husband needed her to be strong.

"Darcy." The word formed silently on her lips. Elizabeth could recall very little of what had happened since she had foolishly permitted Mrs. Ridgeway to lead her upon a merry chase. Obviously, as it was well into the nighttime hours, she had slept through much of the day's drama, but Elizabeth had been well aware of the sacrifice Darcy had made to administer another dose of Mrs. Ridgeway's poisonous mixture. Releasing her husband to follow the housekeeper had been the hardest task of Elizabeth's short life. However, she had no doubt Mrs. Ridgeway would have shot both Darcy and her if Elizabeth had not played along.

The sound of a crunched branch set her nerves on alert. Elizabeth tightened her grasp on the reins and stroked the animal's long neck. Major had heard it also, and Elizabeth meant to keep the horse calm. "Easy, Boy," she whispered.

Watchful, her eyes searched the opening. Another crunch. A shuffled step. A swish of a skirt, and two people entered the open area beside the church. One was Mrs. Ridgeway, but the second was not Darcy.

Elizabeth's heart throttled. She had no weapon. She should climb into Major's saddle, and then ride for assistance, but if she did, the housekeeper could escape. *Oh, where is the colonel?* she thought.

With no hope of surviving this confrontation, Elizabeth boldly stepped into the open. "What have you done with Mr. Darcy?" she demanded.

Not expecting to encounter another person in this part of the churchyard, the housekeeper had jumped from the start, but she quickly recovered. "I know not of what you speak," she declared with authority.

Elizabeth's hands fisted at her side. "I care not if you escape. I care not for the perfidy you practice. I simply want to know of my husband."

The woman gave a disgusting snort, "He is dead. Your husband has breathed his last breath."

Elizabeth's stomach clenched in revolt, and her heart skipped within her chest, but she said, "That is the second time today you have offered me that lie."

The housekeeper growled with disdain. "This time it is true."

Elizabeth's knees thought to buckle, but she kept herself aright. "A prevarication," she accused. "I do not believe you." Even in her own ears, her reply held only a trace of denial.

The man spoke for the first time. "It does not matter what you believe, Mrs. Darcy." He took a menacing step in her direction.

Elizabeth looked at the housekeeper's associate for the first time. "Do I know you, Sir?' Elizabeth asked reflexively.

The man offered a mocking bow. "I am Woodvine's steward, Mrs. Darcy." He paused for an intimidating effect. "I am also the man who has killed your husband," he said bluntly.

This time, Elizabeth's composure faltered. The steward's ominous words rang in her head. A sob caught her, and she pitched forward as if to catch her breath. She knew the man raised his weapon to strike her, but Elizabeth no longer cared. If Darcy were dead, she meant to follow him. As she braced herself for the blow, the sound of gunfire sent her to her knees.

Chapter 28

"Elizabeth? Elizabeth? Are you injured?"

She trembled openly, but she managed to say, "No. No, Colonel." Elizabeth answered twice to convince herself as much as him.

"Then, I require your assistance." Edward Fitzwilliam remained behind the pair. "Remove Mrs. Stowbridge's gun."

Elizabeth looked up in surprise. "You are married to Mr. Stowbridge?" Bits of the conversation between the two at the cottage and memory of what the colonel had told her earlier flooded her senses. Suddenly, everything became clearer.

"I am," the woman said flatly. "Some eight and twenty years."

Elizabeth staggered to her feet. "But why would you continue to live in Samuel Darcy's home if your husband was but three miles distance?"

Mrs. Stowbridge shrugged noncommittally. "Loiza is a fine man. A gentle man, but his idea of obedience is not mine."

"Did Samuel Darcy know?" Elizabeth demanded.

The woman smiled sadly. "Not until right before he died."

"Elizabeth," Edward said with exigency. "We can question Mrs. Stowbridge and…"

"Mr. Gaylord," Elizabeth supplied the man's name.

"Mr. Gaylord," Edward continued, "after you remove their weapons."

Elizabeth reddened. She did not find offense in the colonel's chiding. Instead, she made herself step farther into the circle of moonlight.

"Be wary, Cousin," Edward cautioned.

From where Mrs. Stowbridge still held it loose at her side, Elizabeth retrieved the gun.

"You must run your hands over Mrs. Stowbridge to see if she conceals other weapons," Edward coaxed.

Although she felt awkward in doing so, Elizabeth slid her hands across the woman's waist and corset.

"The lady's limbs," Edward instructed.

Elizabeth bit her bottom lip as a sudden anger flared through her heart. She had permitted this woman to remain too close to her family. The idea had cost Elizabeth her own sense of place in the world. She bent to slide her hands up and down the woman's legs through the lady's gown.

"Not too close," Edward warned. "It would be easy for Mrs. Stowbridge to kick you and overcome you."

The former housekeeper laughed sarcastically. "How bitter you are, Colonel."

Elizabeth removed a small pistol tied to the woman's calf. If she had faced the woman alone, Elizabeth would never have thought to search for the extra weapon. "What now, Colonel?"

"Bring the weapons here," he instructed. Elizabeth quickly joined him behind the pair. He accepted the small gun from her, but insisted she keep the other. "I will search Gaylord. If either of our assailants moves, I trust you to shoot." Elizabeth was not certain she could purposely inflict pain on another, but she nodded her agreement. "Just remember they likely hold information on Darcy's whereabouts."

That fact played well to her resolve. To find her husband, Elizabeth would be willing to exact bodily harm on these two.

Edward leaned closer. "Darcy has taught you to shoot, has he not, Mrs. Darcy?"

Elizabeth nodded almost imperceptibly in the affirmative.

Edward smiled deviously. "If you must shoot, aim for Gaylord. I can easily overcome the woman."

Elizabeth appreciated the flash of levity. It helped her to relax and to concentrate on the task at hand. "I shall endeavor to hit the gentleman, Colonel," she said smartly.

Within a minute, he stood beside her again. The colonel placed the long gun and a shovel beside the brick wall. We must secure the pair before we can conduct our investigation," he explained. "I have rope in Major's saddlebag. Would you retrieve it?"

Elizabeth nodded. However, before she could return to Edward's side, a whistle sounded, which the colonel returned, and Cowan arrived on the scene. Without comment, the Runner automatically took the rope from Elizabeth's hands and set about tying the couple together.

Once the pair was secure, Edward asked Gaylord, "You taunted Mrs. Darcy with tales of her husband's death. Tell me what you know of my cousin's whereabouts."

"How would that benefit me?" The man's expression did not alter. "I hold no information, which would save my life."

As this questioning proved futile, Cowan asked Elizabeth. "Where did you encounter Mrs. Stowbridge?"

Elizabeth pointed off to the right. "She and Mr. Gaylord came from that direction."

Cowan frowned dramatically. "From the cemetery? There is nothing beyond the gravesites but a rocky drop off. What business would Mrs. Stowbridge have in a church cemetery? By her own admission, the woman has never set foot in Mr. Williamson's church."

Elizabeth's heart lurched. She shot a quick glance to Mr. Gaylord's *weapons*: a shovel. "My God!" she gasped. "They have buried Fitzwilliam alive!"

* * *

Darcy's panic had risen to a point of insensibility. His heart faltered. The box held him easily, wedged him into the space. There were but six inches or so between his head and the wooden roof. Possibly three inches remained between his arms and the box's side. There was no way to raise his legs, and he could feel a heavy weight attached to the left one.

A weight to hold me down. But he was not in the water as had been the men his cousin and McKye had pulled from the lake. If not to keep him in the box, what was the weight's purpose? *To keep others out.* The words exploded in his brain.

* * *

"They have buried Fitzwilliam alive!" Elizabeth called as she raced for the cemetery. She hiked her skirt and skipped over headstones and angelic statues to reach the cemetery's center. "We need light," she shouted to the two men who had followed her. "We need to find a fresh grave." In a panic, she turned in a circle. There were so many graves for such a small village.

"Go!" Edward ordered Cowan. "Pound on every door. We need lanterns."

The tears rolled down Elizabeth's cheeks, but she did not bother to wipe them away. "Where do we start?" she pleaded.

Edward's eyes grew in disbelief. "I have no idea," he admitted.

Elizabeth's heart screamed against the injustice. "Find the curate. Locate the sexton. Beat Mr. Gaylord senseless," she demanded. "Someone knows which grave does not belong."

The colonel swallowed hard. "Could you be mistaken, Elizabeth?"

She did not want to think of her dear husband buried beneath her feet, but Elizabeth did not doubt that it was so. "He is calling for me," she said weakly. "Fitzwilliam believes he will die soon." Her eyes fell on her husband's cousin. "He needs you, Colonel. Fitzwilliam needs us both."

Edward nodded his agreement. "Holbrook is bringing Williamson with him. I will seek the sexton in the wait house." He disappeared into the night.

Suddenly, Elizabeth was alone in the cemetery. Her eyes searched for any clue. "Not in the center," she reasoned. "Those are the village founders."

Methodically, she began to pace off row after row of markers. "Mr. Gaylord could not have had enough time to dig a proper grave alone," Elizabeth said aloud as she stepped around yet another headstone. Surprisingly, the moonlight seemed to brighten the polished stone. "If the man could not accomplish the task alone, then it was likely the grave had been dug for another. *Was the earth even now stealing her dear husband's last breath?* The thought rocked Elizabeth's composure. A violent shiver ran down her spine.

* * *

How long could he breathe the little air which remained in the box before it would be no more? Darcy thought to scream, but he knew the futility of the act. He could smell the fresh earth surrounding the box.

"Elizabeth." He mouthed the word. "My God. I will never see her again, and she will never know my fate. How long will my wife grieve? If they do not find me and identify my body, Elizabeth will be forced to remain married to a corpse. She would never be free to find happiness." Sweat beaded his forehead, and his teeth clenched. The thought of how his wife would suffer tightened Darcy's throat in grief. He had thought to die to save Elizabeth's future. Instead, his dying would condemn his wife to a lifetime of mourning.

* * *

"The new graves from Woodvine," Elizabeth said as she recognized the number of freshly dug graves. "Dear God, where do I begin?" She had worked her way along the rows of more recent headstones to arrive at a line of new graves. "Fitzwilliam!" she yelled in frustration. "Fitzwilliam!" But only the echo of her voice remained in the silent burial place.

"Elizabeth!" She turned to observe the colonel's hurried return. Behind him was the familiar face of the curate and a man with whom she had no previous acquaintance. Out of breath, Edward caught her hand. "Holbrook has brought both Mr. Williamson and the sexton, Mr. Sharp, with him."

Elizabeth's relief nearly took her to her knees, and Edward caught her to his side. "Oh, thank you, Sir," she gushed. "I fear a great injustice has been exacted against my husband." Her words tumbled over one another as her anxiety rose. "I believe Mr. Darcy has been buried alive in one of these graves." Elizabeth gestured to the newly turned earth behind her. "Can you tell us which of these sites should not be occupied?"

Even in the moonlight she could see the man's countenance pale. "Aye, Ma'am." The man's voice betrayed his anxiousness.

"Unless the deceased be one of the founding families, we place the departed in rows from the center to the outside boundaries. Of late, we have had more than our share." The man laughed nervously when he realized what he said. To cover his *faux pas*, Mr. Sharp led the way along the path. "The gypsy known as Besnik and the stranger who assisted him in dishonoring the late Mr. Darcy's resting place be in the row with the charity cases, as is the one who attacked you, Ma'am." Elizabeth shivered, and she pulled Darcy's coat closer about her. "Go on, Mr. Sharp," she coaxed.

"I apologize, Ma'am, if I sound insensitive." When Elizabeth did not respond, he nervously continued. "The two men not identified by Mr. Williamson or Mr. Holbrook be mixed among those."

Edward encouraged, "A new grave, Mr. Sharp."

"Yes, Sir." He led them along a narrow path between the rows. "These graves be awaiting a marker," Sharp observed. "This first one be Mr. Hotchkiss. Then Mr. Bates. Mr. Pugh." The sexton counted his recent work on his fingers. "Falstad. Clarkson. Lawson. And Mr. Glover."

Edward's voice asked the question Elizabeth could not. "Is that all of them?" A thirteenth grave remained open.

Sharp frowned noticeably. "The last one be for Mr. Barriton. Mr. Williamson asked me to prepare it today. We must put the Woodvine butler on the row with the gypsies and the other thieves and charity cases. Considering his crime and all. In most villages, those types would not be afforded a place within the church's land." The man appeared proud of the village's benevolence.

Elizabeth clutched at Edward's arm. "There must be some mistake." Her voice sounded hauntingly empty. "I am certain Mrs. Stowbridge and Mr. Gaylord have executed a most grievous crime against my husband. They had no time to dig a proper grave, and I am convinced the pair meant to place my husband in an open gravesite. As bizarre as this story sounds, are there any other possibilities?"

The man shifted his weight fretfully. "I kin think of none, Ma'am. All those in this area be accounted for."

Edward pressed, "Are there other open graves on the property? Perhaps one for a villager not involved with the chaos at Woodvine."

"Can't say that there are, Colonel," Sharp responded. "Only one not occupied be the one reserved for Samuel Darcy. I prepared that one again after the incident with the explosion. I be thinking that someone would recover Mr. Darcy's body."

"Why not bury Mr. Darcy in Mr. Darcy's grave?" Elizabeth murmured.

"Show us where Samuel Darcy's gravesite is located," Edward demanded.

Sharp gestured behind him. "It be beside the Darcy crypt." He led them toward the revered sites of the village elite. "I thought it best to keep it close so Mr. Darcy could be moved into his memorial once it was properly repaired."

Elizabeth and Edward trailed close on the sexton's heels. "Please God," she whispered. "Allow us to be in time."

"The grave be right over…" The man stopped abruptly. "Someone has filled her in."

Edward pushed past him. "How deep is this?" he demanded. He was digging the loose dirt out with his hands. "We need shovels, Mr. Sharp, and make it quick."

Elizabeth dropped to her knees beside the colonel. She dug her hands into the packed dirt. "Hurry!" she yelled at the astounded sexton. The man scurried away. "Dig, Colonel," she encouraged. "And pray."

* * *

The air had grown thin, and Darcy knew his time had drawn near. He held no doubt Mrs. Stowbridge had exacted a most well-devised revenge: Darcy would know he was going to die and, therefore, grieve for his inability to change his fate. She had drugged him long enough to place him in another's coffin and lower him into a grave. A blanket lined the bottom and sides of the box. Darcy could smell the scent of freshly cut wood, but also the distinct smell of gunpowder. And it was that odor which worried him. He feared he had encountered Samuel Darcy's great treasure.

Darcy had no doubt the explosion which had killed Besnik Gry had been because of the torpedo with which Samuel Darcy had experimented before his death. "Likely placed in Samuel's coffin by Mr. Crescent," he murmured. Samuel's valet had been willing to face Society's censure by preparing his master's body in the manner of the ancient Egyptians, so it only made sense that the valet had protected Samuel into the next world.

"Why did I not see the possibility earlier?" he chastised his foolish pride. "Because you were not on Death's threshold previously." Darcy answered his own question. *Because your own mortality brings clarity.*

Suddenly, Mrs. Stowbridge's words came back to him. "One lives. My youngest has recently passed. But the elder is a strong leader of my husband's family."

Besnik Gry, Darcy thought. *The lady ran off with a gypsy. Drewe's poem spoke of Mab and nomadic tribes. And Andrzej Gry argued with the woman we knew as Mrs. Ridgeway. These revelations explain why the housekeeper sold the horses to the gypsies and also why Stowbridge objected to their presence in the area. His wife's sons reminded the magistrate daily of everything the man had lost.*

"Now, if some miracle would permit me a means from this death trap…"

* * *

Cowan and Sharp reappeared with shovels in hand. "Here, Colonel." The Runner handed Edward the tool they had retrieved from the sexton's work shed. "Move away, Mrs. Darcy."

"I want to be of assistance," Elizabeth protested.

Edward pulled her to her feet. "Then assist Mr. Williamson with the lanterns. We will require light to see what we are doing."

Reluctantly, Elizabeth stepped away from the grave. She watched anxiously as the three men attacked the gravesite.

"Mrs. Darcy," the curate said softly beside her. He handed Elizabeth a lantern and struck a flint. "Here is the candle," the man offered. Elizabeth automatically lit several candles, but her eyes never left the spot where the men worked frantically. As soon as the lanterns were lit, Elizabeth placed them along the rim of the memorial so they would shine downward into the hole.

"Would you wish to pray?" Mr. Williamson suggested as he set his lanterns beside hers.

Elizabeth did not wish to leave her husband, but she nodded her agreement. With the curate's assistance, she stepped to the other side of the Darcy family crypt.

Initially, the curate's reverence and benevolence was a soothing balm on Elizabeth's anxious heart. Mr. Williamson spoke of hope, of love, and of compassion, but when the man's words spoke of accepting whatever happened as God's will, Elizabeth interrupted, "Forgive me, Mr. Williamson." Elizabeth gave herself a sound mental shake. "I realize this is blasphemous, but I shall never accept Fitzwilliam's death as God's plan. I cannot believe that God would take him from us. And until that moment arrives I will not entertain such thoughts." With a quick curtsy, Elizabeth returned to the site.

"Colonel?" she asked uneasily.

"A few more minutes." Edward strained to lift a large shovelful of dirt.

Elizabeth stood at the foot of the grave. She swayed from side to side, and soon she lifted her voice in song.

* * *

Running out of air, Darcy fought to keep his senses about him, but his eyes felt heavy. He dreamed of Elizabeth. He could see her teasing him at Sir William Lucas's party. He could visualize how he had foolishly followed her about the room because he had begun to wish to know more of her, and as a step toward conversing with her himself, had attended to her conversation with others. He could hear Miss Lucas insisting upon Elizabeth's lending her beautiful voice to the evening's entertainment. Could hear Elizabeth's singing the same song as she had that evening. So close, it seemed his wife stood above him. Looking down upon him. If only he could touch her, speak words of affection in her ear.

Automatically, Darcy's hands reached for her. "Elizabeth," he said weakly when his fingers grazed the wooden lid. "Sing for me, Lizzy."

* * *

"We have hit something hard, Colonel," Cowan said as his shovel's tip struck the wooden frame.

Edward lifted another shovel of dirt to the side. "Keep digging," he ordered. The sweat poured from his face and down his back, but Edward would not stop. Elizabeth had been correct. Someone had buried a coffin in Samuel Darcy's grave. God! Was his cousin even now taking his last breath? "Sing louder, Elizabeth," he encouraged. "Sing for Darcy."

She raced to the grave's edge and began her song again, directing her voice to the outline of a box, which had emerged from the pit. "Fitzwilliam!" she called through her sobs.

Edward struck the box with the tip of his shovel. "Darcy!" he shouted, accenting his efforts with the tap of the metal to the wood. "Answer me, Darcy!"

* * *

Crazy as it seemed, Darcy could swear his wife's voice had moved closer and that she called his name. In addition to Elizabeth's pleading was a complementary sound of his cousin's commanding baritone. Darcy made his mind acknowledge their pleas. Forced his lids open to stare into the blackness. A thud vibrated the box. "The torpedo!" Darcy's brain formed the word, but his lips would not cooperate. Necessity caused his heart to race. He must stop them! If his cousin and Elizabeth meant to rescue him—to remove him from the coffin—they would meet Besnik Gry's fate, which was exactly what Areej Stowbridge had planned.

Chapter 29

Darcy attempted to make a fist, but his hands had lost all sensation. So, instead of pounding on the lid for attention, he slapped at it, creating a musical tattoo to accent his wife's singing. "No!" he called over and over. "No!"

Edward was the first to feel the vibration beneath his feet. "Quiet!" he ordered. "No one move."

Weakly a dull thud came from below, deep in the grave. "He is alive!" Elizabeth squealed. "Fitzwilliam is alive. Oh, hurry, Colonel."

Elizabeth scooted to the side, where she could scoop armfuls of dirt from the grave. "Oh, please, God," she prayed as tears streamed down her face. "We must reach him. Dear God, we must reach him." She slung the dirt behind her, handful after handful, clawing her way into the earth.

The three men redoubled their efforts, and within minutes, Edward straddled the upper section of the coffin. On all fours, he crawled along the edges, knocking dirt from the surface. "Darcy," he called as he tapped on the lid. "Darcy, we are here." Placing his ear to the lid, Edward listened carefully. Nothing else moved in the cemetery. He looked up with a frown.

"What is it, Colonel?" Cowan asked the question no one else dared to ask.

"Whoever or whatever is inside this box appears to be saying 'No.'"

Elizabeth grabbed another armful of dirt. "I care not for my husband's objections," she asserted. "I want him out of this box. Out of this grave."

"Give me a hammer, Mr. Sharp," Edward demanded. "Cowan, assist Mrs. Darcy with the dirt behind me. We do not want it to collapse in on my cousin."

Edward placed his mouth as close to the lid as possible. He brushed more loose dirt away. "Darcy," he shouted. "Turn your head to the right. I mean to tear part of this away." With that, he wedged the hammer against the edge of the wood. Using the claw, Edward ripped away at the upper left corner of the box.

Within less than a minute, the colonel had opened a small hole, perhaps two inches by three. "Hand me a light," he yelled, and Elizabeth scrambled to do his bidding.

"Are we in time?" she pleaded as she lowered the lantern into the hole.

"Fortunately, Mrs. Stowbridge and Mr. Gaylord have wedged the coffin into the hole at an odd angle," Edward explained. "The coffin has not been buried as deeply as I had originally expected." He did not confide the fact that he kept his full weight from the lid in fear of plummeting the box deeper into the earth. It would prove of no use to have Elizabeth in more distress. Straddling the sides of the box, the colonel balanced precariously on the edge. Lowering his weight onto the coffin, he lifted the light to peer into the small opening. "Darcy? Can you hear me?"

A quick inhale of air rewarded the colonel's efforts. "Move away," a weak familiar voice ordered. "Dangerous."

Although muffled by the wood and the depth of the hole, the message's urgency stayed the colonel's efforts. "Everyone, step away from the grave," he ordered.

In the soft lantern light, Elizabeth's eyes flared with disapproval. "Why?" she demanded.

Edward's shoulders stiffened. "Your husband claims it is dangerous to be here." The colonel spoke with more calm than he felt. "Please step clear of the area until I can ascertain what Darcy means by the warning."

Kneeling at the grave's edge, Elizabeth defiantly refused to budge. "I will not leave him."

"Elizabeth, please," Edward implored.

"You know my mind, Colonel. Be on with it." She lay out full on the ground where she could reach into the hole.

Edward nodded to Cowan and Sharp to step behind the crypt's solid wall. "No sudden moves, Elizabeth," the colonel warned. "Allow me to assess the situation." When his cousin's wife made no further protest, Edward eased forward to where he could speak into the opening. "Are you injured, Darcy?"

A weak "No" escaped the small hole in the lid. "Only what… what remains of my earlier…confrontation with…Mr. Barriton and…this afternoon…with Mrs. Stowbridge." Behind him, the colonel heard Elizabeth stifling a sob of concern. However, Edward felt no such emotion. A breathless panic had taken its hold on the colonel's heart. Darcy should be begging for a quick release from his prison; instead, his cousin had ordered his rescuers from the site.

"Why would you send us away?" he asked slowly, enunciating each word clearly.

A long silence told the colonel his cousin considered his words carefully. Edward concentrated his full being on understanding what Darcy meant to say. "There is something…something attached to my left leg." A hesitation followed. "It is my opinion…Mrs. Stowbridge has buried…buried Samuel's torpedo model with me. I fear if you remove me…from this hard bed… the torpedo will explode."

A sick feeling spread through Edward's veins. He had an overwhelming desire to discover if Bedlam was to be his next home. The dire situation had magnified. "You cannot expect me to walk away," he said cautiously. His chest tightened in a frightening manner, and Edward swiftly pointed out, "We must do something."

"What does Fitzwilliam say?" Elizabeth pleaded. Her eyes widened in fear.

Edward waved away her apprehension. Instead, he listened for his cousin's honest response. "See my wife to Pemberley," Darcy's choked response spoke of the emotions flooding his cousin's chest. "I charge you, Cousin, to see to Elizabeth's and Georgiana's futures."

"Damn it, Darcy," Edward growled. "No one is prepared to abandon you to an early death, so set your mind to our salvation." He bit back his fear of inadequacy. "I plan to rip more wood from this coffin so Mrs. Darcy might look upon your countenance while I devise a means to extricate you from this hellhole." He retrieved the hammer from the lip of the grave. "Now close your eyes and turn your head to the opposite side."

As he ripped away at the wood, anger filled Edward's heart. Anger at Mrs. Stowbridge and the Woodvine steward for their felonious actions. Anger at himself for not recognizing the depth of madness into which his cousin's honor had led Darcy. Anger at his cousin for his willingness to die in order to save them all. Also, anger at Darcy for not realizing his cousin's sacrifice would destroy Elizabeth and Georgiana. And anger at the idea that he would never know such unselfish love.

Fortunately, the second board, which had run horizontally across the top of the coffin, came free easily. With the larger opening, Edward was able to pull the nails holding the planks free. He tossed the offending pieces of wood from the hole to expose his cousin's pale face.

* * *

Darcy sucked in his first full breath in what seemed a lifetime, and, in fact, it had been just that. He had been given a second life. Slowly, he opened his eyes to take in the worried countenance of his cousin. "Thank you, Colonel," he said honestly.

"No gratitude yet," the colonel said brusquely. "Not until you are free of this latest puzzle." Edward reached into the box to squeeze Darcy's shoulder. "I will remove myself from this hole so you might feast upon your wife's countenance. Meanwhile, I will confer with Cowan to determine how to proceed."

Eager to see Elizabeth well, Darcy nodded his agreement. When his cousin had climbed from the hole, Darcy's eyes searched the open space above his head for Elizabeth's fine features. For a long moment, Darcy recalled the first time he had seen her standing with her sister and Miss Lucas as he and Bingley had made their way across the Meryton Assembly hall. There had been a stunning sense of recognition, as if he had known her all his life. Finally, Elizabeth appeared above him. Like a hovering angel, she gazed lovingly at him. The shadows kept part of her face in darkness, but it was comforting to know she had survived her ordeal.

"Fitzwilliam," she said on a rasp, and Darcy had instantly understood his wife's sentiment.

"Be strong, my Lizzy," he said to comfort her. "We will see this through together."

"I love you." His wife leaned precariously over the grave's lip. "I feared we would not be in time."

Darcy licked his dry lips. The taste of laudanum remained, but he refused to grimace so as not to worry his wife. "You never gave up," he said simply. He knew enough of his wife's personality to know she had bullied the colonel and Cowan into submission.

"I could not," Elizabeth confessed. "I shall not know life without you by my side. Set your mind to it, Fitzwilliam," she said determinedly.

Darcy filled his mind with her voice and her features. He would not promise Elizabeth that they would spend their futures together. He doubted he could escape this trap. However, he said, "There is no place I would rather be, my Lizzy."

Edward joined Elizabeth upon her perch above him. His cousin's expression remained grim. "Cowan will ride to Woodvine to retrieve Samuel's sketches. We think it best if we wait until daylight to execute a plan for removing you from this hole. Meanwhile, you must remain still."

Elizabeth spoke anxiously. "I should speak to Mr. Cowan. I hid Cousin Samuel's journals in my quarters. I shall return in a moment, Fitzwilliam."

His wife scurried away, and Darcy took the opportunity to speak privately to his cousin. "You are to protect Mrs. Darcy, Colonel. My wife will plant herself on the lid of this death box if you permit it." Darcy battled down the smothering panic. It would do none of them any good if he acted rashly. "When you are prepared to put into play whatever plan you devise, you must first remove Elizabeth from the area. Remind my wife of her duty to Pemberley and to Georgiana. Otherwise, Elizabeth will follow me into the abyss."

"I understand," Edward said solemnly.

"As I have always done," Darcy assured, "I give you my respect and my devotion." Darcy swallowed hard. "If some part of your efforts go amiss, Cousin, and if I do not…"

Edward insisted, "Do not speak so."

Darcy shook his head in the negative. "Permit me to say this before Mrs. Darcy returns. If I do not survive, I beg you to consider making Elizabeth your wife. You once held an interest in Mrs. Darcy, and you should know I would approve of your joining. Elizabeth will have a substantial fortune, and you could assist her with the running of Pemberley until Georgiana comes of age and marries. Georgiana's children will inherit Pemberley if I do not produce an heir, but that is many years in the future."

His cousin scowled. "I do not intend to permit such a scenario to occur," he said adamantly.

"Promise," Darcy insisted.

Edward's mouth thinned into a disapproving line. "I promise," he growled.

The words brought Darcy the peace he required to see this craziness through. His cousin would secure Elizabeth's future and that of Pemberley. With those assurances, Darcy awaited the return of his wife. If this were his day to die, he would spend the last of his time on Earth gazing upon his wife's countenance.

* * *

For hours, Elizabeth had hung over the edge of an open grave, as if she were some sort of bird, spreading her wings to float above him. They had talked as if nothing unusual surrounded their conversation. As if the most bizarre of events had not occurred. They spoke of their mistake-ridden courtship and of Georgiana's future, of the advancements Darcy hoped to install with his tenants and of the investments he had recently made to ensure the wealth of any children they might have. Elizabeth confessed how overwhelmed she had felt as they had departed Longbourn on their wedding day, and Darcy had assured her that he could not have been more pleased at how well she had acclimated to his world.

Elizabeth had left her perch only once during those long hours. When Cowan had returned to Woodvine to retrieve the plans for Samuel's torpedo, Hannah, Sheffield, and Fletcher had commandeered Darcy's coach to arrive on the scene, along with Murray and Jatson. The loyalty of his servants warmed Darcy's heart. The Pemberley staff had brought blankets and clean clothes, as well as fresh food and drink. Darcy had found it amusing that Hannah had, literally, dragged Elizabeth into the church offices for a clothing change and a quick meal. Neither he nor his wife had had a meal for some six and thirty hours. Darcy thanked his stars for Hannah's caring ways. When Elizabeth had returned to her vigil, she still wore his jacket over her gown, and Darcy marveled at how she draped herself in his protection. His wife understood that he would give her all his worldly goods, just as their vows had declared.

"I shall return your coat when this idiocy has ended," she had said when no one was listening. "I shall drape it about your shoulders so my warmth envelops you," Elizabeth said devotedly.

Darcy smiled easily. "Sheffield will likely burn it as soon as we return to Woodvine." His valet's worried countenance had kept Darcy company while Elizabeth had seen to her own needs. While they were alone, Darcy had exacted a promise from Sheffield to serve Elizabeth in whatever manner his wife required in the eventuality of Darcy's passing. Although the grizzled countenance had hardened, the man, who had served Darcy for some fifteen years, had stoically agreed.

Elizabeth giggled—a delightful sound Darcy would always treasure. "You will never be rid of this jacket, Mr. Darcy," his wife declared in her usual teasing tone, "because it will remind you of how we survived this night together."

"More likely because it carries your scent, Mrs. Darcy. Unlike my other jackets, this one will constantly remind me of your unconquerable spirit."

* * *

"Then we are agreed," Edward said solemnly. Since the first streaks of light, he, Cowan, and Mr. Castle had studied the sketches in Samuel Darcy's journals. They had attempted to question both Mrs. Stowbridge and Mr. Gaylord, but neither would speak to what they knew of the device.

In the light of day, they had discovered the standpipe protruding from the earth. "What prevents this thing from exploding in our faces?" Cowan had growled in frustration. "I mean once a person has set the trigger and has filled the grave."

Castle examined the sketches closely. "It is a most intriguing invention," he mused distractedly. "I can imagine resurrectionists might not be too pleased to know such a device exists. There be a rich trade in bodies for the medical schools."

Cowan and Edward exchanged a knowing glance.

Edward had been pleasantly surprised to learn that Castle had had experience with explosives. "A person puts the gunpowder into the standpipe and then drops in a cork to protect the powder."

"That much I understand," Edward encouraged, "but how do we disarm this?"

"One thing is certain. We must secure the device before Mr. Darcy moves his legs. I suspect the trigger line is attached to your cousin's limbs, Colonel."

* * *

"Do you understand what we propose, Darcy?" Edward had ordered Elizabeth behind the cover of Samuel Darcy's crypt. His cousin's wife had not gone willingly, and the colonel knew it would take all of Hannah's physical strength to detain her mistress. It was only with Mr. Sheffield's reminder that Mr. Darcy would wish it so that Elizabeth had acquiesced.

Darcy said sardonically, "It has been many hours since my legs knew feeling. Therefore, I suspect we have no concern for my moving them; however, if they should choose to act upon their own, I will endeavor to divert the urge."

Edward smiled easily. His cousin's testiness announced that Darcy had abandoned his sacrificial attitude. His cousin wanted to live. That would prove well in their knowing success. "Then we will proceed."

Cowan and Castle had volunteered to assist Edward with this unusual rescue. They began by removing more of the dirt from the hole—digging around the standpipe. "Not too much," Edward warned. "Remember that this coffin is wedged into the grave. It rests but two feet below the ground's surface, which means another foot or two of empty space is below it. If we jar the box loose, the coffin will drop into the space, and Darcy will move whether he intends to do so or not."

They had laced ropes beneath the coffin to suspend it from the thicker branches of a nearby tree. It was difficult work to thread the stiff rope under the box. He and Cowan had carefully dug hand holes on either side and hung upside down to pass the line to one another. After the third rope line was in place, they had agreed they could proceed. With a deep steadying breath, Edward announced, "I will remove the standpipe, Darcy."

"Do your worst, Cousin." Darcy closed his eyes. When Edward glanced his cousin's way, Darcy's lips moved in a silent prayer. Edward said his own supplication for divine guidance. His hands were calmer than he had expected. He wondered, as the fingers of his right hand caught the tip of the standpipe where it showed above the ground, how his life compared to that of his cousin's. True, he had known success in his career, but Edward had nothing personal beyond the moniker of "Colonel." He played but a supportive role in his family and in life. "Take me, and not Darcy," he had begged God.

With his left hand, Edward brushed away the dirt which surrounded the pipe. Then, with a grip of determination, he lifted upward on the metal. Unfortunately, the standpipe proved longer than Edward had expected, and he could not pull the end of it free from the coffin without changing his position, which he could not do without either sending the coffin plummeting into the grave or removing the pipe at an angle, which he suspected would jostle the trigger. Sweat dripped from his chin to splatter in the dirt below.

"Allow me, Sir." Mr. Sheffield stretched out opposite him beside the grave."

"The pipe cannot tilt," Edward cautioned. "I must lift it upward at a perpendicular angle to the ground."

The valet nodded. "I understand, Sir. I will not fail either you or Mr. Darcy."

Edward nodded his approval. "Wrap your hands about the pipe, and hold it steadily."

The valet swallowed hard. He stretched forth his hands to catch the pipe below where Edward currently held it.

"Excellent." Edward whispered. "Do you have it, Sheffield?"

The valet's voice was shaky, but he responded in the affirmative.

"Do not move," Edward said softly. "I shall release my grip." The colonel peeled away one finger at a time. "Hold the pipe in place until I can change my position." Edward scrambled to a foothold he had carved in the grave's side. He caught the pipe at a point closer to where it disappeared into the top of the coffin. "We will lift this together. On three, Sheffield. One. Two. Three. Lift." Wonderfully, the pipe slid clear of the box, but it dumped gunpowder as it rose into the valet's capable hands. Edward looked upward in admiration. "I am in your debt, Sheffield."

"As am I," Darcy said from where he lay perfectly still in the coffin.

The valet stood stiffly, the pipe firmly in his hands. "Acting heroically is not what all the books imply," the man said shakily. Sheffield turned and dropped the offending pipe. "What is next, Sir?"

Sheffield's countenance remained pale, but Edward had seen such bravery often on the battlefield. That one moment of glory lived long in a man's memory, especially for one who knew an ordinary life. "I had originally considered opening the coffin more and then disarming the trigger, but I believe we cannot risk a chance that the box in which Mr. Darcy lies goes crashing downward. I think we must lift it from the hole to set it aright."

Cowan gave Edward a hand up from the hole. "I have followed you through hell, Colonel. Whatever you choose is my course."

"Then let us set the lines," Edward said. "Cowan, you and Sheffield have the first line."

Jatson and Murray stepped from behind a tall oak. "We have the second line, Colonel."

Edward nodded his gratitude. "I am by your side, Sir." His own valet appeared from beyond the row of founders' graves.

"Thank you, Fletcher." The man had followed Edward through a decade of battles and poor living conditions, but Edward had never been prouder of having Fletcher's acquaintance.

As a group, they stretched the lines in a pulley system over branches and walls. "Everyone has his lines?" Edward asked as he surveyed the small gathering. The men removed their jackets. "Darcy, whatever you do, do not move."

"Easy for you to say, Cousin," Darcy grumbled, but Edward observed how Darcy braced his arms against the sides of the box.

"Again on three," Edward ordered. "One. Two. Three. Pull."

The coffin tore free of the earth and rose slowly toward the surface. "Harder!" the colonel encouraged. The wood groaned, and the earth collapsed inward, filling the grave in its wake. Finally, the coffin cleared the opening, but it hung precariously above the hole. "Hold tight," he ordered. The men strained to keep the weight from crashing into the open pit. Tying off the lines would be difficult.

Suddenly, Elizabeth and Hannah were beside the swinging box. Mr. Sharp and Mr. Castle joined them. "This way," Elizabeth ordered. She and Castle caught one end of the coffin, while Sharp and Hannah took the other. They positioned themselves where they might direct the coffin to hang above the solid ground lining the gravesite.

"Lower it slowly." Edward spoke through gritted teeth. Gently, the men set the coffin on the ground. Elizabeth and Hannah braced it while the men slid rocks under the coffin's edges to steady it.

"Elizabeth Darcy," Edward's cousin said in exasperation. "I begged you not to place yourself in danger."

"And I promised to guard your heart, Mr. Darcy," his wife retaliated.

Darcy smiled at her. "We will finish this argument later, Mrs. Darcy. Remove yourself from the area, and permit my cousin to prove himself my superior."

Edward shook out his arms. He gathered the hammer and a small saw. "Thank you for your assistance," he said to the group. "But I must finish this last bit alone."

Elizabeth kissed Edward's cheek. "I promise to see you happy, Colonel. Even if I must wear my mother's matchmaking mantle to do so."

He spontaneously wrapped his arms about her—embracing his cousin's wife. "Darcy has made an exceptional choice. If you choose to be my herald, please know that I have been spoiled by your kind heart, my dear." Edward kissed her forehead before turning to his task.

He straddled the box, and without preamble removed yet another of the horizontal slats. "Where do you feel the weight on your legs, Darcy?"

His cousin said softly, "At my knees."

The colonel did not look up. He concentrated on where the nails and the wood connected. With the removal of the earlier pieces, those from the middle section came more easily now that he understood the box's construction. "One more," he said to Darcy.

"Then what?" Darcy asked solemnly.

"Then we either celebrate with your finest brandy or we greet your parents in their heavenly home."

"Edward."

"Do not say it, Darcy. You would do this for me if the situation were reversed. It is the way with us."

Edward squatted beside the coffin. Leaning across what remained of the dismantled lid, he peered into the open space. "You were correct, Darcy. There is a small, globe-shaped orb resting between your knees. It has an arced shield over it and a line leading to the opening through which we removed the pipe."

"Cut the line, Colonel." His cousin's voice held his acceptance of what was to come.

Edward refused to question his decision. He grasped the small knife, reached into the narrow space, caught the line, and cut it.

Epilogue

"Darcy!" Lady Cynthia Sanderson gasped when she saw him. He had not looked in the mirror for several days, for his wife had forbidden him even to consider leaving his bed until Mr. Newby had pronounced him well enough to travel. As Darcy was satisfied simply to be with his family, he had allowed his wife her way. "My goodness!" The countess fluttered in that annoying way of Society ladies, but then she caught up Darcy's hand to kiss the back of it tenderly. A tear rolled down her cheek, and Darcy caught a glimpse of the girl he had known in his youth. "When Barth said you had arrived in Dorset to set Uncle Samuel's affairs aright, I had no idea how you would have suffered. It is abominable."

Darcy sat propped against a half dozen pillows in his own bed. Elizabeth had insisted that with the arrival of the Earl and Countess of Rardin that he should rest in his own quarters rather than to ignore propriety and enjoy hers. "It has been an experience I would not wish on an enemy," he confessed.

"Oh, my dear cousin," the countess said honestly, "I have heard no tale so twisted. More than a dozen deaths, and our dear Samuel's defilement." Evidently, Elizabeth and Edward had shared the events of the past two weeks with the Rardins. Among those details had been the tale of Thomas Cowan's discovery of Samuel Darcy's body hanging like a side of meat in a private medical school in Manchester, the same school where Geoffrey Glover had served as an instructor and where Mr. Newby had received his medical education. The Runner had also discovered the infamous Mr. Crescent. Samuel Darcy's valet had followed his master's trail, and with the assistance of Cowan and the Fitzwilliam brothers, they had recovered Samuel's body to return it to Dorset for a proper burial.

Lady Rardin leaned close as if sharing a secret. "Do you think it prudent for Rardin to have a new resting place drawn for Uncle Samuel? It appears inappropriate to use the grave in which you were held prisoner and from which Samuel's body was snatched." She shivered violently.

"Cynthia," Darcy said calmly. "The gravesite has no special powers." He patted the back of her hand.

She protested, "But you do not understand, Fitzwilliam. There are already numerous rumors swirling around the mysterious death of Samuel Darcy, and then, subsequent reports of your literally rising from the grave have added oil to the flame."

"Nonsense," Darcy said, although he no longer questioned the power of superstition. He had lived with it for the past month. "Allowing others to determine your choices leads to disaster."

She teasingly tapped his arm with her fan. "You sound like my husband. The Earl is always so practical." She rose to make her exit. "Rardin has released a number of the Woodvine staff, and, with Mrs. Holbrook's recommendations, has rehired an adequate staff from those dismissed previously. When we depart, we shall have in place those necessary to see to Uncle Samuel's legacy."

"Rardin and I have spoken briefly regarding the estate. I believe it would be a great legacy for Perdita. It would add to your daughter's dowry."

His cousin pursed her lips as if to silence a response. "Uncle Samuel would have been pleased to think on it." The Countess straightened the seam of her dress. "I must rescue your wife. Mrs.

Darcy has been entertaining the children while their governess and nurse organize the nursery."

"I am certain that with Barriton's demise the house is in disarray."

Lady Rardin smiled. "It is a bit chaotic, but Mr. Crescent has proved valuable in setting matters to order. Rardin means to offer Mr. Crescent the butler position at Woodvine so the man can end his service under Uncle Samuel's roof."

Darcy said, "That is very generous of the Earl."

She bent to kiss Darcy's forehead. "Rest. We have plenty of time to renew our acquaintance. I have missed you."

"And I you," he said with a smile.

The countess started for the door. "By the way, I should tell you that I thoroughly approve of your choice of Mrs. Darcy as your wife. Any woman who risks what Mrs. Darcy did to save you is of the first tier. Her connections are of no consequence."

"The lady's connections are my connections, Cynthia. Elizabeth is all I require for my happiness."

* * *

The colonel arrived for their nightly game of chess. Darcy had remained in bed for three days, and he thought he might go insane if he had to spend many more days in his quarters. "Thank goodness, you are early," he said in greeting.

The colonel assumed the chair Darcy's many visitors had used over the past few days. "I have heard from Cowan," Edward announced. The Runner had seen Stowbridge, the magistrate's wife, and Gaylord to London. With the truth of the trio's crimes becoming common knowledge, Edward and Cowan had thought it best if the threesome were removed from area.

"And?"

Edward relaxed into the chair. "It appears Cowan had the right of it to take McKye with him for additional protection: Stowbridge attempted to kill both his wife and Gaylord."

"Then our assumptions proved true?" When he and Edward had deconstructed the crimes, they had come to the conclusion that Gaylord had been Mrs. Stowbridge's current lover.

"Even more nefarious than we anticipated," the colonel shared. "Merrick Gaylord was actually Merripen Gry, the man with whom the Baronesa had made her escape all those years before. They had been together all this time. The man is Andrzej Gry's father."

Darcy's recognition arrived. "Mr. Gaylord was the man I saw climbing from the back of the gypsy wagon when we called unexpectedly about the horses." He hated that he saw everything so clearly in hindsight.

Edward added, "It is likely why Andrzej asked that you send for him. If we called upon the band without notice, we would likely have found Merripen leading his people."

"I should have noted how both the housekeeper and young Gry referred to my cousin as *Mr. Samuel*. No one else used the appellation in speaking of Samuel Darcy. If I had taken notice, we could have saved ourselves many headaches." It was too late to regret the blinders he had worn during the past several weeks.

"And what of the Baronesa's relationship with Glover?" Because of his interest in the answer, Darcy pushed himself higher in the bed.

Edward steepled his fingers and then folded his hands across his waist. "As Mrs. Darcy previously discovered in Samuel's journals, your father's cousin had received news from Mr. O'Grady of a woman who matched Mrs. Ridgeway's description. O'Grady spoke of a woman who lured men with a promise of marriage and then did away with her suitors. What we did not know is the woman had an accomplice: a surgeon, a man who paid for the bodies she provided."

"Glover," Darcy said in amazement.

Edward nodded his agreement. "Likely, if we had discovered the bodies of any of Mrs. Stowbridge's suitors early on, we would have recognized how each had been a victim of an anatomy lesson. However, as the bodies were badly decomposed, we had no means to recognize the degradation exacted upon the bodies. The markings on Mr. Bates's grave were meant to divert attention from their true intent. To place the blame on the coven."

"Did Glover and the housekeeper arrive in Dorset at the same time?" Darcy's interest had piqued.

"According to the Holbrooks, they did." The colonel hesitated for a fraction of a second. "Likely, the surgeon and the woman singled out your cousin on his return journey from America."

Darcy's mind raced with possibilities. "Glover's examination room?"

"Was used for anatomy lessons," Edward confirmed. "Mr. Newby has verified that he attended several such sessions in Mr. Glover's quarters. Of course, no one suspected from whence Glover had acquired the bodies. The late surgeon was a respected teacher in his students' appraisals. Evidently, the housekeeper convinced Glover to use her son and several others from the gypsy band as his body snatchers. Glover's minions were given permission to line their pockets with whatever jewels or coins they could discover within the coffins. The man who escaped the night Besnik was killed was Vandlo Pias, which explains how Mrs. Stowbridge manipulated the gypsy into his attack upon Mrs. Darcy. The housekeeper must have threatened to speak to the authorities if Pias did not exact revenge for your interference in the Baronesa's life."

Darcy shook his head in belief. "No wonder we struggled with making sense of this puzzle: There were multiple culprits and multiple motives."

Edward clapped his hands in anticipation of the game. "Enough of this maudlin history. I came to best you in a game of chess."

"It has been a long time since you have won, Cousin," Darcy reminded him. "What makes you believe today is your day?" The smile had returned to Darcy's lips.

Edward set up the board on a small table. "I plan to play on your guilt by reminding you of the danger I faced in liberating you from your grave."

"If you mean to blackmail me, Colonel, you have sorely misconstrued my kindness on your behalf." A chuckle and a knowing nod of affection proved the strength of their everlasting relationship.

* * *

His wife slipped into his bed well after the hour that country society would have retired. Newby had removed the bullet in Darcy's shoulder and had properly stitched the knife wound, but Darcy held no qualms about plastering his wife's warmth along his frame. Elizabeth was his healing balm. "You went to the nursery again," he said as he snuggled into the curve of Elizabeth's neck.

"I want a dozen children, Fitzwilliam," she announced without preamble. Her breath warmed his chest. "May we return to Pemberley soon and make beautiful babies to fill its halls?"

He smiled against her skin. "I knew you would find inspiration in the Sandersons' brood."

Elizabeth crawled up his body. "I miss our home, Fitzwilliam. I miss the park and Pemberley House and Georgiana and Mrs. Reynolds."

"I thought you wished to call in at Hertfordshire?" he said with hesitation.

Elizabeth kissed the line of his chin. "May I not ask Kitty and Papa to come for a visit? I have no desire for my mother's drama in my life. I wish to know Papa's calming presence and my sister's spontaneity. Papa would be happy to live in Pemberley's library, and Georgiana requires another young lady with whom to share her secrets and desires. All girls should have multiple sisters." Clutching at Darcy's arm, Elizabeth pressed her cheek against Darcy's chest.

He rested his cheek against the top of Elizabeth's head. "And what of you, Elizabeth?"

Her emerald eyes flashed with a familiar fire. Her chin jutted upward. "I require only one thing to know happiness: you, Fitzwilliam Darcy. I wish to return to Pemberley where I might nurse my husband to health and where we might finally know the happiness of a family of our own."

Darcy kissed her tenderly. "We could begin our family tonight," he suggested.

She peppered his chest with a series of kisses. "Are you well enough?"

Darcy chuckled. "Not well enough to demonstrate my love to my wife? I can assure you, my love, that possibility does not exist." He kissed Elizabeth again with more passion. "To tonight, Lizzy. To a new beginning."

She accepted his kiss eagerly. "To a dozen Darcy children."

Historical Notes

Internal Decapitation

A rare medical condition, atlanto-occipital dislocation or internal decapitation, occurs when the skull separates from the spinal column during severe head injury. With nerve damage, severance of the spinal cord, or strangling, the injury is nearly always fatal. Although this situation sounds as if it is a recent discovery, the idea of internal decapitation is the basis behind any hanging, in which a person's neck is broken under his own weight. Although survival of atlanto-occipital dislocation is a long-standing medical mystery, in the past eight years, there have been numerous cases of people surviving severe injuries of this nature. Generally in such cases, neurosurgeons perform an occipital cervical fusion to keep the head from coming off the spine.

Belle Gunness

The character of Mrs. Ridgeway is based on the real-life Belle Gunness, a woman known for the many murders she committed. Belle was the archetypal black widow killer. She attracted multiple husbands and suitors, many of whom she murdered for their money. Using cyanide, Belle would dispatch her "loved ones." At 280 pounds, she was also ready to rid herself of her latest "lover" by striking the man with a hammer or an ax.

Born Brynhild Paulsdatter Storset on November 11, 1859, in the Norwegian fishing village of Selbu, she emigrated to Chicago in 1881. Among those who lost their lives at Belle's hands were her husbands: Mads Sorenson and Peter Gunness. Belle often advertised in Norwegian-language newspapers for a "relationship." Those who arrived in La Porte, Indiana, to meet the "comely" widow often did not return home. Farmhands on Belle's farm sometimes went missing, as did her foster daughter Jennie.

In April 1908, a fire at Belle's house left behind the bodies of two of Belle's foster children, as well as an adult female's body. Identifying the body was difficult because it had been decapitated. When investigators searched the site for the missing head, they discovered fourteen other corpses on the farmland. They were able to identify two handymen, Belle's foster daughter Jennie, and five of the Norwegian suitors. Belle Gunness was the U.S.'s first known serial killer.

Cemetery Alarm

When I lived in Columbus, Ohio, I often traveled to Huntington, West Virginia, to visit my mother. In doing so, I would cross Pickaway County and the Circleville area of Ohio. On one of those excursions, I discovered a little-known fact: A man named Thomas Howell had patented (in 1881) an exploding device commonly called a "grave torpedo." If someone attempted to rob a grave protected by the device, the torpedo would explode, killing the robbers. In the 1800s, many medical schools would rob fresh graves to find cadavers for teaching purposes. The Church objected to the dissections, and only those who died in mental institutions or were put to death for their crimes were readily available to the medical students.

In Ohio, the body of John Scott Harrison, the father of future President Benjamin Harrison, disappeared. His body was later found dangling from a rope in a hidden shaft at a medical college. Attempts were even made to rob the grave of Abraham Lincoln.

History Detectives episode 703, titled "Cemetery Alarm" from series 7 devotes itself to the story of Howell's invention and of the prevalence of grave robbing during the 1800s. One can view the full episode at http://video.pbs.org/video/1169415042.

The character of Peter O'Grady is based on Thomas Howell, and, yes, I did use dramatic license in the dates for the prototypes of Mr. Howell's efforts.

Lewis Tregonwell

A captain in the Dorset Rangers, Lewis Tregonwell is known as the founder of Bournemouth. Tregonwell and his wife Henrietta (Portman) came to Mudeford so that Henrietta might recover from the loss of their second child. While in the area, they visited Bourne Heath and fell in love with the area. In 1810, Tregonwell bought 8.5 acres for £179 11s from Sir George Ivison Tapps, the Lord of the Manor of Christchurch. It was to be the Tregonwells' summer home. They slept in the house for the first time on April 24, 1812. The house survives today as a wing of the Royal Exeter Hotel.

The Monoliths in Dorset

Some 30 meters south of the River Stour in Bear Mead and two kilometers west of Wimborne in Dorset, a monolithic stone can be seen. Located at SY 986–993, the stone, of fine limestone, has a density of 2,650 kilograms per cubic meter, suggesting an approximate weight for the monolith of 1,076 kilograms. The stone is affectionately called the "Bearstone." A similar toppled monolith can be found some 600 meters to the NNE, on the other side of the River Stour in Cowgrove. Of similar quality to Bearstone, "Moonstone" is approximately 1.2 meters high x .75 meters wide x 0.2 meters wide, with a weight of 477 kilograms.

The source for both stones appears to be Purbeck, which is twenty-three kilometers south on Dorset's Jurassic coast. Likely, the stones were transported into Christchurch Harbour and up the Stour to their present positions. An Ordnance Survey map dated 1902 shows five stones in a circle, centered on SY 992–996. The Bearstone is situated 570 meters to the SW of the circle and is likely a "heel" stone for the formation. Most professionals believe that Bearstone and Moonstone were boundary stones used before the Inclosure Act of 1805 to mark the meeting points of unfenced fields. One can find wonderfully detailed pictures of the area and the stones at "Monolith at Bear Mead" (http://www. eyemead.com/MONOLITH.htm).

The Lesser Key of Solomon or Lemegeton

The Lesser Key of Solomon is an anonymous seventeenth century grimoire. It is also widely known as the *Lemegeton*. It is an extremely popular book of demonology. Although the book appeared in the seventeenth century, much of the text comes from the sixteenth century, including Johann Weyer's *Pseudomonarchia Daemonum*. King Solomon is supposedly the author of the text; however, the titles of nobility used within the text were not in use during Solomon's reign. Nor were the prayers to Jesus and the Christian Trinity part of King Solomon's time.

The Circumstance and Manner of Death: Drowning Victims

According to a document issued by the Department of Forensic Medicine at the University of Dundee, "The world incidence of death by drowning is estimated at about 5.6 per 100,000 of population. Approximately 1,500 deaths from drowning occur in the UK each year; 25% occur in the sea and the rest in inland waters; the majority of victims are young adults and children; two-third are accidental and one-third are suicidal; homicide by drowning is rare."

Disposal of a body in water is sometimes attempted in the case of a homicide. In such incidents, an autopsy is directed toward establishing injuries inconsistent with an accident. To discover an excellent source on all things related to drowning victims, I would suggest www.dundee.ac.uk/forensicmedicine/notes/water.pdf.

Arsenic Poisoning

Arsenic was once considered to be the perfect poison. It lacks color, odor, and taste. The symptoms include stomach pain, vomiting, and diarrhea. The perpetrator may give small doses of the poison over a period of time, which makes it more difficult to detect. According to most sources, the Borgia family was renowned for its use of arsenic, although some newer articles suggest that this assumption may be incorrect. One of America's founding fathers, George Wythe, was killed by his grandnephew with a dose of arsenic. In *The Phantom of Pemberley*, I incorporated the idea of women adding arsenic to their makeup as face whitener.

A famous arsenic murderer during the Victorian era was a woman called Mary Ann Cotton (1832–1873). Reportedly, she killed twenty people over a twenty-year period, including her husbands and children. She was known to serve many of her victims an arsenic-laced tea. A postmortem examination of one of her victims sent Cotton to the gallows.

Sheela na gig

Sheela na gigs are figurative carvings of naked women which display exaggerated vulvas. They are easily found throughout Britain and Ireland on churches, castles, and other important buildings. One of the most well-known examples of Sheela na gigs can be found in the Round Tower at Rattoo, in County Kerry, Ireland. Another excellent example is located at Kilpeck in Herefordshire, England.

Resurrectionists (or Body Snatching)

The secret disinterment of corpses from graveyards was a common activity in the nineteenth century. Bodies were sold to medical schools for the purpose of dissection or anatomy lectures. Those who practiced body snatching were often called *resurrectionists* or *resurrection-men*.

Before the Anatomy Act of 1832, the only legal supply of corpses for anatomical purposes in the UK were those condemned to death and dissection by the courts. The court system would condemn those of more violent crime to dissection. However, the courts did not supply enough corpses for research purposes. It is estimated only an average of fifty people were condemned for such purposes each year, while the medical schools required five hundred cadavers annually. Therefore, a business in body snatching evolved.

The Minster

In the novel, I have taken the liberty to create a small church serving the Wimborne community. In reality, Wimborne Minster, known locally as the Minster, is the parish church of Wimborne, England. The Minster has existed for over thirteen hundred years and is recognized for its unusual chained library, one of only four surviving chained libraries in the world. The Minster is a former monastery and Benedictine nunnery, which houses the resting place of King Ethelred of Wessex.

Roman Roads

The earliest roads built during the Roman occupation of England connected London with ports used in the invasion (Chichester and Richborough) and the earliest legionary bases at Colchester, Lincoln, Wroxeter, Gloucester, and Exeter. In the eighteenth century, Roman roads were built over to create the turnpike system. When roads on their land had not been built over, farmers ploughed under many sections, and the original roads were stripped of their stone to use on turnpike roads. However, there were numerous tracts of Roman road which survived in the form of footpaths through woodland or common land.

Jack Ketch

Jack Ketch was an infamous English executioner employed by King Charles II. He became famous because of his enthusiasm for performing his duties. Ketch was often mentioned in broadsheet accounts circulated throughout England. He executed the death sentences of William Russell and of James Scott, the first Duke of Monmouth. Ketch's notoriety rose because of his barbarous ways and his sometimes-botched executions. The name "Jack Ketch" became a term for those who performed the duties of a hangman at Newgate and other prisons.

DARCY'S PASSIONS: PRIDE AND PREJUDICE RETOLD
THROUGH HIS EYES
Regina Jeffers, $14.95
This novel captures the style and humor of Jane
Austen's novel while turning the entire story on its
head. Darcy's duty to his family and estate demand
he choose a woman of high social standing. But after rejecting Elizabeth as being unworthy, he soon
discovers he's in love with her. When she rejects
his marriage proposal, he must search his soul and
transform himself into the man she can love and
respect.

CHRISTMAS AT PEMBERLEY: A PRIDE AND PREJUDICE
CHRISTMAS SEQUEL
Regina Jeffers, $14.95
It's Christmastime at Pemberley and the Darcys
and Bennets have gathered to celebrate. Bitter
feuds, old jealousies, and intimate secrets surface.
En route home from a business trip, Darcy and
Elizabeth are delayed by a blizzard and take shelter
in an inn. As the Darcys comfort a young woman
through a difficult labor, they're reminded of the
love, family spirit, and generosity that lie at the
heart of Christmas.

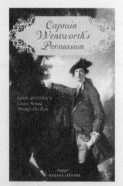

CAPTAIN WENTWORTH'S PERSUASION: JANE AUSTEN'S
CLASSIC RETOLD THROUGH HIS EYES
Regina Jeffers, $14.95
Insightful and dramatic, this novel re-creates the
original style, themes, and sardonic humor of Jane
Austen's novel while turning the entire tale on
its head in a most engaging fashion. Readers hear
Captain Wentworth's side of this tangled story in
the revelation of his thoughts and emotions.

THE PHANTOM OF PEMBERLEY: A PRIDE AND
PREJUDICE MURDER MYSTERY
Regina Jeffers, $14.95

Happily married, Darcy and Elizabeth can't imagine anything interrupting their bliss-filled days. Then an intense snowstorm strands a group of travelers at Pemberley, and mysterious deaths begin to plague the manor. Everyone seems convinced that it is the work of a phantom who is haunting the estate. But Darcy and Elizabeth believe that someone is trying to murder them. Unraveling the mystery of the murderer's identity forces the newlyweds to trust each other's strengths and work together.

VAMPIRE DARCY'S DESIRE: A PRIDE AND PREJUDICE
ADAPTATION
Regina Jeffers, $14.95

Tormented by a 200-year-old curse and his fate as a half-human/half-vampire dhampir, Mr. Darcy vows to live forever alone rather than inflict the horrors of life as a vampire on an innocent wife. But when he comes to Netherfield Park, he meets the captivating Elizabeth Bennet. As a man, Darcy yearns for Elizabeth, but as a vampire, he is also driven to possess her. Uncontrollably drawn to each other, they are forced to confront a "pride and prejudice" never before imagined—while wrestling with the seductive power of forbidden love.

To order these books call 800-377-2542 or 510-601-8301, fax 510-601-8307, e-mail ulysses@ulyssespress.com, or write to Ulysses Press, P.O. Box 3440, Berkeley, CA 94703. All retail orders are shipped free of charge. California residents must include sales tax. Allow two to three weeks for delivery.

About the Author

REGINA JEFFERS, an English teacher for thirty-nine years, considers herself a Jane Austen enthusiast. She is the author of several novels, including *The Disappearance of Georgiana Darcy*, *Christmas at Pemberley*, *The Phantom of Pemberley*, *Darcy's Passions*, *Darcy's Temptation*, and *Captain Wentworth's Persuasion*. A Time Warner Star Teacher and Martha Holden Jennings Scholar, Jeffers often serves as a consultant in language arts and media literacy. Currently living outside Charlotte, North Carolina, she spends her time with her writing.